GLASS SHADOW

ELLE KAELEE

GLASS SHADOW

GLASS WINGS SERIES
BOOK 3

ELLE KAELEE

To the ones who search, the answer is self-love.

1

Hadley | Kinnari Temple

There would be no moon in the sky that night.

It had shattered like glass. The echo lived on, a scream embedded in bone, an image stitched into every blink.

Not even the dark could silence the echo. It pulsed behind Hadley's eyes, haunting the jagged corners of her thoughts.

Hadley lay frozen beneath the weight of that memory, tucked inside her coat with her knees hugged to her chest. The fabric itched, but she couldn't bring herself to move.

It was safer not to move.

Heavy thuds rattled the temple walls, booming, jarring, as if the world outside had become a beast trying to claw its way in.

Her breath caught every time. She gnawed at the inside of her cheek, staring up at the stone ceiling and waiting for it to fall. Her teeth pressed hard enough to draw blood.

Around her, the Kinnari temple was overrun. Army-green cots

filled every inch, bodies huddled beneath mismatched blankets. Some human, some not. Fur-covered faces, snow-pale skin.

Wings. Horns. Claws.

You did this. You broke the world. You called the end with nothing more than a broken vow.

Her promise to the Goddess, to the sun, lay shattered.

She clutched the edge of her pajama shirt tighter. The wind screamed through the cracks in the temple's stone, and each gust felt like judgment.

So many were dead.

Hadley sat up. Sheng lay only feet from her, head resting on his arms, too close, too watchful. Always watching. As if she might disappear.

His skin had returned to its honey-toned glamour. The beautiful disguise he wore when he first handed her a thorned yellow rose.

She had bled then, when she was mortal, powerless, wings still dormant.

Hours ago, in the snow, she had cradled his demon form. Venom in her veins, but fear no longer clutched her chest.

She wasn't afraid of him anymore.

They were nightmares in different skins. His, all jagged shadow and razor teeth. Hers, quieter. Guilt and grief and a darkness she couldn't name.

That's you. That also describes you.

Nightmare. Monster. Demon.

At the table across the room, her makeshift family whispered around flickering pendant lights. An amber glow, an ancient power born in the Kinnari temple. Djoser, Roksana, her father, and the twins were all hunched together, plotting in whispers she strained to hear.

Your family's temple.

Hadley's mother had once walked these halls. Hadley might have even been here, growing in her mother's womb.

I miss you, she thought, just in case her mother's soul was somehow here. Someone had to be watching her.

Hadley buried her face in her knees. The cold was numbing. The guilt was worse.

Then the whispers from the table grew louder, and she could make out the words. She had something new to focus on, to drown the guilt.

"The pressure built up inside me after your death was indefinable," Amis's voice drifted across the room. The man she once knew as a protector, as Sheng's bodyguard.

Hadley watched his flat eyes flicker to the child he held in his arms, distracting him as he continued. "My balance flared out. That power just left me. I still don't know the effect."

A child with dark glossy hair twitched in his arms, its wing lashing his cheek. Hadley managed a small smile. A flicker of light in the unrelenting despair of her thoughts.

"It went somewhere," Djoser's voice was deeper, rougher, as it cut through the air. "It manifested. Wouldn't it?"

Hadley's throat closed. His words struck like flint against dry kindling.

Did it find me? Did his magic crash into me?

Was that why she changed in Bangladesh? Why she became this?

A woman wilting with a shadow that could manipulate. One that turned people into glass, that cracked them, killed them.

Hadley saw a flicker of movement in the corner of her vision, her shadow self appearing, reading Hadley's own thoughts.

"Can you still do it?" Roksana's harsh voice cut into the conversation at the table.

"Should I test it out? How about on you?" Djoser purred.

Silence followed, and the air felt suddenly sucked out of the room. Djoser's voice held no malice, but his words were laced with finality. Death wrapped in velvet.

When the figures crumbled, when that dragon glass broke apart, so did their life and their personality, but the pieces and debris remained. Djoser's darkness left no trace behind. His murders were cleaner.

No, she doubted she had received Djoser's power, his magic.

"Psst."

Hadley was so wrapped up in trying to hear the conversation that it took several times for the whispers a few cots away to register.

"Hadley, are you awake?" the whisper hissed again.

Yes, I certainly am.

Hadley turned her head over her right shoulder, searching for eager eyes waiting for her. Staring into the dark, away from the amber light, made it harder to see, but she knew that bright, genuine smile.

She found comfort in those dimpled cheeks, the gleam of a necklace around his neck. His hair curled at the ends like he'd stepped from a dream, not a nightmare.

Thud-dud.

The wind crashing into the stone was getting louder.

But she was fine.

Everyone was fine.

Everything was okay.

"Hey, hey, I've got you. I'm here." Reifoel jumped off his cot and hurried over to her, hands and knees. His arms instinctively wrapped around her shoulders and cradled her head against his chest. She breathed, letting him hold her and listening to the sound of his heartbeat.

What a beautiful sound.

"I was worried." She tried to clear her throat. "I saw you. You looked dead."

The vision of his body, lying on a metal beam twenty feet in the air, plagued her. She was able to keep focusing on the threat, telling herself not everyone would be saved, but the world maybe could be. Still, it didn't negate that she had saved Sheng and hadn't even moved toward Reifoel when he needed her.

His Serelune tail, thick and black, nearly iridescent, shone blue, multi-dimensional and filled with hidden colors within. But he'd looked frozen then, despite the spectrum, when Ayurveda was in Glaciel, destroying the town and killing so many. The skin on his face and his arms had turned gray. The water from the building pipes kept him hydrated, but the cold had pinned him down like a fish on ice.

Guilt wrapped around her with the same relentless pressure as her memories.

"I'll take that to mean you're glad to have my arms wrapped around you," he whispered, his lips moving up the small ridge of her ear. Hadley's stomach plunged, and her eyes fluttered shut.

Definitely something more.

"Come with me." The warmth was gone as he inched away, standing upright, his arms no longer around her but sliding down to her hands, holding them tight.

"I need to properly thank you, for saving all of us," he said.

Hadley peeked back at the table. The twins, Djoser, her awful father, and the others were still huddled, too deep in conversation to notice.

The two tiptoed towards the closest hallway, with no option for a private room. A long, dark hallway where their bodies wouldn't be seen would have to do.

Reifoel's hand moved across Hadley's back and wrapped around her waist, pulling her into him. They made themselves as small as possible as they moved down the narrow aisles of sleeping creatures, creatures of magic that might not have been alive without Kismet's sacrifice. That wyvern would always be the best thing about her.

What Hadley didn't see as she stepped into the black, her bare feet chilling on the stone floor, was the slightest turn of Djoser's chin. He hovered there momentarily, not long enough for anyone else to notice her movement.

Reifoel stopped pulling her forward and turned, his back hitting the wall behind him as he brought her body into his. His breath hit her neck. His hands trembled. His hardness rubbed against her inner thigh.

"But you said no," she whispered.

It was wrong to remind him because she wanted him to touch her, just like she'd needed it before. Her nerves writhed, a faster pulse in her veins, selfishly hoping the reminder wouldn't shake him free from the moment.

"I'm sorry, Hadley. I'm so sorry if I hurt you." Reifoel lifted his hands and touched her chest, then her neck, then cradled her face as if he needed to feel every part of her to believe she was real. "I couldn't do it then. It felt like I was taking advantage of you. There were tears in your eyes, and that's why I pulled away."

He pulled her closer until her body pressed so tightly to his that she let out a soft gasp. She hooked her legs around his hips, squeezing him with her thighs and shutting her eyes as the rush of want drowned out her doubt.

"But this is all I've thought about since I walked those beaches in Bangladesh."

Reifoel kissed her. It was slow, deep, and careful, as if he meant to memorize the shape of her mouth. When she pulled away to catch her breath, his lips moved lower, brushing down her throat and over the hollow at the base of her neck.

She wore the same pajamas he did, pulled from the pile by the cots earlier that night.The elastic waistband on the pants was flexible enough for Hadley to climb right into his. There was no barrier between want and action as he struggled with the buttons on her shirt.

"I want this. I want you," he confessed. Hadley's hands slipped into that stretchy waistband, her hand moving down his thigh, brushing up against his cock. She moved her fingers up, then down the tip, the shaft.

"I want you so much," he repeated, gasping for air between his words.

Reifoel finally got the buttons on her shirt free, pushing back the satiny fabric, his hands moving down, touching her bare skin, skimming over her nipples, and cupping her breasts. He leaned in to kiss her again and again and again as if he could only breathe air if it came out of her mouth.

It was the most peace she had felt in a long time. Her mind could be blank, only feeling. Cold brushed her skin. So did his body heat, his hands, his lips—the cock she gently squeezed between her thighs.

"How do we get you to breathe under the water?" Reifoel pulled his mouth away, panting, head back as Hadley caressed him, her unoccupied mouth now kissing up his chest.

"What?" she asked before gently biting into his side, squeezing her hands a little harder, not at all focusing on his words.

"You know, so that you can return with me to Serelune."

That she heard.

Hadley looked up, releasing her grip, staring into the dark toward where his face would be. Her moment of quiet was gone in an instant, the anxiety flooding back into her. Once again, she was too painfully aware of her surroundings.

Thud-dud.

The storm outside seemed louder in the hallways. The space was smaller, and the ceilings felt slightly lower than the ground.

"You could be queen one day, Hadley." Reifoel's lips found their way back to her throat, his hands locating her hips before sliding down the elastic on her pajamas. Her stomach fluttered, his fingers touching the sensitive part of her inner thigh, inches away from her center.

"You can be with me. Others would worship you, but, more importantly, I would always worship you." His fingers found the lips around her entrance, pressing down and rotating in small circles. Her eyelids fluttered. Her breath hitched. "My hands, my lips, my whole self, worshipping you forever."

She let out a cry, a gasp, as his fingers slid inside her.

"You would never have to look over your shoulder; no one could touch you, except me, of course." He plunged deeper, and Hadley's shoulders, legs, and core tensed. She was so close, her moment of panic or reality fading again as she focused on the words he whispered, his breath against her ear. It nearly sent her over the edge.

"We could be married,"

Thud-dud.

A loud crash against the temple door jolted her, though the alarm could have just as likely been Reifoel's words. The impact sounded just feet away, right on the other side of the stone they leaned against.

pulling Hadley out of the moment. She stepped back, Reifoel's hand pulling out of her pants as she let go of him.

"What did I say?" he asked breathlessly.

"I, I, need to think," she said, memories of the Vrae circle flooding into her vision. A priest joined her and Sheng in matrimony while she was drugged, then bitten, fully exposed for a room filled with monsters to see.

I can't be someone's wife. I can't belong to anyone.

Less than a day ago—before the attack, before Precession split the earth—Hadley had been devastated by something else. Something that now felt trivial. But it wasn't something that she could just let go of.

She had needed Reifoel then—needed the safety of his body against hers—but he had left her, regardless of his reasons. Would he abandon her again when she needed him most, deep beneath the ocean where she wouldn't be able to breathe but wouldn't be able to drown either?

Hadley lifted her hands to her throat, pressing her fingers to the tightening skin, certain the stone walls around them could collapse at any moment and bury her where she stood.

Safe. I just want safe.

As if the walls abruptly expanded and took the Serelune male with them, Reifoel felt so far away. He was the complete wild card she didn't even truly know. He was someone who wanted her to join his world, but maybe not someone who would be willing to join hers. She couldn't be a tourist to land. Her world, no matter how much it grew, was still her home.

He stepped away.

Reifoel had stepped away from her in Bangladesh—when she was scared, unsure of what she'd done, or how to react. He had fallen back two times, not to let her grow or breathe, but because he didn't know how to handle it.

"No," she blurted out, no longer speaking in a whisper.

"No?" His voice sounded hurt and confused.

Maybe now he will know how I feel.

"I cannot be with you, not like that, Reifoel. I cannot live under the sea, away from anyone and anything I know. I haven't even grasped things here, with magic, with my family. You can't seriously expect me to want to do that."

She could stand up for herself. She would stand up for herself. She would be her best advocate, and that feeling, that reassurance from herself, that it was more than okay to be alone, made her smile.

Thud-dud.

"Am I interrupting?" a smooth voice asked from the darkness, one coated in sweetness, in strength. It was a voice that generally would make her blood boil. Now, however, there was a very different feeling.

Because she had saved him.

See, he is worse than you.

"Go away, Sheng," Reiofel barked as Hadley stepped away. "We are not done here."

"Let's pause this conversation," Hadley said sweetly as she began to step back toward the dim light on the other side of the hallway, buttoning up her pajama shirt. Red eyes appeared before her, glowing, visible even in the blackness.

"I just came to check on you. It seemed odd that you would be missing from your cot after you made such an effort to get everyone here to safety."

"How did you know where we were?" Reifoel snorted behind her.

"Oh, you know," Sheng chuckled as he casually stepped backward. "A big, intimidating Kinnari is sitting at the table. His chin turns, always in your direction, even when you don't seem to be in the room."

Djoser.

"Don't touch me," Hadley reminded Sheng as she walked by him, heading down the hallway toward the main room, leaving the two males behind, following her like the puppy dogs they were.

"Hey, hey." Sheng jogged to catch up with her. "What's wrong with you?"

"I'm assuming you're joking," she spit back at him. "You bit my leg."

"I think you meant to thank me," Sheng scoffed, stepping into the light as they reached the end of the hallway. "You were about to just go off with a Goddess who wanted to destroy this planet, maybe even the galaxy. Mothers are always trying to ruin our lives, aren't they?"

Wrong audience.

He stopped walking, letting her move past him into the rows of cots. More of the creatures occupying them had begun to stir. Hadley turned around, looking back at Sheng, her eyebrows raised, waiting to hear what he needed from her.

"Oh, you thought I went down that hallway looking for you." Sheng smiled wryly as Reifoel caught up to them. The Serelune's eyes were squinted, creases and lines etched on the bridge of his nose, his annoyance obvious, the bulge between his legs still protruding.

"Do you not know how to put that thing away yet?" Sheng rolled his eyes, shrugging his shoulder closer to hers. "Oh, and wife, the next time you need to let off some steam, I'm also available. I suppose we haven't established those clear boundaries yet in our relationship"

Hadley crossed her arms over her chest and frowned.

"No—"

"Touching, I got it," Sheng finished the sentence for her. "You, merman, we need you and that necklace. You, glass wings, are not invited to the table conversation."

"I am not a merman," Reifoel growled.

"Oh, Gods, calm down," Sheng muttered, rubbing his forehead as he cut diagonally through the maze of cots. The large table ahead pulsed with ancient power, as if every soul gathered around it owed their existence to nothing more than a careless kiss from the Gods. The Kinnari standing guard looked even larger now, their wings half-unfurled in a silent warning to the approaching Vrae and the lone Serelune.

Behind Sheng, Reifoel dragged his feet, shoulders hunched and eyes downcast. The sting of rejection clung to him like a shadow, visible in every hesitant step.

Hadley watched as her father, Arryn, threw his arm around Reifoel's shoulder and pulled him to the table. Sheng stood awkwardly by, his hands fiddling with his own set of pajamas, next to the redheaded twin, Roksana, who had her hands on Amis' back, neck, and shoulders, carefully avoiding the still-sleeping toddler in his arms. They spoke in hushed voices.

Reifoel grabbed the necklace and raised it over his head, handing it over to the other red-headed twin, Precession.

"I'm bored," a small voice said down by Hadley's waist, tugging on her pajama top. Hadley remembered this girl; she had seen her being dragged out of the burning, exploding inn. Reign had likely saved her life.

Salome took a bite of the piece of bread in her hand, stacked with meats and cheeses from the trays that were displayed in the small kitchen. Hadley had binged through it hours ago, when she first decided that she wouldn't be able to sleep, but any empty spaces seemed to have been refilled.

"What would you like to do?" Hadley asked Salome, a smile playing on her lips as she tried to ignore the wounds on the child's neck, the bruises that peeked out from under her pajama sleeve.

The little girl shrugged her shoulders, putting all the responsibility on Hadley.

"Do you know where we can get some paper and something to write with?" Hadley asked.

"I'm Salome," the child said, her long black hair partially singed, giving her the appearance of having crispy layers. Her dark eyes and thick eyelashes lit up, understanding her mission. "I'll find some," she said, heading straight for the Kinnari table, the secret meeting that Hadley was not invited to.

She'd be a good spy.

Salome wrapped her small little hand around Amis', who looked down at her, his expression softening. Hadley watched as he leaned down, the girl whispering in her ear as he focused, ignoring the table.

The rest of the Kinnari passed around Reifoel's necklace, murmuring, making quick eye contact, and shaking their heads.

What could they be talking about?

"Arryn," Amis interrupted the hushed voices, loud enough for her to hear. "I need some paper and pens. It seems like quite an urgent situation."

Amis smirked and nodded his head towards Salome. Arryn then handed Salome a set of colorful pens and a delicate artist's notebook, as if they had been in his hands the entire time.

Hadley frowned at her father. One conversation hadn't mended anything between them. It wasn't enough, and he would never be enough—and that was fine. Their relationship had never really existed, and she could live with that now. She didn't need to hold on to hatred or rage every time he was near. He wasn't Sheng, always lurking close whether she wanted him or not.

There was a healing in that, in accepting that her father only existed, not relevant to her in any way.

Thud-dud.

The bangs against the stone exterior were growing louder and more violent. The anxiety that ran through Hadley with each one coursed through her wrists and traveled into her chest. She let her breath out.

The party at the table continued their hushed murmurs once more as Salmone bounced up and down towards Hadley, victoriously holding the notebooks and pens tucked under her armpit.

"I got it, I got it! Uncle Arryn's pretty cool; he can give us whatever we need," Salome said, slapping the supplies down next to Hadley, now sitting on her neatly made cot.

Uncle.

She tried not to roll her eyes. This girl didn't deserve that.

"Now, what do we do? Make a picture?"

"Yes," Hadley said, sitting on her knees while using the cot for a table. "I am not very artistic, but I can write. How about we make a book together? I'll write the story."

"And I draw?"

"Exactly." Hadley smiled and put a black pen down to paper, letting the wet ink dance across the page as she wrote and read aloud simultaneously. "Let's see, we can start with *Once Upon a Time*."

"Oh, I know!" Salome bounced up and down, "there was a queen. She was the queen of her village."

"That sounds good," Hadley said, writing down the words as Salome quickly started drawing a figurine on the top of the page.

"Once upon a time, there was a village queen. She loved her home, her village, but one day, it was empty." Hadley looked over to the table. Sheng turned, meeting her eye. He lifted his eyebrows, and she turned away, pretending she didn't notice him.

"Empty?"

"Yes, and soon, she had no other choice, no other tools to survive, other than selling her . . . heart to anyone who could pay the price."

"Poor Queen," Salome said, "this is a sad story. I should go find Luca; he will know how to make it happy. He can always smile, even when the world is burning down."

She means that literally.

"Rangi and Ahora won't come. They haven't stopped sleeping." Salome added. "I think they are sad."

"But there can be no shadow without light," a rough voice interrupted. Hadley looked up from her writing, pulled out of the moment that had felt so safe and so much like the version of herself she missed being.

"Luca, Luca, we are writing a story," Salome yelled, ignoring the newest writer. Angry, sleepy creatures peered from under their blankets as the girl bounced on her tiptoes before running off towards one of the cots in the room's opposite corner.

She looked up from her notebook, clutching it like a treasure, and met a face hovering over her—olive skin, full lips, and eyes that shimmered with nightmare depth. Still, upon second glance, ones that held slivers of green. The complexity was something to get lost in.

"No shadow without light, Djoser? Would that mean good created evil?"

Djoser smirked, his broad shoulders shrugging.

"I need to get out of these matching pajamas before I can discuss philosophy," Djoser said, his voice husky, deep, raw.

Hadley smiled; he did look ridiculous in the identical pajamas, the silk and softness of the fabric on such ferociousness, on such strength. Her eyes trailed down to his fingers. He flicked them against his sides, showing no sign of the black wisps she knew from their time together on the rooftop.

"We haven't gotten to have another conversation yet." Hadley paused, gulping, her throat dry.

It was true, that moment of disbelief, that feeling of butterflies in her stomach when she and Kismet had landed in the temple just one sleep ago, to see this man, this Kinnari, walking towards her with an expression in his eyes that she could tell was just for her.

That moment was ruined, though, as Amis and the rest of them all grabbed him, claiming he had come back from the dead.

"You want to talk?"

"You had made me a promise, if I remember correctly. A promise of a painless peace. Then you left, like everyone else."

Djoser shook his head and crouched down, hand on her cot.

"I'm not sure that it's all worth explaining, but I'm sorry that I broke my promise."

He looked at her, his gaze reassuring, his eyes not faltering, not leaving hers.

She shivered.

"What's it like, coming back from death?"

Djoser rose, holding his hand out to her, "It's like waking up and remembering that you are severely late."

"Late for what?"

"Late for you."

Hadley blushed and put her hand on Djoser's, letting him pull her to her feet. As she stood, his lips pulled back, his teeth bared. She felt it, too, a sharp sense of nothing.

The two jumped apart. Black wisps had wrapped around her palm and her fingers, and a numbness suddenly existed, as if her blood was no longer pumping and her hand had been asleep. The most minor spot on her skin was now invisible, as if it had been completely erased. The air, the room, was visible through it.

"What did you do to me?" she asked, eyes wide in disbelief.

"I could ask you the same question," Djoser responded, holding out his own hand. The skin that had made contact with hers had crystallized, specks of dragon glass glimmering in the dimmest fire-light from the open wood-burning stove in the Kinnari temple.

Thud-dud.

2

———————

Precession | Kinnari Temple

There was no feeling like it—pure, selfless sacrifice. To love so fiercely that your body and soul were no longer your own—claimed not by one, but by all. These few days of peace, of letting go and letting the planet tear itself apart, were indescribable.

Complete bliss. Like watching pink-streaked skies.

Like the quiet after a scream.

Even without a moon, she still had to keep the Earth spinning. It was a crushing burden on its own, but she hadn't done it. Not since she'd faced Ayurveda in the sky. Parts of the world had stayed in darkness for over twenty-four hours now. The ocean tides would wreak more havoc than she could predict. Many had died already. More would follow.

The world was cruel.

Freedom came tangled with guilt, each feeling fighting to smother the other. Every breath felt stolen—borrowed moments she shouldn't have. Every glance from curious eyes tucked under blankets pierced her heart with imagined whispers: *You could do better. Don't you love all life? Don't you love us?*

Love was starting to seem inaccurate, something Precession wouldn't normally admit. She had once called it devotion. Now it felt more like chains.

Obligated.

That's how her heart spoke now, whispering reminders of her duty to the life the Kinnari had nurtured.

She loved her sister.

She'd loved Percy. That chicken was everything to her.

Everyone else, though, Precession might be fine without. Fine without the tug, the expectations.

She did quite like that Hadley girl, though. A new friend, one who wasn't so quick to turn to hostility. That was something Precession never thought she could have. They could be wounded souls together.

Barely existing with such a self-imposed physical handicap had really put some things in perspective. Precession couldn't run. She could barely wobble to and from the gardens in her once lovely home, a home that her entire heart had gone into. That home was gone. Those chickens were gone.

Percy was gone.

The Vrae were dead, burned in her French estate. Their chaos died with them. Never again would they mistake backroad human murders for village mischief. Ayurveda had killed so many in such a short time, and considering the attack on Myrilosis, it apparently hadn't been enough.

What a bitch.

Ayurveda had obviously never fallen in love with a chicken. She should try it.

Precession's cheeks warmed just from thinking the curse, as if everyone who sat and chatted around her could hear her thoughts. They were not paying attention to her. They usually didn't. Still, it was such a vulgar word for such a delicate little thing as her. Precession understood how others saw her. Being strong and able would likely not be an easy perception to force upon this strange family after millions of years, especially if it was temporary.

It has to be temporary.

Now here she was, free and untethered. Once her magic settled, once the thrumming in her veins found its harmony, she almost forgot it was there. Those faint phantom wobbles from her past still urged her to struggle, to shrink, even as she stood at the communal table in the Kinnari temple. She'd made this choice alone, though she'd argue it was never truly hers to make.

"I will be unable to assist in events from here on out," she announced to the table. The eyes of Amis, Reign, and Arryn locked on her, each face reacting differently as they remembered the strength hidden inside her.

They'd already forgotten.

Precession felt the cracks in her heart, but they'd need to mend quickly. Luckily, as a Kinnari, they would.

Roksana's hand rested gently on hers. Her twin met her gaze, mouth a thin line, nodding once. Roksana understood what Precession was about to surrender.

The only one who ever did.

"It's a shame." Reign's soft, unexpectedly kind words filled her ears. Precession needed that—needed the comfort, the reminder that the creature inside her would soon have to chain itself again.

It's not really like that, Precession reminded herself. *You're choosing this.*

"But I understand. You can't leave half the world in darkness," Reign continued, voice calm for once after months of anger. "And if anyone says otherwise, they don't know you. They don't see the beauty inside you, Precession."

The words wrapped around her like gauze. Not healing, just covering the wound.

"How touching, coming from someone usually so vicious," Sheng chuckled, flicking his fingernails.

"I heard you were the closest to death in the attack, Vrae. I'd watch your mouth," Djoser warned.

Precession watched tension crackle between the Kinnari of darkness and the Vrae prince, first of his kind, maybe the last.

She glanced around the temple. Dozens slept soundly on cots, blissfully unaware of the anger echoing off the stone walls. The storms outside would grow worse the longer she delayed. Restoring the moon felt impossible, but what choice did they have but to try? What choice did she have but to find her center and spin the globe again?

If the storms continued, both realms would become lifeless, dystopian shadows.

Roksana squeezed her hand again. Her sister knew how hard this was, but life had to go on.

Closing her eyes, Precession reached inward, as if dipping into a pond to find the chest that held her magic. She hesitated, one last breath of freedom. Once she reclaimed it, it would be forever. She couldn't justify this release again.

Hesitation vanished.

Precession opened that chest of power, a geyser inside her, seeking direction. Outwardly, she looked calm. Then she opened her eyes: the whites and irises were gone, replaced by pure, liquid gold.

She braced herself, forcing the magic outward. It pulsed through her and down into the Earth's core. The pull grew heavier each second, a rope sound her waist dragging deep with each second. The loose end swayed deep below; she had to seize it and hold tight.

With an incredible force beyond measure, beyond comprehension, Precession turned that weight. The planet's rotation, so minuscule at first, would pick up speed and return to normal with time, as long as she didn't let go, as long as she never stopped the pull.

"Those fish are going to be happy about that," Arryn said, his eyes even broodier than his words.

"The . . . fish?" Reign asked.

"The mermaid . . . men, those two who came up to me at the inn spouting about kings and queens and the Earth's rotation slowing down."

"I don't think they call themselves either of those names." Reign rolled her eyes.

"I can completely understand now why all of Myrilosis hates you." Roksana's face was smug. "You are such a complete ass-"

"Speaking of the Serelune . . ." Sheng cleared his throat. "I believe ours has gone missing from his cot. I can go look for him."

"Just don't eat anybody," Reign snarled at him.

"You've got quite the attitude." Sheng cocked his head, a single eyebrow raised.

Reign stood, her child-bodied arms pushing down on the table. Precession thought it was rather cute.

"You ordered your piece of shit crew to eat me, just as a friendly reminder," Regin said.

Precession watched Sheng's face shift from confusion to something devilish. The curve of his mouth twisted, part smile, part sneer —too knowing, too cold.

No, she didn't like that smile.

"Hmph," Sheng said. "I forgot about that. You barely caused a scene, so polite while they pulled you apart."

Reign's mouth opened, ready to scream, but Djoser's hand slid across the table and pushed her back.

"That's too far. And you're vastly outnumbered," Djoser's voice dripped with sophisticated malice. His power meant that had never known fear the way others feared him.

Precession's head spun. Dizziness swelled as the planet's rotation picked up speed. The pull inside her deepened; her body begged her to stop. She hated this shift, nothing to everything, calm to overexertion in a breath.

She wondered if she'd vomit while the others glared at each other, oblivious to the toll on her. Her sacrifice, hidden, unnoticed. Maybe one day it would fester, but for now, it was her choice.

But is it?

Of course, she'd sacrifice herself to protect everyone else.

"If everyone's done throwing their cocks on the table," Roksana said coolly, though Precession saw the storm behind her porcelain calm. Roksana hated reunions—she was always the first to slip away once she wasn't needed.

"Who are you looking for, Djoser?" Amis asked.

Djoser just shook his head and shrugged, no words offered.

"The fish, maybe?" Amis teased, weighed down by the toddler snoring across his chest. "He might be romancing the girl."

Precession caught the stiffening of Djoser's shoulders, the tight line of his neck.

"That girl," Sheng interrupted, that same twisted grin crawling back across his lips, "is mine. I won't hesitate to rip flesh and tear organs while they're still conscious. To draw out screams, mute but full of regret if it protects what's mine."

Silence.

Precession swayed, black spots flickering in her sight as Roksana's hand steadied her belly.

"Poetic," Djoser said dryly, eyes boring into Sheng's. A silent battle the rest of the table wasn't invited to. "You should fetch her then. I doubt she knows yet, does she? That she's your . . "

"Wife? She does. She just likes a challenge," Sheng shrugged, hands buried in pajama pockets as he drifted toward the cots. "I'll find the Serelune and that moonstone around his neck."

Moonstone.

Precession's lashes fluttered. That tiny piece of the moon was her reason for letting go. It might save the world, but the path ahead would still be long and maybe impossible.

"I don't like him," Reign huffed, arms crossed as Sheng disappeared from earshot.

"We can tell," Roksana smiled at her.

A bouncing seven-year-old ran up to the table, her face stern but otherwise unharmed and secure. She tugged on Amis' shoulder, the one without a toddler's sweet snoring face, and he turned his head towards her.

"I'm bored," the girl announced.

Precession watched Amis, saw his gentle smile, his caring eyes, and was suddenly so sad that she had never really known him. The stigma he carried suddenly seemed just like her own. Were his decisions even decisions at all, or did his magic push him into a direction, push him into a fate?

She wanted to call down her creator, the Goddess Karmakura, and beg for her counsel.

"You'll need to wait until Luca is awake to play; right now, we are talking," Amis sent the child away, only to be met with Arryn's gaze, intense, unwavering.

"We brought him back. You and I, together," Arryn said like he had been holding the words inside him for an eternity. "If we can bring Djoser back, then we can bring her back. We can bring Allienna back."

"Here we go," Reign threw her hands up in the air and then covered her eyes with her hands, her head lolling back.

"No, Arryn. We cannot defeat death. Not in an arbitrary way," Amis answered.

"But—"

"There isn't a way, friend. I know you grieve. I know that your soul hurts. You might even feel dead inside. We've all felt that to a degree, but Allienna left no imbalance in her death. It was a perfect transition once time caught up.

That magic was realized by Hadley, however it may have manifested. With Djoser's death, the cycle of life in its entirety was eliminated. Some of that had been transferred to someone, but we don't know anything else. There is still a void, there is still a correction to be made.

"Everything inside me screams for correction. And for all we know, the Life Gifter will return—ready to undo everything we've defied. In fact, I would be shocked if that's not what happens here soon."

"Thanks for that comfort." Djoser grinned sadistically.

"So." Arryn gulped, staring at his outstretched fingers walking on the table's surface. "If Hadley's magic was eliminated, there could be a chance."

"You have got to be fucking kidding me, Arryn," Reign exploded, unsuccessfully lifting the table to flip it. "This body can't do anything," she yelled out again, her frustration palpable, growing to an extreme.

"Ah, that one's on me," Roksana raised her arm. "I really don't want to be here, and every single word that gets spoken puts me further on edge."

My sister, always so truthful.

"Don't let that Vrae hear you speak about your daughter like that," Djoser smirked. "Or do; that could be an entertaining evening."

The sound of cots being pushed by legs walking down the tiny aisles grew nearer as Sheng approached with a pale-skinned man, eyes the deepest blue, face perfectly chiseled.

"Jesus, you're beautiful when you don't look dead." Roksana raised an eyebrow.

"Table, let me reintroduce Reifoel, the Serelune, and his moonstone to you," Sheng said.

Precession wished she were back with her chickens.

3

———

Arryn | Kinnari Temple

That dragon will destroy this temple . . . again.

Arryn ran his fingers through his blonde hair, gripping hard in frustration as the thudding against the stone walls grew louder and more rhythmic. The storm roared; it had been hours since they made their plan at the table. It demanded too much.

Why must I do all the damn work?

Arryn glared at Hadley, sitting on her cot, twiddling her thumbs. She was useless, playing with children while everyone else hustled in preparation. Djoser hovered near her, never further than twenty feet away, brooding in silence.

He's going to be a problem.

His soulkin—his rival, his twin in chaos—was clearly smitten.

Nothing could annoy Arryn more.

He forced himself to look away, focusing instead on Amis' idea of releasing Hadley's magic. It seemed plausible to bring Allienna back the same way Djoser had been.

Hadley just had to die.

At worst, she'd have to die twice. It could be arranged. He could convince the Vrae to keep his hands off her.

Sheng walked up to Hadley. Arryn tried not to watch but failed, the plotting flickering behind his eyes. He kept his gaze low.

The Vrae was smiling with all his teeth, crouching to match her eye level. She looked as repulsed as Arryn felt, yet her body didn't move away.

How interesting.

A single bite was all it would take. She'd be the instrument of her own death and the key to unleashing what Arryn craved most.

All that work to save his daughter was now the opposite of what Arryn wanted.

"Are you almost ready?" a sweet, soft voice asked. It belonged to the barmaid with mousy brown hair and a generous bust. Her hands slid to his shoulders, rubbing and massaging. She still smelled of ash, her body drained and soot-streaked from Ayurveda's attack on Glaciel. She wasn't shy; she seemed proud and wore the pajamas Arryn had conjured like a badge, like she was on a team.

His team.

"Celestine." Arryn grabbed her left hand and held it against his cheek, feeling her soft, warm skin against his. "You bring me so much peace even when everything is falling apart."

It was true—something about her calmed him despite also irritating him.

Celestine beamed at him.

A single tear dropped from her chin onto the top of his hair. Arryn nearly groaned, all anxiety leaving his body. She wasn't Allienna, but her warmth would do for now.

That woman is always crying.

"I want to get everyone out of these pajamas. They'll need something warmer if they choose to travel," he said.

"I suspect many will choose to stay here if you're offerin'. They don't wanna go into the cities, not with the cruelty we can hear from the wind outside. It can be scary. But you're real sweet for wanting them to be prepared. I think you should do it."

Arryn sighed.

The thought of his home being filled was overwhelming. He wanted only the family he'd chosen.

A family that often doesn't choose you.

"I'm tired of being the only one who tries," he mumbled, barely audible.

Arryn turned back toward Celestine, who didn't seem to hear. He preferred her silence.

He closed his eyes and shut the world out, then reached. Arryn arranged the atoms around him, pulling them from the air until a heap of heavy coats and boots appeared on the floor.

"A girl can never get tired of that." Celestine winked. "You're just making clothes appear."

Celestine was so simple. The constant comparisons to his real love would never end.

He could sit in their . . . situation . . . take comfort in Celestine, use her. She had to be using him for something too. He just hadn't discovered what yet.

She likes you too much.

The barmaid swooped over him, her hair cascading down to peck his cheek before she skipped off to join the few others sorting through Arryn's latest offering.

"Are you going to try to go back?" he heard her ask the surviving residents of Glaciel. Most of their expressions were wary, and questions were answered by either silence or head shakes before they backed away from the clothes. There seemed to be the impression that taking them meant agreeing to leave the temple.

Arryn put his hand to his cheek. It seared.

Such a delicious burn.

His magic's heightened power lingered under his skin, dulling the edge. He was using his magic more than ever these days, creating freely. He would need to get used to this, becoming the Kinnari he'd avoided for so long.

Restoring the moon would take so much from him, maybe too much. Arryn wondered how long he would be unconscious this time, how drunk from power he would feel. He couldn't believe he'd agreed to it. This was why so many avoided families; they were always taking and taking and taking, never giving.

"Will we be starting at Glaciel, then?" Reign asked, walking up to him. "I don't understand why everyone didn't vote to do this work in the Earth realm; if anyone would need help, it would be humans and puppies. They are utterly defenseless."

"It will be easier to use my magic around beings that won't question it, Reign," Arryn said, clenching his fists as he closed his eyes.

"Are you okay?" Reign asked.

"I'm not enjoying this chapter of my life too much, no," he said.

"Well, that's unfortunate," Reign clapped back. "I thought we were all having so much fun. Guessing when the temple falls down on us has become everyone's favorite game. You should join in."

Sarcastic bitch.

"And if you curse at me in your mind," she added, "don't forget that I'm just a poor, innocent child. I know not what I do."

"Yeah," Arryn huffed, "I guess you could use some extra years to grow a brain."

"Rude!" Reign laughed, pretending offense. "Come on, I think everyone's almost ready. They're waiting on you."

Arryn paused, gathered all his thoughts, his sadness, his depression, and tucked them away into a small pocket of his heart. When he was ready, he nodded to his best friend.

Reign's determined, stern but youthful face indicated that she would stand by his side, even when he was an ass, though he didn't have many moments of that. He was more composed than someone like Djoser.

That was the problem, though. He had everything, yet never what he truly needed. It could never be enough, and in turn, he could never be enough. Healing felt like a cruel joke. There was no light at the end of his tunnel. He could still move forward, still function while showing only glimpses of how broken he really was.

Arryn began marching toward Hadley, trying to hide his smirk as he watched Djoser's face snap to him.

So protective, are we?

Of course, Allienna's daughter would be the subject of every male's attention, even the few men Arryn respected. It was massively inconvenient in his quest to continue to ignore her existence.

Or plot her murder. You miss every shot you don't take.

Sheng appeared behind Hadley in an instant. Of course the Vrae had to shadow her. It made Arryn's skin itch.

"Let's go," Arryn said to Hadley, perched on the edge of her cot, looking so delicate. Arryn knew better; the girl was far from frail. He has seen what she did, what she could do.

Arryn resisted rubbing his temples in front of everyone. If this were up to him, he would let the planet ride out the storms. It could take centuries, maybe more, but eventually a rhythm would form. The land would not cease to exist, just the life that thrived there.

I could always make new life.

"I haven't been filled in," Hadley replied, looking up at Sheng with a lifted brow. The girl, his daughter, might actually trust the Vrae demon, judging by her gaze. There was more reliance than he expected.

Better look out, Djoser.

If this were a dark street, if the three of them were alone, Arryn and Djoser would have ripped the Vrae apart, piece by piece. He would not be allowed to exist.

Aren't you lucky?

"Yes, surprising isn't it? We need your pet fish, and he behaves better when you're there. Time to save the world, or something to that effect." Sheng's teeth gleamed at Hadley. Arryn watched her shake her head, nudging away a notebook with scribbled writing on her lap.

"I want you there," Precession's lovely voice cut in gently. Arryn hated it. It was the type of loveliness that made a person flinch, the type that could take on a sun goddess with immeasurable power right before cuddling with a teddy bear.

Precession tossed her blazing red hair over her shoulder as she approached. Roksana held her arm with a promise written on her face to deck anyone who bothered her for the rest of the day.

"Thanks." Hadley smiled at both of them. Roksana looked away.

Arryn lifted his hand, reshaping the atoms of Hadley's pajamas. She now wore a warrior's outfit—brown leather pants and layered pelts, loose over her wings.

Arryn was a personal stylist now. He flinched at the thought.

"Well, she looks badass. I'd like something just like that. I just picked from the boring black jacket pile," Sheng said.

"Go fucking die," Arryn said politely through his teeth.

"How welcome my father-in-law makes me feel."

"That Vrae really knows how to get under your skin," Precession mused. Roksana almost smiled, the judgment apparent.

Arryn tried to hide his grimace to mask his obvious irritation.

You're stronger than this asshole. You are the leader here.

"My lady." Reifoel walked up to the group, holding his hand out to Hadley to help her up.

I don't like the merman either.

"I'm going to go home," Arryn heard Reifoel say, pressing his forehead to Hadley's.

"Hands off, she doesn't like touching," Sheng growled, stepping up and pushing Reifoel and Hadley apart.

Arryn's daughter just stared down at the floor, cheeks slightly red, not saying anything. Maybe that could work to Arryn's advantage, a fight between Djoser, Sheng, and Reifoel with Hadley right in the middle, trying to stop them. She could get hurt. Then destroyed . . . accidentally from the mess of their magic, of course.

A man had to have hope.

"Can we get serious? Every wasted breath means another death. Another soul in agony, praying to a god who either doesn't exist or doesn't care," Djoser's rough voice said, turning to the hallway that led to Myrilosis.

"Since when do you care about life?" Arryn snapped. He regretted it instantly. He was irritable.

Too many people. Too much noise.

Djoser just stared back, eyes full of savage promise. Djoser had spent eternity building worlds within worlds, trying to bury the darkness that rang through him. If Arryn wanted a fight, Djoser would sure as hell bring it to him.

"Since he helped human culture by starting one of the greatest ancient civilizations in the world." Roksana rolled her eyes.

Yeah, I fucking know.

"Always glad to have you here to lighten the mood, Djoser," Reign said, winking.

Salome and Luca were pretending not to listen, but doing a terrible job, watching Reign and stifling giggles while the tension crackled.

Reign pulled the two of them close. "The three of you will be staying here, okay?"

"But we don't want to leave you," Salome's bottom lip trembled.

"We don't know what waits out there. Most of us have never seen some of these cities. It's not a risk we can take."

"What if you don't come back? We hate people not coming back," Luca asked, his voice solemn.

"You're already so grown up, Luca," Amis said, joining them all with Noah in his arms. The toddler boxed Amis' shoulders. "And I'm sorry that you've had to be. But we cannot fail, we will be back. Please, stay here and take care of what's left of your tribe, and try not to leave out the wingless children. I've noticed them keeping to themselves in the south corner today."

Luca gave Amis a stern nod. The teenage boy seemed to run on pride, his eyes masking the fear betrayed by his clenched hands and the breaths he would not take.

"Celestine knows the cities the best besides Balzathar, but he's choosing to stay here. We do as she suggests," Arryn added.

"That's right. I'm not a man of action," Balthazar's grumpy voice rumbled from behind. The furry creature somehow still found another newspaper to frown at.

Celestine bounced up upon hearing her name, her arms instantly wrapping around Arryn. They were always wrapped around him.

"Oh sure, how fun, I've done quite a bit of travel." She smiled. "Let's just start with the closest cities. We can head south. There's Ebsonspire and Phoenix Rest. The Serelune can be dropped off at the ocean in Phoenix Rest. Then we can decide if we want to go elsewhere. I have some ol' friends in New Eldhem. It would be great to see if they didn't die, if we get a chance to cross the continents, of course."

"That's our plan then," Arryn said.

He already felt exhausted.

This might destroy you.

"Let's go south, and figure out how to restore the moon."

4

———————

Djoser | Kinnari Temple

Djoser stared at his clenched left hand. He normally felt on edge, the darkness inside him always trying to claw its way out, but this time he was holding something else back. He ignored the usual threat of his wisps, focused instead on something new—Hadley's magic still pulsing where she'd touched him.

Chin down, eyes on the blonde Kinnari with glass-like wings, Djoser fixated on the lingering chill on his hand. It throbbed like living bone trapped under frost, a curse etched into his skin. He didn't pretend to not want more. He would stare at her until she told him to stop.

That crystallized patch on his hand pulsed with fragile power, like it might shatter and take him with it.

What would happen if it shattered?

Despite the unknown, Djoser wanted her touch again. He didn't want her to be scared off. He certainly wasn't.

Hadley was no longer the girl Djoser had met in the desert heat.

He could feel it. She wasn't the same lost soul begging for death, for peace.

There was still something there, lurking behind her eyes.

Am I the only one that sees it, or just the only one looking?

If there was any purpose for dragging him back from the void, a reason to breathe death back into this world, it was her. And yet, he didn't understand it. Not fully. Was it her magic? The fracture in her that called to the ruin in him?

If his path to her must remain distant, buried in shadows, he would watch. He would not turn away.

He had come back from the darkness, a state of nothing. He had a body again. Energy pulsed inside him, violent and unfamiliar. Then suddenly, he was there in the temple. Dragged back and anchored to Earth like a chained animal.

For a moment, there was relief: no more deaths to deliver, no more kingdoms to drown in blood. But beneath that calm coiled something jagged. Nothingness had been mercy. Now he remembered what it cost to exist, to want, to hunger, to need.

But he knew Hadley was there. Not her warmth, not her laughter, but that hidden spark. A fracture that hummed like a promise and a threat. His darkness stirred at that crack in the world. It wasn't love. It was a fault line begging to split him open.

That was the only truth he knew now. He needed to get closer, to touch whatever inside her refused to die.

But no. Too many soulkin hovered near her, tugging him back from the spark.

Hadley was magnetic. She burned to exist, and after nothingness, that burn hurt more than death ever had.

That's how it will have to be.

At least for now. They would find their way.

Djoser was not interested in jostling between Sheng and Reifoel, fighting like bears over scraps of steak. He would let that implode on its own.

"Is everyone ready? Let's get this over with," Arryn said, pushing

Kinnari toward the exit. It was time to save the world, as if Djoser had any real place amongst heroes.

Djoser moved down the temple hallway, Hadley just behind. He could touch her again if he turned and reached for her, but he looked down at his hand again instead, steadying his needs as he reached the heavy stone door to Myrilosis.

A prickle shot down his chest. His intuition warned him.

It isn't the time. It's not right.

"It won't open," Djoser announced, putting all his weight into his push. There was no groaning of the pivot, no budging of the stone. He might as well have been pushing against a solid wall.

The world does not want us out there.

"Let me help," Arryn said, edging through the group gallantly. Djoser tried not to roll his eyes.

Arryn failed immediately.

Djoser smirked.

The two alphas worked together, jaws tight with forced calm.

Hadley quickly looked away from him, tucking her own hand under her arm.

What are you thinking? Who is it that you were really looking at?

Djoser couldn't be sure that her attention was actually on him. It was that magic, that gleam in Hadley's eye.

"Can you just destroy it? There must be so much snow; we barely even hear the storm anymore," Arryn said lowly, covering his mouth.

Thud-dud.

"I can hear the storm just fine." Djoser smirked, trying to distract from an awkward insecurity he had been harboring since his resurrection. He'd felt off, in a way he didn't have words to explain, since his return.

Could you even destroy the door if you tried? Are you the same monster? The same man?

That was a valid question. Arryn didn't realize the depth of his ask.

Djoser's ability to pull atoms apart had swirled such a darkness around him since that first Vrae attack. He often felt lost, like he'd been plunged into a whirlpool where he could never be saved, but now, there was almost none of that.

What he accidentally did to Hadley, an instant touch of demise, made him nervous that he could no longer channel it, no longer choose.

Am I still powerful?

It didn't feel like it. It felt thin. Hollow.

The threat he'd once worn like a cloak had nothing behind it.

What if you can't?

He hadn't wanted to know, until now. Now he needed it. For her.

He'd seen the wisps crawl over her skin. Only once. Since then: nothing.

"I don't want to destroy what I can't see," Djoser grunted. Arryn turned, stoic but weary.

"Everyone back, except Hadley," Arryn ordered, and the group stumbled back, Hadley already stepping forward.

"Using my name now, are we?" she teased, arms crossed.

"I'll pretend I care about that attitude," Arryn snapped. "Kismet's waiting. If we're buried, we need the dragon."

"It's a wyvern." Hadley blinked. "So ... we're stuck?"

"Yes." Arryn looked like he wanted to headbutt the door.

"I'm not seeing many perks to this soulkin thing yet," Hadley said to Precession, voice playful.

Precession didn't notice, eyes down, smile trembling, clinging to Roksana.

"I don't ... know how to call her. She can't just read my mind."

"I've seen her act like she can," Reifoel murmured, stepping to her side.

"It's not ... it's not that," Hadley said, eyes drifting to the stone, chasing something only she could see. Fooling everyone but him.

"What exactly is it, dear?" Precession asked softly, her voice all exhaustion and sugar.

Thud-dud.

Hadley's shoulders squared. Ready to shove back at the men who needed her power but never her peace.

A tool. Like him. Maybe that's why he couldn't stop circling her.

Her eyes dulled. Her face said she owed them nothing.

Good. Fuck them all.

"Do you hear that?" Reifoel asked, looking up at the ceiling.

He didn't.

Djoser didn't hear anything now that everyone had quieted, focusing his ears only to detect how utterly loud some of the creatures around him breathed.

"It's water," Reifoel said, his head falling back, closing his eyes. "It was trickling, but now it's streaming, calling for us, whispering lullabies and telling us that it will be okay."

"Ha," Arryn snorted. "Serelune are . . . something else, then."

"No, wait, I hear it, too," the brunette woman with the lightest blue eyes Djoser had ever seen said. She grabbed Arryn's hand and put it on her . . . heart.

Gods, you can't be serious.

"Shhhhh, just listen," Celestine continued, her face filled with wonder, her eyes exposing a degree of fear.

Djoser did, and finally, he heard it too. The soft whistling, the rushing of small streams of water getting heavier, gaining more speed.

Then more speed.

And more.

As they all stood there silently, the groaning against the walls became different, almost alive. Djoser felt like he was in a submarine, stuck at the bottom of a shallow sea with waves crashing all around.

"That can't be good," Roksana huffed, biting her lip.

It isn't.

"Look," Hadley said, pointing towards the door, where a small puddle had started leaking through.

This is going to suck.

"We need to create a seal, Arryn. Who knows how much water there is? There are creatures, children staying behind," Amis said. "You know what? No, let me go back. I'm going to stay. I won't abandon them."

"Is anyone else going to change their mind and stay?" Arryn asked gruffly. "Any other cowards? No?"

No one breathed.

Arryn waved his hands; the sound of stones stacking on each other at the end of the hallway echoed. The hair stood on the back of Djoser's neck.

Good. They would have all drowned.

The hum of death lingered thickly in the air though, as if waiting for someone to slip. And as always, too much of that heavy promise tangled itself around Hadley's shoulders. Keeping her alive was quickly proving to be more trouble than dying ever had been.

"Are we ready now?" Djoser asked, his tone even, though inside he felt the pull of the coming flood wrap cold fingers around his ribs. Water lapped at the tips of his boots. He braced his hands on the door handle. "Everyone get behind me," he commanded, and when no one argued, he pulled with a sharp snap of strength.

The door flew open. A wall of snowmelt and stormwater crashed through the breach, swallowing the hallway and slamming him backward so fast he didn't even have time to curse. His head struck stone, and the force jolted through bone and teeth as the current dragged him under.

His lungs burned, desperate for air he couldn't find. His arms flailed once before the freezing dark took his sense of direction, folding him into the chaos like a ragdoll tossed in a whirlpool.

Somewhere in the blur he caught a shape, a tail, dark and sinewy, moving with calm purpose through the storm. The Serelune. Reifoel glowed faintly in the icy murk, with Hadley clutched safely against his chest, her eyes open and defiant even underwater.

Reign's hand grabbed at his shoulder. He felt the squeeze more than he saw it, reminding him there was only one direction left: up. He kicked, limbs leaden and screaming in protest, until his face broke the surface and the roar of the wind swallowed the pounding in his skull.

The temple spire jutted out of a lake that had not existed an hour ago, the storm having buried them alive under snow that now melted into this coffin of water.

"You have to go back for him!" Hadley's voice cracked through the wind as she shouted at Reifoel.

Reifoel barely turned his head, his expression calm in that infuriating way only the Serelune could manage. "Do I truly have to? Wouldn't it spare everyone a great deal of trouble?"

Hadley's voice trembled with exhaustion and fury. "He's not like us, Reifoel. Sheng will drown. Please."

Of course she would care about Sheng. Djoser bit down on his tongue to keep from laughing at the absurdity.

"I'll go," Djoser rasped, tasting blood and snow on his tongue.

Reifoel rolled his eyes. With a single flick of his tail, he dove, vanishing beneath the ice with a grace Djoser would never possess.

A shriek echoed deep beneath the frozen surface, and Djoser's heart clenched at the reminder that fear, for him, was always about losing control—not about dying. Reifoel was a relic of ancient terror given a patient face and gentle smile, but no one who had seen the old world would ever call him gentle.

Not unlike himself, Djoser thought, managing a grim smile despite the biting cold.

Across the lake, the wyvern rose through the mist and sleet, each massive step breaking through the newly frozen crust as if reminding the world who truly ruled these storms. Its scales steamed under layers of sleet and hail, and when it exhaled, the heat of its breath lingered just long enough to remind Djoser what warmth felt like.

Reifoel surfaced again, Sheng's limp body draped across his arms like an afterthought. Their eyes locked for the briefest moment, and the disappointment in the Serelune's glare was enough to say what words could not: the problem still lived. Problems always did.

Heat billowed from the wyvern's snout, but the wind claimed it instantly, flinging shards of ice back in their faces.

One by one they climbed the creature's broad back, boots and claws scraping wet scales. Hadley pressed her palm to its massive nose and murmured something soft that Djoser couldn't hear but felt echo in his bones, nonetheless.

Precession rose first, wings cutting through the storm with grace. Roksana followed, her voice lost to the wind as she spoke to Hadley.

Djoser forced himself through the numbing water, dragging his aching body onto the wyvern's spine as Arryn lifted Celestine next to him. She was too pale, her lips almost blue, and even Arryn's fury softened as he settled her safely between them.

Once they were all perched among the creature's warmth, Djoser risked a glance at Hadley. She met his eyes just long enough to stir that ancient hunger under his ribs, then turned back to the beast, fingers tracing a quiet promise into its scales.

Behind them, the lake sealed with a hiss of new ice, the wyvern's tail snapping it like fragile glass. Its wings stretched wide, each beat of muscle sending another flurry to the distant ground below.

Djoser cursed the creature's existence, Arryn's arrogance, and the truth that saving the world always demanded sacrifice. He would clean up the aftermath in shadows—always in shadows. Egypt would have to wait. He would not leave her.

Not unless she asked him to.

He dug his claws into the ridge of scales before him, planting himself just behind the Serelune's flickering tail.

"Don't you have legs of your own?" he shouted over the storm, his voice nearly lost to the roar of the wyvern's wings.

Reifoel looked back, calm as a ghost, and tapped a claw to the rain streaming off his shoulder. "Rain is water, Djoser."

It almost made him laugh. Almost.

Maybe the Serelune wasn't entirely insufferable after all.

The wyvern hurled them into the storm's heart, wings cleaving the sky open as sleet bit through leather and flesh alike. Djoser gritted his teeth against the wind, reminding himself with every bone-jarring gust that at least this time, he wasn't rising alone.

5

———————

Allienna | Sacramento, Ca | 1994

The sweetest little fingers brushed Allienna's cheek, a bright-eyed four-year-old smiling at her with band-aids scattered across her face. They were decorative, but the one on Hadley's eyebrow would be a fight to peel off later.

Her daughter, without knowing it, filled every space of Allienna's body with a love so deep it ached. Hadley would never know the peace, the fierce tenderness, she brought her mother. And Allienna would never tell her. Living among mortals meant secrets. It was safer if Hadley didn't know any of it, not even a whisper of magic. Allienna had kept it all secret and always would.

It's safer this way.

"Mommy." Hadley blinked. "Can I have a blue popsicle?"

Allienna threw her head back on the too-firm couch pillow, letting a heavy breath slip out, lips pursed to hide a smile.

"We can't have popsicles for breakfast, but I might make a deal with you."

Hadley perked up, her attention that of a navy seal. The girl took her sugar seriously.

"If you eat four pieces of broccoli with dinner tonight—"

"Yuck."

"Wait for it, wait for it," Allienna said, keeping her face stern. "Then I will let you have a blue popsicle, and you can pick the movie tonight."

Hadley gasped, squeezing her tiny fists and bouncing with delight. Allienna tried to ignore the bruises that Hadley's knees were causing her, the girl shifting back and forth on top of Allienna's lap. It was worth it. She would always be worth it.

Hadley pushed herself clumsily off her mom and the couch and moved toward the too-large, beat-up oak entertainment center. The little girl twirled her glittery princess skirt before she flung the bottom right cabinet open and began throwing the plastic white casings of her favorite VHS tapes aside, looking for the right cartoon cover. She usually went for the one about the mermaids.

"This one, this one!" Hadley yelled, jumping up and down while holding a tape over her head.

"Okay, okay, that one," Allienna agreed, standing up and moving to the kitchen to drink her third cup of coffee. She'd been awake for nearly two hours, the sun now rising. All she could dream about was going back to bed.

But she had bills to pay and a daughter to raise.

It had been almost five years since she last saw Arryn. Five years since she'd laid eyes on any soulkin, any piece of the family she'd abandoned for Hadley's sake. Reign lived so close now, just thirty minutes from their modest rental. Yet somehow, their paths had never crossed, not even with the barbershop nestled downtown where secrets were bound to slip.

Allienna still worried.

She always would.

But time had softened the terror until she no longer flinched at every shadow behind her.

What a life that might have been, her daughter having a

godmother in her life. Allienna used to have to fight the urge to reach out, to say, "I'm so glad you survived the Gods. We are here too, we are alive too." But the danger that lurked there, the worry for Hadley's safety if her father had found them, was something she was not willing to risk.

Sometimes she replayed everything in the quiet hours before dawn: how she'd escaped Arryn's hold. She'd landed in Sacramento begging the old barbershop owner to let her sweep floors and until she could stand on her own two feet. Every morning, Hadley's laughter reminded her why she chose this small, mortal life.

Once her daughter was fed and wearing a few less bandaids, Allienna picked up her car keys, walking out of the house with Hadley flopped in her arms, clutching her videotape while Allienna's fingers strained against the child's pink backpack as she balanced it all. The sun had fully risen by then, orange and gold hues drying the dew on the grass. Allienna turned the key in the engine, put the car in reverse, and set out for the barbershop.

"Shoot," Allienna spat out, seeing the traffic piling up at the on ramp.

"What's wrong, Momma?" Hadley asked, holding onto her backpack filled with coloring books and fairytales tightly to her chest in the back seat.

"We are taking back roads today. That's okay, it means we can stop by the drive up coffee stand and get a little treat."

"Another treat?" Hadley squealed, a huge grin on her face.

"It's your lucky day," Allienna cheered as she made a U-turn.

The modern stresses that humans dealt with had undoubtedly been taking a toll on her these past few years, but all in all, Allienna was still perfectly happy to work with these problems, not to have the burning, the agony, coursing through her veins as she comforted, loved and served that male.

Arryn.

He had been occupying her thoughts a lot that day, and she hated it.

Ten minutes later, their old beat-up car was moving along

backroads surrounded by fields. It smelled like cattle and grass, even with the windows up. This capital city was anything but glamorous the moment you drove a little way out.

Allienna heard the siren, her stress shooting up from the alarm, before she realized that there was a cop directly behind her, riding her tail. The siren was for her. She looked down at her speedometer, determined she hadn't been driving too fast, and started to pull over.

"I don't have time for this." Allienna tapped her fingers on the steering wheel. With the car stopped and in park, she opened the glove box to dig for her registration. As soon as she got it, she sat up and gasped.

"Oh my gosh, you scared me," Allienna said to the cop, who stood at her window. No footsteps, no sound of the door closing on his car, not enough time for him to get to her. He motioned with his hands for her to roll her window down.

Something is wrong.

"Mommy, who's that?" Hadley asked, but received no answer.

"License and registration," the cop said, his sunglasses covering his eyes.

"Why did you pull me over?" she asked, complying, the thumping sound of her rolling the window down with the handle rhythmic.

The cop showed his vivid white teeth. "Hello there," he said, waving to Hadley in the back seat. "You're a pretty thing, aren't ya?"

"Here," Allienna cut him off, handing him the paperwork. He looked down at her, chewing a piece of gum wedged in his mouth while leaning his forearm against the top of her car.

The officer lowered his hand to grab the papers from her hand, his fingers brushing against the side of her thumb. That's when she forgot how to breathe, all of his feelings pouring into her.

Go.

What Allienna felt was an undeniable thirst. It was a thirst for blood. Her blood.

She pulled her hand back. It was too fast, too sharp, too obvious. She was going to give herself away. He would notice. He would know that she knew, and that was the only advantage she had. That single touch, that brief intake of his desperation, had been enough to terrify her.

Every time she had looked over her shoulder, bracing to be found, none of it had prepared her for this. She had made a plan to face Reign. She had practiced conversations with Arryn. She had rehearsed explanations that would keep Hadley's life untouched. But this was different.

The fear rooted deep in her body. It swept through her with a sudden wave of vertigo. Her head spun. Dark spots bloomed in her vision. Her stomach dropped. Her muscles went rigid. Her breath caught in her throat.

This was the kind of fear that belonged to prey with nowhere left to run, trapped under the gaze of a predator who had already closed in.

"Can I know why you pulled me over today?" Allienna asked again, her right arm locked on the steering wheel as she weighed her options, trying not to look at him. He wouldn't let her gaze wander away; he was in control. He sneered at her question, his jaw moving in a jolt to check on Hadley before lowering his arms, hands on the top of her window, still a quarter up.

The cop bent down a little lower, a little closer, and pulled down his sunglasses. His blood-red eyes threatened her and stared at her.

"I found you," he said triumphantly, but then his eyes glanced back to Hadley. "Or should I say, I found her."

That was all Allienna needed.

Go!

Her light brown hair went wild as she slammed her foot down on the gas pedal, the tires spinning out for a millisecond on the hot Sacramento pavement before the car shot off. The cop, the Vrae, swore and yelled with a devilry that seemed to cause a cloud of rising dirt around them both. The sudden movement of the car nearly ripped his arms off, but he recovered too quickly.

He was hunting. And he had gotten so close.

Allienna was speeding, but in no time he was behind her again, the gleam of wine-red eyes catching in her rearview mirror while he drove, pushing up on her bumper.

"I'm scared." Hadley screamed. The child's eyes filled with confusion and fear. Hadley sat picking at her nails and watched her mother, looking for any kind of comfort.

Allienna reached her hand back, extending it to her, doing her best to keep her view on the road. "It's okay, baby," she assured Hadley.

But they were driving for their lives.

Hadley took her hand, her chubby fingers gripping Allienna's pinky finger tightly, and her face instantly relaxed. She even smiled as the helplessness, the anxiety that pulsed through that little body flowed through her mother. Allienna knew those feelings well, too well. It was how she felt when she lived in the temple and cared for Arryn. She had never wanted Hadley to feel like that, yet here she was.

You're failing.

Allienna pushed the tears out of her eyes, the cop ramming their bumper again.

"I have to take my hand back, Hadley. Are you ready? We will get to go really fast. It's going to be fun."

Hadley nodded with reluctance, her hand loosening its grip on her mother's fingers, letting her grab the wheel fully. She made a sharp turn down the road, her foot not lessening on the gas. Giggling came from the backseat as the car drifted, and Allienna cheered, her eyes constantly checking her rearview mirror.

They were approaching a red light, but Alienna couldn't stop. With the kind of bravery that she never believed she had, she bit her lip and continued, swerving around an older pickup truck towing a small tractor, nearly colliding. The driver yelled through his window, swerving a second time to avoid the relentless pursuit of the cop.

"Please let this work," Allienna whispered. She prayed to the Life Gifter for the first time in years.

It was the only plan she could identify, her only hope other than jumping out of the car and flying, Hadley tucked in her arms, fleeing for both of their lives. That would lead to so many questions that would blow up her little girl's life. That would be an absolute last resort.

Allienna turned into a fire station, her car bouncing up the curb and her head slamming forward violently as she braked in front of the open garage door.

The Vrae did not follow, but he slowed, and he looked at her with a grin that had shivers running up her back, a grin that told her that this was not the end. He passed, and with her window still open, her hair as wild as ever, she looked up as footsteps approached.

"Ma'am?" A fit man in his mid-twenties, wearing a curiously tight shirt underneath his uniform, tried to smile at her, but it didn't work; he was worried. With the way that she drove into his driveway, it made sense.

"Sorry, I'm sorry." Allienna gulped in some air, looking behind her to make sure the Vrae hadn't turned around. She put the car in park and breathed, her forehead down on the top of the steering wheel.

"I almost hit a dog crossing the road. It scared me," she managed to say as a handful of more firefighters walked up to her car, the firetruck sitting in the garage gleaming in front of her.

"Stay right here, ma'am. I'll be right back," he instructed. Allienna nodded, unsure if she could move if she wanted to.

She's watching you.

"Hey, baby, how are you doing?" Allienna looked back to Hadley, who was sitting there with a huge grin.

"Momma, you went vroom, zoom and slide. It was so cool!" Hadley threw her hands up.

Allienna smiled. "It was something, wasn't it? I think I'm going to call in sick to work today. How about you and I go home and start that movie?"

"Yes!" Hadley clapped her hands.

"Ma'am? For the girl; she's an official firefighter now." The firefighter appeared back in the driver's side window, holding out a plastic golden badge. Allienna took it and smiled, careful not to let their hands touch as Hadley clapped behind her.

6

———————

Hadley | Myrilosis

They were flying south. That was all Hadley knew as wind and rain battered her, ice needling through her veins.

She fought the spiral, the questions about who she was and who she might become. That path was too easy to slide down and only gave back dread in return.

There's nothing you can change. You will move forward. You are who you are meant to be.

But it still hurt.

No matter how strong she pretended to be, no matter what her pep talks sounded like.

You're just tired.

Some pep talk.

The beast beneath her was the only pure source of comfort. Everyone else came with want, with hurt.

Reifoel once had pulled away from her, and that hurt. His next move was to announce that he was going away, going home, under the sea.

No, not only males. You felt peace and trust with Ayurveda. She didn't reject you.

But she made her complicit in mass murder.

And just like that, the spiral began again.

Hadley pressed herself against Kismet's scales, wrapping her arms around the front spike and holding on tight. In the beginning, it had been hard to trust her—Kismet was the first true supernatural creature Hadley had ever met who didn't hide behind a human face. But now, high above the world, she finally understood: in those mountains, it hadn't been Ayurveda who kept her alive. Everything she'd once thanked the Goddess for, every moment she'd felt rescued, protected, even loved, belonged to the wyvern all along.

It was all Kismet.

Ayurveda had only nudged them together. It was Kismet who stayed. The creature was Hadley's quiet half, the part of her heart that never demanded, never took. While everyone else circled with open hands and whispered needs, Kismet simply was; silent warmth in the cold, steady breath in the storm.

Kismet had fed her when she was starving, curled around her when winter came for her bones. She had never been tender by nature, but Hadley craved her calm strength now more than ever. Kismet never dragged her away, never asked for anything. She stayed —fierce, silent, kind.

A sanctuary no lover could offer. Not even Reifoel.

Deep down, Hadley knew it. They could never be more than two bruised souls clinging to each other out of ruin. How could there be space for real tenderness when both realms teetered on collapse? She couldn't imagine a future wide enough to hold them both alive, much less in love.

Hadley pictured it anyway: her childhood house, Kismet dozing in the yard, the back wall gone so the wyvern's tail could curl by the fireplace.

Spiraling . . .

As Kismet's wings moved with power and grace, her mind wandered to another warmth that thawed the ice in her blood.

Reifoel's hands sliding under her waistband, his touch so soft. She closed her eyes and swallowed, the butterflies in her stomach returning.

He's a hot idiot. Don't get distracted.

It had always been just sex. Her old life taught her how hollow it could be, how easily traded. Now, that truth barely even stung.

What did matter was how safe she felt, and she was very comfortable with Reifoel. It was as if they had once been childhood sweethearts, shooting arrows, sneaking kisses behind summer camp tents.

She missed that kind of summer. She missed yellow school buses and her mother's waiting arms in some church parking lot. That was really the comfort she longed for. The older she grew, the more she realized she'd never find that again. It was better to hoard the memory than chase the ghost.

Safe and comfortable were never the same.

She turned her head over her shoulder, her neck stiff from the hours spent in the brutal temperatures. Someone tapped on her back. Precession was seated right behind her, the twin's red hair dulled to ash, frost clinging to every strand. She pointed off into the distance with a blackened fingertip and a weak smile. Hadley's gaze followed.

She didn't see anything. Not at first—but something flickered on the second look. It was a city hundreds of feet below them.

At least, she assumed it was a city.

It was still the dead of night, and despite the storm, she could make out something tall and dark, shadow-esque, where Precession had pointed. The rain, the hail, and the wind seemed to stop, skipping over that spot as if there were an invisible dome over it.

Hadley squinted, trying to see more, and as if on cue, Kismet turned sharply, causing her stomach to float up to her ears as they all plummeted, the wyvern diving.

Kismet let out an ear-piercing shriek, the kind that hurt and made one's shoulders tuck up toward their heads. Hadley had to decide whether to cover her ears with her hands or stay on the wyvern as they continued to descend. If she let go, she'd fly like a kite in a crosswind.

The dive ended and was followed by a swoop up before Kismet thudded down on the ground with an icy plop. It was like seeing the world for the first time. She'd been lucky, soaring above it all.

No matter what she had recently endured, those who lived here had it so much worse.

"What is this place called?" Hadley looked out before her, her words caught in her throat after sliding down Kismet. She held onto the beast, her hand resting on the side of its belly, its thick hide rough and warm. It was the only thing here that could feel good, that could bring some light to a city wrapped in death.

Rain still pelted them. Hadley feared that it would never stop. That it would rain for years, that floods would take over the planet. That it was irreparable. The rain had erased any dream of a winter wonderland, replacing it with something deadlier.

Is this my fault?

It was.

Had she turned Ayurveda's sun into a dark star? Traded a swift, willing death for this slow suffocation of ice and famine? Maybe fewer would have perished. Maybe more would have lived.

She buried the thought where all the ugly ones went, deep, festering. She was good at that now. Good enough to survive this half-life she'd been thrust into. It was better not to feel at all.

Her gaze drifted to Djoser at the far edge of Kismet's massive flank. He wouldn't meet her eyes. He hadn't since their hands had brushed in the temple. She traced her thumb over that patch of numb skin, craving the ruin he left behind. She wanted it to devour more of her.

A voice, low and velvet, pressed against her ear. "Welcome to Ebsonspire."

Sheng. Always too near. Always too amused.

She turned her scowl on the ruin behind him, refusing to give him her eyes.

"I told you—"

"Easy. I'm not touching you. Unfortunately for you," he teased, teeth flashing.

"Didn't you almost die—again?" Reign's small voice cut through the wind as she approached, childlike and cruel all at once.

Hadley tensed. She didn't know what to be with Reign anymore, this girl who'd once been death and rage wrapped in grown skin. She'd watched that fury splatter on concrete. She'd watched Reign fall apart piece by piece. There was no rescue for that.

"I was saved. Who bothered saving you?" Sheng laughed, eyes sliding over Reign's dripping hair, the frost curling along each strand. She only shrugged, imperious even in a child's bones.

"No one dragged you here," Arryn drawled, one arm flung over Kismet's warm scales as he caught Sheng in a rough embrace. Hadley caught the stiff line in Arryn's jaw, the way his shoulders twitched, rage half-shackled.

"Careless as ever," Sheng mused, voice edged with delight. "Family reunion, huh?"

For a heartbeat, warmth flickered among the cluster of riders, then snuffed out just as quick. Fists were clenched, but silence ruled.

A throat cleared. It was her father, watching Hadley like she was a ghost come back to haunt him. She didn't flinch. She let her shadows curl closer, whispering against her boots:

Hold it. Hold the fury. You'll need it soon enough.

In this moonless world, she'd have to learn to kill and wear the smile it carved on her face.

"If you idiots are done catching up, shall we remember why we're here?" Arryn spat, voice sharp enough to crack bone.

Hadley turned back to the blackness, to where Djoser stood like a statue in the storm.

Ebonspire.

There was nothing there, and that emptiness terrified her more than monsters ever had. But she saw the gap in the rain, a clean wound in the downpour.

"North side," Djoser said, drifting closer.

Hadley squinted, praying she guessed north correctly. Then she saw it: white specks drifting like snow, clinging to a hidden shape buried in ice and shadow. It called back Glaciel's ruin but felt wrong, like ash that bled poison.

She breathed it in and it scorched her throat, stung her eyes raw. The cold here crawled deeper than temple stone. It wasn't cold alone; it was death, sifting into her lungs.

It's as if the air around her is . . .

"Poison," Hadley stammered. "We are breathing poison."

"In a way," Precession said calmly before adding, "Your description is quite vague."

Roksana glanced at her sister, looking like the physical manifestation of the phrase *"What the fuck?"*

"I feel it too," Reifoel said, stepping into her view. "I wonder if we are more sensitive to it, those of us who are not Kinnari. . . or Vrae—"

"She is Kinnari," Reign interrupted, defending Hadley so passionately that it made her raise her eyebrows, though her sandpaper eyes quickly reminded her that moving her face was ill-advised.

"Look." Reifoel pointed to the fleshy part of his arm, and through the rain and the world of wet, she saw the rough red skin forming as if it were the desert terrain. Reifoel's skin looked how her eyes felt, and the panic started to set in. They needed to leave, they needed to get out of there. Whatever they needed to do, the reason they were here wouldn't matter anymore if they continued to deteriorate. If Hadley couldn't even move, she would be useless, worthless.

"I quite like all the powder." Sheng shrugged, completely unaffected. "It makes this city much easier to see; it was nearly impossible before."

"Can we stop being cryptic?" Roksana's vicious and bored voice was being carried away with the wind.

"I can break this down as simply as possible, sure," Sheng said before Reifoel jumped in.

"Ebsonspire is invisible. It's an invisible city."

Everyone stopped to stare at Reifoel as if they realized he was more than just a fish.

"Ahem," Sheng cleared his throat, looking for attention, "Yes, the city is invisible, which is great because I wouldn't have ever visited. Bad vibes, I hear."

"What are you talking about? It's the single most beautiful city in Myrilosis." Reifoel shook his head as if Sheng was just so silly.

Roksana slapped the palm of her hand to her forehead. "You guys are going to give me a headache. Say everything it is that we need to know, please, so we can move on. It's fucking cold outside, and we are casually standing here like there isn't an apocalypse happening."

"I couldn't have said it better myself," Reign agreed.

"There's a transparent dome that covers the city; I'm not sure what it's made of," Reifoel offered, "it covers the entire city. Normally, you would need to know exactly where those points are to enter and exit."

"Are the inhabitants of the city invisible, too?" Hadley asked.

"When you go into the dome, you are part of the city. It protects everyone who is inside," Sheng said, his lips much too close to her ear. She blinked, and it was agonizing. She bit her lip, her body caving into itself from the pain as it simultaneously tried to heal.

"We really should get Hadley out of the radiation. It seems to affect her," Precession sang. "Him, too." Her gaze moved to Reiofel, whose face was starting to turn into the same texture as the piece of arm he had just shown.

"Radiation, sister?" Roksana asked. "Really, all of this is entirely too exhausting."

"Well, that makes perfect sense actually," Sheng chimed in, suddenly chipper. "Everything that happens to one realm happens to the other. We are in an area with maybe five nuclear power plants close enough to cause damage. If even one were to melt down, that would explain this ash. It must have been quite a distance away."

Hadley's feet were no longer on the ground, but she didn't protest at all as strong arms cradled her.

"I've got you," Sheng said, holding her tight into his chest.

"She doesn't like it when you touch her," Reifoel said.

"Guys, you can touch your tips and sword fight later." Reign stomped her foot. "Now, where is this entrance, and what do we do with the wyvern?"

Hadley could hear Sheng's heart rate racing once he realized how close Kismet was to him, the creature's black nose wet and hot just a foot away from his face. She was protective; she was concerned. Kismet's eyes were that of a hungry lion, waiting for Sheng to put Hadley down.

"Come on, beautiful," Sheng said to Kismet. "You and I bonded once—we can be friends."

Riding atop of the wyvern was Hadley's shadow self, in all her dark glory, smiling widely in a beam of light that bounced off of the ice below.

What a pair those two make.

Arryn yelled as his hands reached over them, creating a metal enclosure around Kismet, around them. It wasn't sealed, so Kismet could come and go as she pleased.

"There is some protection," he said.

"She'll probably leave. She likes to hunt." Hadley offered a half smile, the closest she could ever come to saying thank you to him.

Arryn turned around, pulling Celestine by the hand with a little too much force as she stumbled behind him, the two walking toward the ghost city, the city of Ebsonspire.

"You'll never find the entrance that way," Reifoel yelled after him, but he was ignored.

Djoser started running after them, trying to catch up.

"I guess we run into an invisible wall now. This is a joy," Roksana said with tight lips as she and her sister began to follow.

Sheng beamed. "These Kinnari are so arrogant. It's truly entertaining."

He kidnapped you and let Amis lock you in a closet because he knew you were Kinnari.

The reminder was good; that the monster he was was not the monster she was. She hated him and she hated that he loved her, wanted her, possessed her in any way. She hated that she thought of him at all, that he wasn't a forgotten, irrelevant thought in the back of her mind, like any of the clients she had met before him.

That's all he was really: a past client who thought he had unlimited access, a season pass.

Despite that hate, there was a truth she would rather ignore. One that told her that maybe they were the same.

She tried to struggle against Sheng's arms, but stopped immediately when she realized every new motion on her skin created a new burn wound, a new agony that maybe was not worth her dignity, that was not worth this fight with Sheng. At least, not right now.

"You're struggling against this element," Sheng said, surprised. "It looks like you have discovered a new weakness."

Hadley thought back to when she was drowning under an ocean but couldn't die. Would she be burned through by the dust, eaten alive, conscious of it all?

There was always something.

Her shadow self followed, dancing around them, making eye contact with Hadley whenever she passed right in front of her, just waiting for permission, for the nod, for the acceptance of her to do what she was good at. Hadley was still scared of what happened, what her shadow self had done in Bangladesh.

If it happened again, even by accident, she would become the monster. Just like him, holding her now as if she were precious, watching her like prey. He was gentle only until the hunger returned.

Demon. Devil. Monster.

Not spiraling. The truth.

They marched after the group, the two of them now last. Small bursts of flame burst through the rain as Kismet blew air kisses meant for Hadley's warmth and comfort.

"I could get used to this, you know." Sheng's smile widened. "Just the three of us."

Four of us.

Hadley watched her shadow stalk after them as they headed toward the powder that hung mysteriously in the air.

7

Reifoel | Wyvern Back

Reifoel was once again perched on that damn wyvern. The winter clothes Arryn provided before they left had helped a little to protect him from the wind. The fabric, waterproof, dried out too quickly. His pants, shredded by his tail, flopped uselessly at his sides.

He kept the pants on this time, the band groaning against his waist. The remaining cloth was in ribbons, flailing and hitting his bare skin raw. He had learned some things and walking around without pants was apparently so taboo that this level of brazen pain was worth it. It also helped that his tail was such a rich black that the chafing and bruises would never show.

He tugged the damp cloak closer, grateful it hadn't fused to him like before. Altitude and wind made him feel brittle, an ocean creature dragged too high from his depths.

He'd rather be anywhere but here, riding this giant flying death bus.

You'll be home soon.

He had to master turning tail to legs on command, wet or not. This world was all rain and flooding now. Until it was deep enough to swim, he'd need carrying.

Like a useless, spoiled prince.

Once he rode dolphins instead of dragons. He wondered if his old dolphin friend was safe.

Could the ocean have changed so fast?

I hope you're well, friend.

He gulped, the air too frigid, too cold. At the ocean floor, cold wrapped him like silk. This cold clawed him raw, drained him, begged him to go still.

Is this dying?

Reifoel jerked his head up, chasing away that thought. He glared at his tail, dragging in the wind. He pressed his chest to the wyvern's spike, arms around it and the redheaded Kinnari in front of him.

If my dolphin's alive, my parents must be too.

"My King, My Queen," Reifoel imagined saying to them, "I've returned without my moonstone and without my cousin."

Guilt split him open. He'd be coming home empty, with only lessons to share.

Loss was fast, love vanished faster, and burritos didn't make you belong.

Reifoel swallowed down the ache in his chest as he pictured that insufferable, sharp-tongued, golden-haired Serelune who'd trailed him halfway across the world. They'd protected each other, grown closer than brothers. Just when Isadore had begun to dream of going home, the bed beneath him and the floor that held it crumbled in a single blinding blast.

Isadore should have easily had three hundred to three hundred and twenty years of life. He should have been old, with a beard that matched the length of his hair, tangled with seaweed and great-great-grandbabies hiding within it.

Reifoel flexed his tail, feeling like an idiot, trying to make something happen, trying to make it change, trying to make those legs appear.

This is pointless. You're too wet.

The wyvern swooped, bored in the sky, jolting Reifoel's pulse. Ahead, the second redhead turned her head and looked directly at him. Her lips were blue, her teeth chattered, stunning like frost on a cliff face.

Reifoel realized that words were leaving her lips. Sound was lost to the wind, but she exaggerated her mouth to repeat the same message.

Reifoel tried to put it together.

Her feet?

She shook her head and kept mouthing.

Hair piece?

Trying something new, she lifted her hand and patted her chest with a quick rhythm.

Heartbeat?

He mouthed it back, palm to his ribs. She nodded, a faint grin, and turned.

He drummed his ribs, syncing the rhythm. Too slow.

She twisted back again, as if she could feel the sag in his shoulders. Her heartbeat was a drumroll, far too quick for a normal rhythm.

Unless that was her regular heartbeat, a human's regular heartbeat.

Reifoel lifted his face, rain striking his skin like sparks. He reached inward, searching for the thread that stitched mind to muscle. His heart kicked harder, then harder still. A mental shove urged it faster. It felt ready to tear free of his ribs, but he clung to that single path: match her or drown.

He sucked in a ragged breath and pressed his forehead to Roksana's back. She twisted to scowl at him, but he didn't flinch, stealing her heat for courage.

He stayed there, chest heaving, until her pulse thrummed steady against his ribs. Had he never felt it before? That wild drum, so different from his calm Serelune beat. Eyes shut, he let his own rhythm stumble, race, sync. One heartbeat answered another, beat for beat.

Keep pushing.

He imagined this is what a heart attack must feel like.

Keep pushing.

He was close, so close to her rhythm.

Go. Go.

Reifoel felt as if his veins were filled with rocket fuel. His pulse pounded twice as fast as normal, but the discomfort soon faded. A strange ease was injected into his veins.

The tail surrendered to human flesh, each inch of peeling skin clinging, then letting go.

Reifoel opened his eyes and stared at his naked legs hanging over the side of the wyvern. The rain hit them, beads of water welling and streaming in trails through the thick, dark hair that covered him. It was a thin layer of protection, but protection, nevertheless.

A stunned laugh almost escaped, but he swallowed it down.

Djoser sat behind Reifoel, looking a little upset at the sudden butt against him.

Thank you, thank you, thank you, thank you, he mouthed to Precession. She clapped her hands a few times.

REIFOEL WAS the first to leap from the wyvern when its claws scraped solid ground. He nearly dropped to his knees to kiss the frozen mix of ice, snow, and drifting white ash, but caught himself just in time. Bare feet burned against the cold, but he welcomed the wet bite. His eyes found Hadley, and his relief soured to a scowl as Sheng materialized at her side like a shadow that wouldn't leave.

She's his wife.

Reiofel pulled at the collar of his jacket.

But she doesn't act like it.

Reifoel had moved on fast from rejection. Hadley might not have agreed to marry him, but he knew that the proposal was preposterous, brought on by lust and grief. A flame still lingered there, though. He knew she ached after him, even if it wasn't in the way he wanted.

Maybe we just need time.

Maybe Reifoel just needed to settle for a nice girl with a tail.

It wouldn't be a stretch to call him the settling type. Anything for his mother, after all.

Maybe it was time to think less about wanting and more about mending the world he'd helped break. That seemed nobler. Though the persistent itch below his belt disagreed.

Underwater, life was simple: scatter some seed, drift away. Up here, with legs and heat and soft skin, the ache was constant, a restless animal prowling his thoughts.

Isadore was right; this penis was a hell of a lot more fun than not having it at all.

"Are we just going to ignore the pants?" Djoser asked Reifoel as he walked behind him.

"My lack thereof, I'm assuming?" Reifoel shrugged. "Maybe I can find a pair when we get there." His legs were numb, each step through snow like glass. He was even less thrilled about his partial nudity than Djoser was..

They caught up to Arryn, who stood stiffly while Celestine hugged her arms around herself, shivering just behind him.

"Damn it," Arryn cursed under his breath as he kept kicking at the air and meeting something hard.

"That can't feel good," Reifoel said. "I know where the entrance is. Let me help."

Arryn looked Reifoel over, his frown deepening. The broad-shouldered, stone-faced Kinnari extended a hand, his mouth set in a hard line. In an instant, it was like Reifoel had never been half-naked at all. Dark blue pants, sturdy brown boots, and warm waterproof socks materialized snugly around him. Arryn didn't spare him another glance, turning away as Celestine bounced beside him, words tumbling out faster than the wind could carry them.

"Oh, thank gods," Djoser said. "Something that hangs down like that is best put away. You might give someone nightmares."

Celestine blushed, hiding her smile behind her hands. She'd stolen a glimpse before those tattered ribbons betrayed what he'd been so casually dragging through the snow. Hadley knew, too. He couldn't help hoping she liked what she saw.

"Go," Arryn said, his voice rough, his blond hair soaked and plastered flat against his head. "Show us the way."

"No use kicking an invisible wall." Djoser smirked.

Reifoel didn't hesitate and began leading them east, circling the dome. He moved fast, knowing that Hadley was in Sheng's arms but not wanting to see it. He'd leave them a blip in his peripheral vision.

Vrae scum.

"Where is it? The entrance? We've been walking a while." Celestine's voice an odd mix of confidence and sweetness. She didn't fit in here, amongst all of them, but Reifoel couldn't pinpoint why. She wasn't non-magical, that he was confident about, despite her human appearance.

"We are almost there; it's just up ahead." Reifoel pointed to two trees in the distance that intertwined and looped through one another without a single bloom or leaf to decorate the unique shape.

The flakes of radiation burned his exposed skin. He hoped he was imagining the blood running down his cheeks. Cracks etched their way in, refusing to give up until his bloodstream was tainted.

They had been walking for miles. The wyvern hadn't really chosen a convenient drop-off point.

"Why are we walking when we could have flown ourselves?" Roksana asked through her teeth, supporting Precession's weight.

"Not all of us can fly," Sheng said.

No one cares.

But you can't fly either.

"If you're playing a trick on us . . ." Arryn's threatening voice erupted.

"I have no reason to be here other than kindness." Reifoel stopped walking and turned over his shoulder. "I am set on finding the ocean. I do not belong here with you. You needed my moonstone. You did not need me."

Reifoel made sure he did not look at Hadley.

If Reifoel had had any worry of a sudden, violent death, then it had washed away. He could make his needs known, he could stand up to Arryn, to any of them.

You are not their puppet.

Isadore might have approved.

"So, you've been here before?" Reifoel glanced back at the scarier redhead marching up behind him.

"Are you trying to catch up with me?"

"No. You walk slow," Roksana said, pulling her sister behind her. Precession looked like a puppy struggling against its leash, staring at the sky as the rain continued to pelt her face.

"How is it that she seems to know . . . things?" Reifoel asked. "I don't understand how she knew what I was trying to do with my tail. I didn't even really know."

"You know, fish boy—"

"Love that nickname," Reifoel scoffed.

"I know, it fits so well," Roksana snapped back. "She is a person. You can talk to her yourself."

Reifoel looked at Precession again, the euphoria on her face blissed-out, like she'd taken something illegal and magical. He couldn't disturb that, at least not now.

I'll talk to her later.

Reifoel felt a spark of energy, of life, building inside him. Roksana walked next to him now, a curious smirk on her face whenever he glanced at her. His blood warmed, his face flushed. Her smile grew wider.

"So, do you belong to any of the males?" Reifoel asked as they approached the twisted, naked trees.

"Oh yes, all of them, really," Roksana said. Reifoel raised an eyebrow. "I just bend over whenever anyone asks. Why? Do you need a ride, too?"

Reifoel's eyes widened. He just stared at her, slowing his step.

"My sister jests," Precession sang.

Roksana let out a closed-mouth, unenthusiastic giggle.

"It's there, the entrance," Precession told her, pointing to a spot in the air towards the city.

She's right.

"I can feel the air shift. What beautiful magic," Precession continued.

"How is this a place you've ever been to? What was it that you were doing here?" Roksana asked him, shaking her head as she took a few steps forward with her arms out in front of her, waiting to run into a wall.

"Oh, you know, that *I want to see the world phase* hit me pretty hard in my adolescence. I had a pretty wild night here. It's best if you're drunk, honestly. You can't see what you're dealing with."

This time it was Roksana who raised an eyebrow.

Reifoel smiled at her with all his teeth, and his blood heated again.

"Luckily, this time around, you can see me."

"No, I have a feeling he won't be able to, dear sister," Precession said.

Roksana huffed as they all stopped walking, Arryn and Celestine just a few steps behind them.

"Let's wait for the group," Reifoel said.

"That's not a very Kinnari thing to do," Roksana said, one left side of her lip curling up as she cast a shot toward Arryn.

"I've done nothing with my life but wait for you all to return to the temple," Arryn said gruffly.

"Here we go, everyone," Roksana threw her hands up, laughing, mocking.

"It's so lovely to hear you laugh," Precession sang to her.

The clipped words and attitudes felt less threatening by the minute. This was just how these completely dysfunctional, powerful beings showed their affection.

"I'm not usually one to insult a lady," Arryn said to Celestine before his eyes moved back to Roksana, "but you are a bitch."

Well, maybe sometimes *it wasn't threatening.*

"Oh, rest assured, dear Celestine," Djoser said, marching up.

"Arryn here does nothing offensive to anyone. He's the literal saint of our planet."

"And you're the devil." Arryn's eyes narrowed. Djoser chose to ignore it, not to engage.

Even he doesn't poke.

"Hey, that's my role," Sheng yelled from behind them.

Arryn's gaze locked on the moonstone resting against Reifoel's chest, the weight of it suddenly crushing. Tension coiled through Arryn's shoulders as his eyes lifted to meet Reifoel's, accusing, as if every disaster traced back to him alone.

His mother must have known. Of course she did, pressing the moonstone into his hands before sending him up to the surface, Isadore at his heels. She'd seen this path long before he ever stumbled onto it.

"I think we should start here before we go inside," Arryn said.

"I am ready to get out of this rain, Arryn," Reign said, stomping up to the group, Sheng behind her, carrying Hadley.

Her blonde hair was a tangled halo, frozen strands clinging to her flushed cheeks. Reifoel caught the raw ache in her eyes, the cold, the misery, yet still he stared, selfish and helpless. Those eyes were still home to him. That same deep blue he once longed to escape beneath the waves was now an ache to return.

Take her with you, tucked safely at your side.

"She doesn't like it when you touch her," Reifoel said to Sheng, who held back a laugh.

"I didn't see you carrying her two miles through a storm."

"I wouldn't assume she needed to be carried. We all know that she's much stronger than me. Stronger than you."

"Shut up all of you," Arryn shouted, "and throw me that moonstone."

Reifoel pulled the necklace up and over his head, the thin black leather wrapped around the small crevices of the stone and knotted in a way his large hands could never replicate. He felt the cool surface, sliding his thumb over it before tossing it over to Arryn.

Arryn held it up. "I don't know what I'm doing. I don't know how this will go."

He pushed Celestine back away from him, her eyes wide with concern.

Reifoel was concerned, too.

"I'll fly it up," Reign offered. "If you pass out, someone has to fly it up. Then we can build on it."

Arryn just stared at the stone, the evidence of his lack of confidence clear, unabashed.

"Be ready to step in," Arryn said, looking at Djoser, "if there's a threat."

$$8$$

Arryn | Ebsonspire, Myrilosis

The whole world, the whole galaxy, dared to rest in the cradle of his hand. Of course it did.

Who else could command it?

In one palm, the moonstone pulsed obediently. In the other, he coaxed atoms to kneel, teasing calcium, nickel, iron into perfect submission. The crust of this new moon would remember him, its creator, not some faceless chaos of collisions and stardust. Billions of years of chance and ruin, now rendered obsolete by a single mind.

His mind.

Let the gods watch him succeed after they tried to tear them apart. Reluctance was for lesser men. Arryn was inevitable.

Arryn drew in the faintest trace of the moonstone, a whisper of weight, less than a picogram balanced on his will alone. He hunted for more, commanding stray atoms to bind into minerals: olivine, pyroxene, forging the unseen core of this newborn moon. Another fraction joined the stone, a full picogram now beating like a promise in his palm. This fragment, this seed of rock, would swell into a sentinel in the sky. It would cradle tides, anchor seasons, and spare the world from the ruin waiting to devour it.

Here we go.

He widened his search and began pulling in masses and masses of atoms that hung in the air, ones that clung to their bodies, the ground, and the trees.

His body trembled under the growing weight. He had to be precise. This wasn't just some abstract fantasy. The implications of creating a false moon could be just as damaging as no moon.

"Nothing is happening," Arryn heard someone whisper.

"No, look," another voice said, maybe Celestine's.

The rock was growing, the band on the necklace breaking as the stone expanded. The exterior began to harden, turning a subtle gray. It was still smooth, volcanic eruptions and meteors not yet having broken the surface.

Arryn continued pulling, morphing, pushing and growing until the moonstone was nearly the size of Reign. His hands waved with the same grace of a ballerina, every fingertip reaching for harmony with the objects he created. Etches of black crept along the edges of his vision, but power wrangled through him like a mother lifting a car off her child.

"Can you still carry it up? It's a few hundred pounds at least," Arryn asked Reign as it hovered, balancing on his hand.

"If Precession can keep it lifted, if she can get me clear to the atmosphere, then yes." Reign braced her hands against the seed of a moon, testing its weight as her wings tore free.

"I can keep going for a few more minutes," Precession said. "I'm connected. I can feel the new tether. It's making me dizzy."

She was building the tethers to the moon while rotating the planet. It was almost as much work as he was expected to do.

"You should keep going, Arryn," Djoser urged him. "I can help lift. We all can. Add as much to it as you can."

Arryn looked around, most of the faces staring at the thing he'd just made. No one was marveling at him.

It's just a big rock.

The atmosphere around him was breathless, haunting. Eyes pierced into his work, hopes tied to quiet pessimism.

"Fine," he said.

He continued. The burning in his skin was already gone, but now, something else began to stir.

It was wonderful.

The rush was filthy, glorious, power spilling from his hands like a drug he'd never quit. He'd drown in it, given the chance. Every scrap of rock fed to this half-born moon was another hit, another drag of a cigarette down to the filter.

He wanted it dirty, reckless, endless. It was the same chaos high he'd ridden when he stitched that corpse of a town back to life in Myrilosis.

And in that haze, there she was.

Allienna.

Always fucking there when he was too far gone to fight it. He imagined her lips on him, her fingers sinking deep, promising the soft death he'd decided he deserved. He'd stitch the sky with moons if it meant her ghost would stay curled in the wreck of his chest. He'd wire galaxies together with his bare teeth if it meant she'd show up behind his eyelids when the come-down hit.

He was the Life Gifter now. Not some brittle old god, not some distant priest. Just him, starved, drunk on himself, building whole worlds because it hurt too much to sit still. He'd keep pouring out until nothing was left to feel. And even then, he'd find a way to feel more.

"Arryn, that's enough." Djoser's hand touched his shoulder.

No, I won't stop.

"Arryn, you can go too far," Reign's voice sounded. It was sweet, full of worry.

It wasn't as sweet as the feeling that rippled his skin, a melancholy song that lingered in his blood. It was a gulp of air that had him feeling addicted, that had him pushing further.

His head was both heavy and light. Concern sounded around

him, but he couldn't bother with them. He was focused on his hands, on his body. This was the purest he'd ever felt.

There was only this.

"Take it, take it away from him," a male voice said.

He heard that. He didn't like that.

"No," Arryn yelled.

But he was too dizzy, too lost in the spell. Djoser and Reign ripped the moon out of his hand.

I will destroy—

Before Arryn could finish the thought, the darkness bled out, a full vision of black. He passed out cold in the snow, two twisted trees over his head.

9

____

Allienna | Sacramento, Ca

She stared into the dark, her eyes tracking the ceiling as she listened to the raspy, noisy air conditioning clicking on and off. The curtains danced a waltz in the air as the floor vent partnered them with a ghost, a draft, a haunting that kept the room heavy.

Allienna wasn't scared, not exactly. It was the crawling weight of doubt, her four-year-old daughter's head heavy and warm on her stomach. Hadley was fast asleep and hadn't said anything about the incident with the Vrae. Popsicles and cartoons had worked like magic.

There was tomorrow, the next day, and the day after that. Each would be harder, knowing that something had found her. Not only her, but it wanted Hadley.

Why was the Vrae interested in the tiny human she'd created? Would a Kinnari somehow find out where they were? Would Arryn show up one night, uninvited, unchanged?

Allienna squeezed. She pulled Hadley closer and kissed the crown of her head.

"Stop," Hadley said in a grumpy, sleep-talking dream state. "I don't want any more hot dogs."

"Got it, no more hot dogs." Allienna smiled.

She would gladly give her soul, body, and heart to protect her daughter. Maybe she should make her way back to Arryn. She wouldn't be happy, no, but Hadley would be safe. Allienna could already feel the years slipping off her, her immortality fading. She mattered so little to the future, to Hadley's story, other than these few big decisions.

Allienna felt the burn, her skin on fire, as she imagined herself groveling before that power, begging him to accept what he'd once called his. She would receive his touch despite every promise she'd sworn to herself. She had once vowed to be lonely to protect her and her daughter's hearts.

Yet here she was again, and it didn't seem like she would be able to escape that cost.

Eyelids growing heavy, Allienna blew air through her lips and pulled the second pillow out from under her head as sleep fought its way in. She let it overtake her. Just this one night, this last night, she would let her eyelids shut.

10

Amis | Kinnari Temple

"I am not a doll," Balizar said, clothes piled on his furry head, wrapped and knotted to create a makeshift wig.

"Just stay still; stop complaining," Salome instructed, pulling out one of Hadley's colored pens, the red one, and putting it up to the creature's lips.

"No, no, stop it." Balizar swatted at the child. "That's where I draw the line. My boundary has been established!" He stood up, his posture like a corseted woman's in the 1800s, and marched off towards the cots.

"Now, what am I supposed to do?" Salome pouted, throwing her hands down on the large communal table and putting her head to her forearms.

Amis sat at the other end of the table; his sudden role as the temple's leader might have gone straight to his head if everyone around him weren't so damn competitive. Noah's cries drifted over from the cots—Balizar was probably the cause, scaring him as usual.

It wasn't a cry of pain or danger; no, Amis knew every tone of that wail by now and exactly how to read it. That wail could shatter nerves or summon gods.

He had chosen to stay behind. He couldn't leave these kids.

Salome. Rangi. Alohra. Luca. Noah.

Amis looked out into the temple, his normally tied hair now loose, dangling over his shoulder. He could hear some creatures talking amongst themselves, but mostly, everyone looked precisely how he felt, how Salome felt, now that everyone seemed awake and alert.

Bored.

He stood up and paced back and forth, his hands behind his head and his eyes darting around the room, constantly categorizing everyone and counting.

Three of the bright-yellow-haired ladies. Two small, angry old men with flowers sprouting from their ears.

Amis had always been anxious, but the stress had dramatically increased since adding innocent lives to his list of beings to keep alive.

It's not something I'd recommend, kids.

Thudd-udd.

Amis jumped at the sound. Even the reinforced wall Arryn had built hadn't kept the water out.

"Noah is scared," Balizar yelled across the temple. "I know because he won't stop crying, and we all enjoy listening to it."

Amis made eye contact with a group of female . . . whatever they were, trying not to make accusing faces at them. They just stared back, rolling their four different colored eyes, tucking that bright yellow hair back.

I mean, would it kill them to help with the kids?

Thudd-udd.

Amis felt the entire building shake.

"Shit," he said, ducking down and covering his head as the rest of the creatures around him screamed and hid themselves in various ways.

Again, these kids were so hard to keep alive.

"Is anyone injured?" Amis asked loudly, standing up after a few breaths.

It's okay. You're okay. They're okay.

Noah's cries rose to a frantic pitch, the toddler teetering on the edge of hyperventilation. Salome folded her arms around him, wings flared wide, her eyes locked on the walls, flicking back and forth like she was tracking the world's most dangerous tennis match.

"Stop," Luca said to Amis, who had hurried over to them.

Amis did. He stopped in his tracks. He didn't move. Hell, he didn't even breathe as he stared at those five children huddled in the corner of the temple, Salome's eyes still focused on the walls.

"What—"

Thud-dud.

That one wasn't just a thud. It was more.

The temple shook again. The movement felt deeper, farther away. Amis could feel the vibrations in his teeth, and his cheeks jiggled.

Get to them. Get to them now.

Amis decided in an instant. While everyone else stayed frozen in terror under cots and tables, he sprinted for the children pressed into the stone corner. He threw his arms wide and gathered them all against his chest, protests muffled, even Luca too frightened to argue.

Thud-dud.

Memories of Mt. Maunganui slammed into Amis's head. He could smell burnt flesh, feel the heat of bodies he'd dragged off screaming children—wide awake but trapped in the same nightmare. They'd done this before: cornered, shaking, no escape. Death had never stopped hunting them. They weren't meant to make it this far, and deep down, he knew it.

Something about that thought stopped Amis's heart from beating.

They were supposed to have died.

Amis stopped it from happening. He had saved them.

Karmakara could be chasing them, looking for the souls that would have been claimed in her woven timelines.

It filled him with shame that he hadn't put it together before. He vowed to protect these children, the remainder of Waihema, a village that was never supposed to exist, a people that were plummeting to destruction.

There was too much death in the world; it was out of balance. He'd thought it was Djoser's power, but what if it was this?

Gods.

The vibrations didn't cease; instead, they strengthened. Walls and floors rattled as everyone's stomachs plunged and heartbeats rose. Noah's cries quieted, the toddler too scared to make a sound.

"Will you throw yourself over the rest of us, too? I could use protection," Amis heard Balizar mutter. The creature's voice was drowned out by the stone wall to the north crushing down, toppling in, and taking some of the hallways with it. Screams erupted but were drowned out by high-pitched, powerful winds that roared through the space, snow and slush barreling in and spreading out; the wood stove was instantly put out.

Those winds were so loud that Amis felt like his head was being split apart. His arms squeezed into himself instinctively as he let his weight fall heavy on the children he worked to protect. Their protests muffled, their bodies trembling, their sobs breaking through the rush of anxiety that had Amis unable to move, reminded him that he'd stayed behind for a reason.

Dark gray stone that served as structure was now loose, flying through the temple like snowballs. The temple pieces hit more walls, causing what remained of the walls to groan as creatures screamed and ran out, looking for more cover that didn't exist.

Amis bent down to his right knee, pulling his weight off the children, who all stayed in place, not moving, with their eyes closed. They clung together, some shaking, while other hands in between their bodies made motions to comfort.

Their new normal.

Amis's chest ached, and in a moment of weakness, in a breaking of his soul and his heart, he got ready to say goodbye. He looked up, the whistling intensifying, the sound of a singing teapot whipping into one eardrum and filling his entire body, adding to his despair, to his sudden understanding that he needed to let go. He needed to let them go.

In the corners, edging into the now clear view of the sky, was something dark, something massive. There wasn't just one. Amis counted two, three, then four.

A sudden chill ran through him. If there was a time to say goodbye, it was now.

"What is it?" Salome roared out, arms holding Ahora.

Brave, she was so brave.

Amis said the words, he answered her, trying to summon up the courage and find her source of bravery within himself.

You've done this before. It's no different. Let the winds take them.

"It's a tornado." He found his voice this time, yelling out what was coming.

Salome was only confused, which made sense. There were no tornadoes in Waihema. That was not a word that she knew.

Luca, though, had a different reaction. He stared at Amis, his eyes cold, almost as if he understood that Amis's posture meant something different. There was anger and judgment there, and the boy raised up and put his back to Salome, Noah, Rangi, and Ahora with his arms out wide as protection.

"Keep your heads covered," he yelled, a battle cry. This boy, this teenager, was not giving up on his people, on his friends. He stared at Amis, his teeth visible as his body struggled against the struggling bodies behind him.

They were so scared.

Noah reached out with his chubby arms, his hands opening and closing as his face begged him to come to him, hold him, and protect him.

I can't. I'm sorry.

It wasn't like the newborns, this type of goodbye. It was so much more; a sadness he had never experienced before ran through him. Creatures around him screamed as more stone rumbled and flew off of walls.

"What do we do?" he heard voices call out. Amis could at least stand there, say goodbye, as the tornadoes came, as they overtook the temple and all the mortal bodies within it. That was the least he could do.

This was what Sheng felt when he had watched that little girl get torn apart all those years ago.

Helpless.

That feeling within him, those eyes that stared at him, were so sad and so scared. The sky blackened more, the wind popped their eardrums, the children's pleading held Amis rooted. There was nothing to fight. Nowhere to run.

Was there?

They all had their roles, balance, and peace to keep here on this planet. If death required these children, one of Amis's hypotheses, then there was nothing to be done.

Noah pushed through the hands that held him back, practically floating in the air with all four tornadoes fully in view, the ground shaking so violently that a step was nearly impossible. He tumbled through, throwing himself towards Amis.

Despite his instincts, Amis lunged to catch him, his torso falling to the ground as the toddler's head bounced off of his forearms. Amis curled the toddler into him, tucking his legs towards his chest and putting his arms over his head as he stared at the sky. The tornados were seconds from ripping through the temple.

Fuck it.

He couldn't do it. That coldness that he'd once had, that ruthlessness for the better good, to support destiny, seemed like a cruel joke that the Gods had played on them.

Maybe it was love, maybe just the raw instinct to live—whatever it was, Amis let his wings tear free from his back, skin splitting around the sharp rise of his birthmarks. The wings propelled him upright into a low crouch, Noah still curled tight in his arms, pressed against his chest.

"Stay low, be fast," he screamed as loud as his lungs could.

Luca's eyes shifted from hate to disappointment to something like understanding. Without a word or a glance back, he crouched low, gripping the hand of whoever he could reach. The Waihema children clung to each other, trailing after Amis, weaving through flying stones and cots that spun overhead like enchanted debris.

Other creatures saw them and followed, too, though Amis couldn't help but notice some getting swept up in the air, their hands clawing for anything they could hold on to. Some were on the ground, bones visibly broken underneath pieces of large temple blocks.

We are going to make it. We have to make it.

There was a thunderous sound as they inched towards the hallway. More stone, more walls destroyed, more bodies, some with fur and some with skin, trapped under the debris.

Amis turned his head, just for a second, to look back.

"Don't stop, don't look, keep your heads down."

A cot blew and swept under Amis's legs, knocking him down and landing flat on his back. Noah cried out, though there was no sound, the both of them having the air knocked out of them.

A hand grabbed Amis by the wrist, pulling him forward. Luca, his other hand grasping the back of Salome's shirt. He held them all together, and he refused to let anyone give up on him or give up on them.

Amis regained his footing. All of their lives depended on it. The wall behind them, where they had huddled against a few minutes ago, was gone, and the base of the tornado was only a few feet behind that spot. Their time was over.

Amis pulled the group and shouted.

"Run." He lifted whoever he could, throwing Ahora over his shoulder, Noah still against his chest as Luca struggled to keep up with Amis's movements. He let the wind launch him, skimming over the ground like a figure skater. He hoped Rangi was holding on to someone, being dragged by someone. He didn't have time to look back as he clung to the ground, doing everything he could not to be lifted and thrown like all other objects around them.

One more step, one hand, one knee, one foot.

They were in the hallway now, snow plummeting from the wall missing, the cold burning against his hands as they crawled. Amis could hear the youthful cries behind him, but he worried that if he looked back, even for just a breath, a tornado would rip through the very spot they moved through, and they would be lost through the air and the wind and the cold.

He reached the door and laughed, thinking about how used he was to these catastrophic events. Something inside him tugged, a reminder that there was much more to come. The children he was saving, the lives he vowed to protect, were already ghosts in a sense. A death waiting to happen, life and stardust that was meant to go back into the world, meant to become something new. Maybe something beautiful, maybe something horrific.

What it was didn't matter because they would not be here. Who they were now was what he wanted.

Amis placed his hand on the latch, his skin bright red from the snow and ice as he clawed it away from the joint until he could pull the door, fighting the snow on the floor.

Someone tapped his shoulder, and like a fool, Amis turned. A tornado lunged toward them, roaring as bodies, furniture, and shattered stone whipped through the swirling darkness just ten feet away. The children clung to him and each other, feet lifted off the ground, their combined weight anchoring him as he forced the door open against the snow.

The tornado ripped through, destroying the door, destroying where they stood, leaving nothing behind. Even the stone laid as the foundation was dug up and thrown, the Kinnari's stories etched onto the broken, dislodged exterior stones sent flying.

Amis stood, his breaths shallow, his back on the other side of the shut door, staring out at Myrilosis. The vibrating sounds were muted, but still there as the four tornadoes passed, heading down the mountain, away from them.

Sobs grew louder, flagging Amis for the first time. He could look again. They would still be safe if he looked.

Salome slumped down, sitting on the snow, her eyes empty, her skin prickled. Amis saw no blood and no injuries. His breathing started to steady as Noah stirred against his torso, returning to life.

The threat was gone.

Salome's shoulders curled forward and she started sobbing into her hands.

"Hey, hey, it's okay, we are safe," Amis said.

For now.

Luca bent down to hug her, to pat her back, pushing back tears of his own. His eyes flickered up, meeting Amis before his lips parted, before his words shook Amis to his core.

"We lost Rangi."

11

Reign | Outside of Ebsonspire, Myrilosis

Reign slowly inhaled. The air felt crisp and fresh, as if the ashes held no consequence. But her body recognized the lie. The particles in the air carried death in quiet, microscopic movements. She could not see it, but she could feel its weight in her bones.

They had remained outside the protective wards for too long, and even she could sense the toll it was beginning to take.

Her body had healed, as it always did, but that did not mean she was unharmed. The Kinnari were resilient, but even their resilience broke down when the world turned against them. The poison did not scar her skin or break her bones, but it nestled deep, clinging to her blood and nerves.

Reign tried to speak, but the words did not line up the way they should have. They broke apart in her mouth, turned into soft mutterings with no meaning. Even she could not understand what she was saying. The sounds tasted like memory, like prophecy, like something important unraveling before it could be understood.

And still, her body stood, her breath steady, her heart slow and unyielding. Immortality had preserved her, but it could never be its own savior.

Wind snapped at her hair, carrying it across the edges of her vision as their group settled near the twisted dead trees. There was a goal. There was always a goal.

You just have to get the moon into the sky.

That was her job. All of their jobs.

Reign looked towards the sky, tucking her thick, pin-straight hair out of her face, ignoring the others while memories that seemed like dreams crept behind her brown eyes. She had endured a cold like this before, a dark sky, an abysmal world she hadn't recognized at the time. The memory of the last of the Waihema pressed into her heart.

They were stuck.

There was a door frame that could have been to the temple, made of remnants of gray and warm stone. Pairs of large yet young eyes were upon her. It almost hurt to go back so far.

She was so young then, so naïve to the horrors her present kept delivering. When their group had left those creatures, those children, Amis, they were safe in the temple. She hoped they were still there, that her younger self had stumbled upon a changed scene, that the time jump she had completed no longer existed.

But she had been there. She had met them there for the very first time.

How many times have you crossed paths with them?

The memory of the time jump started to piece back together, the threads attaching, connecting, and making a new story.

You just left them there.

Even if she had known, she couldn't have interfered. She had broken so many rules.

"Where are you right now?" Roskana's seductively cruel voice wrapped around Reign's heart.

Reign looked up and blinked, bringing herself back, seeing

Arryn's unconscious face cradled in her hands. His skin was burned from reentering the atmosphere, the smell making her nauseated. She sighed, debating whether she was concerned or wanted to rip out his very full, thick, yellow-blond hair.

Her anger swelled, thick and all-consuming. Worry was easier, horror even better, anything to drown out the itch under her skin that made her wrists burn and her arms stiff.

She looked up at Roksana's judgmental face and then back down to Arryn's again. She could claw that nose right off his face.

Is this how you feel, but with burning instead of anger?

Reign tried to put the intrusive thoughts away.

Of course, she was angry.

She was in this small body, her home, her world destroyed, and the one person who could make it alright, the one real friend she had in the world, passed out when he used too much of his magic. She sat in the snow, the wyvern's sour breath the only thing keeping her from freezing. Better that than nothing, even if it reeked like a giant burp.

Roksana. Roksana is hanging over you.

There was a slight sense of relief in that thought.

You are not the problem.

Roksana was likely amplifying it, that anger buried under memories that she wasn't even sure really happened.

Don't lie to yourself.

"I think that human is getting jealous. She's pacing around, staring at the two of you like a lioness in heat." Roksana frowned, tilting her head toward the pretty brunette from Glaciel.

Arryn's new pet.

"I look like I'm nine." Reign narrowed her eyes.

"Romantic attention isn't the only type," Roksana replied.

"Celestine," Reign's voice rang out, "I think it's best if we figure out how to get into the city and get his body out of the snow. Would you be able to look after him? The last time he did this, he was out for days."

The barmaid's heart-shaped face brightened, and she stopped pacing. "Okay, I'm in."

Reign looked around, the two twisted trees hanging over their heads. The sky was still filled with clouds, dark and gray. She couldn't see the progress; she couldn't see if there was a moon, however small, in the atmosphere.

The plan had been for her to fly it up and push the moonstone up into the sky, but instead, she'd caught Arryn, or should she say that he passed out right on top of her.

Instead, Djoser had taken the lead and carried the moonstone, now the size of a small boulder, up into the air. He disappeared. He hadn't come back yet.

Reign couldn't tell if he had been gone five minutes, ten, or sixty, but she didn't love that he was still absent.

"We should wait until Djoser returns before we move inside," Reifoel said, leaning against the side of the wyvern, moving as the creature's breathing expanded and retracted its belly.

Hadley stood at its nose, her hands moving across the side of its face. The creature's eyes were closed as it sat in pleasure, in the comfort of their connection. On the other side of the wyvern's head stood Sheng, his arms crossed and his eyes never leaving the girl's face.

"That thing should be in its shed," Reign's voice held too much irritation.

"Why does it bother you? The beast will always follow the girl," Precession could somehow hum while forming words.

It's damn lovely.

"It doesn't bother me," Reign snapped.

It does. But it shouldn't.

"If there's ever another pet dragon up for grabs, you can have first dibs," Celestine said assuringly.

Stupid. That was so stupid.

"Those who have never entered Ebonspire before will never find the entrance without a guide," Reifoel added, glancing at Hadley once he saw Reign's eyes were on her. He looked a little sad, a little awkward. Unsure about what to do with his body, uncertain of where he belonged.

"So unless someone can carry Arryn here, we all have to sit in this ash."

"We wait for Djoser," Sheng said.

Don't defend Kinnari, you piece of shit.

"He should be back soon," Roksana said. "My sister is steady. She no longer needs my support."

Precession stood alone, her eyelids closed and her hands out. An ethereal beauty in the night, her skin pale as the surrounding snow, her fire-red hair knotted and tangled from the weather. The serenity and focus that was hinted at along her jawbone told Reign that she was working, she was working hard.

Roksana moved, reaching her hands back out to hold onto her sister as if she were worried that she would float away, gravity not applying to her. Reign knew that Precession was caging herself, sacrificing her body to save them all.

Precession was the tether. She cast herself onto that moonstone like a fisherman casting his line, and as soon as it traveled past Earth's atmosphere, she pulled, she anchored, and she turned the planet.

Of course, that's what she assumed would happen if Djoser was successful.

Why is he still gone?

A flare of anger hit Reign again, her hands practically shaking. She would be up there if she hadn't been crushed or pinned. She wouldn't have messed this up. Reign's lips parted and pulled back into a snarl.

What the hell are you doing?

She stopped immediately, forcing her expression to return to neutral.

"It's done," Precession said, a sweet melancholy wrapping around her words, her voice.

Reign watched the twin; the dazed, airheaded look in her eyes was back again, the underlying strength that had made itself known these past few days completely gone.

How cruel. How unfair.

Precession stood there, trapped in a world where she could walk free.

Arryn suddenly felt heavier on top of her. Reign was done. Nothing she did here could help. She was not a replacement for Allienna. She didn't want to be.

Reign rolled Arryn off her with a grunt. "Of course you passed out on me."

Arryn had driven Allienna away. Her best friend was gone because of him. She had pushed Reign out of her life, too, likely because of the association. Deep down, it boiled Reign's blood. She closed her eyes, taking deep breaths as the snow began to get through the waterproof parts of her coat, her boots, and her pants.

Focus on something else.

Reign opened her eyes, her chin to her shoulder, her gaze flickering up to the wyvern, Hadley, and Reifoel. The two barely stood, each highly affected by the poison falling from the sky.

Sheng moved fast, jumping right in front of Reign, turning his back to her as his boots skidded in the snow, ice hitting her cheeks.

"Look," he said, pointing up into the sky. "He's back."

Reign bit back a curse and looked up, seeing Djoser coming back down through the clouds, a dark angel of death, with his legs hanging below him, his arms casually down by his sides.

"You're welcome," Sheng whispered to Reign once all attention was on Djoser. Sheng put his hands in the front pockets of his jacket and kicked at the ground before pacing away.

For fucking what?

Djoser landed, his hands on his knees, doubled over.

Silence. There was so much silence.

"It's done?" Roksana finally asked. "Can we get into this invisible bubble now?"

"It's a dome," Reifoel said, his voice meek.

Djoser lifted his head, eyes gazing over them all but lingering over Hadley's face, her blonde hair flying, tangling in the wind. They all looked positively feral.

"It's up there, just over two hundred thousand miles from Earth. Now we have to make it bigger."

"How much bigger?" Reign asked, trying to get a sense of how often to expect Arryn to pass out.

"The moon's diameter is two thousand one hundred and fifty-nine miles," Precession sang.

"How big was what he put up there?" Reifoel asked, his chest puffing slightly.

Precession smiled meekly. "Our moonstone was maybe eight or nine feet across."

Sheng let out a long whistle.

"Is this even possible?" Reign asked. Her voice cracked. "Is this a fool's errand?"

Silence.

Reifoel stared at the sky. "Even if it is, we try anyway." His next words came softer. "I have a family. Serelune are not immortal. I don't want them to die."

Hadley coughed and looked down at her feet, shifting uncomfortably. Reifoel eyed her. Reign couldn't make the exchange out, but Sheng seemed to understand.

"What if we are not meant to be heroes?"

Reign could see the tears streaming down Hadley's cheeks even at their distance. They did not have time for whatever morality she was dealing with.

"Of course, we are the heroes. Look at us," Reifoel said with the most emotional energy that Reign had seen from him, which was still not much. The guy was a pushover. "Let's go inside, come on," Reifoel said, putting his hand on Hadley's back, trying to get the energy up and get everyone moving.

"You don't have to ask me twice," Roksana said, closing the distance between her and Precession, taking her sister's arm.

Hadley looked back at the wyvern, who was sleeping and unmoving. She didn't like leaving the creature; that much was obvious.

"Go back to your cover. Go hunt. Don't sit in the ash," Hadley said to it, petting its belly as it continued to sleep.

Everyone began marching behind the pair of them, boots crunching in the snow.

"A little help here?" Reign said, straining under the weight of Arryn, Celestine by her side like his loyal dog. Reign prayed she didn't look so desperate.

Celestine dug her arms under Arryn's back and pushed, barely moving him. If anything, she just caused more pain for Reign as his body weight shifted onto the more sensitive, fleshy parts of her leg.

"Just stop." Sheng's low chuckle hovered over her as the tall, broad Vrae male bent down and scooped up Arryn's overly large body like he weighed nothing. "You'll need to walk a bit, wife. You're strong. I know you don't need me."

Reign watched Celestine's mouth drop as Sheng began walking behind the rest of them, right on Djoser's heels, barely visible underneath the too-large mass bundled in his arms.

12

Djoser | Ebsonspire, Myrilosis

It wasn't easy, watching someone else's hands on Hadley's body. Djoser had never been the jealous type—but this was different.

This was fear.

Fear that if he touched her, they'd erase each other. Their friendship would end on a tragic note. So he stayed where he was: the grim reaper the world feared, watching her from a distance.

He didn't need to touch her to love her. He'd kill for her happiness, destroy for her smile—even if she never knew the gift was his. He could swallow the ache, let the others take what he couldn't. That loss he'd grieve in silence, wearing the mask of a friend.

Hadley's head turned over her shoulder, their eyes locking before her cheeks brightened. She was struggling out here. Djoser's body stayed tense; he wouldn't relax until he knew she was healing, the first contact of a radiation cloud lingering in her lungs, her eyelashes, her dainty little ears.

He counted the seconds before she turned away, unsure what she saw in his face. He reached seven before she looked away.

But she looked. She held your gaze.

That was enough.

Djoser would not bow to her like Sheng; she was not a queen, and she would not thrive with that kind of attention. What she needed was a gentle yet firm boundary. Someone to let her be, to cope with the sadness that lingered in her sad, sweet smiles.

He wasn't like Reifoel either, seeking approval and pushing her into discomfort in the same breath. Neither man held her heart. Not even him.

A wicked smile spread across his face. She could be his secret. They could lock eyes across a room and know they were the same animal, the only true pair.

Satisfaction pulsed through him, all from that single look.

Then, their small parade came to a standstill.

Djoser watched Reifoel extend his hands, grasping at the air, fists closing over nothing. He did it over and over. Everyone peered at him; most scowled. Everyone, of course, except Hadley. She watched something else, something moving around Reifoel closely. Her lips twitched. She was holding back a smile, a secret joke he could not see.

Djoser would have to get used to not seeing as Reifoel struggled still in this nondescript, seemingly ordinary location. What was on the other side of this bubble, this dome, fascinated him enough that he waited with the rest of them.

Reifoel's hand hit something solid, a sharp smacking sound, his palm against maybe glass or plastic. Djoser couldn't tell, but Reifoel's face lit with victory. He had found what he had been looking for.

"I've only ever seen someone open it for me. But I still managed to find it." Djoser noted the self-doubt in his tone, the lack of confidence.

She deserved confidence

"Welcome to Ebonspire," Reifoel announced, reaching out again, gripping.

The Serelune pulled back, suspended for a heartbeat, then he was flung backward into the snow.

He laughed, barking like a small dog. Djoser's heartbeat jumped, a tick forming over his right eye.

"That door is lighter than I thought." Reifoel got up, brushing the back of his pants free from the white powder that refused to bow to gravity.

"Am I supposed to see something?" Djoser asked, peering at the spot where Reiofel once stood. He didn't appear to be the only one; Roksana, Precession, and Reign squinted too, confusion apparent on all of their faces.

There was no change, no visible door, no city on the other side. Just snow, the same barren landscape he'd stared at since they arrived, so hidden that Djoser would never have seen it.

Sheng chuckled behind him. That sound grated, too.

Djoser noticed that he was carrying an unconscious Arryn like an infant.

What a show-off.

Djoser grunted.

"The Ebonspire rumors are true, then. Reifoel, why didn't you warn us?" Sheng asked. It was barely noticeable, but there was a hitch in the Vrae's voice.

Was he nervous?

"Warn us about what?" Reign asked.

"I had a great time last time I was here. I didn't think it was a big deal. Come on, let's go."

"Where exactly?" Roksana asked, her voice dripping with an eye roll.

Reifoel put his hands out, his hip bouncing against the open door frame. Hadley followed him, her eyes gazing up as if she saw skyscrapers and statues instead of the empty air.

"I've always had reasons to avoid it, but Ebsonspire is a mystery to most," Sheng said as Reifoel kept moving. "Take the Serelune. He has just disappeared from our view simply by walking into the dome."

Djoser looked back and realized Sheng was right. Both he and Hadley were gone.

"We have to close the door, hurry up," Reifoel shouted, his voice faint. "You're letting the radiation in."

Roksana pulled Precession tighter and held her free arm out before her, tucking her chin. "With my luck, I'm going to walk straight into a wall."

Nervous energy surrounded Djoser. He was clear-headed enough to recognize Roksana's magic on its own, but it still took effort to keep his own heart rate from rising much more.

The twins walked forward and disappeared.

Reign followed, her eyes closed, bracing to walk into a brick wall —then vanished.

"Ebonspire is a hidden city, you could say," Sheng said as he walked towards the invisible door.

"Hidden how?" Djoser snapped, black wisps rising from his hands.

Arryn snorted, his breath rasping as he burrowed into Sheng's chest, not waking even slightly.

"Most cannot see any of it. A city of ghosts, perhaps. No one really seems to know unless you're a part of it. I've heard a lot of stories that came out of here. Powerful, strange magic lingers inside."

An invisible city.

"I can't believe I'm going in. Here goes nothing." Djoser watched Sheng step through the doorway, Arryn's hanging legs bouncing and hitting the sides with quick, sharp slapping sounds. Sheng didn't seem bothered by it and kept going until he, too, was out of sight.

The Kinnari male was alone; the wyvern behind him slept on.

"She will be fine."

Djoser recognized Hadley's voice from the doorway.

"I don't like leaving Kismet either, but she's loyal. She won't leave me. I think in a way she's a part of me."

He stepped closer to her voice, frowning.

"I don't like being unable to see you," he said.

A hand appeared out of the doorway, an invitation to touch her.

He raised his own, reaching out for her.

Do not touch her.

He pulled his hand back.

"I'm coming in. Please step aside," he said, eyes down, praying he didn't walk straight into her. The wisps in his hands died down, and he stepped through and disappeared from view.

HE WAS THERE, but he wasn't.

Djoser looked down at his hands but saw only air. The Kinnari clapped his hands together. There was sound, the crisp noise attracting the others.

"Are we dead?" Reign's perky yet irritated words hit him just as someone bumped him, their body warm.

Not dead.

"Why can't I see anything?" His voice boomed, commanding the area, bouncing off objects, and echoing back to him. Objects, of course, that he couldn't see.

"How did you have a good time here? There's no one, and nothing," Roksana's voice brought no warmth, no comfort.

"It's so bright," Precession sang out. Djoser could hear the smile and imagined her childlike wonder. If there was no panic or apparent concern to the queen of beware, then maybe there was no danger.

Otherwise, he felt like a sitting, invisible duck.

"That doesn't convince me that we are not dead," Reign said.

Djoser heard Reifoel laugh, then clap his own hands. "Everyone holds on to the person in front of them. I'll lead the way."

"Can you see something we cannot?" Sheng asked.

"No, I just remember this part from when I was a boy, when my father brought me here. It was one of the few trips he had brought me on to show me what it meant to be royalty, what the job entailed. It was a diplomatic meeting to bring awareness to our kind, the Serelune."

Djoser rolled his eyes.

A royal pain in my ass.

Someone grabbed his arm.

"It's me," Sheng said. "This guy is tricky to carry with one hand. Can you loop your arm through mine?"

Djoser grunted and swung blindly, hitting what he assumed was Arryn's foot, then Sheng's bicep. Finally, he hooked an arm firmly.

"That's perfect, just like you are now, my princess," Sheng snickered.

"Your atoms are touching me," Djoser warned. "One sneeze is all it takes."

Sheng had no rebuttal, but Djoser could feel him pull as he adjusted Arryn's body against him.

"Everyone sound off, so we know the gang's all here," Djoser said, not wanting to be the leader of any of this in any way. He was reluctant to have a voice among them and regretted every word he had spoken. They didn't need to see him, not for who he was. He'd rather keep the distance, keep the shadows over him, shrouding him in mystery.

It was better that way, not to get attached. His heart wouldn't ache when they parted, his body wouldn't fail him in protest of being alone again, of being without anyone who knew who he was or what he was.

He was death.

You are death.

It was best he didn't forget that. It was best he kept everyone far away.

Hadley might have been an exception if he hadn't erased her with a single touch.

"Good idea," Reifoel barked as Djoser took his free hand and stepped forward, reaching until he hit another body, grabbing the puff of their jacket. An audible roll call had begun, and whoever was in front of them began to step forward, the line toward a destination that obviously didn't exist.

"Reifoel."

"Hadley."

"Celestine."

"Precession."

"Roksana."

"Reign."

There was silence before Sheng answered.

"Djoser, Sheng, and Arryn, all present."

Djoser wanted to hate Sheng with everything inside of him, but he smirked just a little. He was the type of asshole that was sometimes tolerable. He was much better than that last human he'd road-tripped with, Greg. He'd take the demon Vrae any day; they could mock and insult each other while they stood awkwardly behind the woman who held both of their attention.

That woman was holding a fish's hand and letting it lead her into the unknown. She seemed to make bad choices sometimes. That was okay, though; he wouldn't hold it against her.

Djoser's foot hit the back of Reign's heel, her delicate voice swearing, using words even he had never heard before.

"We stopped walking," she said once she recovered.

Obviously.

"Found it!" Reifoel's voice called from the front of the line.

"Holy shit," Roksana said as everyone let go and stepped forward. Their world was brought into color and wonder and magic.

Djoser's jaw dropped, then snapped shut. He crossed his arms and reclaimed his usual scowl.

They indeed were in a dome.

Where there should have been sky, though, there was a bright white light, as if the world had been erased. Djoser looked back to see where they'd come from. There was the same glowing light, the end of the dome, the end of this world.

This is what the invisible looked like to those who lived inside it.

"Do you want to set that down?" A creature appeared out of nowhere, its legs thin and long, its torso relatively normal.

The creature smiled, its teeth the purest white, the comfort of the gesture wrapping around him like a hug. It was like it could ward off who he was, the monster beneath. Here, Djoser felt redeemed.

"Is this heaven?" Roksana asked. "Did we die, along with the rest of the world?"

The creature was not alone, Djoser realized, looking around to see that the entire dome was filled with them. They moved with solid weight, but Djoser wasn't convinced. Their halos glowed like the dome above—bright, ethereal.

"I'm talking about the oversized male in your arms," the creature said. "Come, follow me. I am Meenio, welcome to our city."

Meenio had no hair. Its head was shaved like Djoser's. If it had a gender, he couldn't tell. As it walked in ahead, its light and luminescence faded, reminding him of his darkness. He followed, as did Sheng, grunting slightly under Arryn's dead weight.

"If I get to put this guy down, I'll follow you anywhere," Sheng said, now fully visible.

Everyone was visible now.

Djoser glanced at Hadley, who was looking around, her curious eyes widening, her hand outstretched and clutching air as if she was holding onto someone for support. The colors and the whimsy of their surroundings overwhelmed her. It overwhelmed him.

"This is insane," Djoser read her lips.

She wasn't wrong. Towering buildings arched and twisted like living vines, encircling them in a maze of color. Between them, plump townhouses squeezed beside open plazas, bustling cafes, and bookshops where more Meenio-like figures drifted in clusters, casting curious glances at the newcomers.

Each building rose brick by brick in bright cerulean, sunlit yellows, and flawless whites — pure eye candy. Flowers spilled from massive clay basins along winding paths leading to painted doors, deep purple petals tangled through pale white hedges. Even the air was sweet, heavy with sugar and potion scents that wrapped around Djoser, lulling him into a syrupy, unwilling contentment.

What the fuck is this shit?

Reifoel jumped around like an overexcited puppy, rushing up to a few open windows in brick walls, accepting small packages of food before jumping back to Hadley, smiling at the results of his hunt.

Djoser watched her reluctantly take a bite out of a creamy type of cake with a crunchy wafer coating as he held it out to her and then forced the rest of the package into her hand.

"These are out of this world," Reifoel exclaimed, popping some bits of something brown and smooth into the air before catching them in his mouth like a performing seal.

Djoser ran to catch up to Sheng, who didn't seem impressed or surprised at all this colorful, angelic perfection. The Vrae's only priority was getting Arryn out of his hands. His boots scraped up bright red dirt that was otherwise manicured perfectly.

Following Meenio and Sheng, Djoser walked through an open doorframe. The building it belonged to had a lemon-yellow exterior. The rest of the group hung back, a few feet from the door, some peering inside but mostly gawking and marveling at the city around them.

The townhouse was larger and more open than he expected. Four wide couches lined the orange walls, with grandiose paintings hung behind them, each depicting a white, ghostly figure against a dark background —a combination of haunting and eccentricity. He couldn't tell if this place reminded him more of heaven or hell.

"Homey," Sheng said, dumping Arryn onto one of the couches without any gentleness. His massive body flopped with a gentle thud while the fabric bowed under his weight. The Kinnari was still out cold, despite the color coming back to his cheeks under the cover of frost and radioactive ash.

"What are these paintings?" Djoser turned to Meenio and asked.

"Those are called Glaciels. They once lived here among us, cohabiting. Their magic is a rare one and, unfortunately, has made this city the way that it is now. We sent them away before any more of our home was erased, here, but not visible. They are doing very well in the new location." Meenio stared down at Arryn's unconscious body and smiled as a mother looking at her newborn baby sleeping soundly in a crib.

"What did they do, exactly?" Djoser asked, reminding himself not to get creeped out by their optimism.

You are death. You are the creepy one.

"Oh, well." Meenio looked up, its eyes, a shade of light purple, irises too big, assessing him. "Everything they touched became invisible. When enough of them passed through certain spots, it began to erase the world. I hear they sometimes pass through into the Earth realm. That brightness in the sky, we assume, is what nothingness looks like."

Djoser shook his head. That was wrong. He knew what nothingness looked like better than most.

"They were also drearily cold; they needed so much ice, and our kind are too warm, too soft. It was an unfortunate cohabitation," Meenio finished.

"Well, I suppose we just leave him here and go explore," Sheng said, shrugging his shoulders and turning towards the door. "My skin was beginning to rot from being left out there for so long. It was a hard choice to come in but here we are."

"What do we call your kind? The ones like you?" Djoser asked, ignoring Sheng, who stopped abruptly at his question, turned, and gave Djoser a warning look.

Meenio laughed as if it had never heard anything so ridiculous. "We are Atheri."

"They are the closest thing to angels that exist. I figured you'd know all about them, seeing that Arryn created them," Sheng said. Djoser noted an edge of caution in the small flicks of Sheng's eyes, darting between anything that moved.

"I wasn't around much after that attack," Djoser admitted. "Most of us have no idea what is in this realm."

"Well, as close to angels as possible with the exception of my wife." Sheng winked.

Prick.

"So, this is the group that is going to save the realm," Meenio said too affectionately, too pleasantly.

He hated that. There was nothing more suspicious than "nice."

"How do you know what we are all doing here? This place looks perfect, unaffected."

Meenio beamed, light coming out of its ears, its smile. The light that seemed too much like the nothingness it described before, supposedly caused by something completely different.

"Oh, I've been watching you, of course. When you started searching for the entrance, I came out to meet you—almost crossed the visibility barrier myself. We love having visitors, especially with him in tow." Meenio glanced down at Arryn. "Sadly, we've felt the moon's destruction too. There shouldn't be snow this far south, not this time of year. Most of you are too frostbitten to notice, but inside the dome, it's colder than it should be. Our beautiful flowers won't survive for long, I'm afraid."

Djoser had had enough of this privileged, optimistic city. He grunted, which seemed to delight Meenio even more, and pushed past Sheng through the door frame, walking back out to their group, instantly met with a small commotion.

What else do we have to look forward to?

A small group of Atheri, some with those lilac eyes, some with eyes more silver, had surrounded Celestine. The overly friendly barmaid looked like she was thriving; all the attention and such bright, abundant light coming from those smiles that surrounded her gave her a glow not too dissimilar from theirs.

Hadley stood off to the side, staring into an empty open space without any vacancy on her face. He ignored the group and marched straight to her.

"When will you tell me who it is that you've been looking at?"

Hadley's eyes met his, and she let their gaze linger again, an unspoken tension burning through the air. She looked awful—always on the brink of death, yet somehow always chasing it off.

His body eased in time with hers, the rhythm anchoring him. He ached to hold her, to breathe her in, but he knew even that gentleness might break her.

For now, he would have to be content with standing two feet from her, looking at her, breathing with her.

He'd take it.

She didn't have to talk. He didn't mind the silence between them when it was there. Those breaths, growing longer and deeper, said enough. She smiled at him just a little.

"Those things around Celestine seem to think she's fascinating, don't they?" Hadley asked.

Djoser still didn't look away from her or give the commotion even one consideration.

"Do you know why?" he asked, his voice more profound, more labored than he intended.

Hadley shook her head no.

He didn't either. He didn't care.

"I was standing here with Reifoel, who suddenly bounced away looking for accommodations."

"Your father is sleeping on the couch inside there." He pointed to the whimsical, stubby, colorful building he had just emerged from.

"Are we in danger here?" Reign crept up on the two of them, Djoser nearly needing to bend down to get a look at her and the scowl she wore on her face.

"We are in danger everywhere, I suppose," Hadley said. "It's been my state of being since those days we spent together in Grant's garage."

Reign turned scarlet. Djoser would have been blind not to notice that uncomfortable shift, the sudden powerlessness that Reign gave off. That was not like her. She reeked of guilt as she picked at her nails, avoiding direct eye contact with Hadley.

"I'm sorry" was all she said. "I promise I tried. If I'm being honest, I don't think anyone can protect you better than yourself."

"I don't think you understand how that sounds, Reign," Djoser interrupted.

"I love you, Hadley." She turned. "Djoser, stay out of this."

Djoser straightened, Reign's command, her magic, instantly taking hold of his body. His mouth felt rigid, his teeth clamped down, his lips shut tight.

"I'd trade the moon to fix us. I know I failed you, but I'm still here. I want to take you and the kids and disappear somewhere normal, somewhere far from all this. That was always my happiest place: no counterparts, no magic."

Hadley smiled, a sad, sweet smile.

"I want to go back, too," Hadley said. "I miss it so much. This world—it's not mine."

"Let's get you back, get us both back. After all this moon business." Reign's words sounded underwater this time. "I need to go check on Celestine. Those Atheri are starting to creep me out. They won't stop hovering over her. She might need some help."

Djoser glanced over to Celestine, who seemed to thrive in an environment of pure joy. He saw a faint glow around her, one that wasn't just the reflection of the light radiating from the Atheri's eyes and their ears.

You're imagining it.

Several of the Atheri glanced at Reign, their eyes lighting up; too much joy was there.

"What do they want from you?" he said through gritted teeth.

"Something gross, I'm sure." Reign put on a brave face.

Roksana walked up to her and put her arm around Reign's shoulder. The two moved closer to Celestine, Reign turning her head to look back at him and Hadley.

Once again, Djoser was alone with Hadley, and that comfort enveloped him, a blanket of warmth.

Her lips were parted. He could see that small, adorable gap between her two front teeth. Hadley's complexion was returning to normal, healthy colors emerging and highlighting the natural pinks in her cheeks.

"I must ask, but are you committed to Reifoel or Sheng?"

She looked at him with surprise, her mouth opening as if to speak. Instead, she adjusted, her eyes squinted, her eyebrows raised.

"If I weren't, would that mean I belonged to you?"

Challenge accepted.

A soft smile tugged at his lips. He watched her mirror it. Her blue eyes caught the overhead light, the faint creases at their corners so human, so perfectly flawed. He'd never wondered if he had them too —until now.

"I could never own a person," he said, watching a spark of confusion make her flare her nostrils.

"Then what are you to me?" she asked. "I can't forget about the peace that you promised."

"I'm here," he said. "That's what I am. I will always be here for you."

Hadley exhaled through her lips.

Was that a pout?

Djoser knew she wanted darkness, his darkness. There was something so beautifully demonic hidden under those sweet, sad smiles. She yearned for death, for quiet.

Not death, you.

They were bound together in a way that no one else could be. One grim reaper to another, both floating, unsure of how to exist.

He stepped back but didn't drop his gaze. He couldn't—not when she was looking back.

"Should we go join the group?" Hadley bit her lip. Her gaze finally fell, a slight anxiety-driven bounce in her knees.

"Let's go," he said, holding his hand out to let her take the lead. She could forever be his lead.

The two reached the group, and the number of Atheri lurking had doubled. Djoser was sure he counted at least fourteen of them, each touching Celestine. They played with her hair, providing a general atmosphere of celebration, of victory.

Reign stood off to the side with Roksana, both of them frowning. Precession stood a few feet away, muttering to herself as she stared up at the bright nothingness, smiling.

Sheng sat up against a building, closer to where they had entered. He picked at his nails, not a care in the world, except for the occasional glance towards the group of Atheri.

"We need to leave. I need to leave," Reign said as she noticed their approach. "I'm panicking."

"That's just Roksana," Djoser said.

Roksana shot him a glare.

"I feel like a mouse in a cage of falcons. I can't understand why," Reign whispered.

"I know that feeling," Hadley said, keeping her arms tucked.

Djoser saw that mixture of pain, panic, and guilt. The range of emotions was bigger than her small body. Reign looked like she might implode or lash out, but at whom, he couldn't guess.

Sheng is an easy enough target.

"I'm done with no longer having control," Reign whispered.

Djoser saw a flash of red in Reign's eyes, light that must have bounced from the colorful buildings mirroring her.

"Hadley, let yourself be angry," Reign continued. "You deserve it, to heal in that way. I might let myself be angry, too."

Shit.

Djoser saw Hadley's back straighten, the familiar magic of Reign's command running through her. Those pink cheeks disappeared, an eerie calm washing over her face.

Her blue eyes now told a different story, one of rage.

13

Allienna | Sacramento, 1994

A quiet blanket of white draped over ancient stone—the stone that had once held her prisoner. No one would ever understand that they'd abandoned her here. She had spent her years alone with the male who gave her everything.

Good and bad.

Did roses make up for pain? Could a smile heal a broken heart? Allienna's skin pricked, goosebumps whispering memories of past anxiety and the life she'd fled.

Hadley cannot be used. Not like I was.

Allienna couldn't believe she was back here. The only sign of life was migrating geese in the sky, a vast triangular formation above the distant Kinnari temple.

The mound of snow gave way to the curves and angles of shaped stone. Through another lens, it could be beautiful, a wonder of the world.

But she knew better.

Pain lived there.

You were supposed to break it. You were supposed to break the cycle.

Tears froze the moment they fell. She couldn't stop crying anymore. Everything she had built was collapsing around her.

Allienna had nowhere left to run.

She was ready to fall to her knees. She would do anything if Arryn could protect their daughter.

Because you can't do it yourself.

There were memories of love. Love so intense that it often felt overwhelming, burdensome. That compassion was what she clung to as she made a heavy choice, one that should have only existed in nightmares.

Arryn could be tender. She could convince herself.

There were touches that sparked passion. His devotion felt absolute, like worship. But now she knew it was suffocating. Between his outbursts, she'd cherished every scrap of affection, grateful for anything at all.

Allienna begged the wind to spare her his rage—a fury as legendary as the goddess who'd cursed her womb.

Wind nipped at the small areas of her exposed skin, the back of her hands. The faded purples and oranges of her mismatched flannel pajama set were no match for the altitude, for the cold that could cleanse the world. Here, a fresh start could exist.

Allienna's slippers were soaked through, the water and ice from the snow contact bleeding through the faux sheepskin. Her wings were tucked away.

Wait, the realization hit her.

You're not really here. You've made no choices.

This was always a last resort, an option saved for desperation.

But are there none left?

The unmistakable sound of steps trudging through thick snow came from behind her. Turning over her shoulder, she stared, not afraid. She was curious.

A lump covered in blankets moved toward her. Small flurries of snow made it easier to see the contrast with the fabrics.

Stopping, the lump straightened and shuddered. Then, it uncovered its face and smiled at her.

It was a wonderful, boyish smile with bright pink lips and curly brown hair.

"I've nearly grown old waiting for you to get here," Tristan said, standing proudly as an eight-, nine-, maybe ten-year-old human boy.

"You don't look a day older. I'm guessing you don't actually age then?" Allienna raised her eyebrows at the Kinnari. He was older than time, older than the dirt and the air, as old as she was.

"No. I believe I'm the eldest. The others don't age either."

Allienna blinked, then opened her mouth and closed it.

"Did you say others?" she asked.

"I did." Tristan smiled, but it didn't match his eyes. There was something else there, something that he did little to hide. It was an emotion she knew well, especially since motherhood.

Guilt.

"Do you feel anything while living in the dreams of others?" Allienna asked.

"I do. I can feel that mixture of dread and curiosity coursing through you, too. Come, walk with me."

Allienna let him move past her, then followed. His magic was similar to hers.

No one ever talked about Tristan. He was a ghost, a bad memory, a reminder of a childhood plagued with fear and uncertainty.

He had always kept his distance since that first Vrae attack. No one had ever questioned it, even after realizing that his appearances were not a product of their imaginations.

No, Tristan was a living, walking mask.

More ice and snow and sky lined her vision; it was so peaceful, so quiet.

"Can you feel those things in the real world?" Allienna asked as she trudged through the fresh powder that came up past her calf.

"What makes you sure this world isn't real?" Tristan smiled.

I am dreaming, aren't I?

"For a moment, I felt so hopeless, Tristan," she murmured. "I looked up, and somehow ... I was here. Maybe my mind brought me back on purpose. I want to return to Arryn if he can keep Hadley safe. Something found us. It watched me with eyes like the monsters that once hunted you."

Tristan stopped moving. "You don't need Arryn. You don't need anyone."

A small sense of relief, even pride, crept into her, her shoulders lowering just slightly.

I know that.

At least, she did sometimes.

"I'm here to help you protect Hadley," Tristan said. "That's why I brought you here. They've been looking for her."

Allienna could hear the pulsing of her own heart. She gulped down air so cold that her throat burned.

"Who are they? The Vrae?"

He nodded.

"Why do they want her? How do they look so human? How many are there?"

Tristan shifted uncomfortably; it was just a millisecond, but Allienna noticed. There was something he wasn't saying, something refused to tell her.

"Spit it out," she demanded, her vision tunneling, thinking only of Hadley, her safety, and her future.

"They plan to lock her away. She will be prized cattle, used for breeding due to her unique lineage," he said, looking down at his feet.

No.

A wave of shock hit her. Her blood, already cold, turned to ice.

She hadn't escaped this place just to watch her daughter suffer worse. She hadn't escaped him to see Hadley caged. She wouldn't allow it. She would crawl back if she had to. She would fall at Arryn's feet. There was no other way.

Djoser would come when Arryn called. Together, they would tear everything apart if that was the price. They would prove they were worth something. They would keep Hadley safe.

If you can't avoid them, use them.

Allienna flopped heavily into the snow, her mind numb. She could do it; she could be submissive, blank out her mind for their lifetimes. She would die one day. Then she could be free, her job, her wants and needs, the person she loved more than anything, more than herself, taken care of, safe.

"Don't do that," Tristan said, his brown eyes staring back at her. He held out his hand, only the tips of his fingers visible. "I told you I have a plan. I'll be handling this one. You need to come with me. We have a few dreams to travel through."

She reached out to take his hand, but he had already dropped it. She turned away, his voice still beautiful and soft, with a loving tone that reflected the youth his body held.

"Are you ready to begin now?"

14

Hadley | Ebsonspire, Myrilosis

Let yourself be angry.

That's what Reign commanded.

Drops of blood formed in Hadley's peripheral vision. Blood vessels burst from the strain. Her body was ramping up, slowly but violently. It felt like a mudslide of pure mania, tearing through her without mercy.

Complete and utter disgust hit Hadley first. It came in waves, crashing through her like a tide she could not turn back. Each surge burned her from the inside out. And yet Reign stood there, so small and so pure. This was the same child who once watched Hadley strip and pose under the flash of a cheap camera.

She had been angry before, but never like this. Now she was molten, the ground beneath her primed to collapse. She did not think about the Vrae who locked her away. She hated herself more for letting him stay close enough to charm his way into her heart.

You were wronged. But it's your fault, too. You let everyone take what they wanted.

She did not care about the months of starving in the mountains, wings breaking, and bones splitting until her body bled. She cared more about the truth she could not avoid: the only guidance she'd ever had came from a Goddess who wanted to break the world.

It says you're no one. Just your magic. Something to use.

Maybe she was meant to be the villain. Maybe it was easier than clinging to the child she once was, safe in her mother's arms. It felt too right to say yes now, to burn the world down for all the others like her who wanted the darkness but did not know how to find it.

Villain to some. Savior to others. No, you cannot be like him.

She was not her father's child anymore. She was not nothing to everyone, not anymore. Her dreams stayed buried where no one could steal them, but the fury would not.

Magic scorched through her veins, white-hot and blinding. Her hands trembled until she forced them into fists, arms locked at her sides. She stared down at Reign's feet, willing herself not to lose control.

Numbness spread under her skin, a crawling ache that pushed her higher than any high Hector's poisons ever gave her.

Djoser and Reign were watching, waiting for her to break or burn. Reign looked away first, back to Celestine and the Atheri she hated so much. Hadley stayed still. The anger coiled deeper. She would let it out when she chose to.

You can control it.

Hadley could control it. She could control her response to how utterly unfair and victimized she had been.

"It feels bad, haunting, around you now," Precession's voice, filled with its usual beauty, whispered.

"Are you okay?" Djoser asked, leaning in, trying to get Hadley to look at him.

She couldn't. She couldn't look at him. She might unravel. The rage pulsing inside her stacked up, one brick at a time, echoing the gaudy city walls around her.

She shook her head, blonde hair whipping against her neck.

"What can I do?" Djoser asked.

A glimmer, not a shadow, flickered across Hadley's vision. It was a shape hungry for vengeance, ready to strike to kill. It was her true partner, her constant ally when Kismet was not near, always waiting at her side and asking for nothing in return. Her shadow self needed only her silent permission to unleash the chaos buried deep in her heart.

Hadley lifted her chin, ignoring Djoser, ignoring the redheaded twins who kept a cool distance with expectant eyes. She ignored Reign, too, who didn't bother looking back.

No surprise there.

"I'm back," Reifoel called from deeper in the city. "I found lodging for all of us, and I think you will all be really impressed. I call dibs on the bathtub."

Hadley forced a laugh; the entire thing was ridiculous. She stood here, fighting for control, when her shadow self was begging for permission to act.

Djoser knew her intentions. He saw that lethal vengeance radiating from her and recognized the murderous gleam in her eyes. She couldn't hold it back any longer, the magic of Reign's command burning through her veins.

Let yourself be angry, Hadley.

She moved, the supernatural grace and strength nearly elevating her off the ground, her wings bursting through her back, shredding her jacket as they blossomed behind her. She couldn't feel the pain; she wondered if she would ever be able to feel anything other than hate, distrust, or malice.

She suspected not.

Though swift, she was a perfect picture of collected, calculated, and cold.

"Where are you going?" Hadley heard Roksana ask. She didn't slow.

"When you see someone that calm and that deadly, I would recommend you not get involved," Sheng yelled.

"Hadley, wait," Reifoel called, though he didn't go after her.

Hadley was at the door of the townhouse that housed her father. Her shadow self danced around her with the excitement of a puppy with a new ball as she pushed the daisy-yellow wooden door open.

She could hear rushed footsteps behind her, multiple people running to watch her, to stop her. It didn't matter who, because suddenly, she was that girl again, that girl in the middle of a room filled with Vrae holding her captive, with venom coursing through her veins, with no one there to help her, only to use her as some political hostage, some kind of breeding tool, a bird in a cage.

There were so many to blame.

She knew where to start.

With the one who should have stepped in.

The one who could have spared her those last hollow years of childhood—motherless, anchorless.

The one who was meant to love her.

But never did.

And never would.

She walked into the building, seeing the orange couches, the art, and the too-large male body sleeping atop them. It was rest he didn't deserve.

If he wants to sleep, he can sleep forever.

The glimmer of that now-familiar figure should have given her chills, should have made her stomach flip, but instead filled her with joy, a rush of adrenaline as her rage built higher. Hadley suspected that if it were possible to breathe fire, she would be unstoppable, an explosion of flames.

Exploding like that would feel so good, but she couldn't.

So she did this instead.

Hadley let go of her heart.

Her shadow self jumped into Arryn, a streak of shimmering color.

Fuck you, she thought.

"What's happening?" Reign asked from the doorway.

But Hadley didn't care. She lost herself in that rage, a new type of box she'd cracked open inside herself. The world needed healing as badly as she did. But she couldn't heal. She never would. So she would put that world out of its misery.

Hadley turned toward the door, ignoring the Kinnari, ignoring Reifoel's face. They were staring at her.

Behind her, she could hear a sharp sound, the type of whistle that no one else could hear, a crack meant only for its maker.

"Oh, gods," Reifoel said. "It's happening again, Hadley. Look,"

"What is it?" Reign asked, panic edging her voice.

Hadley did not look back as her father turned to dragon glass behind her. Light from the windows and skylight struck him, scattering prisms across the walls. She stepped forward, ignoring every face she passed.

She owed them nothing.

She reached the doorway just as everyone rushed in. Celestine appeared first, panic and grief twisting her expression as she searched for Arryn. Reign nearly collided with Hadley, scrambling out of her way to avoid the newcomers crowding behind.

Hadley's shoulders and wings brushed aside Kinnari and Atheri alike as she pushed through. Behind her, Celestine's gasps and cries rose. The woman would cling to the cold shard left in place of the man she loved. He had always been just that to Hadley; something clear but hollow, sharp where there should have been warmth, a father only in name.

Her mom deserved better.

She deserved better.

"Don't worry," she reassured herself more than Celestine, "I did it for your own good."

She turned from the townhouse and faced the city again, trying to figure out how to exit the dome.

A long whistle cut through the air. Hadley looked down and made eye contact with Sheng, still sitting with his back against the wall of a building, one leg stretched out and the other tucked in, knee up towards the sky, or the light, or whatever passed for a sky here.

"I don't need your judgment," Hadley said.

"And you certainly won't get it." Sheng chuckled, letting his head fall back, the top of his hair touching the brick wall. "The exit is that way. Good luck navigating that invisible bit, though; it seems tricky."

Her shadow self glimmered and danced around her. It pulsed with want. It wanted to jump into Sheng.

That bastard.

She was about to give it permission; the glowing yes, the satisfaction, and the hit of dopamine already coiling in her chest as she began to nod.

"You know, Hadley," Sheng interrupted, standing. The sounds of screams and weeping came from inside the house. "If you need help killing Kinnari, I can surely assist."

The yes in her mind disappeared, and the glimmer of her shadow self froze, feet from Sheng's body, looking at her as if it were screaming, *"What the fuck?"*

"Not from you," Hadley whispered.

"Sorry, I didn't quite catch that," Sheng said, closing the distance between them.

"I would never ask for help from you."

Sheng's breath was cool, a breeze compared to the heat and anger that poured off her. He was now inches from her, his face almost touching hers. His hand was raised, lingering before brushing his fingers under her chin.

"I could kill you," she struggled to get the words out.

Sheng's eyes lit up. "Only if you promise it would feel good."

"Death isn't supposed to feel good." She jumped back, her hands trembling again, the glimmer circling them like a caged predator. She pushed it out of her mind, begging Djoser for death, for the tranquility that she imagined would come with it.

Her fury was all that she could feel, and now that one problem was out of the way, her father, she could focus it on her captor, her supposed husband.

"For you, Hadley, only if it feels good for you," Sheng corrected.

He wasn't scared of her. He wasn't judging her.

But he still was going to force you to carry his children.

"No touching," she forced out, tears filled with hate and confusion spilling down her cheeks.

"Hadley," Reifoel shouted, "Hadley, what happened?"

"Uh oh," Sheng said, "you are losing your chance to escape. Go, I'll be a distraction. I'll find you later, I promise."

Hadley looked into his eyes again—the eyes of a demon, the eyes of her captor.

She hated that it felt good.

It felt too right to look at him and not look away.

What the fuck are you doing?

"Don't follow me."

She saw Reifoel and Reign coming toward her. Djoser was just behind them, moving carefully like she might vanish at any moment.

She did not wait.

She ran, wings lifting her just enough to glide through the streets. Atheri watched from their windows as she passed bright buildings and flowers that deserved none of her mercy.

The glow ahead sharpened—an outline of nothingness, a gate to nowhere. She reached for it, but stopped just short.

"Hadley," someone called behind her.

She did not turn.

This is it, she thought. *There's no one to fix me now.*

She sprinted harder and burst into a pocket of silence, nothing but snow waiting on the other side. Her palm struck the invisible barrier. She slid her hands along it, moving sideways until she found the seam she needed.

You're not going to be someone's daughter anymore. Not someone's mistake. Not someone's weapon.

She found the seam—the faintest pulse in the air.

She pushed.

And the world opened like a wound.

Kismet was there, fifty feet away behind the twisted trees, a sight for sore eyes.

Hadley's heart lightened as she lifted off the ground and flew to her wyvern, her heart bursting as her skin connected with those scales. Kismet shot out a groan of approval, of joy, signaling that it was just the two of them.

"It's you and me, Kismet," Hadley said. "Let's put this world out of its misery."

The wyvern huffed and spread its wings before launching into the air. Hadley's stomach lurched at the sudden lift. She looked down and caught a glimpse of Reign stumbling out of the dome, staring up at them as they climbed higher. Hadley did not look back again. Her anger stayed with her, burning steadily as she disappeared into the sky.

15

Amis | Myrilosis, Outside of the Temple

"You're a coward," Luca said through vacant eyes, his voice direct but distant. The accusation weighed heavily on Amis.

Snow fell like endless buckets poured from a sky torn and moonless—a sky that would rage long after these children were gone. This place was not meant for survival, yet somehow, they were still alive.

You kept them alive again.

Luca was sharp, his focus moving from Amis to Salome, Ahora, and Noah. The toddler was still huddled against him, trembling and freezing in Amis's arms.

"We have to go back in," Ahora choked out, her breath growing steadier with every word. She turned towards the door, her hand on the latch, her youthful face filled with desperation.

He kept his back to the door, as did Salome. Luca only blinked, his silence an echo of Amis's buried helplessness.

"No," Amis said. His tone was soft, blending with the sadness that clung to the air.

But you didn't save them all.

Salome's eyes widened, staring at Amis. She looked crushed, her heart unable to process more trauma, new trauma. She was done, though Amis knew how much more was still to come.

"I'm trying to protect you," Amis replied.

"We no longer require your protection," Luca said, grabbing the handle on the door and pushing. The door opened easily, as if there was nothing on the other side. There was just a frame with nothing beyond.

Amis saw Luca's face, stoic and still. He stared into the doorway and saw only snow. No temple, no floor, no foundation, no scattered cots or injured bodies. Just pristine drifts, undisturbed and already smoothing over what the tornadoes had erased.

Erased. They had all been erased.

Luca knelt, slamming his knees to the ground, but kept his head lifted.

"Where do we go now?" the teen asked, his gaze fixed beyond the threshold.

Noah whimpered, shifting in Amis's arms, forcing him to adjust. There was only Ahora now, without wings. He could carry her and the toddler together.

Difficult, but doable.

"We go down the mountain. That's all we can do," Amis said, offering Luca the choice.

Luca didn't move. He just stared through the door, frozen in a choice he refused to make.

No more dead children.

That was to be his new golden rule—until the tornadoes came and he'd stepped back anyway, watching the last of Waihema huddle against a wall that vanished moments later. In the chaos, he'd reverted back to the Kinnari who sacrificed when balance demanded it.

Sometimes it took sacrifice to keep the realms whole, to keep the gods at peace.

Roksana was his opposite. She was only a scapegoat, something Arryn could blame his anger and abuse on whenever she was around. Amis knew others did it, too. Roksana was not so careless about her power, so naïve regarding how her magic worked. Neither was Amis.

Better. We are so much better than the others.

How he could not have seen it, how he could not know it, was ludicrous. That ended today.

Luca still didn't move, he didn't blink, not even when a light blue, purple, and oil slick black appeared in the sky, traveling toward them through the snow that fell, that began to cover their feet, their limbs, erasing their bodies like the temple, the ones saved from Glaciel had been.

"Look," Salome said, her voice hardly more than a whisper.

Amis looked and saw the wonder blooming in her face.

That kind of strength—frail, human, and enduring—was not Kinnari. It came from her ancestors, from Mother Waihema's leadership, from the sacrifice she had made to ensure her tribe survived.

And Amis had almost let that go.

Right and wrong blurred too easily here.

The glow in the sky shimmered with buried stardust and hidden worlds, like a crow's feather catching the sun—dark at first, then suddenly alive with color no human eyes could truly see. That was the unfortunate thing about having eyes like these, human-esque eyes, never being able to truly understand, to see the colors of a crow, nor the celestial colors of Karmakara.

Amis had never been visited by this Goddess, not on her own. He had only ever seen her once before, even though he had shaped lives in her name. It was a slight comfort, however, to see her. Though his eyebrows were raised, he felt no fear for either himself or the surviving children.

There was comfort in destiny, in the woven threads she held: choice, future, past.

Noah seemed in awe, his cheeks rosy and grinning from ear to ear as he took in the figure in human form, the swirl of black and stardust, the hints of blues and purples evaporating into the air, revealing silver and golden hair woven into plaits that came down over both shoulders.

Snow continued to fall, but its heaviness had lightened; what once felt like menace now melted like kisses from the sky.

Amis just stared at Karmarka as she lifted her left arm, stardust, bright like the burning debris of a welder, trailing her movements, falling like sand. Her body was wrapped in a large cloak—purple, no, cerulean, no, gray and pink, and copper and onyx blended together, appearing as the fabric moved through space and time. It shifted constantly, revealing layers of woven futures.

Karmakara turned her head, scanning Amis but quickly looking past him, disinterested. Her gaze instead fell to the boy who was still on his knees, staring out the door. Luca kept his back to the goddess, but his fingers twitched, his hands resting at his side as he visibly held tension in his wrists and forearms.

"I know why you're here," Amis said, interrupting the frown that Kamarkara's lips began to press into. She was not used to being ignored. The appearance of sweetness, of a cozy magic, would garner a certain amount of attention. People wrote myths about her. Portraits, poems, devotionals. They mistook her kindness for motherliness, but she was no one's mother.

"Is there even a point to any of it? Of speaking to you, of telling you something?" Amis followed up when the Goddess refused to give him an audible reply. "Do you know what I'm going to say?"

"I know much, dear Amis," Karmakara glided forward, her cloak dragging as she kept the single side hung open, small images etched within the threads, a collage of choices, fragments of their futures. "I know what is in your heart," she continued, "but it is not you I am here for."

Amis's stomach dropped.

She was here to weave fate, or so he had believed.

"I am not a grim reaper, Kinnari. I do not carry out futures. I do not alter time or destroy the trust in the fabric that clings to me, that makes me whole. I am here today to present options to someone who feels like they have none. If he chooses wrong, the web will tear, and fate will bleed."

Amis gulped, her eyes sliced through him like blades.

Wrong.

That boy, devastated on his knees, needed to choose his own, and an option for him to consider could be wrong.

"You there," Karmakara's voice whispered, calling Luca to her.

He still didn't move.

"I have your choices." She motioned toward the inside of her cloak, where small reflections, hundreds, thousands of them, were webbed together by stardust and more colors than mortal eyes could process.

Amis wasn't close enough to see the choices up close, the futures that flickered with every breath, every stubborn nod Luca might make. But he knew only one being had ever seen their path before.

Reign.

And Reign had twisted fate so completely that even Amis still felt the ripple of it now, the balance shifting under his skin. Whatever Luca chose next, another web was already spinning itself into place.

"Why are you here, just for me?" Luca's voice was filled with anger and hurt. He turned his head, finally taking in Karmakara, his eyes adjusting to the unexpected beauty of light and dark.

Luca lunged for her, his hand outstretched and closing around emptiness, just the air as his hand traveled right through her.

He stumbled.

Did not expect that.

"Curious that you think I am really here," she said, unfazed by Luca's sudden outburst. "If you caught me, what would you have done?"

Luca raised himself from the snow, his hands red, reminiscent of blood, his fingernails beginning to purple.

"My home, my life, have been taken from me. All of us were robbed. Make it make sense," he demanded.

Karmakara smiled, and Amis winced at the kindness.

There were moments when gentleness felt more terrifying than violence. This was one of them.

He had no trust in the Gods, not even this one. The Kinnari were nothing to them, irrelevant, the blades of grass underneath their feet. The rest of the living were the dirt.

"I can be patient should you need me to be," Karmakara said, ignoring Luca's question as Salome hugged Ahora, the two girls hovering in the empty door frame, preparing for their own escapes.

They were growing more intelligent, even more skittish. Amis felt a little proud; they were adapting.

Noah thrashed in Amis's arms, the toddler's tiny fists hitting against his cheeks as he whined and whimpered from the cold. Amis shushed him and held him tighter against his chest, hoping his body heat would help.

They were all supposed to be dead. None of this should matter.

Noah relaxed against him, though his small body still shook, still shivered.

But it did. It mattered. It all mattered.

"You are about to make a choice," Karmakara said, her eyes laser-focused on Luca as he stood at nearly the same height as the form she presented herself in. Their faces were only a foot apart, and the boy didn't flinch.

He had given up.

Amis suspected he knew that because he had once been around a human who felt like that. That grilled cheese he'd made to comfort Hadley as she watched Reign get ripped apart in front of her eyes had been such an irrelevant gesture. He realized that now, how she had given up, that look in her eyes was the same as Luca's.

Was the choice he was supposed to make to stay alive willingly?

"Show me," Luca said, pulling his gaze off the Goddess's face and letting his eyes trickle down to the cloak. Tears flowed, his shoulders slumped as he studied and watched.

"All of this could be?" Luca looked up after a few minutes.

Karmakara nodded.

"Only your choices can bring this to pass. This is what is woven, but I can feel that choice on the tips of your fingers and the tip of your tongue. Do you know what choice I'm referring to?"

Luca shook his head no, and Karmakara only frowned.

"I'm afraid that's all that I can say to guide you. Anything more, and the others would say I had an agenda."

Karmakara's face turned to that of an angel, so genuinely innocent, so pure. She was light, time, and space. It was funny how much he saw Precession and Roksana within her.

Amis's cheeks warmed, thinking of Roksana, thinking of the chaos she brought to his life. They balanced each other perfectly.

"As a Goddess, do you answer to others?" Luca asked, his face stone cold.

Amis, on the other hand, froze.

Ayurveda had burned Glaciel to the ground. The sun hadn't risen since. That goddess was ruthless, far more terrifying than Karmakara could ever pretend not to be.

But Karmakara was still powerful, and her schemes were tangled up with the Life Gifter's all the same. Luca had the nerve to talk to her like she was just some soft, harmless woman.

Poor kid.

He was a lamb dressed for slaughter, pushed toward a choice he didn't even understand. Amis almost laughed at that.

Almost.

"We will travel through Myrilosis," Amis said. Luca stood there, staring at the tethered web of paths his life could take.

"No," Luca said, turning around, his hands balled up into fists, his expression still so sad, so angry. "Let that life get lost. I don't want that; I can't want that."

Karmakara's serene expression held, though a small mark of tension etched into her brow.

"He knows what else waits for you," she replied, her chin turning towards Amis. "He knows what chases you, what hunts you all."

Death.

Luca didn't bother looking at Amis; at least right now, that relationship would be strained. It didn't change his vow, though. Amis would still follow him, still follow them all, just like death.

"What do we do?" Salome asked.

"We survive," Luca said.

"What did you see?" Ahora asked.

Luca only shook his head as the Goddess behind him shifted back into her colors, shadow, darkness, light, and radiance. Feet lifted off the ground, eventually not feet at all. The celestial body floated to the sky.

"It's nothing; let's go," Luca said, pushing his dark, matted hair back. "How far away is it? Do we fly?"

Amis nodded but was hesitant. He wished Sheng were with them. He didn't know this world, didn't know it at all.

Salome and Luca let out their wings, ripping through their clothing. Salome cried out in pain. They were still adjusting; the skin on their shoulders and backs was still turning to calluses, still toughening.

"Tell me," Amis said, scooping Ahora towards him while holding Noah. He was getting much better at multitasking, he had to admit. His brain was always working, never quiet, never in balance. If his mental health could override his balance and magic, then things would be very concerning.

"I saw myself, old and gray and withered. I saw Waihema behind me. I took the role of Mother, leading Waihema, the next generations that would follow me, Salome, Ahora, and Noah."

"We get to go back home," Salome whispered, the smile on her lips not quite reaching her eyes.

"I can't go back," Luca said, lifting off the ground.

"We have to go back. It's written, it's destiny," Ahora sang out.

Luca drifted back down, hearing those words. Amis just stood there, watching, waiting, fascinated by whatever this was, whoever this person was, suddenly growing into. He'd been nearly silent when Amis met him.

Well, fleeting was maybe still right.

"You're not old enough to know." Luca shot Amis a look that

explained his feelings and silence. "But Amis knows. Amis knows what Waihema was and how lucky we all are to be here and alive."

Amis wasn't ready to have that discussion.

"You can follow me," he said, preparing to take off, but a muffled crash interrupted him. It was a sound like metal smothered by silk.

Salome jumped, and Luca moved into a fighting stance. His arms were too skinny, and his posture seemed like the breeze would be able to push him over. These kids had so much heart but were emaciated, living in a constant state of stress.

A woman, full-grown but petite, had fallen into the snow, and it puffed up around her. She'd hit the ground with force, as if she had been running.

Then Amis saw her wings.

Their newest visitor had been flying.

The long black hair on the back of the woman's head was a dramatic contrast against the white surrounding it. A soft moan came from the body before she started to move, her head tucked into her chest. She looked hungover as she pushed herself up.

"When am I?" She stood, her heart-shaped face instantly familiar, her high cheekbones fierce, her eyes defensive, her body ready to attack.

She saw Amis and the Waihema children.

"Do I know you?" Salome asked, and the woman stared right at Amis, cocked her head, and smiled.

"No, I don't think so, little girl." She shook her head. "But I know him. Does this count as breaking the rules, Amis? I certainly did not mean to run into you here," adult Reign said.

16

Amis | Myrilosis, Outside of the Temple

"What year is it?" Reign asked, her wings retracting into her adult body. Her posture was impeccable, nothing like the modern-day woman-child Amis had known.

"When was the last time you saw me?" Amis countered. They were at a stalemate, each asking questions neither wanted to touch.

"Will it ever stop snowing? What is going on with this weather? I'm soaked," she grumbled, flicking slush from her sleeves.

"Oh, that's because of the moon," Salome started, but Amis cut her off.

"Do not say anything."

"Why not? Oh, little cute girl, do you have wings like me?"

Salome looked at Amis, puzzled.

"You know this person," Amis told her, "but she does not know you yet. Salome, let me reintroduce you to one of your favorite beings, Reign."

Salome's expression changed from confused to excited, a genuine beam of delight, while Reign shot a glare towards Amis that said the exact opposite.

This version of Reign lived beyond his era—after the temple, after Waihema, after he'd thrown himself into preserving balance. He didn't know her, not really.

"Do you often time travel through realms or do you sneak into Myrilosis underneath Arryn's nose?" Amis asked. Reign's face dropped. A hint of fear showed from the distinct gulp of air she took, the strain on her neck too sharp to hide.

"We are on the wrong side of the door," Reign said, her steps long and hurried as she moved forward, past Salome, and Luca, and Ahora. Her hands grabbed the door frame, the solid stone door not moving as it stood fully open.

"There's nothing there," Salome said. "You're all grown up now. That's so cool."

Reign snapped her head, glaring at the girl. "What's that supposed to mean?"

"Don't tell her," Amis was direct but gentle.

"Tell me now." Reign looked directly into Salome's eyes. There was no mistaking her command.

Salome straightened, the magic kicking into her, flowing.

"You left the temple, left us, a few days ago. You were just a little older than me."

"Your clothes are so funny." Ahora snickered, pointing out the pale blue dress on Reign. The sleeves came down to the center of her palms, the pointed fabric wet from the snow she fell in. The shoulder sleeves were puffy, highlighting her tiny waist. A hoop skirt billowed out like an umbrella. Amis wondered if it might protect the children from getting wetter if they hid underneath it.

"Oh, this ridiculous thing?" Reign laughed. "I completely agree. I just returned from visiting Roksana and Precession in France. They had been scouting for a new home. I was sent away wearing this dress. French fashion is so fussy." She giggled. "At least they had the sense to leave the back low for wings, though I imagine it's rather scandalous without a shawl."

"What year did you leave?" Amis asked.

"Eighteen-thirty-two," she said while smoothing out her skirt. "I have to say, I'm getting rather tired of all this fabulousness. It feels disingenuous. I am thinking about heading to the United States and seeing what all the talk is about. I might even ride in a ship."

There was an uncomfortable silence as everyone stood there, staring at her. She couldn't have looked more displaced. Amis smirked. Then, with perfect timing, Noah—annoyed at losing the spotlight—reached up and slapped Amis on the cheek.

"I like the ruffles down by your feet." Salome pointed to the bottom of Reign's dress as her teeth audibly chattered.

Reign let out a polite sigh.

"Well, I suppose I should fly until I get back to my correct year. You all are just standing here in the snow, and it seems improper."

"You are not the most proper individual, so I'm told." Amis chuckled. "Even throughout history, you tend to make more noise than you should."

Reign gave him a stern look, one that was familiar, that attitude he had gotten used to hidden there. There were fewer than two hundred years between this woman and the child he knew, but it felt like a millennium.

What happened to you?

"We were about to fly, to go towards a city here in this realm."

"What's it called?" Reign's curiosity piqued.

"I don't know. I don't know where we are going. You are welcome to come with us. Unless it breaks any rules."

Reign considered momentarily, her brow furrowed as she weighed the options.

"If I go, we will be captured, hunted. Arryn, he told us we are not welcome here, that we are hated. That we will be punished."

"Is that true?" Luca asked, his chest puffing, his skin showing the dull colors of hypothermia.

"If it is true, Luca," Amis said, "I doubt it matters. Not with everything that has just happened. I imagine everyone, every place, is struggling and fighting for survival. I'll take my odds finding you shelter. And if we're lucky, maybe we'll find Arryn. That would be the best scenario. He's the only one who can save us all."

Reign lifted a single eyebrow. "Arryn is not a savior."

"Arryn is the only hope we have," Amis shot back. "One day, you'll understand that when you get to this time."

Reign shook her head and rolled her eyes.

There's the Reign I know.

"Maybe I shouldn't leave the temple then," she said.

"You cannot make decisions based on these conversations," Amis said with urgency.

Shit. Shit. Shit.

It couldn't be different. The choices she made had to happen precisely as they had.

"It's time to make a choice, then, Luca," Amis tried to change the subject. "Should we fly west, north, east, or south? The rest of the group went south. That will be our best chance for comfort."

"Hungry!" Noah yelled, his tiny hand slapping against Amis's nearly frozen skin, causing waves of pain to flow down into his neck.

Luca looked down at his hands, flexing his fingers, not letting his limbs stop moving.

"West," he said.

Of course. Why would we make it easy?

"I don't think you could convince me to ever want to come through that door," Reign said, turning her back to them and heading toward the open threshold.

"You're leaving us already?" Salome whimpered.

"Don't be sad," Reign said. Salome straightened instantly, her frown flipping into a wide, impossible grin.

"Maybe I'll know you one day, too."

Reign took off, her feet hanging awkwardly behind. Her chunky black heels and stockings flashed beneath her skirt as she moved through the air, pumping her wings hard as she disappeared into the clouds and falling snow.

Amis lifted Ahora again.

"Let's go," he said, offering no space for questions or hesitation as he took off into the air, heading west. Noah and Salome followed behind, their flying shaky but improving with every lift. Gray and snow stretched endlessly ahead. The two children in his arms were so cold, so still, they barely felt alive.

More death was coming. He could feel it in his soul.

TIME LOST all shape when Amis flew. Usually, there were signs to track it: light, shadow, and stars. The world they flew through, scarred and scorned, offered none of it, just endless snow and cutting wind no matter the altitude. He was already sick of it. He'd take desert heat and cracked earth any day.

It might be a better trade-off, honestly.

His magic coiled like spiders beneath his skin, like worms crawling up his spine, desperate to escape. Balance begged to be restored, and he didn't know what would break when it finally snapped. Rot lived in that magic. There was too much of it. He had to hold it in. He couldn't explode. If he did, who knew what would die?

It could be a plague. It could be a command to Djoser to eliminate Waihema at the demand of the Life Gifter.

Amis tried to lead them higher, to fly above the worst of the storm, but it was useless. Ahora and Noah dragged his wings down, and their faces were pale with the creeping edge of hypothermia.

They're fighters. All of them. You've been here before.

They were flying too high. The air thinned. Lungs would soon give out. Bodies would start to fall.

There were no breaks. Chaos bled into the bones of anyone still breathing.

Something dark flickered in the corner of his eye. A shadow below. A body falling. Wings were limp, just barely catching the air current. Then another dived after it, arms and wings tucked for speed.

Amis twisted midair. Salome and Luca were gone.

You've got to be kidding me.

"Hold on, everyone," he said, though his words were lost to the wind.

Amis plunged.

Noah tensed, a silent scream held in his small body while they chased the shadowed figures.

Ahora let out a light scream, followed by whimpering cries.

Amis was gaining on both figures. He had more mass, more speed.

You can catch them.

He'd slow them down somehow.

That was the plan, right until the ground rose up at him like a threat.

Amis picked up speed as panic surged through him. He pulled his wings back out. The force nearly knocked the breath from his lungs, but there was no time to recover.

He drove his wings harder, large and dragon-esque, too big for this kind of maneuvering.

Ahora's screams blended in with the whistling air in his ears.

It sounded like the tornadoes had come back. His body wanted to shut down, to protect him from the stress. His magic protested too; the feeling of needing to implode was overwhelming. The death clinging to them all pulsed against his bones.

You know how to fix it.

Let them hit the ground.

"No," Amis growled to no one.

He shoved the thought aside and pushed harder.

Amis was flying too fast, way too fast, but there was no way to slow down without turning into a crater with two half-frozen kids in his arms.

That's a problem for later.

He was close now. Close enough to see Salome, hair whipping in the wind, her face stretched in terror.

Luca was further, arms slack, wings rag-dolling behind him. His eyes were closed.

The teen had passed out.

Amis reached Salome. Her cheeks pushed upwards by the air, her lips peeled back over her teeth.

She looked at Amis, her eyes wide and wet. The ground raced up to meet them.

Amis didn't have a way to pull her in. His arms were full.

"Pull your wings out," he mouthed, he yelled, he screamed. His voice went nowhere.

She didn't respond. No movement. No sign she understood.

Luca had rotated to where he would land on his back. His limbs were loose.

Salome reached for him, and when she grabbed hold, finally, miraculously, she snapped her wings out.

A makeshift parachute. Smart girl.

Amis angled his wings too, dragging hard.

It wasn't hard enough.

Two hundred feet turned into one hundred feet.

One hundred feet turned into fifty feet.

They hit white fog, no, steam.

Then, a crack.

A surface shattered like thin glass beneath them. They plunged into water.

Hot water.

It burned. It stung. Amis screamed.

They had fallen through steam thick enough to hide everything.

His wings dragged him under. His legs kicked, but the resistance was all wrong. He wasn't rising, just thrashing.

Noah still clung to him, but the boy's tiny fingers loosened their grip. Ahora was gone, freed from his arms in the chaos.

Amis had to get the toddler up to the surface. He had to keep pushing. His left arm stroked upward. His right arm clamped tightly around Noah's small, limp body.

Then something touched his leg. It was sharp and pointed.

He panicked.

Air escaped his mouth in a rush of terror and bubbles.

Again, something scraped his ankle. It stung, nearly tearing his flesh.

He looked down, but Noah's body blocked his view. The child wasn't moving. His eyes were closed. There were no bubbles.

He's dying.

Amis felt that awful, familiar feeling, his balance weaving inside him like Karmakara's web.

This is your fault.

Something shoved him upward, hard.

He fought against the sting still wrapped around his ankles, the sharpness biting into his skin. But then his face broke the surface.

Air.

Sweet, stinging, hot air from a boiling hell.

Amis raised Noah's body above the surface, kicking to stay afloat.

Noah sputtered and then cried.

The sound had never been more beautiful.

I've got you. I've got you.

The water around him cleared, revealing a surreal turquoise hue that faded into navy as it deepened.

The ice they'd broken through was already reforming, a thin sheen glossing over like the spring wasn't even there.

Amis scanned the water. Nothing.

Salome, Ahora, and Luca were nowhere in sight.

Maybe they didn't fall in. Maybe they're already dead.

The pressure inside him stayed.

Noah's breath steadied.

Amis dipped his hands beneath the water, trying to draw the warmth into the boy's frozen fingers.

"Look," Noah said, voice faint and shaky.

A head emerged from the water. The figure moved with fierce calm and balance as it rose, like walking up a staircase. Amis studied a gray body highlighted with streaks of red and orange across its torso. Little legs were hanging over its left shoulder.

Salome.

The creature carried Salome out of the water. Its long antennae sprouted out of the top of its oval-shaped head. As it fully emerged, Amis saw legs. This being had too many legs of various lengths. They moved continuously, even when no steps were taken, like it was treading water even on land.

The creature laid Salome down on the shore. Her body sat on top of snow that quickly melted under her. The heat from the water, still on her skin, steamed and hissed. Her eyes were closed, her mouth open.

The creature pivoted on its swarm of legs, revealing a chest plated like a shell. It had no arms, no fingers. There were only two massive claws, twitching like they had opinions. Amis had little doubt that this creature could crush full-sized rocks between those pointed tips.

Beady, black eyes peered at him and Noah. Noah decided that now was the best time to resume crying. The toddler's head wobbled, weak. Amis needed to get him to rest. He glanced at Salome.

They all needed rest.

It was going to be hard to get the two of them out of this water. He already felt so relaxed, so sleepy, but they couldn't stay here forever. The storm still hounded them from above, and no break in the clouds was visible from anywhere. Painful cold, like thousands of needles, pierced every inch of his body that rose from the water. It radiated through him, through Noah.

The sound of splashing made Amis turn back around. The same creature breached the surface, moving much quicker than he could through the water. Nestled harshly against its shell-like chest and pincers were both the bodies of Ahora and Luca.

One would assume them dead, but Amis knew better. That feeling in his chest led him, gave him hope that there was no relief from the pressure, from the build-up. As long as he was uncomfortable, these children were alive. His promise was still being fulfilled, and he would hold on to that as long as possible.

Amis and the creature were side by side now, stepping onto the snow. Amis's wet boot squished as water seeped out at the seams.

Noah was asleep or passed out; either way, he needed the rest, needed to ignore the cold that hit completely differently after being submerged in a natural hot tub. Amis wanted to get back into that water so badly.

The creature looked at Amis, setting the two children down on the snow beside Salome. It held up its claws and started tapping the tips together rhythmically. When Amis stood there and stared, confused, it tapped again.

Talking. This is it talking.

Amis shook his head.

"I don't understand," he said softly. "Help. These children need help. Shelter."

The creature stood there and lifted its pincers, tapping again. The rhythm was slightly different, but there was still nothing that he could understand.

Again and again, it tapped out a rhythm, and Amis began to realize he needed to do something more, that he would get no more help here. It had done all it could, this primitive thing that stood as tall as he did.

The sounds of splashing erupted behind him, and Amis turned back to the hot springs as more pairs of clicking pincers emerged, followed by the heads and bodies that they were attached to.

Amis counted three, three more of these creatures. Their eyes were similar, beady and black, but their mass was double, maybe even triple, of the original creature that had saved the children, saved Amis from drowning.

What the fuck did you make, Arryn?

Giant. They were giant, lobster-like beings.

Amis gulped.

The creature that stood on the snow held up its pincers, making more clicking sounds, and the newcomers reciprocated. They were having a conversation, and the three larger bodies moved their eyes over to Amis, their attention obvious as they moved out of the water, coming closer to them.

"Please don't eat us." Amis couldn't help but let out some nervous energy, his mouth in an awkward smile.

Gods.

"What is that on your back?"

Amis jumped, the larger of the creatures stepping onto the snow, speaking his language so perfectly with a voice so deep, so smooth like pavement being rolled underneath a large truck.

"My back?" Amis asked. He activated the muscles in his shoulder blades and pulled his enormous wings out in their full length, each side as long as he was tall.

The creature grunted. "These are real children. Otherwise, their kind is not welcome here."

Amis looked down at the unconscious children, the heat from their breaths making small, lovely, puffy clouds. Their wings, tucked back underneath them, were twisted but visible enough.

"We need help. These children are not immortal. They can die from this cold."

The leader looked at its companions, who were silent during the entire exchange.

"Walk them up to the village," he said. Swift movements came next as the creatures all joined in picking up a body each, the small one who had pulled them out of the water empty-clawed, moving away as the others followed.

Amis gulped and began marching. Trust was not something he was willing to give easily, but there was little choice in the matter. If these terrifying creatures did not kill any of them, the weather surely would.

Once Amis emerged from the steam that perfectly wrapped and hid the hot spring within the snow from above, his lips parted, his eyes in awe as he stared at the side of a mountain. This mountain was only partially covered in snow, its walls sleek black rock with no slants, no ridges to hold snow, mud, or debris.

There were large, grand houses with floor-to-ceiling windows and flat roofs built into the sides of the mountain. They shone and glistened despite no reflective light in the sky. The looming weather only made the spectacular homes seem even more cozy and gave them a wealthy ski resort feel.

It was beautiful, but more importantly, it looked safe. It looked resilient. Amis's heart lightened. Somehow, Luca made the right choice. The right direction to fly, the right time to close his eyes and fall. It was unbelievable how they'd ended up here.

A hard-shelled pincer pushed against him, the creature that led him gesturing to a different area, pointing away from those houses. Down below, on a plateau, existed smaller homes that looked like mushrooms but were dull green, mined gems that went unpolished.

These buildings, this plateau, were where they were going, instead of the glass fronts of the homes embedded in the mountain. Amis saw small waterfalls spouting on both sides of the plateau, the water pouring aggressively as an endless resupply of water came down from the skies.

Shelter was shelter, and as Noah stirred and whimpered, Amis was glad to get his little frozen fingers inside one of the small homes. They moved past ten of them, small walking paths and patches of garden lining their perfectly aligned structures that still somehow blended in with the mountain behind them. From far away, Amis could see how this little town camouflaged itself: even the smaller homes could look like boulders.

Their group passed another ten, then another, and Amis realized there were hundreds of these homes on the plateau. Though they were all made out of the same material, their shapes and sizes were not uniform. Some were simple, others grand. There was no hierarchy in structure, only function.

Eyes peered out of glass windows, following them as they finally stopped at one of the homes. It seemed like they were directly in the middle of the plateau, and Amis imagined that he'd be running for miles if he did a full lap around the outskirts of this community.

"In," the larger creature among them commanded, locking his small beady eyes on Amis as he pushed through a front door. The others followed. Amis was the last to walk through and was instantly hit with the aroma of onions and potatoes.

Amis's eyes nearly rolled into the back of his head from the immense pleasure he took in simply breathing it in.

The pressure in his chest thrummed, reminding him that death still chased him, but he was able to push it away as the warmth of fire gently sparked. The creatures holding Salome, Ahora, and Luca set them down on the plush taupe carpet.

"Where are we?" Amis asked, unsure how many of the creatures in the house could understand him. The same one, the only one that spoke to him, stood up and turned, communicating with the group by clicking his pincers.

"Emerald's Peak" were eventually the words communicated back to him.

17

___

Hadley | Wyvern Back

Kismet shrieked, a chilling and eerie sound, as they soared through the air. Dark clouds churned below them, an endless roil of storms stretching in all directions. Hadley couldn't see an end, but she watched them flash and strobe. The lighting and blast of fire that followed Kismet's eldritch cries illuminated the skies.

She felt lighter being away from them all. The anger still burned in her, but it had turned inward again to its closest target, herself.

Even if she had never met Sheng or gone to the masquerade, the choice still would've belonged to her. She had made it with full awareness of what it might cost. She had tried other paths without enough conviction. That failure had carved itself into her.

No one else had ruined her. She had done that herself.

Even if she kept it a secret forever, the knowledge would still live inside her. She would always know what she was capable of when fear and desperation backed her into a corner.

That was the person she was. Those were the types of choices she made.

She grieved for her mother, her past, but she also grieved herself. She grieved the woman she had become, angry that she was made to make choices that led her here.

Kismet ducked and spiraled down. Hadley lowered her upper body, pressing into Kismet's back. The wyvern's spike pushed into Hadley's side, and gravity pulled her harder into it.

Hadley brought her wings in, bones cracking, ghostly and soft. She could see the ground as they emerged from the bottom of the storm clouds. Lightning struck all around her, electricity buzzing in her ears.

There was no snow. The air was warm, heavy.

If it weren't for the whipping wind, she would have been too hot. The humidity soaked her skin with sweat.

They continued to descend, the ground now more visible to her eye. She could make out the mounds, some ashen, some warm from the rain underneath them.

Sand dunes.

Kismet didn't stop her descent until they were thirty feet from the tallest one. Hunger gnawed at Hadley, too.

Anger took a lot out of her.

Lightning struck just ahead, and Kismet pulled up, nearly knocking Hadley off the sudden shift. Kismet shrieked and let out a burst of fire that seemed endless as Hadley struggled to hold on to the wyvern's black spike. She held on so hard that she could feel the blood trickling out beneath the spike, the blue liquid making it harder and harder to hold on.

Kismet corrected herself, tossing Hadley's body back violently onto her stomach. Hadley shoved herself upright, just in time for Kismet to lurch forward again.

Then she froze.

Right in front of her, the dune right below now looked like her wings.

Translucent specks of color flashed against the lightning, warm sand trapped beneath thick sheets of dragon glass.

Kismet let out more fire, torching the dunes in front of them. Every dune below glinted with glass. Hadley thudded her hand against the wyvern's hide as they dodged the lightning that seemed mere feet away from Kismet's wings. The beautiful beast twisted mid-air and landed on the glass. Her weight made the surface crack beneath her, small glass spikes jutting out beneath her feet.

Hadley slid off of Kismet easily, thanks to the wet, slick scales. She landed hard, pain blooming through her knees and wrists. Her ankle throbbed with every small movement, but she pushed through it. Blood ran down her arm, but she kept her focus ahead.

She stood, blinded by rage, on a glass mountain, wyvern behind her as lightning came down violently from the raging storm above.

The gleam of her shadow self made itself known, always there, always watching.

It exhausted her being so powerful yet feeling so weak.

Hadley looked back up to the sky with the wind tousling her wet blonde hair.

Something more than just lightning illuminated the clouds. This light was warmer and constant. It did not disappear or follow the rhythm of the storm.

She knew what it was. She knew who it was.

I wondered where you were.

Fear was not something she had room for in her heart. If it still existed at all, it was buried deep where she could no longer reach it.

A ball of embers, a woman's silhouette surrounded by deep reds, oranges, and yellows, descended toward her. The glass turned molten upon her arrival.

Hadley unfurled her wings, hearing the already ripped fabric of her jacket tear further as she hovered. She wished her body could withstand flame like Kismet's.

"There you both are," came the soft, echoing threat of Ayurveda's voice as it swept across the clearing.

Hadley blinked at the Goddess goddess and wrapped her arms around herself, savoring the extra warmth from her flames. It felt good, stewing in anger, soaking in the heat of something that could burn the world down.

"What are you doing here?" Hadley asked, voice clipped and hard.

Ayurveda paused, her face blank and unreadable in her silhouette phase.

"Hadley, that rage you feel is yours. Reign's magic doesn't hold power over your actions when you get far enough away from her."

Even if that were true, Goddess, you are still a source of that rage.

"They told me that you had taken advantage of me," Hadley told the Sun. "They told me that my life was no different than when I was held captive in Sheng's home."

"Sheng," Ayurveda mused, "what a complete disappointment. Entertaining, but beneath us."

"Are you here to kill me?" Hadley asked, refusing to waste words.

Ayurveda's fire fulminated blue, purple tips reaching like claws toward nothing but wind and glass.

Hadley's shadow self stood stoic and strong to her left side—a silent sentinel, radiating readiness for battle, for loyalty that might finally matter.

"What is it that you're looking for, Hadley? Because I thought it was a family. I thought you wanted closeness. I thought I had given that to you. Even now, surrounded by your own blood, you don't seem content."

"I realized that killing all living beings on this planet was likely against what my mother would have wished for."

Ayurveda almost laughed. "Your mother would have happily killed everyone if it meant she could have you. She wouldn't have even thought twice about it."

Her seething cooled, and Hadley could feel that pang of sorrow rise again in her chest.

"That line is thin, isn't it?" Ayurveda asked. "That line between anger and sorrow. It hurts. It hurts to be alive. There are too many passions, emotions, and things to hold on to and care about. You crave that darkness, Hadley. I see it. There's a reason for that."

Hadley stepped back closer to Kismet, looking away from the Sun, and the tempting darkness she tried not to want.

"What is that reason?" Hadley asked.

"It seems almost a rhetorical question," Ayurveda answered. "You were never meant to be the simple flesh that populates this world. You were born from a deity with the aid of something even more powerful. You are meant to be my companion, dear girl. You are meant to be a God."

Hadley didn't know what to do with that. She looked down at her hand.

Say something. She's waiting.

"What does it mean to be a God? What do I have to do?"

Ayurveda smiled, her grin curling like flame, sharp enough to make Hadley's skin prickle.

"We finish what we started, dear little one," Ayurveda said.

The dark star.

"I don't want to destroy anything," Hadley said, her shoulders sagging. "It isn't me."

"No? But you seem so accustomed to killing now. All it takes is a little provoking."

She wasn't wrong. Hadley had been wrestling with this, with her lack of humanity, with what she was becoming.

"Is a God a devil?" she asked, her mind going to Sheng. He was the one who seemed not to care, the one who seemed like he wouldn't abandon her if she were a murderer, if she was power hungry, if she had a spell of rage.

"Everyone is a devil to someone," Ayurveda said simply.

Hadley supposed that was true. She figured that even Sheng thought he was a hero, somehow. She supposed Djoser thought himself to be a villain. She supposed Reifoel . . .

Well, she wasn't sure what Reifoel thought about himself. She didn't even believe he knew how he felt about her.

She was tired of passion. She was tired of declarations, of longing, of not knowing what was real.

"Why would I want to be a God?" Hadley asked.

Ayurveda's flame calmed, flickering softer, almost approving.

"It's written in the threads of time. Only one small detail can derail it. If you are struggling in any way, then I'd say it's time to grow. It's time to step into that destiny."

"What do I have to do?" Hadley asked, petting Kismet, who let out a purr.

Lighting struck only eight feet away from where she stood, from where Kismet lazily lounged under Hadley's light mass. Glass shattered, and the dune nearly exploded. Hadley covered her face with her arm as shards dusted her.

There was a crack, one that reminded her of the earth opening underneath her, when Precession pulled hidden underneath geysers for aid in their battle against the Goddess that stood before her.

"That is something you will no longer feel," Ayurveda said, not affected by the lightning that continued to strike around them. "There will be no fear, no sadness, no anger. Your emotions will cease, and your existence will become a to-do list. What is human about you, lost, recycled back into the life of this planet."

Numb.

She would be numb.

It was all she craved. All that she had wanted. No more pain, no more wishing that she could have drowned when Reifoel and Isadore pulled her out of those caves. Here, Ayurveda was again, offering her exactly what she needed in the exact moment she needed it most.

"What do I have to do?"

Ayurveda's flame was now nonexistent; an almost human form stood in front of her. She hadn't seen that since Coachella, since the house in Joshua Tree. Hadley couldn't believe what she saw. It was a version of herself made divine, radiant, terrible. She held the future within her own hands, a destiny to command that was all her own.

"I will burn you alive. The wyvern could help as well."

Hadley's eyes widened as shock rippled through her. Another bolt of lightning struck the glass nearby, sending a spray of glowing shards into the air. Kismet groaned beside her, the wyvern's body tensing, aware of how vulnerable her size made her in the open storm.

"This will not kill you," Ayurveda said, her voice calm but resolute. "Not exactly. A simple death would lead you to a very different fate."

She stepped forward, her form pulsing with heat.

"Your body will heal. It will repair itself. The pain will not last, though its shadow will linger at the edges of your memory. After the fire, you will have nine days to keep your body alive. That is the test."

Ayurveda's eyes gleamed, her flames flickering brighter.

"The fire will mark the death of your humanity. It is a sacred transformation, an ember from the cosmos itself. A star's heat is unlike anything you have known."

She lifted a hand, letting the fire spiral between her fingers.

"If you can survive those nine days, you will shed your human self entirely. Like a flower losing its last petal, your former life will fall away. What remains will not be mortal."

Ayurveda tilted her head, studying Hadley.

"You will gain power beyond what you can currently imagine. You will pull the strings not only of this world, but others. You will take your place beside me, alongside Karmarkara and the Life Gifter."

Hadley didn't know these names, these Gods, not really.

"When I join you, will you restore the moon?"

Ayurveda's flame instantly responded, growing brighter and hotter than the glass dunes underneath her could handle. The dune turned red, molten, and gold. The colors were so blindingly beautiful she nearly stepped into them.

Ayurveda seemed to want just that.

"I do not have the power to create in that way. But when you have turned into a deity, when you have become my counterpart in power, you will not care what happens to this world. You will see a bigger picture."

Such seductive words. Ayurveda was telling her exactly what she wanted to hear. Not caring anymore would be a luxury. Letting go of the battle between who she was and what she had done would be a kind of bliss.

Hadley continued to stare at the colors, the molten glass dune that called to her underneath Ayurveda's form. Kismet nudged her in the back, and the heat coming from her nostrils made Hadley close her eyes and savor it. She wanted to wrap it around herself.

Here, she had a true partner. This beast had appeared from nowhere. Kismet had stayed loyal, dependable, and fierce. The thought of losing her made Hadley's stomach twist.

Since Glaciel, Hadley always knew when Kismet was near.

"I can't leave her," she said. "I can't leave the wyvern behind."

"As a God, you can have your little pets. I have my Vrae. Karmakara and the Life Gifter have their Kinnari."

This was enough for her. Hadley nodded, turning to kiss Kismet on her wet, too-hot nose. Hadley's lips burned, but she counted it as a good warm-up for what she was about to do.

"I accept. I'm ready now."

You will do this. You will do this and not cry.

Another strike of lightning hit between Ayurveda and Hadley. Glass shattered, and blood rolled down her cheek.

"Step into the dune," Ayurveda instructed, the flames around her turning back to that familiar blue, those threatening yellows that seared the glass.

Hadley stepped forward. She gathered her strength and closed her eyes, waiting for the darkness, that promise of nothing. That hadn't worked out. She hadn't been able to let go. If she did this, though, she could let go of everything.

She closed her eyes and breathed.

You can do this.

"Will it hurt?"

She couldn't help it.

Of course, it will hurt.

Kismet shrieked, lightning struck, and more glass shattered.

"Step into the dune, Hadley."

And she did.

18

Reign | Ebonspire

"So . . . is he dead?" Roksana asked, popping out her hip.

Celestine had dramatically thrown herself over Arryn's body. Reign wasn't even sure it qualified as a body anymore. He looked like he was made of crystal, of ice, of glass. She had seen this magic before, when she huddled with shaking children and watched the sky burn. She had stared at Ayurveda as she'd turned into something that should sit on top of a Christmas tree.

The Goddess had not died. Arryn wasn't a Goddess.

Celestine turned her head, her long brown hair a tangled mop matted with tears. She shot a nasty look at Roksana.

"What?" Roksana asked, flinging her arms back behind her. "Like none of us are thinking it."

"I can't feel him," Celestine wailed.

Whatever that means.

"It's better," Reifoel said. "It's better that she left him like this. He is whole; he isn't shattered. He might not be dead yet."

Reign turned to Djoser, tall, dark, and handsome, sulking against the end of the bright orange couch, his fist against his chin, trying not to look Celestine in the eye.

"He's not dead, I'd think I could tell," he said, rolling his eyes. "Does anyone know where I can get a good stiff drink around here?"

Most everyone in the room nodded. Reign didn't think it was possible for him to look any grimmer, but here they were.

"I can't wait to see what her tears do," Reign heard an Atheri say to the small group of them that tried to funnel in behind her. Goosebumps crawled up Reign's arms. She didn't like how close they stood, how unnaturally bright they looked.

"The answer to your question is yes," Precession's sing-songy voice chimed in.

"I didn't ask a question," Reign answered.

"It's still yes," Precession giggled.

"She means that yes, all of this is your fault," Sheng stepped into the room, sliding through the Atheri carefully, slithering like a shadow and avoiding any accidental touch. "It's okay—no one can blame a child. Is it ever really their fault at the end of the day?"

Reign lifted her chin and closed her eyes, that anger simmering inside her.

"Make sure you collect yourself before you open those eyes again." She could hear the smirk in Sheng's voice as he taunted her.

But he wasn't wrong. It was her fault.

Hadley had composed herself so completely that Reign had turned away. Maybe the command she'd given hadn't been clear enough. Or maybe she had let herself get distracted. She hadn't expected the blonde Kinnari woman to stay calm, to not pick up a chair, to not throw a fit like one of those wrestlers Reign flipped past on her new silver TV.

"I'm going to go after her," Djoser said, standing. Reifoel stood weirdly at attention as if he regretted not saying it first.

"No," Sheng interrupted, "the only one who should go after her is Reign."

Right again.

That damn demon Vrae. Scum of the earth. Piece of shit.

Reign opened her eyes slowly and brought her chin back down, pushing out a slow breath between her slightly parted lips.

"Good girl," Sheng said, stepping into her view. She didn't like how he looked at her, like they were a team. "Now go get her."

She froze, not taking her eyes off of him. Celestine's wailing in the background grew so obnoxiously loud that she supposed doing anything else was much better.

I hope you're not dead, dickhead.

Reign walked out of the room, avoiding the Atheri whose eyes lingered on her when she passed. It felt like they could see right through her, but not knowing what it was that they saw was terrifying in itself.

Once she was outside, once all eyes that lingered were no longer paying her any mind, she ran. She ran hard.

She ran for Hadley. She ran for herself. She ran because everything hurt, and the only thing she knew to do anymore was run. She was supposed to make it up to her goddaughter; she had promised Allienna that she would take care of her.

Gods, she sounded like Arryn.

Reign was getting sick of Allienna, sick of hearing about her. Her best friend had lied to her and left her in the dark. Worse, she hadn't trusted her. Whatever that Kinnari was hiding, she didn't feel like it was safe in Reign's hands.

I'll show you trustworthy.

With her arms swinging around, with more rage that crept up each vertebra of her back, Reign made her way out to the nothing, to the light, and found the knob that took her back into the snow outside of the dome.

That's when she looked up, falling out of the invisible door, to see the wyvern flying overhead. She wasn't too late; she could catch them, small wings be damned.

Reign kept running, her boots sloshing in snow, passing the two twisted bare trees as her wings ripped out from her jacket, as the bones fused together so fast that she no longer even considered that they were not always there, ready to take off and soar into the sky.

The clouds were ominous, a signal she would ignore as she fought wind and cold while she rose higher and higher and higher. She soared, and she turned in the direction she hoped Hadley had taken off in.

A storm began to rally around her, so she pumped her wings harder. She was going so fast that she could barely see straight, barely comprehending what direction she was going in.

She looked for any sign of them, but they were gone, lost in the endless sea of storms. It wouldn't faze her, couldn't faze her. She wasn't going to fail.

The higher she flew, the faster she pushed herself.

Reign thrust her arms forward, then pulled them back, willing her body to fly faster, fast enough to rival a wyvern. She pushed ahead once more. A ripple passed through her, faint and easy to miss, until the sky split. She dove headfirst into a time jump, hurled far from the one she meant to reach. Far from the apology still waiting on her tongue.

REIGN WAS PULLED THROUGH TIME, the air around her filled with a pulse that physically shoved into her. pressing and rolling over her skin in waves of heat and static. It was an unmistakable feeling.

This had to be the most inconvenient power that any of them had. Time travel was rarely useful and always unpleasant.

The sky turned black. The air cooled.

She looked down, relieved to see grass, green and lush.

There was a beautiful village.

There were canals.

There was a moon in the sky.

It felt like breathing, being somewhere with no rain, no snow, no threat of apocalyptic weather.

The past few days were very grim. She was over the excitement of it.

Reign swooped closer to the ground, passing a gorgeous orchard, the fruit so ripe on the trees that she could smell its sweetness even from her height.

She would have been embarrassed to admit how long it took her to see how familiar it all was to her, how she knew exactly where she was when she was, but it didn't happen until she saw a large man passed out on the grass with a child kicking the shit out of him.

She knew that man; she knew that child.

It was her, and that was Arryn.

Reign quickly dropped out of the sky, landing behind a barn-like structure near the orchard, and peered around the corner. That's when it hit her.

There was a Vrae around here. She remembered seeing those red eyes through a bush. This was her chance to find them. Hell, maybe she was responsible for making sure Arryn and past Reign weren't slaughtered. That's probably why she couldn't find them. She was there, commanding them to leave, to disappear.

Without hesitation, she crept up and around the building and followed the canal down until she could hear her own voice, sighing and muttering to herself.

Poor me, I'm having a really hard time.

Reign knelt behind a tree and then moved slowly under the cover of a few bushes. She tried to avoid studying herself, tried to avoid looking at Arryn. He would surely piss her off again.

Instead, she scanned the greenery, looking for flashes of red eyes.

Pixie-like creatures flitted between branches, tiny bodies glowing and weaving like birds in love.

They startled her.

Every moment made her flinch.

She was on edge and took her new mission seriously.

If she was the only one stopping this potential Vrae attack, then she would accept being jumpy.

"Gods, you suck," she could hear her past self yell out loud to the sky and then slump down next to Arryn in frustration.

Reign bit back a laugh.

She really had been a mess.

I feel you, girl.

She crouched low, pulling her chin into her chest. Her hands were braced down on the ground. Leaves scratched her neck. Thin branches jabbed the backs of her knees.

She tried to shift her weight to avoid the pain and immediately lost her balance.

Her arms bucked. She nearly face-planted into the dirt. The sound of snapping twigs and thrashing branches echoed louder than it should have. It was a betrayal of every bush she had ever tried to hide in.

Shit. Shit. Shit.

She saw the flicker of awareness, muscles tensing in her past self. Reign held her breath, quiet as death.

She expected Karmakara to appear any moment to save her, to scold her. But that moment did not come.

Instead, she heard footsteps.

Reign tilted her chin up and saw her past self walk towards the bushes. That familiar face rippled with fear, then confusion.

Reign's heart dropped.

This was when she saw the Vrae.

Which meant that the demon . . .

Is here, in the bushes, with you.

Reign gulped down her panic. There was no time for that.

You need to run.

She tore through the back of the bushes and ran through the dark, lush green grass underneath her feet. Her heart thundered. Emotion swelled to an explosive level.

Her legs carried her further than she anticipated as she slumped behind a thick, tall tree to catch her breath. Unfortunately, that's when she realized that she was being chased.

The Vrae.

The Vrae must be running after her.

She didn't dare look back.

Reign gasped, lungs burning, and launched forward. Her arms pumped, wings catching the wind just enough to lift her feet from the ground. She skimmed through a narrow grove, heart hammering, doing everything she could to stay aloft and unseen.

Her eyes burned—her tears had dried to salt. She scanned the trees below, the ocean gleaming in her periphery.

She didn't see red eyes or jagged teeth. The memory of them curled at the edges of her vision like smoke, motivation to keep her speed up.

And then she felt a pulse.

No.

That horribly familiar, bone-deep pull. It shivered through her hands, down her spine, up the back of her skull.

She didn't have time to curse it.

The jump had already begun.

19

Amis | Emeralds Peak

mis woke up to silence, to warmth. He couldn't remember the last time he'd felt this held, this safe. Wherever he was, it felt like a small piece of heaven, the weight of constant danger finally lifted off his shoulders.

You're too relaxed. You're all barely surviving.

There was a heavy blanket over him, the material so soft against his cheek. It was not quite cotton, not quite silk, something in between. He lay there with his eyes closed for minutes, enjoying the feeling while ignoring the nagging voice trying to pull him back to reality. It was too easy to swat away.

Peace like this didn't just feel rare; it felt wrong.

Little hands touched his face, and he smiled. There was no crying, no need nor want, just tender little hands that needed him, maybe even loved him.

Love.

Amis opened his eyes to see Noah, who was busy grabbing his ears, his cheeks, and his lips and pulling, pushing, shaping them in every way as he played. Amis winced, Noah gradually getting more and more excited and engaged, seeing that he was awake. Awake and smiling.

Do I have their love? No.

Amis pushed the thought away. The horrors he had committed took up too much space in his mind, too much focus and attention. Letting it go felt easier than holding on. Easier than the constant back and forth between protecting them and accepting Karmakara's fate. Those webs she spun in her glittering tapestry were tangled for a reason. If fate was changed, the Goddess seemed to be prepared to let you know in that passive-aggressive, princess sort of way.

Noah squealed, delighted by whatever silly beast Amis looked like with his cheeks squished together, somehow reaching the sides of his nose.

"They fed us," Salome's gentle voice sounded behind him. Amis lifted his head, realizing that the amazing, comforting place he rested on was the floor.

How low my standards have gotten.

He used to sleep in silk sheets, serve Vrae royalty, ride in bullet-proof cars he never actually needed. And now, he was grateful for the floor.

Amis laughed to himself. Everything they were trying to accomplish had directly brought him here, thankful to be present, to have a child giggling on his chest.

His stomach growled loudly for the entire room to hear.

"What was on the menu?"

Salome looked confused at his word choice, tilting her head like she was trying to translate him.

"I mean, what did you eat?"

"Some kind of stew. It smelled of the ocean. I'll go get you a bowl," she said, skipping away, a glow on her cheeks, light in her step.

"There is no ocean around us," Luca said, making Amis jump a little. He appeared out of nowhere, a ghost. His normally tanned skin was paler, the purple under his eyes more prominent.

"Did you get any sleep?" Amis asked.

Luca scoffed, as if he didn't look like something undead.

"I've fallen into the lap of the most terrifying-looking creatures I've ever seen. There are families of them, hundreds of homes all packed together where they can all group at a moment's notice. Their claws look like they can tear us apart. How could you sleep knowing that? How could you sleep when Salome, AhoraAlhora, and Noah are taking food from these things?"

Ah, so he hasn't eaten either.

"You're sounding a little crazy," Salome giggled as she walked back from an awning that led to the kitchen, holding a steaming bowl and a spoon.

Luca shot her a look that painted a portrait of someone manic, someone who was falling apart.

"The first rule about crazy people, Salome," Amis said, trying to break the tension, "is not to tell them that they are crazy."

"That doesn't make any sense," Ahora interrupted, stretching her arms lazily lounging near the wood fire stove in the corner of the room. "You should know who you are, what you are becoming. Just like you, Amis." She smiled tenderly.

Amis accepted the bowl, doing his best not to spill on Noah, who just wouldn't get the hint that he, too, could use some food. His brain worked better when he wasn't malnourished. Amis didn't even get thinner; he was just more oafish.

He could feel that now, even in this strange peace.

Those were emotions for the fools, the dreamers. The ones that lived in their heads and ignored the realities around them.

Happiness was for those who got eaten first.

Maybe I shouldn't eat.

"And what am I becoming?" Amis asked as he tipped a spoonful of the broth past his lips. His senses heightened, and his stomach growled louder at its salty, buttery, savory flavor. He might need another bowl of this.

"Good," Ahora said. "You're becoming good."

Amis's heart sank and sang simultaneously. He froze, staring at his bowl, doing his best not to let his emotions get the better of him.

You're not going to cry over those words. You're just out of balance.

He held back a sob and looked up at the rounded, overly tall door frame, which made a small squeak in front of them. Amis watched the door handle, vertical and long with indents made for pincers and claws, turn ninety degrees.

The door opened, letting in the dreary cold, the gray light. Light sounds of thunder purred off in the distance.

One of the creatures who had saved them—who could just as easily un-save them—stepped inside. Its shoulders were so broad that they seemed barely able to squeeze through the frame, and its dozens of pale legs reminded Amis of tentacles.

Immediately as it stood before them, it held out its pincers and began to communicate in the rhythm that Amis had seen them use once before. It still meant nothing to him, but the thing was trying.

Amis shook his head no and gave his shoulders a quick shrug.

"Sorry," he said, a delayed smirk creeping across his face so as not to betray how utterly nervous he felt around the thing.

It turned around and put its pincer out into the open air, signaling.

Shit. It's calling more.

Instinctively, Amis wrapped his arms around Noah and made eye contact with the girls as he tried to signal for them to get behind him with a quick toss of his head.

They didn't move.

"Don't be silly." Salome bent down next to Amis. "They have been treating us so kindly."

Amis was aligned with Luca on this one. He didn't trust the situation, not one bit.

The creature backed up as a second one joined. This one was slightly taller and could speak.

"Have you had enough time to recover?" it asked.

Amis couldn't answer; his mouth was so dry, and his stomach was aching for more soup.

"Are you wary of us?" it asked again after the silence.

They stand so still. Too still.

"I am," Amis finally spat out. Luca slapped his hand on Amis's shoulder and nodded his head at the creature, teaming up with him. The teenager's approval oddly had so much weight, so much pull on him. Amis couldn't help but smile.

"Why?"

Amis's smile turned into a chuckle. He couldn't help it. He was starving, and his balance jumped around the inside of his body like a children's game of dodgeball. He was protective and reckless; he was starting to feel similar to how Luca looked.

"Look at you," Amis said, "you are the most terrifying thing I have personally ever seen, and a week or so ago, I was on the back of a dragon."

"Wyvern," Luca corrected.

Amis waved him off with his hand and rolled his eyes.

That seemed to pique the creature's interest a bit, its shockingly still body swaying almost a centimeter to the right.

"How have you survived since the moon fell apart?" Amis asked, starting to feel just a little more comfortable after the creature didn't eat him after being told his kind looked like monsters.

The stillness returned, other than the movements of a jaw hidden by a lower set of antennae that hung like a mustache.

"We are miners," it said as if that were enough explanation. "We are called Marthrend."

Amis shifted, trying to hide his discomfort, his mistrust.

The Marthrend continued, "Our homes and our community are built on the emerald we mine. Our claws are powerful, able to crush the rocks and cut the gems. After the moon fell, we felt horror. Soon after, our mines were filled with water. The gases beneath kept it warm. The steam has helped ensure we are not buried in snow. I imagine we are more fortunate than most."

The creature paused, letting his words settle. Amis took another sip of the stew, his spoon clinking against the bowl.

"So you were trying to mine then when you saved us all?" Amis asked.

"Yes," the Mathrend said. "Not all of us are used to swimming, so just a few are risked each day to please the merchants."

"The merchants?" Amis repeated back to it.

"Those homes above us, built within the mountain, belong to the other half of our kind. They are able to sell our gems and make the community prosperous for us all."

Amis nodded, understanding.

"Will you go to Mytholm? Are you traveling east? You have a safe place to stay with us here until you are all healed from your fall from the sky."

"What is Mytholm?" Salome asked, her voice light and shy, inching a little closer to Amis.

The Mathrend blinked its beady black eyes.

"Mytholm is a town filled with beings that look just like you." He pointed at Salome. "It is isolated, hard to get to. I suspect that it is for a reason. I have never left Emerald's Peak but have heard stories from visitors."

"Filled with me? There are many children there?" Salome's eyes lit up, and Ahora's knees bounced up and down.

"Indeed. A town of children, only children."

The two girls were delighted to hear this. Amis only frowned. If there were such a thing, a town filled with children, he suspected it would be a very grim scene to enter. The few of them could barely survive even with his help.

"What is your name?" Salome asked the Mathrend.

It bowed, and Amis jumped back at the sudden movement. It did not seem to notice.

"I do not have a name. I am not an individual. I am of Mathrend. I am like water—I fill any space that needs such. When I die, when my vessel, my body, can no longer be useful, I will be harvested for stew. Mathrend is a cycle. Mathrend is one with nature. We will endure long after others are gone. "

Amis looked down at his stew. A frown formed; pulling the left side of his lip down.

"I am eating one of you?" he asked.

The Mathrend nodded. "It is nutritious. A staple meal for us all. How long will you stay?"

"Not long," Luca croaked.

"We would appreciate at least one more night of rest," Amis jumped in, giving Luca a look that he hoped conveyed how easy it would be to tear the flesh off of his bones.

Fucking teenagers. Impossible.

Amis would love to believe that he wasn't this big of an asshole at this age, but he was probably a bigger one even now.

The Mathrend tapped its pincers in a rhythmic pattern while it stared at their little, meek group. Amis plastered a grin across his face, watching, being as agreeable as possible as he pretended that the thing that stood before him didn't still creep him out.

They had to know. That they look like nightmares.

Tap. Tap. Tap.

Tap. Tap. Tap.

Tap. Tap. Tap.

Amis took a bite of his stew. His slurp of the broth, the root vegetables, and the meat was so loud that he felt the tension increase in the air.

Damn, that's good.

Tap. Tap. Tap.

The Mathrend ended its message and took a step forward while turning on his back tentacles or legs. Amis wasn't sure how to categorize them.

It exited the house, closing the door behind him with a soft thud. Luca was there, ready to verbally pounce on Amis the second the latch clicked.

"How can you eat that?"

Amis shrugged and took another bite. "They don't seem to have a problem with it."

"Can we go?" Ahora all but pushed Luca out of the way. "To the city of children? There must be families, someone that can take care of us."

"Amis takes care of us," Salome interjected.

"Play!" Noah yelled, hands in the air, feeling left out of the conversation.

After getting to his feet, Amis sighed. "What we need is to find Arryn."

"But what if he's there to protect the children?" Alohra asked.

You obviously don't know Arryn.

"They flew south, sweetie. We probably shouldn't head any further east."

Sweetie? Who are you turning into?

Amis grimaced at himself.

Ahora looked crushed and fell to the floor, her arms crossed over her chest as she pouted.

"What I need right now," Amis said. "Is for Luca to sleep. I have a feeling that he'll be a little less of an ass then."

Luca's eyes narrowed into daggers, but Amis only laughed. Gods, he was starting to feel like an old man.

"I already said that I wouldn't," Luca said.

"I will stand over you all. You will be safe. They will be safe. You are putting them in more danger by choosing not to sleep, not to recover when you have an opportunity to."

He really wished he had Reign with him right now. She would say three words, and this problem would be solved.

It took several more minutes of convincing, of pleading. Salome joined in, and Luca caved, laying down on the carpet. Amis draped the heavy blanket over the teen and watched until his blinks became heavy.

Luca couldn't have fought harder, but sleep eventually won. It always did.

20

———

Allienna | Sacramento, CA | 1994

"Momma, Momma, it's morning. It's time to wake up," young Hadley said, trying to shake Allienna's shoulders.

Allienna pried her eyes open, the crust creeping under her eyelid causing immediate irritation. She winced, rubbed hard at her lashes and blinked into the blurry room.

"The phone keeps ringing. Can I answer it?" Hadley asked, jumping up and down as Allienna covered her face, expecting her fairly uncoordinated daughter to fall on her at any moment.

She heard it too—the high-pitched rhythmic tones of their house phone.

"Yes, go see who it is."

That must be why Hadley was waking her up so early.

It's not like the sun is up.

Allienna laid on her pillow, feeling the warmth and brightness on her cheek, snuggling in her blanket, but then jumped out of the bed like it was on fire.

The sun is up. What time is it?

"Momma, it's Zade. He asked if you're still sick. I didn't know you were sick," Hadley yelled from the doorway with the nine-inch silver cordless phone pressed against her left ear.

Shit.

Allienna leaped over to Hadley and snatched the phone from her.

"Hey," Hadley protested and crossed her arms over her chest. "Not fair."

"Zade? Hey, yes, I'm coming in. I feel better. My alarm forgot to set itself. See you soon."

Allienna pressed the squished rubber button in until the phone let out a high-pitched beep and moved to place it back on its home station in the kitchen.

Moving as if she had five hands instead of two, she began the monumental task of getting the two of them dressed, fed, and packed up even though it felt like someone was physically pulling their fingers down the bottom of her eyelids. She was tired. There was no doubt about that, but there was something else, something nagging in the back of her head, a headache brewing.

No, it's not quite the same.

"Let's go," she yelled to Hadley, who came waddling out of her room, holding far too many dolls in her arms.

"I'm ready," Hadley declared.

Ignoring the fact that Hadley was wearing two different shoes, Allienna stared at her front door and paused. Her throat dried. She couldn't even swallow, unable to push an intrusive thought out of her head.

That cop, that human-looking Vrae, could be out there. Right out there, steps from her door, just waiting, smiling, ready to hunt.

You are a terrible mother, she thought and placed her hand on the round gold-painted doorknob, then turned.

Birds chirped, welcoming the two of them to the sunshine that lingered in their lower-income neighborhood. Suddenly, everything that Allienna had worked so hard for, that she had been so proud of, seemed not enough.

She saw the house across the street with eight or nine broken-down cars parked in front of it, the overgrown, dead grass that forested her neighbor's yard as its elderly tenant walked around holding a cat, always a different cat. The rest ran amok in the neighborhood, breeding, multiplying, and sitting alongside driveways as they stared at and judged her.

Hold it together.

Allienna held Hadley's hand to walk a few feet over to their car and tried not to jump at every noise she heard. The skin contact helped. Her daughter was generally always gleeful, always appreciating the daffodils that grew in the cracks of their driveway.

She helped Hadley buckle in her seat belt as she continuously looked over her shoulder. As soon as she sat in the driver's seat herself, she locked the doors immediately, a small amount of security blanketing her. They weren't in the open anymore, and the barbershop was in an area that was too populated for her to be attacked.

Wasn't it?

Maybe thinking that a Vrae would hold back was a mistake on its own. She knew so little about them.

Goosebumps rose on her arms as she put the key in the ignition and turned until the engine roared.

"I want country music," Hadley pleaded as Allienna kicked herself for never fixing the stereo. It had only been four, maybe five years. She hadn't needed to replace it yet. Doing it now seemed silly.

That ache in the back of her head came back in a wave.

"I can't make it work right now, Hadley," she said. "I'll try again later."

As she put the car in reverse, the ache began to reveal itself. No, it wasn't a headache.

A memory.

She had a dream last night. She had dreamed about Tristan.

He said he had a plan—a plan to protect Hadley. That wasn't a dream, not really. It had happened.

She finished pulling out of the driveway and continued the drive to the barbershop, looking in the rearview mirror once every other breath. She couldn't live this way for long.

"Auntie Paisley," Hadley yelled out an hour later as she ran through the open glass door of the downtown Sacramento barber shop. She ran into the arms of Allienna's boss, the barbershop owner who wore dark brown lip liner and seemed to have a new hair color every other week. Today, it was sea green with chunky pink highlights that closely matched the rose gold pendant that pierced her nose.

The two hugged near the black check-in desk covered with stickers, most of them collected from Warped Tours or sneaker outlets.

"When are you going to get that child into school?" Zade said, popping out his hip and pursing his lips, already working with a client with corded headphones over his ears attached to a CD player. "Hey," Zade poked the client, a young male in his twenties. "I don't know how you expect me to cut your hair when your headphones cover most of it, dude."

"Whatever, man," the client said, rolling his eyes.

Allienna tried to hide her giggle as she could practically see the black spikes in Zade's hair trembling from his annoyance. She moved past them into the break room while Paisley let Hadley play with her hair, grabbing an apron from behind the curtain and tying it around her waist, filling it with clippers, scissors, and a small purple spray bottle.

"She starts preschool this fall, actually," Allienna answered Zade as she walked back out, ready to wait for her first appointment.

"Good, momma, that child needs friends. She's starting to get my attitude, and I'm not convinced Paisley won't try to color her hair green with her leftover dye of the week."

Allienna smiled softly, watching Hadley, so content in here, running around the barbershop like this was her family. It was her family, though, as far as she knew. It wasn't a bad one to have.

No, if this had been a week ago, Allienna would have had to pinch herself as a reminder that her life was real. What she had built for herself and for Hadley was something that was all hers.

You did this.

Allienna pushed back, tears welling as the door opened. Her first client of the day arrived, and Paisley pulled Hadley to the back room, where the TV and coloring books awaited.

Allienna smiled at the tall woman who walked in, though her mind would think of little else that day besides going back to sleep, finding Tristan to protect the one person she had worked so hard for, who she loved so much.

21

A rryn | Ebonspire, Myrilosis

He was alive. His thoughts scattered like ash.

Celestine's heat spread over the surface around him. There was a warmth there that was comforting, not threatening.

Subservient.

He liked that. He craved that.

Anything else was always a fight. Always a battle.

He couldn't move. He just . . . was.

Am I stone?

Now, there were no worries of the moon. There was only silence, only stillness.

He supposed he was supposed to love it. He did love it. He loved it so much that everything else, everyone else, could go to hell.

There were whispers—-faint, weightless—that only felt half real. They floated around him like ghosts pressing through the crystal.

It was so bright, but he couldn't squint. He couldn't blink. Light splintered his vision.

He hated it. He hated that light.

He couldn't lift his hands. He couldn't turn his head.

Crack.

The whispers, the ghosts that lived in the light, grew louder as small crevices formed in the veil.

"Get it off, get it off. Don't help me."

He heard a woman's voice. She was sobbing.

A snap burned his cheek. There were pinpricks of pain, material torn away.

"Arryn, oh Gods, my Arryn."

The sobs continued, more frantic.

Something trickled. He realized that it was air.

That was what air felt like: a drink, a stream, hope that almost made him smile.

"Get it off, get it off," the crying woman sobbed. "Don't help."

One eye opened. He winced and shut it immediately.

"Arryn, oh Gods, my Arryn," the sobbing continued.

"She did it, did you see that?" The other whispers were whispers no more.

The crystal peeled away, piece by piece. Snaps, then tears, then heat dominated his senses until his face was free, then arms, then shoulders.

Someone was clawing at him, pulling the pieces of crystal off. Liquid hit his skin and sizzled, minty and sharp.

"I would have never believed it if I hadn't seen it with my own eyes."

"Look at her; she's otherworldly."

"We need to keep them here."

Arryn blinked at the new voices, familiar voices. Celestine's face swam into view, tear-streaked and trembling.

"I'm not staying anywhere," Arryn said. "Why can't I move my legs?"

Celestine let out a partial laugh, followed by a partial sob.

"I was so scared, Arryn. I thought we'd lost you."

"We did lose you, in a way," an Atheri said. A group of them with their blinding angelic light swarmed around him, around Celestine, smiling at her like she was smiling at him.

Fucking creepy.

He knew exactly what that was, though he didn't remember the light. It made sense, he supposed, to battle that type of darkness.

"Oh, look who woke up." Sheng swayed on the other side of the room. He was the closest one to the door.

Arryn couldn't help but smile, but he was able to hold back a full-on laugh. What he would have given to be able to see Sheng's face when he'd walked in here. Even if he had never seen an Atheri before, there was no way he couldn't sense what they did, what they were for.

"I can't believe you're still here, out of everyone," Arryn said. Celestine's face looked confused and pained. "I'm talking to that asshole over there," Arryn said, meeting her eyes but pointing to Sheng.

"Proof, I suppose, that age doesn't automatically gain you intelligence. Though I'm sure you knew that," Sheng said, walking up to Arryn, careful to stay clear of the Atheri.

Arryn smirked, wondering if he was the only one to notice.

Probably.

"Your girl here," Reifoel jumped in front of Sheng. Arryn sensed a nervousness that existed on moral high ground with no real strength to match. "Your girl here is amazing."

"I don't want to talk about Hadley," Arryn said flatly.

"Not her; don't worry. I can tell Hadley that she's amazing every day. Plus, I'm pretty sure she tried to kill you." Reifoel laughed nervously, "I'm talking about Celestine. She seemed to bring you back to life."

Reifoel motioned towards Celestine. Arryn's eyes gazed back over to her tear-soaked face, pale from worry, and watched as her cheeks pinkened and a new kind of sparkle, one from recognition, showered over her.

"Where are we?" Arryn asked, looking around. "What happened?"

Celestine opened her mouth to speak but was interrupted by a flighty, ethereal, sing-songy voice. One that Arryn could tell immediately meant that they'd been successful, that there was a moon in the sky.

The strain with which Precession spoke was now more stable.

"We are inside Ebonspire. You had passed out from the moon creation, and then your daughter . . ." Precession spun in a circle, nearly falling. Roksana's hand met her forearm as if catching her sister was the most natural, most harmonious motion that could be made.

They were a dance, a ballet, the pair together.

"Hadley turned you into glass," a dark, gruff voice came from the furthest corner of the room. Djoser was sitting on the floor, looking for the darkness in a place that only seemed to emit a heavenly light. The poor devil.

"More of a cocoon, really," Precession sang. "She somehow wrapped you inside a glass cocoon. We thought you might be lost if it were not for Celestine's tears. She's such a beautiful bird."

Celstine's hands were on him again, breaking apart the already splintered glass that still was holding his legs and hips down.

She cried again, the tears hitting the glass, casting sprays of colorful light on the walls, giving the illusion that for seconds, for moments, they were underwater.

Blood was on that glass, on her hands, as she kept clawing.

"I almost have you," she said between sobs.

"Hey, hey, I'm okay," he said.

That crying was hard to deal with.

Arryn couldn't handle it when Allienna cried, either. He would have rather flown away for weeks at a time, figuring out ways to punish himself.

Any punishment was better than listening to the crying.

"But I have to cry," she looked astonished, as if his words didn't make any sense. It took a lot for Arryn to feel stupid, but as Celestine went back to moving her hands erratically over him, as she wept, her tears splashing on glass, on his skin, on herself, he suddenly felt like a pile of rocks.

"If you're asking yourself, what am I missing? The answer, buddy, is a lot," Roksana said. Her words were so unwelcome.

Reifoel nervously fiddled with his hands, the skin cracking along the back of his thumbs.

"It's been more than twenty-four hours since that moon was placed in the sky. I think that's it for me. It's time for me to go home, to protect my community, my parents."

"Oh yeah, it makes sense; Hadley's gone, so there's nothing keeping you here," Sheng said. Reifoel shot him a look of disdain.

"I'll find her," Reifoel said.

"Correction, little boy," Sheng replied, "I will find her."

Arryn's head raised towards Djoser, his opposite unnaturally still, his lips forced into a tight, straight line.

"It seems like Hadley tried to kill me, Djoser," Arryn said. "I think that means that I can ask you to kill her."

Maybe this was his chance to find Amis and bring Allienna back. If the girl died, her magic, whatever it was, would be free, floating without aim. He could argue how dangerous it could be to float unattached. Amis would have to agree.

Djoser didn't move. He didn't react. Arryn wasn't entirely sure if he'd heard him.

But Reifoel did. The Serelune winced at his words, his shoulders squared, and after a gulp, there was a protectiveness there. There was a decision to defend, despite the fact that they were talking about someone who'd just tried to murder him.

Ludicrous.

At least, he was pretty sure the intention was murder.

Even if it wasn't, it had certainly helped Arryn achieve what he wanted: to play the victim.

You should be a victim more often.

"Please stop crying," he said, his voice more firm, a command was there, a threat that he let linger in his voice.

Celestine looked up at him again, her bloodied hands filled with large shards of glass.

"If she had touched you after," Reifoel said, "you would have broken into pieces. There would be no body, no cocoon around you. You would be shattered dragon glass. You would have also deserved it."

Reifoel bowed.

That was weird.

When he stood upright, he walked backward towards the door, his focus shifting between all the bodies in the room, somewhat huddled over the oversized orange couch.

He was protecting himself.

He was expecting to be attacked for that comment.

Reifoel ran into an Atheri, and Sheng winced.

I saw that.

Arryn watched the Serelune disappear on the other side of the door frame, leaving a little more oxygen in the very crowded room. Arryn's right leg was free, and quickly after, his left leg was free. The tears loosened the glass that had molded to him.

The Kinnari raised his hand to Celestine's cheek to wipe away that tear, but the wet spot on his skin felt like oil. The scent of menthol and salt awakened his nostrils as he pulled his hand back into himself, staring at her curiously.

"I think he's finally realizing why she cries," Precession sang, a too-large smile painted across her delicate face.

"Finally," Roksana scoffed.

"Isn't she amazing?" an Atheri commented. The group that surrounded it clamored to agree, speaking over one another, overwhelming his senses from the sudden nose stimulation.

"What if we kept her here?" one asked.

"If we trade the Vrae for her, maybe they would accept that?"

"I don't think either of them are cared for much."

Roksana cleared her throat, the sudden palpable annoyance filling the air. She wasn't even trying to hold it back.

Arryn wondered if it would be best to be stuck in the glass a little longer, even if he was relieved to hear a discussion around the Vrae. He did create these annoyingly optimistic creatures for a reason.

"You know what I am, Meenio?" Sheng asked the group of Atheri. Arryn thought he detected a tremble under Sheng's false confidence.

The Vrae wasn't stupid.

Sheng knew why the Atheri existed.

Maybe today was the day they got rid of Sheng once and for all.

It felt like a good time for justice, for his side to win, for the false pretense of their truce to break.

Justice for Tristan.

The one called Meenio tensed and turned its head a full one hundred and eighty degrees. Its body continued to face the opposite direction. The Atheri was all brilliant smiles, that light shining out from its throat, its ears, its eyes. The promise of fulfilling a purpose was an excitement that Arryn could understand, since he'd denied himself that for years and years. What opportunity did the creature have to do what it was created for? It probably never had.

"It has been so long since we've seen one of you that looks mature," Meenio said to Sheng. "Did you know that as long as a Vrae stays within a limited area, we don't attack? Your group broke those rules."

"I know," Sheng said.

Limited area? When did my creations get so democratic?

"We were going to kill you when you slept, but so many of you have been leaving."

Arryn wiggled his hips loose. Celestine still stood over him, brushing away excess glass. Her red blood mixed with his blue, both cut from the micro pieces.

"Thank you," he said.

Arryn said the words simply because he felt obligated.

"So, are we still doing this moon thing? I feel like it's time for me to get out of here," Roksana cut in.

"Arryn was about to tell us about the Atheri, I think," Precession said. "Then we can find a bed, lovely sister."

He wasn't. He wasn't planning on doing that at all.

All eyes glanced his way as he stood up. Celestine didn't move, any distance between them disappeared. She was like a desperate pet, a dog sticking its tongue out.

Arryn thought it might be funny to say, "Good girl."

He resisted.

"The Atheri," Arryn said, "are what I created after the first Vrae attack. Tristan was gone. Amis and Djoser had left. These creatures can sear a Vrae as if it has been doused by acid. All they have to do is fully release their light."

Roksana's eyes widened, and she laughed. "I get it now. You stopped creating because you would have figured out a way to kill us all."

"Well, he did counter that with some things. Just like with the phoenix, here," Meenio said, its head still facing the opposite direction of its body.

"Of course," Precession sang. "I'm so happy it's out in the open now."

Arryn blinked, not understanding.

"It's true, Arryn," Celestine said, taking his hand and putting it on her chest. "You created me, and I am goodness, I am healing."

Celestine's human limbs changed shape. A beautiful red hue took the place of her complexion. As she transformed, Sheng took the opportunity to sneak out. Arryn wanted to run after him and show him what Atheri light could do. Instead, he watched Celestine's face grow a beak and her hair turn into tall, thick feathers.

Beating wings now kept her hovering.

"A phoenix," Precession sang, clapping her hands together before she stumbled from the excitement.

22

───────────

H adley | The Eastern Asia Continent of Myrilosis

She had stepped into the dune.

You didn't die.

You became what she said you would.

Something more. Something less.

She had said yes to the silence, to forgetting. Not because she wanted power, but because she was tired—utterly, irrevocably tired. Hadley was tired in a way that sleep could never fix. Ayurveda had called it becoming, but what she heard was surrender. Not a surrender to greatness, but to the quiet.

It was a surrender to the unmaking of everything that had ever hurt.

Now she was awake.

The sand had not buried her. The fire had not destroyed her. But this did not feel like survival. It felt like floating just above herself, too far to touch, too far to mourn.

And somehow, despite everything, Hadley could only think of home. She pictured the front door with its forever-peeling paint that her mother had tried, again and again, to repair. She saw the cracked tiles in the kitchen and could almost smell the burnt coffee on the stovetop. The memory of her mother's voice, singing along to a half-broken radio, echoed faintly in her mind.

That place had always carried pain, but it had been hers. If everything else was fading, she needed to return to it. She needed to see it one last time, before the girl who remembered it disappeared.

Her mind competed for screen time with memories that needed to be replayed. She watched intently, a movie on repeat. She saw herself burning, melting, her mouth open, but her throat unable to scream.

It was unforgettable pain—a death she wouldn't have wished on her worst enemy. Hadley woke up nude, with remnants of ashes clinging to her skin that she assumed once belonged to that ripped-up winter jacket she had arrived there with.

She sat up, shaking. She was cold, so cold—but she couldn't feel it.

Hadley propped her weight on her hands and nearly fell over. Hands to her head, she took stock and realized that her hair was singed off but already regrowing, the length of a pixie cut currently.

Kismet was there with her, her tail making a crescent shape around her. The wyvern slept, but its breath was hitched, uneasy. She wondered how long it had been there, protecting her.

You will never leave me.

As if on cue, a jealous little shadow skipped around the perimeter.

I see you, too.

Her stomach didn't growl. Despite the phantom pain, she felt untouched. She felt perfectly content, apart from the cold, and even that wasn't registering within her mind. Her body shook, but her brain did not tell her to react. If she submerged herself in ice water, she wondered if it would feel like anything.

Ten days.

That's what Ayurveda had said.

Did she step into the dune yesterday?

She would have nine days until she was a goddess, until she was equal to Ayurveda.

That part didn't seem to matter too much to Hadley, but now as she sat there, her body shaking but her mind perfectly clear, not much seemed to matter at all.

How she felt was spectacular.

It was as if she had all the carefree energy that came with having two or three cocktails, but there was no heaviness in her body or silly awkwardness that would make her trip over air. She hoped she could feel this way all the time, but she suspected that with each day, her body and mind would be different.

How long has it been? Is this day one?

Hadley put her hands on the side of Kismet's belly, petting the tired beast.

Her shadow self grew still.

Something glimmered out of the corner of Hadley's eye. The change was obvious.

There was no silly dancing, no playful skipping. Her shadow self changed from that glittering, mist-like state to a darkened hue. The shadow's undefined face was somehow stoic, strong. There was a seriousness that had never existed before—the glimmer of a goddess to be.

What now?

Hadley couldn't wrap her mind around why they were in the middle of a desert, large hills of sand, some glossed over by glass, smooth in some places, broken in others.

That felt a little bit like her, maybe. She couldn't tell anymore. Smooth was a great description of how her mind felt. Easygoing. Broken was all that she knew she'd felt before she stepped into that dune. That moment felt so far away now, a memory that didn't belong to her.

Ayurveda wasn't there. Hadley felt like she had come full circle, sitting in dunes instead of the mountains, waiting for the sun's appearance, instruction, and any kind of attention. She looked up at the sky. Perhaps the storm had been a dream. There was only blue, only a lovely, sweet, hazy sunrise that painted the landscape with warm golds.

That was something that felt special.

A blue sky was something that she'd never expected to see again.

Something had changed. She had a feeling she had been a part of it.

Hadley was forgetting.

She sat there, trying her hardest to remember these things. She knew them. She knew that she did. It felt good, like taking a lazy midday nap, to not remember.

Will I keep forgetting?

The smallest twinge of panic signaled in the back of her mind but calmed immediately. Whatever magic that was transforming her acted as a fire extinguisher, putting out any spark, any ember immediately.

She had her free will still, that was something at least.

Hadley stood, letting the searing hot sand caress her bare feet. She didn't flinch; she could walk through it. The pain, the burning, again not connecting to her mind. She was staring down at herself, no longer a part of her body, knowing that it hurt, knowing that she should flinch.

She reached Kismet's head, putting her full weight against the side of her brow, trying to wake the gentle, terrifying creature.

"Hi, beauty," Hadley whispered, trying to fill her voice with love.

Love.

That was something that she needed to remember. It was a weapon, something to use for self-preservation. She may soon become a goddess, but to get what she wanted, she couldn't forget how to keep that emotion in her voice. She would need to keep it like a secret weapon, the least sinister form of manipulation.

Or maybe it was sinister. One thing she did remember was that she was the one to be feared. She thought someone had told her that. It was hard, so hard, to remember the few weeks that passed before she took that step, before Ayurveda guided her into her dune.

You didn't die.

Kismet opened her eyes and let out a gentle snarl, followed by a long, hot yawn.

"I want to go home," she said. "I don't know how to get there. I don't know where we are."

Hadley wasn't even in the same world, the same realm. The Kinnari temple was the only way she knew to travel between realms, to return to where she once lived as a human, missing her mom.

It could be a final goodbye. She didn't owe it to herself; that part of her would be lost and forgotten, but the compulsion was there. That's where she needed to be before the ninth day hit. After that, she supposed nothing would matter anymore.

She would have that same expressionless stare that Ayurveda did. Her life wouldn't be a life anymore but an emotionless checklist. That was the relief that she had wanted. This was the closest she would be able to get to that quiet, that darkness, that peace.

She had been tired, so tired that she stepped into a molting fire. It was the closest she could get in her immortality to ending it all.

Kismet shook out her body, nearly flinging Hadley off as she rose, spreading her wings and casting shadows on the dunes.

Hadley flitted up, her wings feeling so strong, like they had always been there, moving fast like a hummingbird. Despite the daintiness, Hadley landed on the wyvern's back, her own eyes filled with a calm that swirled with power, a cyclone of dangerous magic combined with ambitions and morals that were fleeting.

Kismet leaped into the air, casually hovering in the cloudless morning sky. They glided east, and eventually, Hadley could smell the salt in the air. The ocean was in front of them while crossing the edge of the continent.

Overhead, a new moon hid in the stars and witnessed the girl who once burned fly home.

23

———————

Allienna | Sacramento, Ca | 1994

Allienna had a dreamless sleep that night.

She woke up frustrated, cursing Tristan in her head while Hadley jumped up and down on the bed, singing with too much energy.

Maybe it had been a dream. Maybe Tristan hadn't come at all.

If he hadn't, then she would go back—back to Arryn.

The thought of flying with Hadley in her arms was enough anxiety for the entire day. But there was so much more than that, Vrae lurking outside their home, Arryn turning her away . . .

Arryn welcoming us.

Allienna sat up, and Hadley squealed with laughter as she leaned in to tickle her. That tiny patch of skin—the warm curve of her daughter's belly where her pajama shirt had ridden up—sparked a joy so pure it nearly undid her. She pulled back quickly, careful not to draw too much from the moment, careful to let Hadley keep it: her laughter, her light, her unknowing peace.

Allienna's head was heavy on her pillow as she stroked Hadley's back. They both fell asleep.

And then they woke up again. Allienna's sleep was dreamless.

Fuck. Where was Tristan?

Another day filled with motions, fear, and anxiety passed. Allienna fell back on her pillow again, holding Hadley tighter, closer.

That night she dreamed. Tristan still did not come.

Her hope slipped away.

A week had passed. Allienna finally accepted it.

It was just a dream.

Tristan hasn't visited her. There was no savior.

A monster, a demon, was out there, looking for Hadley. The Vrae's long, white teeth haunted Allienna. She wasn't sure if she could leave her house again—it wouldn't be worth the risk.

Tomorrow's the day, Allienna decided.

She would start planning. Somehow, she had to get Hadley to the Kinnari Temple.

Allienna laid down on her pillow, her daughter curled up under her armpit.

This was their last night on this bed, under these sheets.

"Goodbye," she whispered.

Goodbye to her life, her peace. She accepted her failure.

A FIRE CRACKLED, its warmth coating Allienna's skin. It temporarily replaced the usual weight she got from Hadley, always sweating on her chest as they slept.

Hadley's not here.

Allienna whipped her head around, too disoriented to tell what was wrong—only that something was.

The air was different. Allenna wasn't in her bed.

Her heart soared. Hope shot from her chest as she spun a full one hundred and eighty degrees to be met with fire.

It was large and roaring, burning in a pool made of rocks,

smoothed by the sea. The smell of salt helped her focus. There was the sound of the shore, nearby, judging from the volume.

Footsteps, light and nimble, approached on a man-made dirt path that wound between huts and cottages.

She saw a figure now, turning around a hut as dawn approached. The body was small and hunched over, just like Tristan had been in the snow.

Please. Please. Please.

"You are the one I've been waiting for, then?"

An elderly woman's voice came from the figure, strong, sure, unwavering. She stepped further into view, her withered face one of judgment, of a tiredness that Allienna couldn't place.

"I've been waiting in my dreams for days, at the boy's command. I'm assuming you know him?" she continued.

Allienna nodded reluctantly, taking in the woman's gray hair knotted on the top of her head. The cloak that draped over her small frame was made of heavy fabric that swayed back and forth with her movements.

"If the boy is Tristan, then yes," Allienna said. "He made me a promise, and I'm desperate to see it fulfilled."

"You may call me Mother Waihema," the elder said. "You are here for binding magic. Protection that can only come from a community woven tight like a fishing net. We protect each other here—with or without wings."

"You know about wings, then?" Allienna asked, her eyes wide.

"We have lost many. Souls have been sacrificed in ways that you could never understand, all to keep the wings alive in our village."

Allienna frowned, starting to piece things together.

She had heard little of this place, its people.

"This is where Amis lives, then?" she asked. "Does Tristan live here too?"

Mother Waihema let out a laugh and gently slapped Allienna's arm. "Neither of those Gods live here. The one you call Amis—he is our creator, our father. Our life and existence are owed to him."

"This binding ceremony—what is it?" Allienna shifted to her left hip, playing with her hair. Her eyes kept drifting toward a small wooden stage beyond the fire. It wasn't distinct, but it pulled her gaze like a secret being whispered into her ear.

Mother Waihema laughed, sharp and ugly.

As if that were possible.

"What is it? What do I have to do?" Allienna asked again, feeling less clear than she ever had.

"I think you're scaring the poor Kinnari, Nyree," said a youthful voice, slicing through the tension between.

Allienna turned, and her breath caught. It was the face she had been waiting for, praying for.

"I take complete offense at you using my birth name, boy," Mother Waihema said, her tone cruel. Tristan seemed unbothered. Allienna flinched slightly.

"Ah, Mother," Tristan said, arms wide in mock affection. "Do you know how many of Waihema's elders I've met in my life? It feels more disrespectful to blur you all together. When you die, I'll remember you as Nyree."

"Hmph." Mother Waihema glared.

"I'm so happy to see you," Allienna broke the silence that followed. She held her arms out. "It's been torture. I wasn't sure if my dream was real or not—if you were real or not."

Tristan did a spin, ducking underneath Allienna's arms as she hugged air.

"Not a hugger, got it," Allienna stumbled.

"Ah, it's not that," Tristan said, putting his hands in the front pockets of his cargo shorts. "It's just that I'm dressed for vacation, for Island life. This pineapple Hawaiian shirt wrinkles easily, and, you know, it's new." He winked.

"Is this my dream? How are we all here?" Allienna asked.

Tristan shook his head. "This is Mother Waihema's dream. See? I can be respectful," he said, giving the older woman a smirk.

Mother Waihema crossed her arms and tapped her foot. The woman looked to be out of patience.

"I have one more person to gather, so I'll have to excuse myself.

It's exhausting to gather everyone into one dream. Luckily, Hadley is smaller, with less brain mass to move."

Alienna's stomach lurched at the mention of her daughter's name.

This was it. Her daughter would be protected from the hideous monster that had found them. They would be safe again,

"And then, then what?" Allienna breathed.

"Didn't you hear Nyree? Then we watch her perform a bonding ceremony."

24

———————

Precession | Ebsonspire, Myrilosis

Silver and pink shone brightly around her.

Precession giggled, overjoyed in this environment.

If there wasn't music playing, she still heard a chirpy tune in her head that hugged her heart and energized her limbs. She wanted to dance, twirl, and play.

The colors reflected the bubbles surrounding her, their heavy, sweet perfume reminiscent of cotton candy, like the most joyous treat that might cross her lips, or rest on her tongue.

"Mhm," she let her voice sing out, breathy, sinful, as her hands fell to her chin and traveled down her neck, her collarbone, the fronts of her breasts, and between her hips.

She laughed, knowing this pleasure was what it sometimes felt like to be her sister, to be Roksana. The highs were indulgent, and a euphoric desire rang through her.

Precession popped a bubble as it floated above her.

The warmth of her bath water stole every ounce of stress from her tether. She could sit in this tub for hours, this beautiful white porcelain bathtub in a pink and white stained tile room. There was a large frosted window to her right, letting light twinkle in as if it were clamoring to get into the water with her.

And maybe it was.

Because what Precession was feeling was pure blissful wickedness as her hands wandered and explored her body. Her wings were out, partially sitting in the tub, and the remaining three feet hung over the edge. She touched those too, and the swirling sensations made her moan, then giggle—pure joy and discovery.

Large silver bubbles rose from the mountain that sat atop her bath, popping as liquid trickled down her head and face. She licked her lips, overjoyed to understand what glitter might taste like.

Her shoulders rolled back, shimmying as her hands continued to find crevices and soft spots. This body wasn't ever celebrated; it wasn't ever worshipped, but she could change that. She could be that self-loving, girls' girl kind of woman.

She thought of her friends, her sister, of Hadley. They all needed support and endless loyalty. They deserved that.

Precession's eyes fluttered as she saw new colors. The bubbles of pink and silver flashed white and black. She moved through a bubblegum scene to one of noir.

Once her body calmed and her spasm left her feeling immeasurably lighter, she opened her eyes to a different reality. She tried to grasp that feeling. Could she carry it with her like a secret in her pocket?

Roksana was masturbating loudly, passionately on the other side of Precession's wall. There was only a closed door between them. The air still held that lust, that elation, but the view was that of a small room, a small bed, inside one of the buildings they retired to in Ebonspire.

Precession rubbed her eyes, her body still very aroused. Roksana's moans were constant enough that Precession wondered if she wasn't alone. When the two of them didn't share a bed, Roksana always took full advantage of that, and she certainly had no self-control with her magic, which tended to rub off—figuratively and literally—on anyone nearby.

That was usually just Precession.

Precession pulled the light blanket off of herself. She stood and tiptoed towards the door. Her familiar lightheadedness pulled her down; gravity held within her a constant chain.

She waited.

She listened until there was a final, obvious climax. With so few pleasures in one's life, who was she to take that away from Roksana?

After the muted sounds of heavy panting calmed, Precession lifted her hand and daintily knocked.

"Shit," she heard Roksana say. A chaotic thump of objects hit the floor. Frantic footsteps came nearer.

Roksana pulled the door open between their two adjoining rooms, her red curly hair as wild as Precession had ever seen it.

"What do we do now?" Roksana asked unapologetically. "We are rested. Do we go?"

"Go back to Amis, perhaps?" Precession giggled as Roksana's face turned the color of her hair, and regret pooled into her stomach.

Roksana was not amused.

"Don't fret, dear sister," Precession reassured her. "I was simply teasing. Don't be embarrassed about what you want. I envy it. I'm embarrassed about how little I want."

Roksana's frown deepened, but the energy around her dimmed as she reined it in.

"We cannot leave yet, though. We must finish what was started," Precession said.

"I am curious to see if Sheng was killed in the middle of the night by those Atheri," Roksana admitted.

"Yes, what a curious question indeed. We are learning about this world, about Arryn's creations."

"It seems the more we learn," Roksana said, "the more I suspect that he kept us out of this realm for his own reasons."

"Of course he did." Precession pulled back and took her sister's hand. "But if you and I don't continue encouraging him, I am confident that Arryn will stop efforts to build up the moon. I am in between states, making the Earth spin and holding the moon in orbit —but it is too light. I worry, sister, that I can be too easily persuaded to let go again."

"You want to be held more captive to your magic again?"

"It is like a muscle, I fear. If I am not using it fully, I will be too lazy to build that strength back up."

Roksana nodded.

"It seems like you do know what you want, then," Roksana said.

Precession smiled, but it was filled with sadness.

"It doesn't matter what I want. I am not a living creature in the same way someone like Hadley is. I am a tool. It lessens the pain to remember that."

"You are not a tool," Roksana snapped, an odd edge to the air. "We are not gods. You are my sister. You have a family. You are loved."

"Perhaps," was all she said. Precession wasn't unwilling to have this conversation, but it would have been easier if they hadn't. It was easier to let her go off and be an object, a utility. A world where she was unleashed was one where many couldn't survive. Not everyone had special domes that protected them from harsh elements.

She wondered how the land fared where her home once stood, if the fire, ember, and ash were a mercy compared to famine and flood.

"Do you think we will go back to France?" Precession asked as Roksana turned toward her room.

Roksana stopped. Without turning around, she shook her head from side to side.

"I don't."

Precession reached for their adjoining door and pulled it closed. That was where she'd cry—where want and need would pool to remind her she was almost human.

But she wasn't.

Thank the Gods for her understanding and acceptance of herself. Even if her sister wanted more for her, it was such a dangerous thing to want.

She moved to a small vanity painted a bright yellow. It overlooked a small side street in Ebonspire. Bright light, the blankness at the top of the dome, poured in through the glass.

She supposed it was cheery enough there, with the buildings opposite her painted bright blues and greens and beautiful cobbled streets that were meticulously maintained for the Atheri strolling in small groups below.

~

Precession stared out the window, listening to the clicks and clacks of her sister getting dressed in the nearby room, the water running, closet hangers lightly tapping together.

She was wearing an oversized, flowy, bright-pink dress. The color washed her out and clashed against her skin, but Arryn didn't provide clothes. The Atheri had their closets stocked with whatever they might need.

It was a kindness that she knew came with strings.

Those strings likely involved Celestine, the newly realized marvel. A phoenix that could take the shape of a woman or a woman who could take the shape of a phoenix. She wasn't sure which one she truly was.

When Celestine was revealed, the Atheri blinded the room. Light poured out of their ears and eyes. Their smiles brought unparalleled joy, like they had been waiting for her, a messiah in the form of one magical bird.

"I need an explanation," Arryn told her, bringing the room's magic and atmosphere to a halt. "I don't like feeling used."

These words visibly wilted Celestine's bubbly demeanor, her neediness for his approval more evident than usual.

"And you"—he turned to face the group of Atheri—"I would like to see you do what you were created to do."

Arryn's eyes were darker and sunken. He looked like he was wearing charcoal eyeliner. His magic, or something deeper, was changing him.

Roksana held her hand out, pressing it gently against Precession's stomach, protecting her from what might come next.

Sheng merely laughed, his confidence unwavering, his hands in his pockets.

"I think we should retire. It's been a long day, and your phoenix is covered in blood."

Apparently, her tears healed others but not herself.

"Curious creatures, phoenixes," Precession sang. "We know so little about them, really."

"A phoenix," Meenio interrupted, "is pure goodness."

"Well, then, that rules out Arryn as their creator." Sheng winked a little too confidently.

"That is why we are so attracted to her," Meenio said, giving Sheng a smile that promised something much more, a level of malevolent feelings that Precession didn't think she would naturally be able to understand. The smile looked lovely, though. From the outside, it seemed like pure goodness itself, like what he described Celestine as.

"We are light. She is goodness."

"They are not the same thing?" Roksana asked, sounding extremely bored. Everyone looked at her with various expressions ranging from amusement to irritation.

"What? I'm trying to move this conversation along. I want to go to bed." Roksana shrugged.

"They are the same as darkness and depth are the same. Darkness can hide depth, but the depth contains the monsters that make the goosebumps on your human-like skin prickle."

"Which one are you in this analogy?" Precession asked, "Depth or darkness?"

Meenio smiled again, and Precession's heart dropped. She knew the answer even if it wouldn't outright say it.

"It is time for bed, then. Some of my fellow Atheri will show you all to your rooms. Even the Vrae."

Sheng shook his head. Precession had a feeling that he'd rather sleep outside in the snow beyond the dome.

"We have someone else to chase tonight." Meenio cast a look at

Sheng, but instead of a look of relief, Precession could see dread creeping into his face.

Sheng knew something that she didn't. There wasn't a hint, a feeling. But she knew that a ball of terror was now rooted in his stomach, that there was care inside him.

"How peculiar," Precession said aloud as some Atheri exited, passing by Sheng, who was obviously holding his breath, chin, and neck stretched high.

"What's that?" Roksana asked in a half-whisper.

"He wants to protect someone. I don't think it's Hadley."

Roksana raised an eyebrow and turned to follow an Atheri out the door. "Are you coming? I'm following them to our rooms."

Precession stole a glance at Arryn, who was being brushed off by Celestine, tiny shards of glass hitting the floor as he took his first crunching step.

"I'm sorry, let me help," Celestine said in a panic, bending down and brushing away glass with her bare hands. Precession couldn't watch. Arryn's attitude towards her was disgraceful, a rockstar sneering at his groupie.

Roksana reached back to grab Precession's arm, pulling her.

"Which one was it, do you think?" her sister asked as they moved out of the building, marching on the cobblestones. They followed three Atheri, who whispered among one another. "Darkness or depth?" she clarified.

"I think they're neither," Precession answered, her voice barely more than a breath.

"They mentioned depth and darkness as a way to hide a monster. But I think the monsters seek out both only to hide from them."

25

llienna | Sacramento, Ca | 1994

WITH A TURN AND BOW, Tristan glided on his back heel and disappeared into the air as if he had never really been there at all.

Allienna was left in the middle of what felt like an abandoned village, surrounded by trees that felt as old as she was. Mother Waihema was the only one to stare back at her, her face giving away no emotion. If anything, she looked quite bored.

"So, I keep hearing the words *bonding ceremony*." Allienna felt a slight uptick of panic rise in her chest from the sudden one-on-one conversation she hadn't expected.

"The child must be hidden," Mother Waihema answered.

Weariness flushed through Allienna's face as she followed the shuffling elder toward the fire, toward the stage.

Allienna could see a larger hut, at least four or five times the size of the others, on the pathway up a hill in front of them.

"What's that building for?" she asked.

Mother Waihema stopped, looked between the hill and Allienna, and shook her head.

"It is a place of worship."

"Oh, like a church." Allienna's voice was slightly more chipper.

"And a place of darkness, pain."

Well then.

"Do you bleed from your womb?" Mother Waihema asked, the two shuffling up the steps towards the stage as Allienna shook her head in response.

"That's most unfortunate, child," Neyee said, taking Allienna's hand without her permission, without her consent.

The skin contact did the same thing it had always done: it flooded her body with raw emotion. The withered skin of Mother Waihema was no exception, not even in a dream. What filled her, however, surprised her.

Trepidation—the feeling that a mistake would be made. It was not about danger, though; there was not an ounce of fear or concern for anyone's safety. It was about deserving.

The elder was being pushed to do this, whatever this was. She did not think Allienna, maybe even Hadley, deserved such protection.

That was a new type of heartbreak.

She had no idea how to proceed.

Maybe you should wake up.

No.

Waking up meant that she was going back. She would be airborne, heading toward the temple, the snow, toward Arryn.

"If only you bled. Womb blood makes the strongest bond."

Mother Waihema bent down and raised her cloak, pulling a jagged obsidian knife out of a small satchel attached to her calf, her skin spotted and unshaven.

"It's a bit dull. I sharpen it before I suspect an upcoming birth, but I don't believe we have one coming for at least a month. Hold out your arm," she commanded.

Allienna didn't move at first. She locked eyes with Mother

Waihema and saw it—that look of judgement. It was an unwavering belief that she didn't belong here.

Gulping air, she pushed out her left arm, offering it to the Waihema elder, staring at the black stone that looked like it couldn't have even punctured a bag of chips.

Mother Waihema wrapped her fingers around Allienna's forearm. She took in a sharp breath, the anxiety draining from her body as those same feelings from before flooded back in. She felt so small and helpless before this mortal, who in reality had to have been quite frail.

"Why do ceremonies always involve sacrificed blood?" Allienna chuckled.

The elderly woman flicked her eyes up, keeping her head steady a foot above Allienna's forearm.

"Would you rather I use the blood from the child? The girl?"

Allienna shook her head. "It was a joke. Definitely not, let's avoid a child spilling blood."

"Are you sure? It happens around here more than you might think." Mother Waihema's knife was pressed against Allienna's forearm now, waiting for that final confirmation.

A chill ran up her spine, making a mental note to revisit what was just said. If she ever came back, if she ever went to this place in person, awake and conscious.

"Do it."

There was no hesitation, no moment for a breath to pass as Mother Waihema pushed her elbow down with so much might that Allienna wondered if bone would break. She just stared at the blade lodged in her skin, the wielder's hand still holding tight, with her opposite hand holding Allienna to keep her still.

Regret.

That was regret flowing through the woman. The one feeling Allienna dreaded. The one that told her it was a mistake. Whether it was more danger or false hope, Allienna didn't know, but something wasn't right. Something hadn't been right from the beginning.

She thought back to every gesture, every glance, trying to figure out where this went wrong. Not knowing how to prepare—that was the worst part.

The pain from the knife, half an inch deep in her skin, began to make itself known as the adrenaline started to wear off. The woman connected her gaze back to Allienna quickly and then proceeded to pull the knife towards her, tearing Allienna's skin with significant effort. The dull blade was unforgiving, excruciating, and Allienna couldn't help but cry out.

She wasn't made for this type of pain. There was no action, war, or battle she had trained mentally for. She could keep her inner trauma inside, but this was exterior pain—visible, gushing, thick, and red.

"That scream is why I do this part first," Mother Waihema said, fully convinced that she was performing something sacred, a favor. "We don't want to waste any of that," she added, tsking as if Allienna's blood hitting the stage was a mistake she had made.

Allienna stood awkwardly, pulling her free hand underneath her arm to catch the flowing blood. Unsuccessful, the elder scowled. Mother Waihema rolled her eyes before her hands moved underneath her cloak to pull something free.

It was a thick fabric, also beige, as if she had ripped it off her cloak herself.

"Here, let it soak into this. We can still use it and spread it. Get it a rich bright red; the more pigment, the better."

"Why is that?" Allienna asked nervously.

"Again, child, that blood is not of your womb. It's not the child's. If we want the bond potent, we will need much of it. You'll need to bleed the entire time."

Oh, that's fun.

"Why are you helping me?"

Mother Waihema sighed at the question, an air of defeat, of despair, pulling down at her lips.

"Because if women don't help women, then no one else will."

Allienna's breath stopped, and her stomach fluttered. The words were so simple, so plain, but supportive.

A fat tear inched out of the corner of her eye, sliding down Allienna's cheek. There was no weakness in that tear, only unwavering appreciation for those words, for that love she had done nothing to deserve.

"Why the regret then?" Allienna blurted out.

"What?" Mother Waihema was bewildered, her head bobbing back as the wrinkles under her chin pushed forward.

Allienna didn't repeat herself but instead matched her gaze, neither woman's eyes faltering as the cloth wrapped around her arm was already painted with her blood, the smell of copper slightly sickening.

"You'll understand my feelings one day," Mother Waihema gave in. "Or maybe you won't."

Before Allienna could protest, she heard, "Mommy," from a voice so wonderfully, heartbreakingly filled with love and admiration. It was the voice of the most critical being in the world, the one that made everything worth it while also feeling like she could never give enough, never stop giving, never stop loving.

Hadley, with her stocky four-year-old legs, ran towards the stage, coming out of the trees, her blonde hair golden underneath the soft daylight.

The toddler's smile was so big, so infectious, that Allienna turned to her, holding her arms out wide. Trekking behind her with hands in his pockets was Tristan, looking worn.

Allienna wrapped Hadley in her uninjured arm, trying not to wipe the bloodied cloth against her cute little pajamas—but winced when she couldn't avoid it.

"Mommy, why are you wet? Is that paint?" Hadley felt the blood from the cloth seeping into her shirt and turned over her shoulder to investigate.

"Yes, baby, we are having a special ceremony, so I have to paint my arm."

"I want some paint!" she shouted, jumping up and down. "Can you share?"

Allienna inhaled, caught off guard, and Mother Waihema jumped in to answer instead.

"Yes, yes, child, you will get your share of the paint."

Hadley jumped back and hid behind Allienna's back, nearly knocking her. She placed her injured arm, unhealed, so ordinary, down to regain balance and clenched her teeth as pain vibrated through her.

"You're not looking too good," Tristan said as he walked up the steps to the ceremony stage to join them.

"You are one to talk," Allienna said, pulling herself upright.

Tristan just shrugged and looked away. "It's exhausting, you know. Pulling you all into this dream. A few more people, and it's possible I might never wake up, always stuck, too tired to move on."

I know that feeling.

"Are we ready?" a whisper breathed against Alienna's ear. She turned her head, startled. No one was there. She looked around. Mother Waihema's eyes were still locked on her. She was several feet from them, but opened her mouth, and the whisper sounded again, as if her lips were at Allienna's ear, as if the words were only meant for the two of them.

"Are we ready?"

Allienna nodded, unsure, her stomach clenched, her hand grabbing Hadley's tightly.

Drums sounded behind them, making Allienna's heartbeat louder.

"Mommy, I don't like it," Hadley said, tugging.

"Hush, child," Mother Waihema's whisper came again, and now, Allienna could see the drummers, half a dozen males who were shirtless, wearing headdresses and knee-length beige skirts, beyond the fire. The black smoke rose, turning daylight into haze.

"What do I have to do?" Allienna asked, looking at Mother Waihema, who was humming as she reached out to take Allienna's injured arm.

The elderly woman unwrapped the cloth, completely soaked in scarlet red blood.

"We should hurry before it browns," Mother Waihema chuffed. "I am going to paint you now, child."

"My turn," Hadley cheered as the elder turned her upper body to the toddler, brushing the cloth across the girl's cheeks, temple, nose, and neck.

"What are you doing? Why?" Allienna demanded, watching as her daughter was covered in blood.

"It's okay," Tristan hissed, maintaining a small distance from them. "This is for both of you. This is how we protect you. You both will be fine."

Conflicting thoughts ran through her. Everything in Allienna's body told her to stop this lunacy, to protect her child. If Hadley remembered this, Allienna would be forced to tell her about the Kinnari and the Vrae. She wouldn't have accomplished much more than falling back under Arryn.

Only moments later, Hadley's pajamas were now painted red as well. The child looked like she had survived a war and had been through so much suffering. Allienna's heart hurt just seeing her like that. Even her joyful smile didn't ease the fresh guilt pressing into Allienna's chest.

Mother Waihema's chanting grew louder. The drumbeat grew faster. Taking center stage, the elderly woman raised her hands to the sky. As she brought them back down, her eyes were black, fixed on Hadley.

Allienna wanted to look away. The sight terrified her, and she suddenly felt like she was in a nightmare. She tried to pull Hadley away and run right into that forest.

Another mistake. You made another mistake.

Mother Waihema moved a few steps towards them, wrapping her hands around Hadley.

"Momma, help!" she squealed as the elder continued to hum and then raised the toddler up, holding her to face the fire, the face of the drummers with eyes still black as night.

"Don't do it," Tristan said, sensing Allienna's tension. "Let it happen."

"It tickles!" Hadley laughed.

Mother Waihema threw back her head, parted her lips, and began her song.

Waimeha, where power hides,
Wings that span the endless tides.
Centuries pass, yet they remain,
Guardians of the hidden flame.

"Wings that span, that is us," Tristan whispered behind her, interpreting.

In unity, their strength is sown,
Silent bonds, by fate are grown.
One in light, one in night,
Invisible paths, woven tight.

"A life will be created one day, tied to Hadley."

When one walks, the other near,
In shadowed realms, they both appear.
Twin-born magic, silent thread,
Through time's weave, their power spread.

"Until it is created, until it is alive, Hadley will seem invisible to anyone who doesn't already know of her existence."

Bound together, unseen, unknown,
Into each other, they are sewn.

"They will be bound to protect one another when they need each other the most. They will be a part of one another, who they are, tied, altered, because of this bond," Tristan finished his explanation just a breath after Mother Waihema finished her song. Hadley, hanging, defeated, covered in Allienna's blood, still held up in the air.

The drumming stopped, the fire seemed to simmer, the heat it provided almost gone entirely as Hadley was lowered down, and the black of Mother Waihema's eyes faded back to the light browns and hazels that were familiar before.

"The ceremony is complete," the elder woman announced as Hadley raced back into Allienna's arms, the skin contact sticky from the drying blood.

"Thank you," Allienna said, "but she's invisible only to those who don't know she exists? That Vrae knows. He knows where we are. This doesn't work. We are not safe," Allienna said, trying to keep her voice calm, a sweet smile plastered on her face.

"Momma, I'm tired," Hadley said, looking up at her.

"She is safe, Allienna," Tristan insisted.

Allienna stood, her daughter in her hands, to face him.

"How?"

Tristan shook his head. "I found that Vrae, I've trapped him in a dream, a memory."

"He's trapped? He's really gone? Are we really safe?" Allienna asked as a flood of relief or gratitude cooled every ember of doubt and panic inside of her.

Tristan nodded and gave her a half smile, the bags under his eyes surprisingly dark.

"Thank you," she breathed, reaching her injured arm towards him for an embrace.

"No," Tristan protested, but it was too late. Allienna's hand brushed the back of his neck, and she felt it again. The veins in her body froze instantly. She stumbled back, eager to get away, her daughter still wrapped in her other arm, wrapped too tightly, no, not tight enough.

Just like when she brushed the skin of the cop, and the feeling of hunger, the feeling of a thirst for her blood, for Hadley's blood had filled her, the same unquenchable maleficent intent came again.

"What? What was that?" Allienna said behind the shaky breath, Hadley protesting from the tightness in her hold.

Tristan's eyes pleaded before they flashed a color that completely broke Allienna's heart—blood red.

26

———

Amis | Emeralds Peak

The spoon was lifted to Luca's lips, filled with the hot and spiced stew he had been protesting. The teenager's stomach betrayed him, growling enough to make the nearest Marthrend tilt its head.

"It's fine," Luca muttered as he sucked in his bottom lip, trying to be sneaky as he lapped up any remaining flavor. It had been a few days of peace, of filling their bellies.

Amis knew better, though, than to let himself heal. He could not afford to settle. Healing invited softness. If death still chased them, he would stay alert.

His magic was unbalanced, itching to escape. It crackled along his bones like static.

He still felt too much death. It sobered him the moment he let himself enjoy anything.

Don't get comfortable. Don't you dare.

Still, Luca was entirely more tolerable once he ate. The tension left his shoulders, and the sharp sarcasm was replaced with complete sentences, still brief, but it was something.

"It's your turn to hide, Ahora," Salome shrieked after Luca opened a cabinet revealing their hiding place.

"Make Noah be it!"

The four children ran around, laughing and chasing each other, no one daring to step outside in the blistering cold. Their laughter bounced off the stone walls, a dissonant hymn of innocence inside a world that had forgotten it.

The front door would open more often now, and the Marthrend family who lived in the home would go in and out, tapping their pincers as they walked by in greeting.

Each day, one of the Marthrend would move into the kitchen, carrying what Amis first thought were stones in a small pack attached to its waist. Amis watched as it scrutinized the scene, walking into the kitchen and pulling the rocks out, slapping them on the counter as its partner began cooking the familiar stew. Amis wasn't sure they ate anything else.

Luca was particularly interested in the process that came with those rocks, pulled from down below the lake where they had fallen from the sky. The Marthrend would bang them violently against the counter, shaping them. It didn't bother polishing them. There was no effort to make it look like a rare gem. Instead, it was used for utility, something more common than concrete in the modern world. It would stir the powdered residue, which had gathered on the countertop from the beating, into a bowl with other materials until it turned into a tar-like paste with a green hue.

Taking the paste with its pincers, the Marthrend would next begin to paint its own body with it. Thick strokes across its carapace, smothered in tight circular movements until the shell looked glossier, denser. It formed a rigid yet flexible coating, preparing them for the elements outside as the weather conditions only got worse.

"Certainly looks more water-resistant," Amis mumbled to Luca. They both stood at the entrance to the galley kitchen, watching the Marthrend work.

Because you certainly need to waterproof a lobster.

Another night passed, and then another morning.

After waking up to the smell of fresh stew, another bowl was handed to him as Amis woke up on the living room floor. At this point, all the kids had taken to scooting around him in their slumber—a head on his calf, a foot in his back, a toddler on his head. He woke with a giggle in his throat and a cramp in his spine. It was terrific how acclimated he was now in his caretaker role. He imagined he could sleep through an apocalypse.

Well, maybe it would be best not to test that theory. He smiled into his stew.

We certainly don't need another one.

That evening, a Marthrend pulled on Amis's shirt.

"You want me to come with you?"

The Marthrend only clicked its pincers before turning away and exiting the house.

Amis grunted, trying to keep the irritation inside him under control. The cold was painful. Amis could not stand to be in it after the days of warmth, food, and kindness.

We must be getting kicked out.

His stomach lurched. The stew threatened to climb back up.

No, they are kicking me out. They are keeping the children . . . probably for the stew.

His magic swirled inside him. Maybe it was telling him he was right.

Or maybe it's telling me I'm a bit dramatic.

One could only hope.

It prickled beneath his skin, a restless thing seeking permission to panic. Either way, Amis followed. There was no use in being a rowdy houseguest after all of this time. He did his best to swallow any hint of terror before it spilled into his expression. He tightened his jaw, focusing on the Marthrend's gait. They were gentle creatures, but still too alien for comfort.

"What is it?" Amis asked out loud, like an idiot, because it certainly didn't understand him. The Marthrend who spoke English hadn't returned, which made no sense to him.

Why wouldn't you want to communicate with your guests who had fallen from the sky?

Amis would undoubtedly be more suspicious, even if they showed up with cute youth. The Kinnari inhaled automatically; the cold so fierce he felt like a knife was stabbing into his vertebrae. His breath turned to crystal in the air, sharp and immediate.

He looked at the houses up on the hill, glistening, both opulent and hidden, their glass walls tinted in the evening moonlight.

Moonlight.

His eyes followed the pincers, realizing for the first time what the Marthrend was trying to show him.

A moon. Those idiots had done it.

"Un-fucking-believable."

It had a long way to go, was barely the size of a star, but creatures of magic certainly understood what they were looking at. It was the thing with magic, how attuned it made their existence with the Earth, with nature. The calm made more sense now. So did the peace in his chest.

He blinked hard, unsure if it was an illusion or a miracle. The tug in his chest, light, not frantic, told him it was real.

His balance had returned. There was no more foot pain or ringing in his ears. It no longer screamed, it hummed.

Amis had assumed it was because he was consumed with the world's plight. Instead, it was a faint pull, a small reminder that there were still corrections to make, actions he could do himself without the gamble of releasing self-correcting power.

The new moon would guide him. The children, the last descendants of Waihema, were his purpose.

Amis stared at the moon. He would find the village of children, as they had wanted. He would let Waihema pride guide them. If something was still out of balance, it was still the injustice of their existence.

He turned to look at the Marthrend, covered in black and

emerald green paste, who was also staring up. The entire neighbor-hood noticed. Door after door, the surrounding emerald-built homes opened, and more Marthrend pointed at the sky.

Luca, Salome, Ahora, and Noah edged their way outside, all bare-foot. Noah immediately winced from the chill of the wind.

"We will leave in the morning."

The Marthrend snapped its head down.

Tap. Tap. Tap.

Tap. Tap. Tap.

Amis blinked, tried to interpret. He was getting nowhere.

I will never learn this way of communication. I don't even want to.

The Marthrend pushed him back inside, which he allowed, picking up Noah on his way in and holding him against his chest as the toddler slapped him in the face and giggled.

"I guess we should gather up our things and start heading on our way," Amis said as the others followed him inside.

"We don't have anything," Ahora said.

"Good point."

The Marthrend walked into the kitchen and returned with a bowl, balancing it on both pincers and shoving it into Amis's hands.

Tap. Tap. Tap.

Amis looked into the bowl, seeing the green-black paste clumped into thick, droopy piles.

"Uh," Amis looked back at the Marthrend, "thanks?"

Tap. Tap. Tap.

The Marthrend shoved its pincers forward toward the bowl, its beady eyes still creeping him the fuck out. It was a good choice to leave. Perhaps this comfort wasn't worth the trust issues rooted deep within him.

The Marthrend dipped its pincers into the bowl, scooped up a large clump of the clay, and then, without hesitation, spread it over the side of Amis's face, from the center of his forehead down to his jawbone. It felt oily, like clay, before it hardened and dried.

"Hmmm," Amis said, not sure how to react.

Another Marthrend walked in through the door. They all looked the same to him, though he was sure there were differences he did not know how to identify yet.

"It's a goodbye," the new Mathrend said.

Ah, the one who speaks English, thank Gods.

"It protects you from the elements; the mixture will harden, and you will be somewhat waterproof. We have begun coating ourselves as we dive since the water is too frigid."

Amis stood there, trying not to be obvious about how upset he was about the texture of the smooth, powdery, and wet clay moving all over him. The Marthrend ripped Amis's simple black shirt down with its other pincer and began slathering the clay over his chest.

"It's a bit forward; I haven't had this much action in a while."

"What's action?" Salome giggled.

"Nothing for you to know about." Amis shook his head, the nearly black emerald paste all over his fingers.

The clay was starting to harden, and Amis did feel . . . waterproof. He wasn't warm per se, but it felt a little more like there was a wall in front of him, protecting him from the elements.

Armor. Maybe the lobsters were actually onto something.

The Marthrend returned to the kitchen and brought more bowls since the bowl Amis had was quickly emptying. The creature handed them to the children, who stared unenthusiastically. Luca shook his head and scoffed, crossing his arms over his torso.

"You're the oldest. Be an example," Amis said from the side of his mouth, teeth clenched together. "Time to lather up." Amis pulled his pants down, to Salome and Ahora's embarrassment, as they screeched and covered their eyes.

"I'm wearing underwear, for goodness's sake," he laughed as he coated his calves, his thighs, and the tops of his feet. He went around the corner to the kitchen and got the bits he'd missed that were covered by his underwear, too.

Moments later, he was a fully clayed-over man, waiting to feel cracking as he moved his limbs. Despite how the clay hardened and formed to his skin, there was none. Amis rejoined the kids, who were laughing and painting each other's arms and faces with it.

"Thank you," Amis turned to thank the Marthrend who had forced the clay over him.

"We are one," the other English speaker said. "You can be a part of that. Come back anytime."

Amis wasn't grateful enough to attempt a hug, so he gave them both a nod of thanks and hoped the sentiment would come across.

He popped a clay-covered Noah on his hip, who giggled and made a monster face. "Let's go."

"To be with our kind, to be with more children." Salome made a monster face back at Noah.

A clamor of goodbyes from high-pitched voices was his backdrop as Amis walked back into the night sky, letting his wings out among the Marthrend, who still stood outside, looking up at the moon.

Hope. There was hope there.

For the first time in a long time, Amis felt as though they were not being chased by death, perhaps doing precisely what they were meant to do. He let that dangerous thing, optimism, bloom inside his ribs. He ignored the balance trying to erupt out of him, a worry for another day. The death that piled within him could be something else, something he wouldn't know about, something he couldn't fix on his own.

You can give them a chance.

He chose hope; he decided on optimism. He chose to get these children to safety so they could live and live fulfilled, happy lives.

He would do it for Sheng and Emere. That little girl taught Sheng that he didn't have to be a monster.

Their hearts broke together. It served a purpose. It did not go in vain.

27

Amis | Air Bound, Myrilosis

Raised skin puckered while Amis tried not to swear, utterly defenseless against the physical assault he was being forced to endure. Noah had been pulling Amis's tightly knotted bun the entire time they had been in the air, flying toward some unknown city with no knowledge other than a general direction.

I guess I've made worse choices.

Flying had gotten slightly easier while carrying the toddler, despite the searing sting of each hair on his head being plucked. Even if Noah could hear him cry out, Amis knew he wouldn't listen.

Don't flip out. Don't flip out. He's an adorable, traumatized child. Don't flip out.

Before they'd taken off into the air, leaving the Marthrend, those terrifying lobster squid giants which were curiously hospitable, they'd worked to fashion a jacket where Amis's wings could comfortably be out. Noah could lie on his back, snuggled into the cloth. Amis figured the worst thing that could happen was him having to dive down and catch the short terrorizer, and it would save his arms from aching, his face from constantly being hit, and his cheeks from being squished.

But you forgot that you have hair—lots of it.

The toddler knew how to use his wings, and he was even proficient at it. He might even be able to catch himself, but the longer unknown distance made Amis feel like it would be easier to wrap him up and keep him from getting spotted and chased down by some feral, terrifying bird creation. At this point, he wouldn't put anything past Arryn.

"Ouch," he growled, but it was lost to the wind.

Just a few days, really, had it been since he had written these kids off, accepted they were destined for death. He would hate to admit it, but he'd miss those hands pulling hairs from his scalp. His heartstrings had been tugged even more than his bun. He was attached. He was in it for the long haul, a choice that felt foolish, a choice he was sure would promise utter devastation.

Eventually, Amis felt his bun loosen completely, and Noah cried; a faint screech in his ear made his stomach tense. Amis's hair blew in the wind and tickled Noah's face, and the scream turned into a giggle. He could feel the staccato pulsing of Noah's stomach as he squealed. Amis smiled. It was hard not to get swept up in it, in love and innocence.

He never hated to love something so much.

Usually, Amis would hold Ahora, the last of Waihema who did not have wings. Still, he would periodically look over his shoulder to see Luca carrying her in his arms, his face determined but not void of struggle.

Amis assumed he would need to take over soon, but he felt a sense of pride within himself for helping Luca act like a man. The boy wanted it too, and fought for independence and freedom. He deserved it as well. Who was Amis in his life to do anything else but aid that?

They all had gotten used to flying over the clouds to avoid the storms raging over the land, but now, they were looking for a place and needed to be able to look down to see a target. They were looking for a city called Mytholm, tucked into the middle of nowhere, with no other civilizations nearby.

A city tucked away, filled with kids. Amis hoped it was to protect them.

He hoped this could be the end of the promise.

Then there's the redhead.

It was hard not to laugh, not to let his cheeks get sore from the love-drunk smile gracing his face whenever he thought about her.

You could fall into her chaos, and she into your calm.

They could lie with each other, stroking each other's faces, taking care of each other as their magic fought and then simmered, a quiet explosion between them.

Don't get distracted. It's been an eternity already, and I can wait a little longer.

The icy cold dampness clung to the air, sliding off them like water off a duck. The green-black clay, the crushed emeralds, which Marthrend found so many uses for, still clung to his skin. He had a newfound appreciation for them and wished he'd had something like this from the start.

Amis suspected they all were far less miserable now and that this emerald paste should be used during all long flights, not only when there was the threat of the world's end.

There was hope now, a new destination, more comfort, a new moon, however small, placed in the sky.

They continued east. Amis noticed the trees first: great, large, ancient trees swaying in the breeze down below them, emitting secrets in ancient languages he would never understand. The night surrounded them, and the crepuscule intensified. There was a lingering eeriness that earlier hope was now on a sliding scale. But there was no denying the magic in the air and the land around them.

We are close.

Luca slowed in the sky, his struggle visible from the strain on his face, the purple under his eyes. Amis tugged on him to reduce Luca's speed, to be ready to do a mid-air transfer, taking Ahora out of Luca's arms and into his own. The sleeping girl mumbled her irritation at her weight being shifted hundreds of feet in the air.

My apologies, princess.

Amis wanted to roll his eyes, but he couldn't. He was starting to care too much about them; even the scoffing and sardonic thoughts in his head felt disingenuous. He no longer knew how to make fun of them. He didn't want to.

She deserves to be carried across the entire world. They all do.

"Look, there," Salome yelled, barely audible.

A low cloud covered an area up ahead, reminding Amis of the steamy lagoon they had fallen into when meeting the Marthrend. It was nothing but alive, growing and spreading rapidly, racing their gazes as if it didn't want them to see the landscape.

As they flew, the fog continued to spread, covering an expansive area. Ancient trees, bogs, and wetlands adorned the land, and their stagnant water was lined with dark reeds, swaying as the air whistled past, inviting visitors from above to fly down and listen.

There was so much water that Amis could see the area being confused for a lake, even an ocean.

Salome flew further ahead with sudden speed, clearly seeing something. Turning towards Amis, she pointed at the moving body of the fog, still following, erasing the water and ecosystems within it.

"Yes, the fog, I know," he grumbled, arms already sore between the two bodies he carried.

We will need to take a break soon.

Amis didn't know how the little girl gliding in front of him kept her motivation. Perhaps Salome was stronger than all of them. Maybe strength is simply what happens when you don't have any options.

Salome kept pointing, bending, and straightening her arm, motioning towards the same spot, although she was moving. She was yelling, her mouth opening wide and eyes squinting from the effort. Though Amis could hear her voice, faint as it was, he could not string together her words.

Luca flew around them in a circle. His face looked withered, even under the clay. Their time spent in comfort and rest hadn't been enough. The teenager would surely never admit that. Amis hoped with all his heart, with all the magic he could manifest inside himself, that this place existed, just as it had been pitched. This utopian world, a safe place for the children of the most vulnerable, would be more than he could ever ask for, ever hope for.

Their group hovered in the air, with no horizontal movement, as Amis watched Salome and Luca staring in the direction she was pointing. The teen wasted no time, though. Amis saw recognition and excitement in his widened gaze before he dove, his darkened hair a blur, blending in the night.

"Luca," Amis yelled. He knew that yell was pointless as he cursed, rolled his eyes, and nodded to Salome. Tightening his grip around Ahora, Amis siphoned the air caressing his wings, which supported him against the gravity that would have him plunge into the earth. Despite the reluctant look Salome gave him, they both angled themselves and flew down.

Salome pointed again; despite the speed of their fall, he tried to focus his eyes on the fog as the force pulled the skin on his face back, preventing blinking, his eyes dry and stinging.

They were closer, and he could see the tops of deep green trees peeking out from the fluffy, thick, white, and gray cotton candy-like fog that continued to spread. There was something else, though, and Amis saw it so late; they were already so close. He was losing his touch.

Luca was heading straight toward it—the top of a pointed clock tower, painted white, camouflaged enough to be missed. Amis's heart beat faster. He was no longer aimlessly chasing a pubescent boy through a surge of his own emotion. No, he had underestimated the teen, who had decisions to make. Karmakara had even visited him and warned him.

Amis was often doing that, underestimating. He needed to stop. Change was so hard, but he knew it was a start.

Amis watched as Luca pulled up feet away from the structure. He turned to look at them, watched them try to catch up, and instead of waiting, he wafted down like a feather falling into fog.

It's okay. It's not like anything dangerous ever happens.

Amis caught up, Salome right by his side, as they floated down the clock tower. The time showed a few minutes after midnight. There were no bells visible, no metal of any kind, only a solid tower the entire way down.

Even though he was a couple of feet from the structure, Amis panicked as it disappeared. As they lowered themselves into the fog, he realized it was so thick that he could no longer see Salome, nor could he see the tower; he could barely make out Ahora, still sound asleep in his arms. The child couldn't be bothered, honestly.

"Scared," Amis heard the word uttered from Noah, who was still on his back. He almost forgot that there was a living thing still clinging to him.

Always spot-on with the appropriate emotions, Noah.

"Don't be scared. You are with me," he caught himself saying.

Who are you to keep him safe?

The doubt crept in again. The death he once felt chasing them, nipping at their heels, might have found them, might have lured their little group back into its clutches.

Maybe Luca chose wrong.

Amis had no choice but to keep floating down, find his two lost kids, and ensure they could all flee if needed.

"Salome," he yelled at the top of his lungs. Noah snuggled into him more, burying himself under Amis's loose hair as much as possible.

"Luca," he yelled again, this time not as loud. The cloudiness and the loss of vision spooked even him. His eyelids were cold; if it were not for the clay, he could tell they would be entirely uncomfortable.

"Hello?" Ahora's meek voice called out. "Who is holding me?"

"It's okay," he said, nearly falling as his feet unexpectedly hit the ground. If it were possible to see even less, then that was what was happening. His vision was clouded with so much white. When he stepped forward, he thought he saw something move, a flash in a different color.

You're hallucinating.

"Salome? Luca?" he called again.

Amis wasn't comfortable putting Ahora down, not knowing what they were standing next to. He knew the clock tower was right near them. That could be the different hue he saw.

"I'm here." Amis felt ten times lighter when he heard Salome's voice. She sounded so far away, though.

"Luca? Salome, can you hear Luca?"

If they were all accounted for, that would be enough for now.

But they weren't.

Luca's voice didn't sound.

"Salome? Let me hear you so we can come together," Amis croaked.

"Here, here," she said. She sounded even farther away.

"Don't move, I'm coming."

"Scared," Noah's voice came through.

"I can't see," Ahora said.

Amis followed Salome's voice, stepping off the curb, hitting Ahora's feet, her hands as he bounced off hard surfaces. He was definitely in a city; it was angular. His boots echoed as he stepped, and he imagined buildings surrounding him, tightly packed, very unlike Emerald's Peak.

I'm starting to miss that place. At least I could see the terrifying monsters before me.

He couldn't see it, but he felt it—a swoosh of air around him. Someone had run past him. There were footsteps he couldn't hear. Either it didn't touch the ground, or it was as light as it was fast.

"Hello?"

There was only silence.

Move. You need to move.

A chilling scream made Amis's blood curdle and his stomach drop. A stream of nerves and chills ran down his body as realization hit him. That was Salome's scream.

Tears welled in his eyes as he walked around frantically, nearly tripping several times, Ahora whimpering in his arms as he ran into structures, Noah trembling against him, whispering he was scared.

Me too, buddy. Me too.

"Salome," Amis yelled. It was risky to yell. There was something there, something hunting them.

Death wasn't chasing them. It expected them to walk into its front door.

And they had.

Again, Amis was hit with dread, with the immediate preparation for detachment, of losing these kids, of the end of Waihema.

They couldn't catch a break.

Or, Luca chose wrong. He dove when he shouldn't have. He was distracted by the story of a village filled with children, of acceptance, of love.

A place like that couldn't exist. He felt like a fool for entertaining the idea now, for getting their hopes up.

For getting his hopes up, too.

"Amis!" Salome's shrill, panicked voice called.

Amis let out a massive sigh of relief.

"Help!" she cried again.

Another swoosh of air, someone passed them, was possibly even circling them.

Music filled his ears.

It was loud, the chimes of little bells gently being played in a rhythm that made him feel like the fluttering of wings was hitting them.

The sound would play, and then he realized that instead of continuing, it reversed.

He was listening to it play forward and then backward, then forward again, and with it, the fog began to thin.

Amis could see the dark outline of his arms, of Ahora's body in his arms.

"Salome!" he yelled, hoping the fog would keep thinning.

Luckily for him, it did.

But he wished it hadn't.

Ahora, in his arms, was no longer the only thing he could see.

There was something else in the near distance, something he could see better, more clearly than his forearm or Ahora in his arms. Through the fog, the cold, and the damp caressing his naked eyelids, chilling his teeth when he parted his lips, there were eyes.

Glowing red eyes.

As the fog continued to clear, they became brighter and multiplied. Amis counted six pairs, an entire group of Vrae blinking at him.

There he was, handing these children over to death once again.

28

———————

Reifoel | Mryilosis

He had been wasting his time.

Hadn't he?

Reifoel reached to his collarbone, where his moonstone had rested for months. It felt strange to be without it—his mother's gift, meant to protect him and Isadore both.

That unease returned, like a whisper in the wind he couldn't catch. He would be returning home without his cousin. The Serelenunians would hear of his cousin's bravery, his dry jokes, which were probably the most honest things he ever said.

Reifoel shook his head. It was a good thing Isadore couldn't hear him now. If he did, he'd haunt Reifoel just to gloat.

"You do love me," Isadore's ghost would say with a sardonic smirk.

Standing at the cusp of the shore, Reifoel was ready to go back, but he wasn't prepared to go back alone. There should be three of them standing there together. Hadley should be with them, too.

It had been a long hike, but the solitude was good for him. Or so he kept telling himself—while dreaming of impossible things like hybrid children pulling at his cousin's hair.

He smiled at the thought of looking into her eyes, ocean-deep and full of home. They would have figured it out together—how she would be at ease in the water.

He had traveled south, through deserts, through mountains. There was rain and thunder that didn't stop, not even for a minute. Earthquakes split the land before his eyes, forcing long detours and making shelter impossible.

It wasn't smart, taking this path alone, but he couldn't stand it any longer. He couldn't stand watching the person he loved fall for someone else—even if she hadn't realized it yet.

Reifoel was no fool. He couldn't wait for her to realize the mistake she was making with Sheng. Their bond was real—messy, but undeniable. After her rejection in the temple, he couldn't shake it.

You're wasting your time.

They'd restored the moon, he'd gotten them into Ebonspire, and his obligations had ceased. His mother would've smacked him if he'd left before finishing what he'd started.

Reifoel bent down, picking up seaweed on the shore. It smelled like heaven, briny and clean. He dusted off as much sand as possible and plopped it in his mouth. Seaweed was slimier out of water, the texture altered by air and surface bacteria, but he was starving.

Reifoel had barely eaten on his journey, ripping apart plants he didn't know and throwing most of them back up. He stared at his wrist, skin dried but not cracking thanks to the violent rainstorms.

He removed his jacket and peeled off his pants, nearly tripping as he fumbled one-legged in the sand. With a final kick, the pants flew off onto the sand, and he stood there nude, staring out into a horizon that stretched forever—cotton candy skies blooming with sunset.

It was the first time he had seen a calm evening since Isadore was murdered. He would consider it a welcome if the sea had also chosen to behave. Instead, towering waves roared onto the sand, leaving barely a foot of dry beach at low tide.

The tides were angry.

They depended on the moon and sea, bound like seahorses to their mates.

Stop thinking about her.

It felt impossible. It felt devastating.

Walking away had shattered whatever future they might've had.

This could be a mistake.

Go home.

The chill of the setting sun washed over him, and the water inched closer and closer to his planted feet. He shook his hips, waving the piece of manhood between his legs back and forth, and smiled in a sort of hilarious goodbye to his cousin.

And Isadore hadn't even gotten to stick it into anything.

Not that Reifoel had either.

Stop thinking about her.

He was a love-sick sea lion, and it wouldn't do. He had to push that aside. He needed to get back to Serelune.

Reifoel stepped into the water, ocean spraying his face, the water surprisingly warm—his skin drinking in the salt, minerals, and magic he was made for.

It had been too long since he'd been in water like this.

His eyelids fluttered, his heartbeat slowed, and even though fifteen-and twenty-foot waves crashed over him, he felt so relaxed.

He let it soak in, the glorious way he felt, as his legs bonded together and the bones turned into cartilage. He sank, sitting on submerged rocks and pebbles as wave after wave hit his face, his torso. He opened his mouth, letting the water fill it, swallowing, then letting it dribble out.

And yet, there was still the memory of those hands on his skin, of those lips pressed against his, her ass filling his hands. It felt just as good.

Reifoel looked back at the land, at the bare cliffs he'd stumbled down to reach the shore.

She was somewhere there, somewhere beyond those cliffs.

If you swim, you might not ever see her again.

His dream would end here.

There would be no hope of getting it back, only the memory of her warmth. Sometimes, no matter how broken it was, specific dreams were not meant to come true.

You have a different destiny. You belong to the sea. You belong to Serelune.

A heavy mass was brought in by the waves, which tossed it ashore. A massive fish had washed up—blue and gray, fin broader than its body, dead and still.

Reifoel blinked at it and then looked back out at the sea before another mass caught his eye again. Then another, and another.

Not one death—but dozens. They were carried in by the tide.

Some were fish, some were sharks. Others were magical beings that had once thrived in these waters.

The ocean was sick, and an old familiar feeling rose to choke out sorrow and longing.

Fear.

Who knew what state Serelune would be in, but Reifoel feared the worst.

There was no extra time.

He had to go.

He had to help.

He had to find his mother and his father and hug them—to prove they were all still alive.

He was already in Myrilosis. All that remained was the swim.

Reifoel waited until the next wave crashed, then angled his tail behind him and shoved off the rocks with both hands, using the flow of the tide as much as possible until he was submerged deep enough to flick his tail.

Relief chilled down his spine. Every flick of his tail flooded his brain with something close to euphoria.

With every stroke, he went deeper, until he could make full, powerful movements..

He hadn't truly swum like this in ages—not just a dip or a float, but real swimming.

The last time, he'd been dragging Hadley from the edge of death.

He'd watched her look for it, call out to it, as her lungs burned. She hadn't found death—but she hadn't found life either.

What kind of life would that be for her?

You would drown her. Suffocate her. Maybe love shouldn't conquer all.

Maybe trying would kill any joy their future could hold. The constant looming stress, fear, and rejection from their worlds would ensure that neither of them could breathe.

Reifoel swam further, propelling himself deep enough that the light barely flickered anymore through the surface.

No moonlight would guide him even ten feet under the ocean's surface. The moon was still too small, the light not powerful enough to cast a glow.

His skin glowed faintly—bright white, edged with a magical hue that warned predators to stay away. Reifoel had ripped a few sharks' jaws open before, grabbing each side as they tried to bite his arm.

Reifoel let the water soothe over his gills, his mind so clear.

He would stop his hurried pace every few hours when he stumbled across bite-sized fish he could scoop into his mouth and swallow whole, seaweed he could pick from the floor, or algae he could lick up from sitting rocks that were likely as old as Arryn himself.

Dark masses of land would haunt his peripheral vision as he moved through the water, following continents down, letting islands guide him. It felt like forever, a loop of swimming endlessly. There was no stopping, though, not when there was nowhere else for him to go.

PRIDE, feral and roaring, surged through him when he saw a faint glow in the distance.

He had made it.

There it was—Serelune. Nothing else glowed like that in the ocean's deepest dark.

Reifoel picked up speed. He could see more faint glows, the

outline of structures, domes built from whale bone, splintered ships, and forests of sunken wood.

He'd made it home.

You did it.

"Who is that?"

Reifoel heard voices as he approached.

"It's him. He came back."

"Where is the other one?"

Whispers rippled through the currents, gossip and questions drifting around him as he swam past structures of agatized coral and paths of carefully curated pebbles.

"He's alone."

Thanks for the reminder.

Reifoel lifted his chin as he passed the uniform domes, heading for the last one in the center path, the one that was a bit bigger than the rest. Glowing bodies turned to watch. Hair floated like seaweed—red, blonde, black, brown. Young and old eyes peered from behind doors and windows, as the city—the home their ancestors had built—seemed to pause just to watch him.

A group of children swam in front of him, intercepting his path. Three faces stared up at him, unsure, hesitant, before they glanced at each other and then smiled.

"Welcome home," they said, wrapping their arms around him.

A familiar figure swam over, someone older, someone Reifoel had spent plenty of time avoiding being in the same room with, not out of dislike, but because she meant accountability.

"Hello, Reifoel," Gasher said.

Gasher sat on the council and was often in the royal hut. Her eyes were tired, red—like she'd been crying at the surface for hours.

She was a middle-aged Serelune female in her late 100s, her skin still tight, and her frown lines beginning to show. Her silver-blonde hair floated dimly, dull and dry, not catching the light the way it used to.

Reifoel blinked, catching the cues: the whispers, the grief behind open arms. Even those he'd once teased—and who'd teased him back —stood together, staring with eyes full of sorrow.

Isadore.

They must know about Isadore.

"I'm so sorry," Reifoel choked out. He hadn't said it aloud before. This pain was new—like knives lodged in his throat.

"I'm so sorry. I took him away from you. I take responsibility."

Gasher's eyes softened, her hand reaching out to Reifoel's arm.

"What happened, dear?"

Reifoel broke. The full weight of his sadness and guilt crashed through him. His body convulsed. The children swam away, back into the arms of mothers who held them close.

"Did you find your father?" Gasher asked gently.

It took a moment for her words to register. Reifoel stopped sobbing, a new realization hitting him. He looked at Gasher. Then at the faces around him.

There were so few of them. They all looked scared.

He'd assumed they were safe. The city looked whole—but the people weren't.

"What happened to my father?"

29

Arryn | Outer Space

She's here because I was broken—am broken.

"Screw Celestine," Arryn tried to say.

His ego was better than that.

Unfortunately, speaking out loud was not an option.

He was in space, and his lungs burned with that familiar tingle under his skin. It was a comfort, a reminder of how far he'd come since he'd tried to be something he wasn't: a Kinnari who spent too much time caring.

He cared about the others, their lives both within and outside the temple. He cared about the species thriving in the mortal realm, unleashing creations to help nurture a world while locking the monsters away.

Most of all, he cared for Allienna.

And he had nothing to show for it.

He was hated. He knew.

And yet, he was expected to save this world. Save his creations.

Why should I care what they want from me?

The world could end. It had before. He was always just fine.

Arryn all but stopped moving, his body floating. The cold was so profound that it made him miss the snowstorms he'd summoned. He had to focus, move slowly, and be precise. Otherwise, his hands could snap off in the process.

He gathered what he could, unable to move, unable to breathe. Arryn was unable to feel anything but that haunting cold—one that gave kisses of death, promises of annihilation. Arryn could pull enough atoms together to glove over his skin, arms, torso, and head.

It felt glorious to breathe in and out, his spacesuit supporting his body's needs. His fingers tingled with a new kind of pain as they defrosted.

Arryn was scared to turn his head and upper torso to look at Djoser. Space had a way of propelling you with one wrong movement. It was like falling into a current, one that would never give you back—not even after you were dead.

The things I do for everyone.

He pushed his magic behind him. He moved slowly, just in case there was propulsion he hadn't noticed. Inch by inch, it reached— until Arryn felt him. Darkness clashed with his light, death touching creation.

Arryn didn't like touching Djoser too much. He was perfectly happy avoiding the sensation altogether. The feeling of balance when they were together was the most unnatural thing he could imagine.

And I've made some weird shit.

With some effort, Arryn pushed atoms together around Djoser's skin, enclosing him in a suit of his own.

"You're welcome," he said.

"You put a microphone in this thing?" Djoser asked, out of breath. "You didn't even have a phone, but you know how to make a mic?"

"You sound like Reign."

"Good."

The two stared at the bright circular boulder in front of them. It was misshapen and already looked like it had been hit by debris and craters—still small, easily damaged.

"How big do you think you can get it?"

"I'll keep going until I can't anymore."

"So my job is to get you back down to Earth after you black out?" Djoser asked.

Arryn grunted. "Let's get this over with."

He already had a slight buzz in the back of his head, that drunken pulse of power that came when he created and created and didn't stop. It was a euphoria that mortals would kill for.

Eyes nearly rolling, Arryn flexed his fingertips. Arms loose at his sides, he drifted farther from the planet. A cord unspooled from his suit, tethering him back to Earth. A subtle tug pulled him backward, making him bounce as the slack tightened, halting his drift. With a quick pulse of magic, a second cord extended—this one linking Djoser's suit to his.

They were now hanging out in space like best buddies.

Arryn watched as Djoser sprang slightly, his body reacting to the new boundary.

"Good idea," Djoser's voice came through the mic. "Are we wearing diapers? Real human astronauts wear diapers. I saw it once in a museum."

Arryn couldn't help but laugh.

"I did not wrap your ass in a diaper, Djoser."

"I'm not the one who's going to pass out," Djoser raised his hands.

Now able to move more freely, Arryn pushed his arms back, propelling himself closer to the moon. He pulled Djoser with him, who cursed in protest as he was dragged.

"If I'm closer, I can spend less energy pulling everything together," Arryn said.

Maybe Djoser wasn't as bright as he had thought.

Idiot.

"That's funny. I don't have any problem with distances," Djoser said. Arryn could hear the smart-ass grin.

"If you think making me mad will help with my magic, then you're wrong."

"Oh, no, it's a hobby of mine, getting under your skin. I want to say I have mastered it, but... you've never met Greg."

"Sounds like I need to find this Greg and handcuff him to you."

"What's with you and handcuffs all of a sudden? A new kink your phoenix likes?"

"I'm not talking to you about that," Arryn said, irritation spiking.

Arryn hadn't meant to be in this new relationship, but he also hadn't done anything to stop it. She was a lost puppy who followed him, and he continued to feed her. Now, that puppy was biting back, saying she was an emotional support animal.

I don't need healing. Everyone else needs healing.

Millimeter by millimeter, Arryn stretched his magic, feeling the microscopic bumps of the atoms. To him, they felt so solid—large grains of sand he could scoop, mold, and give life. To anyone else, they would fall right through their fingers unnoticed.

He had gathered so much, the weight of thousands of pounds on his back, shoulders, mind, and magic. Only he could do this, and he relished the reminder. When the atoms made contact, he was an artist sitting down at a pottery wheel, sculpting the additions as they took shape.

"It is special watching you create," Djoser admitted.

It was exactly what Arryn needed—a compliment.

He closed his eyes and breathed into the muscles, feeling that burn beneath his skin. That kind of pain craved release.

It felt good to be a little dangerous.

Arryn opened his eyes again to see the moon in front of him, its size doubled. He and Djoser could now stand on opposite sides and not touch wing tips.

The energy propelling through Arryn made him bare his teeth and let out a low, feral moan. He could live in this feeling—get trapped in the energy the way someone got trapped at the bottom of a bottle.

"I don't know what's going on, but the sounds are getting a little too graphic for me," Djoser's voice came through his helmet.

But Arryn was already too far gone, his magic still adding to the mass.

"Your head's starting to wobble, man." Djoser's voice grew fainter, like the speaker in his helmet was getting further and further away.

"I'm pulling you back," Djoser's voice was garbled now, but Arryn still kept pushing, kept gathering, kept molding, letting release erase him.

Without warning, the corners of his vision became blurry, then dark, with blackness swirling and forming patterns that he knew were not real. Soon, the patterns completely covered his vision, leaving him in blackness, drowning in nothing but the depletion of his own self.

Before that last strand of consciousness left him, a little voice tapped him on the shoulder, one that he could barely hear.

"This is going to suck."

Arryn would have loved to laugh at Djoser's displeasure, but he was gone. The next time he woke up, his body was sore, his burn insatiable.

Drops of water peppered his face.

No, it wasn't water.

Arryn opened his eyes to a pair of plump breasts in his gaze, peeking out from the buttoned cardigan that tried to hide them.

He groaned.

Tears.

Celestine hovered over him, her hands massaging his hair and his neck. His body was cold, and as he flexed his right knee, he heard the crunch of snow.

"Oh, good, you're awake." Celestine giggled, her cheeks rosy, her smile large. Those dimples he liked were pressing into her cheeks.

"So," Arryn attempted to say, his throat sore.

"Shh, shhh, shhh," Celestine tried to soothe him.

"You did alright, Arryn," Djoser said, footsteps coming closer.

Arryn tried to sit up, his arms protesting under his weight. He wondered if he would ever get used to these magic-induced blackouts. Could he get stronger?

"Are we done yet?" Arryn asked, staring at Roksana, who stood a few feet away and looked down at him, her arms crossed.

"The moon is heavier," Precession's sing-songy voice said behind him. He didn't bother to turn around.

Her words already felt like defeat.

"We still have a long way to go, is what she means," Djoser said.

"Yeah, got it, thanks."

30

Allienna | Sacramento, Ca | 1994

Allienna opened her eyes and gasped, shock freezing her as the morning light crept into her window. Her blood had thinned overnight, and her body begged to tremble.

But she could only find stillness, a slight paralysis.

The warmth of Hadley's breath against her shoulder was the only heat that existed. Only one person in her life was still who they claimed to be—Hadley, the child she had given everything to create.

Tears welled in her eyes and spilled. There were always tears now, and she was tired of them.

Tristan was Vrae. A Kinnari and a Vrae.

How could she believe the bonding ceremony was real when something so protective had turned horrific? That brush of skin on skin, that thirst for her own blood that had filled her body, all from someone she trusted.

She couldn't let this continue. A monster was out there, pretending to be one of them still.

You have to warn them. You have to tell somebody.

Today, she would take Hadley to the Kinnari temple. Today, her daughter would learn about her family. Today, she would be safe.

I should look up plane tickets and get us most of the way there.

Allienna rose, letting Hadley slump over, still in a deep sleep. It wasn't normal. Hadley was usually the one who woke her.

She looked at Hadley and ran her fingers through her glistening, bright blonde hair and bent down to kiss her forehead. She would let her sleep. It was going to be a long day.

Moving into the kitchen, she picked up the wireless house phone off of its stand, pressing the power button until she heard a dial tone, then began to dial Paisley's phone number.

Allienna would have to tell her friend and boss that she wouldn't be coming in today. That she never would again.

Then, she would have to figure out how to get a passport and plane tickets. She couldn't carry Hadley in her arms the entire way back; they wouldn't make it far. Hopefully, by tonight, they could be buckled into a seat on a plane. After they landed somewhere nearby, Allienna could complete their journey with Hadley in her arms and her wings out, supporting the two of them in the cold, frigid air.

The phone rang once, then twice. Then her pupils rolled back, and she collapsed with a heavy thump, her body twitching.

"Hello? Hello?" Paisley's voice was barely audible as the phone lay feet away from her on the carpet.

It didn't matter. Allienna was no longer there.

"Leave me alone," Allienna yelled, jumping up on her kitchen counter. Her knees banged hard. The pain followed her here.

She was in her home—but at the same time, she wasn't. Her daughter wasn't asleep in the bed, and the walls and air seemed drained of color, muted in gray and blue.

Tristan stood in the middle of the kitchen in his youthful, petite body. His brown eyes and brown hair lacked the telltale tint that would mark this as a trick—another vision.

Her breath caught in her chest as she looked frantically for the knife set that usually rested right in the left corner, but it was missing from this vision or dream she'd been unwillingly pulled into.

"Don't kill me. No one will come to check on Hadley," Allienna rasped. "I'll keep your secret. I promise. I don't talk to anyone. I'm isolated, just like you."

Her pleading words changed something in Tristan's expression. The amusement dropped. His face turned soft, sad.

"I'm not here to kill you, Allienna." Tristan shook his head and kicked the heel of his right foot against the linoleum kitchen flooring.

"You'll . . . you'll scuff the flooring doing that," she said, tucking her knees into her chest and resting her chin on top. She tried to look relaxed, even as she wished the knives were still there.

"You left too fast. You didn't give me a chance to explain," Tristan said, bending down to trace the black scuff that he indeed did make.

It's a vision. It's not real. You'll still get your security deposit back.

"My daughter was smothered in my blood, and then, you wanted to eat me. If there was a time to wake up, that seemed like a good one."

Unless, of course, you get mauled down and die in Tristan's dream because you can't keep your mouth shut.

"I didn't want to eat you," Tristan scoffed as if that was absurd. "Sure, I crave Kinnari blood, but I'm not an animal. I have self-control."

Allienna blinked, frowning.

"So, does that mean you are no longer Kinnari?" she asked after letting silence fall between them.

"I am Vrae, Allienna."

"But how? Have you been here to hunt Hadley? Was the whole ceremony a ruse?"

"No, stop," he said, rubbing his forehead with both hands. "I'm trying to explain. You are rather insulting."

"Well, you're doing it badly."

Case in point.

"Just shut up for a minute," he said, his voice raised, his eyes gleaming red for just a moment before returning to their normal color.

Allienna nodded for him to continue.

"The day of the attack, when the Vrae came into the Kinnari temple, I was a Kinnari. I was soulkin. Once I was torn to pieces, I somehow healed. I somehow came back together. Even with immortality, complete mutilation should have been the end, but it wasn't. The Vrae venom mixed with Kinnari blood changed me."

"It changed you into Vrae?"

Tristan nodded. "A child-sized one."

"I didn't notice it for years. I struggled, really fought to not completely hide in dreams, in visions, but I was so scared, Allienna. After that attack, it felt like I needed to die, and no one came looking for me. No one even seemed to try."

"Oh, Tristan." Allienna scooted forward on the kitchen counter, her legs hanging over the edge. "We thought you were dead."

"Eventually, I understood that. So, I made a plan to come back to the temple. I walked in and heard you ... heard Arryn and Roksana. I was just about to call out, to reunite with you all, when I caught your voice. You were talking about wings. You'd just gotten yours, Allienna—and you were soaked in blue blood.

Something in me snapped. My body went feral. I didn't understand it at the time—only that sharp teeth were growing in my mouth and I wanted to use them.

So I ran. Again.

I hid in more dreams, slipped deeper into visions, until I found one that led me somewhere real—a city in Myrilosis. It was full of others like me. Once-Kinnari, turned Vrae. Monsters, yes, but living in something like a society. Something almost civilized."

"You never came back because you were protecting us."

Tristan gave her a melancholy nod.

"I love you, I love Hadley, I love all of you."

"Did you say other Kinnari?" Allienna scoffed.

Tristan grimaced. "Unfortunately, yes. I'm sure he's completely forgotten about them. Ayurveda created the first Vrae and set him loose on our society. Everyone turned. I heard he was moving to the Earth realm. That's why I found you again. That's why I wanted to help you protect Hadley."

"What am I supposed to do now?" Allienna asked.

"Prepare Hadley, perhaps. Tell her about us."

Allienna shook her head. "I won't. I can't. I worked too hard to hide her."

"Then there's nothing." Tristan shrugged. "You are completely taken care of and safe to live out the remaining years of your life."

"Remaining years? Are there so few left?" Allienna laughed.

"They will go by faster than you think. Immortality made us careless. We stopped hugging, stopped showing up for each other's grief and joy. That is probably the biggest difference between our kind and the humans you live among."

The gray and the blue tones around them began to flicker. The vision was leaving her.

"I love you," Tristan said again. His expression was sad, like he'd never see her again.

"I love you, too." She smiled.

Color entered her world, vivid and bright as the daylight flowed through the window. Hadley stood over her, poking her, the house phone broken beside her, and its battery spilled out as if the toddler had been messing with it.

"Momma," Hadley sang. "Why are you sleeping on the floor? That's so silly!"

Allienna sat up slowly, her body sore from the fall, and gently pulled Hadley into her arms, kissing her cheek.

"Good morning, baby. Did you have any nice dreams?"

"I dreamed . . . I dreamed . . . I dreamed about a big dinosaur that could fly and breathe fire. She was my friend," Hadley said with a larger-than-life smile.

"That sounds like a dragon, Hadley," Allienna said, brushing away more tears. Her daughter didn't remember the ceremony, and in the end, they were both safe.

You didn't fail.

31

Hadley | Mryilosis

Dreams were different now.

Everything she saw wasn't real. She knew that.

You're drifting in and out of sleep. Hadley reassured herself.

Kismet held her as they soared through the sky. The cold no longer bit at her cheeks or hands. The numbness that usually followed was simply absent. Pain, too, had vanished. She felt nothing —no pressure, no chill, no warmth.

Instead of sensation, she saw everything.

These dreams were so vivid, so real that she resisted reaching out, knowing she was flying through the air.

She saw fire. She saw her mother. She saw a village surrounded by lush trees and a blue sky. She saw herself, a child, with red and purple colors wrapping around her. The colors weren't just dream fragments. They were magic. They were love. And something else— something powerful, dangerous.

Something just beneath her skin.

But she hadn't grown up with magic. She would have remembered.

So she watched, mesmerized by what her mind could conjure.

Simple.

Wanting was its own kind of suffering. To reach for something you'd never have.

She lived in a different world than the happy people. The ones who never strayed into darkness, who didn't need desperation to justify their descent.

That was her world now. She would rule it.

Everyone already thinks you're something more. You can be more.

Hadley didn't know what it meant to be a Goddess, but she wanted to guide people. She wanted to help. She wanted ...

She began to forget.

Hadley started to forget what she wanted.

Remembering felt like trying to catch wisps of air. Wanting was a feeling, hope was a feeling—and feelings were slipping.

If she had ten days —no longer human, no longer Kinnari—then only two or three sunsets remained. Days had passed while she recovered from the dune. Ayurveda was nowhere to be seen. Hadley assumed she watched from the skies.

Kismet flew high, so close to that new moon. Its fullness reflected off the sun that evening, a deep red hue.

They had done it. The misfit band of Kinnari had healed the moon.

Ayurveda would have to let it go.

Now, it made sense why she would.

Hadley couldn't imagine feeling anger again. Need, too, was slipping.

It was either that, or she had just gotten what she was trying to accomplish. Ayurveda must've been acting on pure logic. Destroying the moon again wouldn't serve her.

Or maybe she'd gotten what she wanted.

She had gotten Hadley.

I'm hers again.

Nothing was stopping the transformation now.

Kismet began her descent in a wide spiral. The air whipped Hadley's long blonde hair, but this time, it felt graceful—gentler than the rest of the ride. They'd flown over oceans, mountains, plains, and forests—across every kind of landscape.

The want was gone now, replaced by a single-minded focus.

This was what she was doing. But with no heart behind it, Hadley knew it was all a waste. She didn't want food. She didn't need water. If she were still mortal, she'd have withered away by now.

The ground below was thick with trees and a wide, raging river that raced toward mountains on the edge of her vision. Kismet circled lower and lower until she finally touched down. The wyvern's body creaked, her knees and joints absorbing the landing.

Hadley slid off instead, her wings unfolding to catch her. She drifted to the ground like a pixie landing in wildflowers.

"You're bleeding," someone said.

Hadley kept her eyes low, but through her lashes, she saw the silhouette of a man she knew far too well.

"You'll never leave me alone, will you?" she asked. "You'd follow me to the ends of the world."

She stepped away, placing her palms on Kismet's belly in quiet gratitude.

"Go hunt," she whispered. Kismet obeyed immediately, wings unfurling as she leapt skyward. A stream of fire rippled behind her, scattering embers that singed Hadley's hair. The scent of burning strands curled in her nose.

Sheng rose from where he'd been sitting and strode toward her in long, smooth steps. His hair was tousled, dark circles bruising the skin beneath his black eyes. His complexion had dulled—pale and rough—as if fear had bled the color from him. But now, a trace of warmth returned to his cheeks, his lips parting the moment they stood close again.

Sheng reached for the smoldering lock of her hair, snuffing the ember between his fingers while she stared up at him, blank.

"I didn't technically follow you," he said, "but I've been here for days, hoping you'd land in this spot." His words were soft, heated, his gaze fixed on her body instead of her eyes.

"You're naked," he observed, one brow lifting, a crooked smirk pulling at the corner of his mouth.

"Yes."

"Did your clothes fly off midair? Or is this a liberation moment? Either way, I support it."

"I stepped—" she began.

"Wait, hold that thought." He spun around, jogging back to where he'd been sitting. He crouched in the grass, retrieved something, then turned and sprinted back to her, grinning with a puffed-out chest like he'd just won a prize.

"I found this here," he said. "It had to be yours."

Sheng extended his hand, offering her a yellow rose. Thorns pierced his skin, and tiny beads of blood welled from the tips of his fingers.

"Just like our first date," he said. "Strip poker. You wouldn't stop staring at me in those sweatpants."

Hadley stared at the rose, unmoving. She didn't reach for it.

Sheng's smile faltered. He stepped closer and gently took her hand, guiding her fingers around the stem, careful to avoid the thorns.

"You didn't say it," Sheng murmured.

"Say what?" Hadley asked, her eyes locked on the rose, her hand still cradled in his.

"No touching."

Hadley looked up at him. His lips were parted—soft, waiting—until he bit down gently on the lower one.

"I can't feel it," she said at last.

"You can't feel this?" he asked, stroking the back of the same hand.

She couldn't. It was like he was a ghost, or air, that wrapped around her—an invisible touch, an invisible blanket that promised sensation but never delivered.

"You can't feel this?" Sheng asked as he brushed the back of her hand with slow, deliberate strokes.

She couldn't. His touch was like mist trailing air across her skin—there but unreachable.

"Can you feel this?" he asked again, his finger gliding up her arm to the curve of her neck.

Then his hand expanded, cupping her face, guiding her closer.

She laid her hand atop his, her other fingers ghosting across his wrist.

Nothing.

She shook her head and dropped her gaze. Sheng's black pants and unbuttoned winter jacket filled her vision.

She noticed his bulge—growing. His blood had already begun to heat.

She wondered if hers had too, or if her body responded while her mind remained still.

Or maybe that was just it.

Sheng lowered his head, his shoulders curving protectively around her. His lips hovered near her jaw but didn't touch; instead, he pressed his forehead gently to hers.

"This?" he asked softly.

"No," she whispered.

His nose brushed hers, their lips nearly touching, and all space between them vanished as he stepped closer.

She didn't feel the press of his body, the tension building between them. But she could see it—his arousal, the way his breathing hitched, the desire bleeding from every attempt to stay composed.

It felt like awakening—being near him without fear, without flinching.

He was just Sheng, no matter what horrors he could conjure, no matter his reputation. And he needed her like she once needed air.

"I can't," she whimpered, the words spilling out as her lips moved.

Sheng kissed her. His free hand threaded through her hair, drawing her in until their bodies were pressed so tightly she couldn't tell where one began.

Hadley didn't breathe. Then she closed her eyes and surrendered to the moment, to the hope that maybe she could feel something.

And she almost did. Not touch—not warmth. But want. She wanted to feel.

She wanted, just once more, to know what it was like to be loved —not for her power, not for prophecy, but for her.

Maybe this was her last chance to feel something fully human.

Sheng broke the kiss with a sharp breath, then dove back in— trailing his lips down her jaw, her throat, her collarbone. It reminded her of how he used to kiss her in bed, while she bled onto his sheets, the mattress, as his tongue licked her up and down from the tops of her feet —ankles, knees buckling—up her inner thighs as she moaned, his venom pulsing through her veins.

"It binds us together," he'd once told her. "It makes me your master. It makes you mine."

But Hadley wasn't his.

She belonged to herself. Maybe to Ayurveda.

Sheng's hands slid down from her face, cupping her chest, gently pulling at her nipples as his mouth continued to claim hers. Hadley's eyes fluttered down, watching his left hand keep going until it found her hips. He squeezed and groaned, his body moving fast as if he thought at any moment she would swat him away.

But she wouldn't. Not this time.

This is how she would say goodbye to the world before she turned into a shell.

His hand moved onto her pelvis, lower and lower, until he found her other set of lips. She watched his elbow bend and softly straighten until she could tell by his forearm that he had moved on to small circles.

"Can you feel this?" He pulled out of their kiss to ask.

"No," she said, and Sheng let out a laugh.

"Hard to please, I see," he said, taking it as a challenge.

Hadley let Sheng gently lower her to the ground, onto plush grass, surrounded by dandelions.

Sheng was over her.

She looked up at him as he smiled, caressing her wings.

"Beautiful," he whispered, bending to kiss her chest. He dragged his tongue up to her neck and fumbled with his pants.

Giving up, he stood again, letting her watch him drop his jacket and rip off his long-sleeved thermal, exposing that hard core, the perfect V pointed towards his bulge.

"Do you see something you like?" he asked, eyebrows raised.

Hadley didn't respond. She just stared, trying to figure out why she hadn't stood up, hadn't called for Kismet. She could hardly remember why she was even there, why they had stopped flying. She was going somewhere.

Where was she going?

"Can I proceed?" Sheng asked.

"Yes," Hadley answered.

Sheng's face lit up—that devilish smile, that familiar look from when she'd once begged him not to leave, his venom in her veins.

"This chase," he said, "following you around the world, has been worth it, wife. I would do it again and again. I would follow you until this world explodes, until our sun dies, and then you would be my star, my light, my beacon of hope. You make me a better man, a better Vrae, Hadley," he said, unbuttoning his pants, not taking his eyes off of hers. He didn't blush. The intensity on his face was unwavering. He was serious, opening his heart and soul to her.

But she didn't need him. Not in any way he thought she did.

Right now, she just needed to see if she could feel anything at all. He was the test.

Sheng's pants were down to his ankles. He stood there proud, his hard cock twitching, hunting between his legs, looking for her. Sheng kneeled, pulling himself over her, his skin sliding against hers. She looked, watching that hard muscle flicker on her inner thigh.

"It missed you. I missed you," he smirked, kissing her hard, fast, chest heaving, heart racing. His arms trembled, barely holding the space between them.

She breathed in, wondering if he still smelled clean, still smelled fresh—tea tree, that shower-fresh scent that used to cling to him.

She couldn't smell it.

She couldn't feel the heat from his breath.

She couldn't feel his bite.

But she saw him pull back, saw the stretch of her lip, the satisfied smile as he let go, waiting.

So she crunched up and took him in her mouth, biting back.

He gasped.

She let go, wiped her mouth with the back of her hand, and saw crimson staining her skin like she'd smeared on lipstick.

Sheng's smile faltered, cautious now, like he was asking for permission. His arms started to tremble, still holding himself in a plank.

"May I?" he asked.

"Yes," she said. She needed to find the line, to see when her body would wake.

Sheng opened his mouth. Hadley watched his jaw expand, fangs longer than her fingers. He hovered, then bit—swift, fluid, like water.

She heard the rip of skin.

She heard his gulp.

She heard his moan.

Her blood—dark blue, metallic—dripped from his chin and pooled at the curve of her breast.

There was no pain. She stared at him without flinching, her mind temporarily lost in the colors from both bodies.

"You taste different," he mumbled.

She had no answer. She softened her gaze.

His eyes darkened.

Sheng's response was feverish, feral. Her blood permitted him to be a monster, to act in his true nature.

He could be himself with her.

There was no holding back.

Sheng thrust into her.

He howled.

She stared—his beautiful face, his carved chest, those biceps that pinned her down.

"You want this," he said, rocking into her, steady, insistent. "You want me."

She knew it wasn't a statement. It was a question—maybe even a plea.

Hadley still couldn't feel him, his bite, not even when he drank.

"Yes," she said. "How far can we take it?"

Sheng nearly choked.

"We can go as far as you can handle," he whispered. There was danger in his delight.

He sat back on his knees, pulling her with him, her legs wrapped around his. His eyes closed, jaw ticking, every motion vulnerable yet dominant. His hips moved—circles, then thrusts, deeper, harder.

Hadley checked in with herself, waiting for the surge of love, of near worship, to hit her. The venom's bond never came. She wasn't fighting with herself. There was no voice screaming to run, no whisper commanding that she stay.

She was the monster now, maybe that was why.

She sat up, wings unfurling. She slammed forward, knocking Sheng flat. He caught her—smooth, continuous—and moaned louder. She rode him harder; the friction she couldn't feel made puddles on his pelvis.

There was still no sensation, but her body reacted.

That was something.

She raised her arms, moved rhythmically, touched herself, danced over her skin, her thighs clamping around him like possession.

"Hadley," Sheng groaned. "Fuck . . . Hadley."

He stared at her, his eyes no longer filled with the flame and fire of something possessive. He stared at her with softness, with awe.

He dipped his finger in the blood on her neck, then trailed it to her inner thigh.

"Mine," he read as he traced four letters.

He dropped his head back, letting her ride, letting her move. It was how he would worship her, giving her the freedom to find her body without understanding.

Sheng grabbed the grass, ripping it in fists to stay in control.

"You're mine, Hadley," Sheng said, his eyes burning into hers. "My wife, my sin, mine to put back together."

Hadley rolled her hips harder, trying to feel, pushing him flat again.

"No," he protested, flipping her fast onto her side. He was behind her now. Her wings were in his face as he kissed and sucked.

"Break for me, Hadley. Scream into the abyss so even the monsters can hear."

She closed her eyes, breathing, listening, trying to feel.

Then he bit her ear.

And she felt it.

A tingle, a ring, vibrated through her entire body as if she were waking up for the first time.

"You're almost there. We can do it together," he purred. "I can feel you. I feel how tight you are. I feel you trembling."

Sheng pulled her hard.

If she were still Kinnari, she'd bruise.

"Straighten your legs," he demanded.

"What?"

"Straighten your damn perfect legs."

She did.

And when she did, he pulsed into her again.

The tingling was now an explosion of stars and power across the sky overhead.

She could see colors that did not exist.

Hadley convulsed in his arms.

Sheng moaned and released.

A harmonious duet.

She stayed there, unmoving, staring at the sky. The swirls and sparkles left her vision, replaced by bright blue.

Sheng buried his face in her neck, his heat fading already.

"Did you feel that?" he asked, smiling against her skin, clinging like he'd never let go.

"Yes," she whispered back. "I did."

"There's my good girl."

32

Reign | Mytholm | 1787

Reign was feeling out of control, her focus previously on finding the Vrae that had stalked her and Arryn. Now she was drifting through the skies, not wondering where—but when—she was.

She certainly expected that after millennia of this, she would have the time jumping more in control. Her stomach fluttered, the little butterflies reviving when she fantasized about being able to choose where she ended up.

Control, she was meant to be in control.

Yet it escaped her, eluding her like someone dedicated to watching thunder.

Another thing that made those butterflies flutter again was the prospect of a bed. It was the middle of the day, the sun blazing so bright, and judging by the architecture below her, she certainly had not traveled into the future. She was somewhere in the past.

It was nice to think about fashion for once. Whatever it was that the ladies were wearing down there, she hoped that they had pajamas.

Silk pajamas.

Blue ones.

With a masseuse on demand.

She fantasized that all the orphaned children in this timeline had those items on call as she hovered down, wishing for cloud coverage. Instead, the sun burned—a stark difference from the cold, from a world still mourning its shattered moon.

She landed in a city. Eastern European, judging by the human faces and buildings that lined the cobblestone streets.

Am I in Myrilosis or the Earth realm?

The ground beneath her feet was filthy. Reign was too aware that it was likely made up of much more than dirt from the stench alone.

Horses passed, some towing carriages and others being led by young girls with a rope tied to them in one hand and a full bucket in the other. Reign was disappointed to see they wore no silk blue pajamas—only full-length skirts, corseted tops, and ruffled blouses that matched the patterns on their hats.

A few of the passing girls noticed Reign and gave her blatant looks that told her she didn't belong there.

She knew that, of course.

She stood in a city square. The buildings were wooden, the men fast-walking with newspapers, yelling at orphaned beggars who trailed them, hoping a coin might drop. Matronly women screamed out of windows while hanging laundry on wires.

"Put those away," someone hissed at her. She could barely hear them. Someone grabbed the top of her hair and pulled up, like they were plucking a carrot from the earth.

"What the fuck?" Reign's hands snapped toward the wrist above her.

A middle-aged woman with blonde hair, wearing an ugly dress and a scowl, looked down at her.

"I said, put those wings away," the woman repeated. Reign's feet touched back down as the woman let go of her hair.

"There's nicer ways to ask," Reign mumbled and slid her wings back into her body, the sickening sound of popping cartilage and slithering skin echoing in her ears.

"You look peculiar," the woman said.

"You look weird," Reign scoffed.

"You speak peculiarly, too. I've never seen wings on a child," she muttered, looking around as people passed by, glancing.

"You've seen a lot of wings, then?"

The woman cocked her head at Reign's reply, confusion creasing across her face.

"The demon stalks these streets, child. A Vrae that hunts for blue blood. Good Kinnari have gone missing."

This isn't a usual casual conversation with a stranger.

"Where am I?" Reign asked, her voice barely audible.

"Mytholm."

That doesn't mean anything to me at all.

"Were you talking about me, Sable?" A man's voice came from behind.

Reign watched boots emerge, kicking dirt up.

The busy street stilled and seemed to watch as someone far too familiar approached with a cocky grin that said everything.

Everyone around belonged to him.

The man nodded to Reign and gave her a wink, his long blonde hair pulled into a ponytail.

"How do you know my name?" Sable, the middle-aged woman, asked, stepping back, exposing Reign fully.

She watched as the man's eyes turned red and realized who it was. It was the very Vrae who'd torn her apart when she tried to save Hadley—then later sat with her, drinking Roksana's homemade limoncello.

Saul.

"It's time for my feed. I was told that you would be my volunteer."

"Don't you have halflings in the other realm to feast on? Can't you leave us alone?" Sable said, though there was no real bite or courage. Reign only heard defeat, the last of Sabel's resistance long gone.

Kinnari wings spread from Sable's back as she turned to flee, but Saul was faster. The Vrae always were. He leapt onto her, fangs sinking fluidly into her neck.

Sable screamed, then faded as Saul audibly gulped.

The street emptied, and only the three of them remained.

Saul released after thirty seconds and moaned in satisfaction.

Reign froze. Her throat tightened. Her senses overloaded, and her control snapped.

Reign stared at the streak of blue blood seeping into Sable's dress.

"Want a taste?" Saul smiled at her, wiping his mouth. "Look at you, little monster. How did we make one of you?"

"Completely slaughtering a Kinnari, at least that's my guess," Reign said, her voice detached, like she was watching herself from far away. The longer she stood still, the less control she had. The sudden surges of anger and the homicidal thoughts clicked into place.

Reign felt her teeth elongate, felt her mouth slide open in an unnatural way to accommodate them. Oily, rubber-like skin ran down to her fingertips, replacing hers. She couldn't hold back. She was gone.

She dove at the middle-aged woman, who was whimpering on her feet, as Saul held her in place by the neck.

"Let's test that theory, shall we?"

Reign wasn't asking for his permission, but the encouragement was satisfying. She opened her mouth, considering how good it felt to extend it, how natural it all was.

There had been too much noise, too many distractions. Kinnari, humans, and creatures all added to her guilt and responsibilities—no wonder she'd never noticed.

Those worries were still there, buried beneath her skin, behind the anger, the thirst.

Gods damn. She was so, so thirsty.

Fuck it.

Her teeth sank into flesh.

"Hey, watch it," Saul said, his fingers brushing Reign's bite. "You little bitch."

The blood was sticky. The flavor profile that coated the inside of her mouth made her freeze for just a second—she almost gagged.

It tasted like dirty pennies, dusty and metallic. It felt like aluminum scraping her enamel, pulling and stripping.

What the hell are you doing?

She loosened her jaw, prepared to let go. But her mouth was full. And when she swallowed, everything changed.

There was no loose trickle down the back of her throat, but instead a waterfall of warmth, a gentle hug, an invitation to the body she now had, a love song telling her: you are not weak.

She was no child.

She was Gods damn terrifying.

What had tasted like rot now melted on her tongue—like fatty steak, seasoned, paired with ancient wine.

Secrets like the one of what her body craved.

Reign's loosened jaw reversed, and the warm body underneath became something she wanted to climb into, wear like a skin— warmth and power wrapped around her like a promise.

Her body whispered, *this is who you are. Let go.*

She let go only to take a breath, gasping from how fiercely she drank. A smile, feral and wide, broke across her blood-slicked mouth.

"Careful," Saul said, "you're going to push me past my limits of self-control."

She didn't listen.

She didn't even hear him. Reign went back in, bit down, and tore.

"Blast it. I suppose we are simply pressing onward, then," Saul said before chomping down on Sable's head. Her body stayed rigid far too long.

Until Reign bit her right leg—and it came off in her mouth.

"We make a morbid pair, do we not?" Saul kept making his little comments.

Reign chewed, her mind screamed to gag. Her body rejoiced.

It was a euphoria unlike any high she'd known.

They kept going until little was left—shreds of skin, bone, hair, and blood soaked into dirt.

"That was me once," Reign choked out through a ragged breath, her stomach growling in sync with the violence she had just unleashed. "And you stood over me, my blood on your chin."

"That scarcely makes sense to me, yet I shall comply and perform my part as required."

"This romantic past-century prose you use doesn't do it for me."

"Do... it? My, you are a spirited little creature. From this moment, you shall be my daughter. We shall wreak much havoc together, and I daresay it will be most satisfying."

Reign ignored him, eyes locked on Sables's remains as they went from still to twitching.

"Holy shit—" She laughed and shook her head, watching as the bones shifted—growing. They were inching toward each other. She counted her breaths, getting up to fourteen before a pinky bone clicked into the curve of a forming hand.

Saul looked at her as if she were crazy.

"Are you responsible for this? Might this be some manner of Kinnari power at play?"

"Shut up, Saul," Reign said, her eyes stretched wide, almost bursting.

Saul's mouth snapped shut at the command as Reign's skin turned back to the familiar color of her natural-born body. Her teeth were smaller, blunter. She barely felt it. Her focus was on the other transformation—the one that was happening on the ground.

She watched the Kinnari body come back together.

She watched what her own body had once gone through.

"I wondered when I might be seeing you here," a young boy's voice said behind Reign. Saul's face paled. He took several steps back.

"I thought we agreed not to kill Kinnari, Saul," Tristan said, hands in his slacks, sporting a white button-up shirt and a gray vest. Reign was surprised by how well he fit in here—how calm and clean he looked without the guilt their kind had buried in him.

"I suppose this means... " Reign trailed off, her eyes meeting his.

Tristan nodded, saying nothing, everything, at once.

Saul, incredibly unnerved by Tristan's presence, stood quiet and still.

"He ripped me apart, too, you know. He was one of them, the original Vrae pack," Tristan said.

"You're never one for casual conversation?" Reign blinked.

"We can talk about the weather if you prefer. I think that a body can recover more quickly in cold temperatures. Less time to cook."

Reign frowned. "Have you ever—"

"Eaten a Kinnari before? No, no, your presence in this timeline makes you the first."

"The first?"

"To tear a Kinnari apart, not counting myself. Before now, it was just samples, sips from volunteers. Not something I liked, but it kept me hidden—kept me from losing myself. Saul, on the other hand, prefers. .. indulgence."

"The farm in Waihema is barely enough to satisfy anymore," Saul grumbled.

"He means thin," Tristan clarified. "Amis is doing what he can."

"Did he know?" Reign asked.

Tristan shook his head. "No, Amis's heart is in the right place. His methods? I can see why those would be questionable."

Reign knew everything she needed to know. And the rest of Sable was coming together before her eyes.

A child lay in the dirt and dried blue blood, her skin soft, perfect.

"Saul, get this one something to wear," Tristan commanded.

"I knew I felt different," Reign said. "I knew it wasn't just that I was a child, but it took me so long, Tristan, to figure it out. It doesn't seem real. Is this one of your dreams?"

Tristan shook his head and shrugged.

"I think, Reign, something was just set in motion. Time seems to be a loop."

Sable's eyes fluttered open.

Red.

She sat up, and Saul came running back, draping a blanket on top of her. Sable clutched it and got to her feet, the purple woven fabric draping around her. She tied the top of it together, forming a hands-free dress of sorts.

"Did you enjoy the taste of me?" Sable asked Reign.

The candor and bluntness of the question, spoken in such a soft, childlike voice, stunned her.

"Yes."

There was no point in lying.

"Did you feel bad about it?" Sable pressed.

Reign's lips twisted. She hadn't fully processed, but guilt wasn't there.

"No."

Sable nodded and then began to look around. She sucked in a breath as another Kinnari, far in the distance, snuck between buildings.

"Good." She replied as she took off—a blur of blanket, her speed unnatural.

Screams echoed, followed by the thud of a body collapsing. Reign turned her head at the sounds of flesh ripping.

"That's going to be a problem," Tristan said.

"What do we do?" Reign asked.

"We do not do anything. You must leave here. Vrae or Kinnari, you are needed elsewhere."

"She just went into one of the buildings," Saul said, referring to Sable. More distant screams haunted the air. Reign imagined more Kinnari on the ground—dead, yet revitalizing.

"This will be a massacre," Reign said, breath catching. "We need to do something."

"Fly away, Reign. Fly away fast. I need you somewhere else. Don't get stuck here. This is my city—the discarded Kinnari of Arryn's past. Creations he hid from you, from everyone."

Tristan began walking away from her as he said those last words.

"Saul," she heard him say, "let's see if we can contain this."

What if they can't?

"Reign," Tristan yelled back at her. "Why are you still here?"

It was a good enough question. She'd just caused so much damage; a weapon, perfectly placed.

Reign's eyes flared, a flash of red as the adrenaline surged.

She'd never be anything useful again, never anything good.

She wasn't upset about that, though.

Why should biology make her feel shame?

And that blood, that blood felt so good.

Reign took off, her body thriving in the air, a strange combination of Kinnari and Vrae. Now that she knew—now that she understood—she supposed she should go home and warn Arryn.

Maybe he had a solution.

He certainly had enough secrets.

She flew fast, blasting through the sky until she vanished.

The town was below her, but now it was night.

No, this isn't right.

Zipping back and forth across the sky, Reign kept jumping, searching for her timeline. Colors painted the sky as she slipped through realms—some cities that she'd never seen.

Finally, she looked down and saw a world that she knew well.

A world she hadn't been sure she'd ever see again.

Reign hovered above it, watching Grant come home to his garage, a look of worry on his face.

She was still in the past. That much was clear.

There were no signs of devastation or an apocalypse.

She wondered if she waited long enough, would she see herself, too?

A full-bodied, adult Reign. Pure Kinnari.

You cannot dwell on the past. Not when you just created a new future.

Reign flew away, leaving pieces of her heart behind.

She missed her townhouse. She missed the life she had built—the one that was hers, not commanded.

It was once real.

A blast of speed, and she jumped again.

This time, she found her mark.

33

Amis | Mytholm | Present Day

The fog had cleared now.

The clock tower's chimes had faded.

Amis stood clutching Ahora—shaking, barely breathing. Noah, still strapped into Amis's jacket, wasn't so quiet.

"Monster!" Noah yelled, pointing at the group before them.

Funny how the youngest could see truth more clearly than most. Even in their human forms, he knew what they were.

Beneath his feet lay the brick path, raised several inches higher than the pathways that led to the building doors. The color was a burned crimson, the same as the buildings, uniform in shape and size. The only real color that was different was the clock tower. The brick was white; it emulated the fog now, Amis realized.

The time still read a few minutes before midnight. It hadn't changed.

"Amis," Salome whimpered, "what do I do?"

Amis didn't know. Guilt swelled in his throat, making it hard to look at them. He didn't want to move, to signal the start of a mass feeding frenzy.

Why wasn't his balance a more powerful tool against creatures like these?

All he could feel was the war of balance inside him, urging him to reach out and push Noah's monsters away. That wouldn't work, of course. They were outnumbered, no matter how small those monsters were.

Salome stood there several feet ahead. A Vrae had backed her against one of those identical brick buildings with one hand on her neck and the other around her waist. Amis could barely see its features—Salome's wings blocked most of his view. The eyes glowed. The lips parted in a full-toothed smile.

Luca was also there, trapped as well. Three other Vrae stood over him while he sat on the ground, his head buried against his knees drawn tightly to his chest. Amis could only see the top of his head, his hair. His dark wings hung wilted, fallen by his sides.

This was defeat. Amis knew it well.

The Vrae around him were nearly giggling, snapping their jaws, teeth extending to full length in half-transformation before snapping back to dull human forms, narrow mouths.

Amis knew the look that flickered in their faces. The same look that the Vrae that surrounded Sheng had before they would feed off of him in that Sacramento mansion. A look of hunger, of desire. A pulsing need to be wicked—to feed off the blood that they were created to drink.

It was the look of a creature deprived, reunited with its purpose.

There would be no chance of a truce here. Amis was no fool.

He wasn't even sure if these Vrae would know Sheng—or Arryn. This was an entirely different world, and they were child-sized. Amis could fly up, right now, and save the two bodies clinging to him—leaving Salome and Luca, just like he had left Reign.

Reign.

A flicker of recognition crossed his face.

"How old are you?" Amis asked, his eyes locking with the one pair peeking out from Salome's wings. It was female, and her chin barely cleared Salome's shoulder. She was a perfect, terrifying doll. Undoubtedly, she was a child.

The doll didn't respond at first. Instead, her feline smile made Amis tighten his hold on Ahora, pulling her even more protectively into him—as if he could pull her any closer.

He could feel the girl flinch. His grip had gone too far.

There would be time for apologies later, to soothe bruises.

At least, he planned on it. He planned on getting out of here. Amis was arguably the most qualified to deal with Vrae.

He reminded himself of that as silence thickened between them after his question—his words lingering like pollution, thick with weakness, soaked in fear.

The Vrae lifted her hands off Salome and left them in the air, fingers dancing. Salome's breath hitched. She let out a sob.

She didn't understand the rules.

Neither did Amis.

"Are you asking about my body or my mind?" the Vrae asked. Her voice was high-pitched, but the tone held no delicacy—only strength.

Salome screamed and sprinted the ten feet between them, arms outstretched, tears streaming down her jawline. The Vrae didn't move an inch—statuesque, ancient, eerily amused. The slight uptick of all their lips confirmed to Amis that they knew they had the upper hand.

"Such pretty wings," the little girl Vrae said, stepping forward. Her black boot hit the ground hard—yet made no sound.

Only now did Amis understand why he hadn't heard them before. Their steps were as light as ballerinas on thin ice, hunters masked by silence while he was blinded by fog.

"I keep my wings tucked away. All of us do. Since the extinction, there's no reason to fly, nothing in the air to chase." She bit the air. "I wonder what it would feel like to let them break the skin again. Do you bleed when you pull them in and out? Is it blue blood? I imagine that it is."

Salome slammed into his leg, nearly knocking him over.

"You lived in the mortal realm?" the blonde Vrae continued, speaking for the group. "All the others are gone, in a way."

"You have a lot of questions for someone who won't answer mine," Amis replied.

The Vrae's smile faded. Her lips pressed into a thin line. He wasn't sure which expression made his heart beat falter more.

He swallowed.

"Do we bite the wings?" she asked, staring at Amis but clearly talking to the other five child-like Vrae, who had varying levels of daggered teeth—some partially transformed, ready for their feast, a slaughter on the edge of beginning.

"It's been so long, I think I've forgotten."

"Let me go," Luca said, raising his head. "You are scaring my friends."

So tough, so broken. Luca was like a porcelain doll, cracked and tossed, glued back together by his own trembling hands.

Amis knew that the Vrae would attack at any second, and taking flight might not help—not after what the blonde had said.

"You were once Kinnari?"

The blonde smiled again.

"I haven't heard that word in so long," she whispered, dazed. "My body was tall, my hips were full, my chest curved. I lived in the clouds with the others until the day I was torn apart by something made for this realm. Something vicious, no bigger than I am now. Something from another time.

She attracted him, and then he encouraged her. Him with long blonde hair, more yellow than mine. He called himself Saul, I believe.

I haven't seen that Vrae in hundreds of years. Once the blood stopped running blue, he never came back."

Her eyes went vacant.

"Go," Noah whispered. Amis hoped only he had heard.

"How many of you were there?" Amis asked, taking a step back.

He was ready—ready to leave Luca. He might have to for the others to survive.

This wouldn't be a gentle bite, not like the blood donation

schemes he'd endured before. He would willingly offer again if it meant that all of Waihema could get out alive.

But they had that pinch of magic in their blood. They'd been bred for it—like baby calves suddenly on the table as veal.

"Are you ready?" Amis asked Salome, his voice low, but he knew Vrae. They could hear him as clearly as a scream.

Amis let his wings go long and locked eyes with Luca—apology in one gaze, understanding in the other.

"Uh-uh," the blonde Vrae said, lifting her index finger, moving it left and right.

"You don't understand what it's like barely being sustained, gagging on rodent blood and magical filth trickling down your throat."

She giggled, then her mouth snapped back into that thin, straight line.

"I'm sorry. I'm just so excited," she said—too monotone for comfort. "It looks like the rest of us are as well."

She raised her hands and flicked her fingers toward the tops of the brick buildings that surrounded them.

Amis couldn't help but glance up, tracking her gaze, drawn to the source of her widened smile.

From balconies and rooftops, Amis saw more bodies lining up, watching with eyes so red. At first, he counted twenty. Then more followed, coming through doors—flooding the streets.

They had found the city of children.

But even in Myrilosis, their true nature had stayed hidden.

Amis didn't believe for a second that the Marthrend would have sent them here if they'd known blood-drinking demons would welcome them so warmly, with open mouths.

There were hundreds of them, and now all Amis could think of was to stall.

"All of them were once Kinnari?" he asked.

The blonde nodded, and she opened her jaw a full one hundred and eighty degrees. Large, dagger-like teeth took shape and protruded from her mouth.

"I'd love to know what to call you—what to call the one who is about to rip open our flesh."

The blonde tilted her head, considering. Amis's wings tensed—he found the nerve to take off just as she spoke.

"Sable." Her tongue shot through the slight separation of her front daggered teeth.

Amis shot into the air; his ascent was sluggish under the weight of too many bodies. Noah clung behind, watching them struggle.

Fly, Salome. Please fly.

The girl was still holding onto his leg. They weren't more than ten feet in the air when rubber-like Vrae bodies leapt onto Luca, swallowing him beneath a swarm.

Sable just stared at Amis, a flicker of challenge—possibly amusement—in her arched brow.

Amis tried to look away, to break their eye contact, to focus on saving them all, but he couldn't.

He wasn't a savior. He was balance—nothing more, nothing less. Sable would certainly know they wouldn't get far.

"Luca!" Noah screamed, trying to throw himself down—but he was strapped too tightly to Amis's back.

Sable opened her mouth fully, the lines of her lips expanding, as if her face was being cut before him from ear to ear as she bared those Vrae daggered fangs, ones that gleamed as Luca screamed.

No, the screaming wasn't Luca. It was Sable.

With her teeth bared and vicious, Amis could see the pain painted across her face, the agony that lay hidden under a primal brutality, a promise of demise. He couldn't hear the cracking of her bones, but he could imagine it. He had been there before, as the Vrae was nearly bent over, the ends of her blonde hair tinted red from the blood that trailed from her back as her wings sprouted.

And when they did, she laughed, and the frenzy of Vrae bodies tensed, stilled. The only thing Amis could hear was his own heartbeat, thudding, the vibrations of his own wings straining just slightly under the weight of everyone he carried.

Why are you stopping? Go. Go.

GO.

He screamed at himself, but his body was as still as the Vrae below him, and that was because of something so stupid, so idiotic, that he never would have relied on if this were even a year ago.

Because of hope.

Because beneath those Vrae—those bodies slowly rising to their feet, heads turning toward someone Amis cared about, maybe even loved—was a threat he could no longer ignore.

Loved was maybe too strong a word.

But he hoped, he hoped so Gods damn hard, that these kids would keep defying death, that whatever destiny Karmakara had weaved for that teenage boy, wasn't one so sad, wasn't one where if he chose wrong, he chose to cease his life.

Amis's wings subconsciously worked a little less, as they barely hovered above the ground now, Salome's feet touching back down to the earth as her body trembled, as she squeezed his leg so Gods damn tight that it was actively falling asleep, numbing.

"I've never met one of these halflings before," Sable said, her smile twisted. "I wonder . . ."

"Wonder what?" one of the fully transformed little Vraes asked her.

"When we were killed with Vrae venom in our veins, when we were once Kinnari, we turned into what we are now. If a halfling dies, will it share the same fate? It's been a while since we've had so much excitement," she said.

They are very mortal.

"It's probably pretty dull, all of you bloodthirsty monsters, having no one to kill," Amis said, no longer hovering and very much in danger.

She liked to talk. He could tell. Maybe she could talk longer; maybe he could save Luca after all. If there was a Luca still there to save.

His heart dropped when enough Vrae had stood up from the pile. He didn't hear sobs or screams for help. He could see blue blood, specks of it splattered. Though the boy was strong, Amis's hope shattered, and he could feel his chest cave in.

The grieving came on so fast.

"Luca," Salome yelled, "get over here now."

A groan, there was a groan, and a bloodied hand that shot up to the air as the Vrae who stood circled the boy seemed to jump at his movement.

Not dead yet. That's my boy.

Sable cleared her throat. "I don't know if we'd kill you all yet. You can be kept for a few days before that blood turns cold."

"Let these kids walk away. It's my blood that's pure. I am not a half-breed."

"No, you aren't, are you?" Sable's eyes gleamed with an expression that Amis didn't quite understand.

"I've done this before. I've been farmed before. Just let that boy get up. Let him heal."

"Do I look like someone who makes deals?" Sable asked.

"You look like someone who's smart. One immortal Kinnari will keep going. My blood will not go cold, not like theirs."

"It's an adorable proposition," Sable cooed.

"Adorable isn't a word people usually pin on me," Amis smirked.

"It's adorable because you think there's a choice to be made. When really, we will just have you all."

Sable jumped into the air, her skin slickening into oily black. She flapped her wings, sloppy and rushed, the push and pull urgent but untrained.

It didn't matter, though—as seconds passed, her body hovered inches above them, her mouth wide open, diving for his head.

She meant to dislodge it—the Vrae signature move.

With Salome still on his heels and no ability to go up, Amis tried to shuffle but wasn't fast enough to course correct.

He looked into those daggered teeth that now hovered a foot away from him.

"Hold on," he yelled, throwing himself forward, expecting impact.

But then a flash—something hit Sable midair, intercepting her path.

Amis's skin skidded over emerald mud, protected by the strange slick coat the Marthrend had given them.

He'd need to go back to Emerald's Peak later and kiss their weird tentacled feet for sparing his face.

It didn't protect him, however, from the smack of his skull on the hard ground, a crack loud enough for Salome to hear.

He heard her cries, Noah's too. Noah always cried.

"Amis, Amis, there's so much blood," she said.

He flipped over despite the pounding in his brain and saw exactly what he feared: a pool forming beneath his head.

No time to care about his wounds. They had to run.

The large group of bloodthirsty Vrae was inching slowly towards him.

He had to get Salome out.

He had to get the toddler out.

He wanted to get Luca out.

You can do this.

There was another flash in the air, and Sable landed in front of him, her wings spreading out and showing a different shade of brown than he remembered. Her claws flexing, her stance dominant as she faced the Vrae that stared at Amis and the blood trickling onto the ground. It almost looked like she was suddenly defending them.

Sable's head turned, looking back at Amis and the Waihema children who clung to him. Her red eyes were different now, the expression still filled with a certain kind of bloodlust, but it was no longer directed at him.

That's not Sable.

The Vrae lunged toward the hoard, and Amis watched as three heads hit the ground, detached from their bodies, blood running free in small streams following the cracks in the pavement.

Amis stared, his mouth open, though that could have been from the brain damage.

The Vrae stopped attacking and then began to change; its skin turned the color of wheat, its hair grew long, the darkest of browns, and was silky and beautiful.

"You will all go back to what you were doing before the fog cleared," the Vrae said.

Amis knew that voice.

One by one, they locked eyes with the commander.

And then, as if obeying some ancient, silent code, the horde of Vrae turned and dispersed—slipping back into the doorways and houses they'd crawled from, vanishing like a bad dream at sunrise.

Luca came into view.

His body was mangled—limbs twisted, bones broken, blood smeared across the mud-caked skin of his chest and arms. His eyes were shut, but his chest ... it moved. Barely, but it moved.

Rising. Falling. Rising again.

A single tear slipped down Amis's cheek—drawn not from grief, but from the desperate, foolish thing still clinging to life inside him.

"They need to stop doing that," he muttered, sniffling as he shook his head. The pain in his skull was dulling. He'd be able to sit up soon.

"Stop doing what?" Salome asked as she peeled Noah from the back of his jacket. The poor kid had been squished, jostled, flung like a rag, but now he whimpered and kicked softly in her arms—enough to make Amis smile.

He'd live.

"Are you going to get up off the ground, or are you pretty comfortable?" That familiar voice, that voice that saved them, asked.

Amis looked up as small, bare feet padded toward them, stopping close.

"You have no idea how relieved I am to be back in the right timeline," Reign said.

34

Hadley | Myrilosis

Hadley rolled up and off the grass. The loose green clippings stuck to her, lower body still wet from sweat and the mix of what they'd shared. She stood, her legs betraying her, buckling. She couldn't feel the weakness in her muscles. Hadley felt only numbness.

"Whoa there, we just did a lot," Sheng laughed, jumping up to help her.

But when his hands reached out and steadied her, she didn't feel them either.

Any sensation was already gone completely, a ghost guiding her.

Where are we?

Hadley looked around—still in an uninhabited forest mixed with grassy plains. Kismet had led her here. The wyvern knew Hadley better than she knew herself, as if she were the fire that once lived in her chest.

"What are you doing? What do you need?" Sheng asked, still

charged from their time together. His smile was large and would have been infectious in another life.

He was so happy.

"I can't remember," she said. "I can't remember why I came here."

"Was it because you found me so distracting?" he said. "I imagine I know why you're here. It's the reason I chose to wait for you."

"You do?"

"You're trying to find your way back."

"Back?"

"Back home. This would be the best path if I were trying to find a portal without risk of running into someone you might know. Plus, you know, you're basically already there. Just step through the portal."

Hadley blinked at him, suddenly so empty.

Her shadow self came into view, shifting between darkness and light, unsure of which form to take. The murderous, mischievous version of her unapologetically danced around Sheng, putting a finger up to him while shaking her hips and thrusting her pelvis, puckering her lips—a promise of seduction laced with death.

"I could be blinded by sex, but is there a possibility that you're acting weird?" Sheng chuckled and then frowned when Hadley turned her face away.

He has something useful—he knows you.

That was slipping too fast. Everything was fading fast.

The fire, the stars, the step she took — the invitation she accepted.

Ayurveda understood her. The Goddess knew her soul better than Hadley did.

Even after it all, she was still there.

Hadley felt it now—every ounce of her humanity draining. There was no room for vengeance, for anger, for lingering too long on moments. There was only the to-do list.

And that's what she would focus on right now, before it was too late.

She would let Sheng help.

"Take me there," she said to him.

Sheng nodded, reaching out his hand. She just stared at it, her shadow self doing everything to pull Hadley's attention, to get her to nod, to give her permission.

Hadley shook her head. He would live today.

"Back to no touching, then?" Sheng raised his eyebrows. "Your games keep me on my toes. I will give you that."

Sheng moved ahead, then turned when she didn't follow.

"You should come with me," he said, voice raised.

Hadley moved, stepping on the yellow rose on the ground. Once she reached him, he held out his hand, stopping her mid-step.

"That's the wrong way," he said, pointing towards the sky. "We will want to go up. Normally, I get a running start, but I figured since you have wings, I can jump, and you can make up the difference."

Hadley stared, expressionless. Sheng sighed and forced his arm under hers, linking them together.

"Ready?" he asked.

Without waiting, he bent his knees. His skin texture changed, the deep black color of a Vrae, the literal night, pulling her up as he hurled himself into the air—ten, then fifteen feet.

Hadley could feel the loss in their trajectory, the pull of gravity slowing them down. It made her eyes brighten. Some life was still there in her.

Did she want it? She didn't know.

Translucent wings beat back and forth, a rainbow-glinting in the sun. Sheng weighed heavily on her arm.

Hadley soared, bringing them up higher. She had so much power; she moved so fast, her wings fluttering at a hummingbird's speed.

Crash.

They hit a large round table, splintering under their weight.

"I should have warned you about that," Sheng said, hissing, nursing his head after tumbling a few feet away from her.

Hadley didn't feel the crash. Physical pain didn't exist. Her time was nearly up.

Memories of Sheng, the Kinnari, and her mother would all be gone.

All the bad. All the good.

But it's what you wanted.

Hadley looked around. The other end of the portal had shot her into a place that seemed familiar but was a different world—tragic opulence. A foyer once grand. A marble floor cracked and chipped. Walls riddled with holes.

She looked up to see a pentagram in the ceiling, a broken chandelier dangling through it.

"We put that chandelier in so we wouldn't fall up," Sheng said, getting to his feet. "Are you okay?"

This was Sheng's home. The memories crept in.

"We are back in your realm," he said. "I don't know where you consider home, but I can help you find it. Do you know how to get there from here?"

She didn't remember. She just knew it wasn't here.

Sheng sighed and held his hand out to her, helping her up to her feet.

"I've got a garage filled with vehicles on the other side of the back-yard," he said. "Let's go."

Hadley moved, bare feet stepping over plaster, broken vases, and fake plants. Her eyes fluttered. Suddenly, she needed to close them.

"Are you okay?" Sheng asked, reaching his hand out towards her. "Don't be scared. I'm pretty sure we are alone."

She wasn't scared. She couldn't remember how to be.

Hadley took his hand. Her steps were fluid and strong despite how she felt inside. She never equated emptiness with weakness— but apparently, the two looked similar from the outside.

"You look cold," Sheng said, leading her out of the foyer and down a familiar hallway.

She'd once walked down this hallway in uncomfortable heels that Reign had convinced her to wear. She wore a dress that was elegant and sexy. That dress played a part in her downfall.

"I'm not cold," she replied, walking so silently she wasn't even sure she was really there. She was becoming her shadow, wondering if anyone would see her soon—or if she'd disappear entirely.

Photos had fallen from walls. She walked on glass, leaving blue, shiny footprints. She didn't wince.

The hallway opened up into the kitchen, where she had first shared a sandwich with the Vrae that led her.

Light poured through dusty windows. Pots and pans littered the floor. The fridge was open—empty except for spoiled milk and rotting vegetables. The power was long gone.

"It's okay," Sheng said carefully. "We can rebuild."

She didn't care, but her face must've said she did. She touched her cheeks, her lips—trying to feel something.

She failed.

"You're bleeding," Sheng said. "As much as I love the smell of your blood, we should keep you uninjured. Here, I can carry you."

"No," Hadley said, long and slow. "No touching."

"There it is." Sheng shook his head. "We will go out the back door," he said, pointing to the white French doors leading out.

She nodded, took a step, then froze.

Sheng's face changed from concern to rage. She stared at an animal protecting what was his. His teeth were bared, his gaze fixed on the floor.

He listened.

He hushed her, but it was already silent.

"Someone's here," he said, cocking his head. A smile curled, feral.

Hadley saw the ruthlessness in his clouded eyes. A red smoke consumed the blackness.

Still as a statue, Sheng waited.

An explosion of glass filled the room.

Hadley watched in slow motion as a bullet came through the French doors, its shooter on the opposite side.

Her shadow self danced between the shards. Her face perfectly matched Sheng's as she sashayed and twirled while in her darkness.

The bullet ripped through Sheng's skin, burying itself in his back.

A low growl rumbled from his chest.

"Get the fuck outta my house," a man yelled through the shattered door. "Ah, you can stay," he added, eyeing Hadley.

The man wore a trash bag over a sweatshirt. A cowboy hat covered his eyes.

"This isn't your house," Hadley said, numb.

"Oh, no?" He laughed—a hoarse, unpleasant sound. His chapped lips cracked with the motion, revealing rotting teeth that confirmed what his stare already promised: wicked intent.

"This is his house," Hadley nodded to Sheng.

Why are we here?

"He seems pretty dead to me," the man said, pistol spinning.

"He's still standing," Hadley said.

"Do you know how many people my crew and I had to kill to claim this house?" He chuckled. "I'm not going to let one little man ruin that for me—or for you."

"For me?" She breathed, barely hanging on to the conversation.

"Of course. You'll stay here. I'll treat you real well. Might even find a diamond for that naked finger."

Hadley stepped toward Sheng. His eyes snapped open.

"I was trapped in this house once before," she said. "I will not be trapped in this house again."

Sheng frowned.

"We'll see about that," the man said, raising the gun again. He pulled the trigger.

The bullet hit the back of Sheng's head.

35

—————

Precession | Outside of Ebonspire

"You blacked out," Djoser said to Arryn. Arryn looked unimpressed, as if this news was barely worth acknowledging.

"Did I fall out of space? Why am I so sore?" Arryn demanded.

"Hey, asshole," Djoser snapped. "I think I deserve a couple of glasses of that liquor you made at the temple after everything I just did for you."

Arryn snapped his fingers and massaged the spot between his eyes with his other hand, as a small table appeared with five clear, short glasses filled with amber liquid.

Djoser grimaced, likely wishing Arryn hadn't done something nice at all. They had a funny way of showing appreciation.

"I spun us down from space until we reached gravity," Djoser said, picking up a glass and shooting it back. His lips smacked, satisfied.

"Spun?"

"Literally. The moment I used my wings to propel us back down, I lost control, and we spun around each other. You can inspect the inside of my helmet if you need proof." Djoser motioned to the discarded suits in the snow before picking up another glass and drinking it as well.

"I think there was one for each of us," Roksana scoffed.

"I don't believe I've ever seen your sister drink," Djoser said, his confidence somehow endearing as he raised the glass towards Precession, not taking her slight frown personally.

"He's an asshole too." Roksana put her hand on Precession's shoulder, trying to provide solace of some kind.

"I want to live in peace again," Precession said, letting her head roll back on her shoulders.

"Why are you saying this?" Roksana asked, brow furrowed.

Oh, how lovely her sister was. How absolutely perfect. She wanted her to live in peace, too.

Precession looked around. The skies were slightly clearer, the gray clouds less depressing than before Arryn and Djoser had ascended to that infant moon. Arryn began to wake up, the most beautiful, peaceful creature hovering over him, healing him, loving him. It reminded her of another woman who had once held that place. Life was just a continuation of cycles.

Another apocalypse. Another forgotten life.

It was beautiful, in a way—being forgotten. Everyone you'd ever known or loved is now in the same place: lost together. Your lives, your loves, a secret the universe kept as your atoms were recycled into new secrets, new life.

Precession knew she was forgotten already. She hummed like a frequency no one could hear. She wanted, hoped, dreamed—to her own detriment. She clung to relationships as if they were as important as the moon. Only then did she feel remembered.

Maybe being remembered meant nothing at all.

"To want is a dangerous line," Precession finally said aloud. "And maybe, today, I feel dangerous."

Roksana smiled, just the right corner of her mouth lifting. "The moon is heavier now, and so is your heart."

Precession nodded. It made sense, this sudden sorrow.

"What if it never passes?" she asked.

"Can I help?" Celestine asked, rising from the ground. Arryn tensed as her body left his, but didn't move or even look at her. "Let me help," Celestine said, large tears welling in the corners of her eyes. She raised a finger to one, letting the wetness roll over her fingertip, and offered it to Precession.

Precession just stared. Her heart was too heavy to think. Her head filled with lead, her body unsure if it could support it.

"I'll take care of you," Celestine whispered, pressing her finger to Precession's lips, tracing the lower, then upper. Precession closed her eyes, breathing in salt and rose. Her knees buckled as something in that tear penetrated her soul.

"I take care of her," Roksana's voice cut through.

"Does it feel better? Do you need more?" Celestine asked, ignoring the jealousy muddying the air.

"Don't give her more," Arryn interrupted, standing. "She doesn't feel the same way as us. You'll make her disappear inside herself entirely."

"You don't get to say things like that. You don't even know her," Roksana snapped.

Precession, as usual, observed. Everything felt normal and far away. She wasn't really there—but she was.

"Whatever these tears are, Arryn, maybe you should keep them for yourself," Roksana spat.

"She's my friend," Precession cooed like a baby. "Don't be rude to my friend."

Precession relaxed as arms wrapped around her.

"Thank you," Celestine said.

"Are you ready for more, Arryn?" Djoser asked.

"I can get him ready," Celestine said, nearly jumping with excitement.

"No," Arryn said, putting his hands out. "I don't need her."

Djoser blew out a raspberry, and Roksana threw her hands in the air.

Precession could almost hear their synchronized 'what the fucks'.

"You should rest, too," Precession said to Celestine.

"We don't get enough rest, do we? The females of the group," Roksana complained, staring daggers into Arryn's back.

"You would all be better off no longer talking," Arryn said. "Otherwise, I'm walking away. I can do one more round today."

"Can we just all admit that everyone sucks and move on?" Djoser shook his head, flexing his wings out but taking care to slam one more drink.

"I want to go," Precession whispered, but no one heard her, or they pretended not to.

Roksana looked at her over her shoulder and shook her head slightly, a warning just for her.

Arryn and Djoser wore freshly sealed spacesuits, their helmets airtight. The silver fabric mirrored the gray clouds and snow. It felt like the world was colorless except for Roksana's bright red hair.

"You had to tether us together before we flew up?" Djoser asked, his voice showing signs of that third glass of liquor.

Precession giggled—Djoser was right. The cord barely looked long enough for both to fly freely.

"I would have paid to watch this happen," Roksana said under her breath.

Djoser grabbed the second cord, the one that was long enough, humped in a large pile, to go up into space with them, keeping them grounded.

"What are you doing?" Arryn asked.

"Looking for the end, it's not attached to anything."

"I don't have the patience for this," Arryn said. Without a word, he pushed his wings back and was airborne, dragging Djoser behind him.

"Whaaaaat theeeee fuuuccccccccck," Djoser screamed, his voice trailing as they soared upward. He twisted and did a few somersaults, getting his balance back, and pulled the cord with a giant yank. Arryn looked like he'd run into a brick wall, his chest heaving out, but the rest of his body pulled back.

Precession could see the gleam of Djoser's teeth, satisfied, the only thing that wasn't reflecting gray, even from the inside of his helmet.

Celestine ran to the pile of cords, now disappearing fast, chasing the Kinnari as they vanished into the sky.

"Let me help you," Precession said, moving over a bit too quickly, her head pounding from the tension, from the other tether she held onto, one that no one could see.

"I've got it," Roksana stepped in front of her, holding her hand out. Precession steadied herself, holding her head in her hands. "Please take a seat. You are still adjusting."

"I've been adjusting my entire life, sister."

Celestine ignored them, dragging the cord toward the tree, tripping and grunting as it snaked around her ankles.

Roksana squeezed Precession's arm and sprinted after the cord, intercepting it before it could trip Celestine.

"I'll feed it through the back," Roksana said, letting the cord slide through her fingers as she followed Celestine. She reached the tree and tied it around a trunk, bracing with her boot and yanking hard.

Just in time, the rest of the cord snapped taut against the bark.

Celestine groaned as she fought against it, still holding the rope.

"It's easier when they send a cord down to us once they're already up there," she laughed. "This feels like an Olympic event."

Roksana walked over to help tie the rope off, making another knot and pulling it tight.

Precession watched, brushing back envy. Her powers could never help this way—only erupt or distract.

You have one purpose. Find peace within it.

Celestine and Roksana walked over, laughing like new best friends.

Precession smiled as they approached.

"How are you feeling? I can give you more," Celestine offered.

Precession shook her head. "I can't tell how it made me feel, but I would prefer not to amplify it."

Celestine's smile faltered. But she nodded.

"I think we should watch that cord," Precession said.

"It's knotted and tied tight. We made sure of it, sister," Roksana said. "I say we give them ten minutes and then the three of us get out of the snow."

"You have such strength," Celetine said to Roksana. "It's infectious."

"It literally is." Precession grinned, but her gaze drifted past them. She couldn't stop staring at the cord, wondering why it demanded her attention.

You should be up there.

"So, you seem like a smart girl," Roksana said, looking at Celestine.

"I can not imagine that is followed by anything nice." Celestine beamed at her.

Precession was beginning to see past Celestine's airiness—it was an illusion.

This was no fool—this was a woman with an agenda.

"I just can't believe this goody two-shoes act about healing Arryn. Why are you really with him? I can't imagine it's because of his winning personality."

"Well, he is hot," Celestine mused.

Roksana nearly choked.

"Looks like you agree."

Roksana collected herself, her brow furrowed. "I would rather fall off a cliff."

"He does look like those paintings of Roman Gods," Precession admitted. "As if their jawlines were sculpted after his."

"Can we agree, though, that a man's worth is more than how he looks?" Celestine smiled.

"Can you even call Arryn a man?" Roksana scoffed.

"What is he worth, then, Celestine?" Precession echoed, curious.

The conversation was a welcome distraction from the pressure bearing down on her.

The tether on her moon grew heavier. It had briefly vanished after Arryn's first flight earlier that day. Now, it felt like someone had her hair in their fist, pulling down, testing whether her neck could hold.

Her stomach turned, and bile rose in her throat. Instead, she closed her eyes and let the weight seep into her blood, her heartbeat, her breath.

"Even before the moon crumbled," Celestine began to answer Roksana, neither noticing Precession. She was used to being overlooked—flitting, odd, like a hummingbird that could never catch its breath. "There was strife here in Myrilosis, so much so that my home disbanded."

Precession listened, focusing on Celestine's voice.

"Where is your home? I'm guessing not where we found you then?" Roksana asked.

Celestine shook her head. "No, it's not far from here, actually, but there are many of us, many Phoenixes that live to heal. We live in a place called Phoenix Rest."

"A little on the nose there," Roksana laughed.

"It is a beautiful city. Many species live among us, many of whom have come to heal from various traumas, both physical and mental. Some even came to mend the traumas of their hearts. Those were always the hardest to heal."

"I would imagine that mental and heart are the same thing," Precession sang out.

"What is the easiest to heal, then?" Roksana asked. Precession kept her head back, her eyes closed, but she could feel someone moving closer towards her, the crunching snow right in front of her.

A soft wetness, unlike the seeping cold, touched her lips—guided by a gentle finger.

The weight that had been heavy on her neck loosened, but her dizziness immediately intensified. It was like solving pain with heavy drinking. The turning feeling in her stomach also pushed through, and she vomited all over Celestine's boots.

"I'm sorry," Precession spat, her voice coarse but still incredibly high-pitched, a tune carried by the air.

Celestine bent, unbothered by the mess, cradled Precession's head, and whispered soothing sounds.

Jealousy flared around Precession, souring the air. Roksana didn't like anyone else caring for her. She'd always known that—and didn't mind. Roksana was the only one who understood her confinement.

"I would say physical pain is the easiest to manage. Cuts, wounds, punctures in the neck," Celestine said, glancing at Roksana. "The hardest I've encountered so far has to be your sister. Her pain is all three;they are entangled within each other. You must have cared well for her, for her to function as she does."

That cut—just a little.

Precession lifted her head and looked at Roksana.

"She is my light when I see darkness," Precession said, smiling through it all.

Their eyes held more words than mouths ever could. Precession's heart swelled—hoping for chickens, for a home Roksana would tease her about with a male Kinnari—deep-skinned, long-haired—who could finally make her sister laugh.

Precession wanted Roksana to have that love so badly that she would consider letting go of her tether again if it meant that love could prevail.

If love was what you would call whatever it was between them.

There was a part of Precession that believed it was their magic that called them to each other. Maybe that was beautiful in its own way and should be honored in the same manner.

Roksana offered her hand, and Precession took it without hesitation. Her sister eyed the vomit on the ground and did everything she could to keep her feet as far away from it as possible.

Precession stood and instantly staggered as the world spun.

No, you're doing that. You are the rotation. You are the pull.

She needed that reminder when everything felt like it was slipping. She used to be so strong, so good at this. It was amazing how much strength she had lost.

"So your whole city's like one giant hospital?" Roksana said, steadying Precession.

"Maybe it is," Celetine said, beaming. "It's certainly an idyllic way to think about it."

"Why did you leave?" Roksana asked.

"Because of the punctures," Precession moaned, rolling her head.

"Are you not okay?" Roksana asked. "Is this different?"

Precession tried to shake her head no, but it required more effort than she had.

"Can I try again?" Celestine asked, plucking a tear from her left eye and holding it closer to Precession to inspect.

"Is it different?" Roksana snapped. "I don't think you made her feel any better."

"It's different. I shape it," Celestine said.

"You can change the healing. It's not universal," Precession marveled. "No wonder the Aetheri were so enamoured by you."

"If it were universal, it would be much easier," Celestine said, her dimples appearing, but her eyes did not match the call of her smile. She took the tear on her finger and rubbed it again on Precession's bottom lip.

"How does that feel?" the brown-eyed phoenix woman asked.

Precession didn't feel a change at first. While the first tear was instant, this one's effect was so gradual that she wondered if anything was happening at all.

"I don't feel much," Precession admitted, hoping the apology was conveyed enough in her voice.

"Perfect." Celestine beamed.

Roksana's glare said she was done. That's when the words clicked into place. She felt as if she'd let go again.

In a moment of inner panic, Precession checked and was relieved to find that the tether was still there. She was holding on tightly. There was no mishap, no slowing in the earth's rotation, no loose moons in the atmosphere.

"It's amazing," Precession said, looking at Celestine in bewilderment.

"You certainly sound more coherent," Celetine agreed.

"It worked? You feel good?" Roksana asked, not trusting, always questioning, always protecting.

Precession gave a slight nod before her eyes scanned the twisted trees again, something continually pulling her towards that cord.

"You know then," Celestine said, bringing her face right in front of Precession. "You know about the punctures, what they mean?"

"I'm not sure if there's any point in speaking like everything is a riddle," Roksana threw her hands up in the air, before they came to her hips.

"I know about the punctures as much as I know about that cord," Precession said, her head turning away, her eyes searching. "I know that something about those words settles deep into my soul, into my mind, and I cannot get them out of my head."

"So, it's not exactly seeing?"

"How could I see the future or the past, when Karmakara's web can change at any moment?" she mused.

"And the coherent side of Precession has left the building," Roksana said.

"No, it hasn't. Look at the cord," Procession said, unable to take her eyes off it.

Celestine and Roksana looked, then sighed and stared at their feet, waiting for something to happen.

"It's been ten minutes, let's go get warm," Roksana said.

"No," Precession insisted, "I have to go up there."

"You are not going up there." Roksana's brow furrowed. She understood how ridiculous it sounded.

"Trust, sister," Precession cooed like she was talking to a baby. "See? The cord, look—"

She pointed at the cord again, still unmoving, still unremarkable.

"Come on, let's go," Roksana said, taking her arm. "I've got you. I'll take care of you."

Celetine's eyes grew wide. "I have to go."

"So soon?" Roksana muttered under her breath.

"But Arryn is up there," Precession said.

"I know," Celestine said.

"No, you don't understand. Arryn is up there, but the cord is down here," she insisted.

She pointed once more at the trees, and the three of them watched as hundreds of feet of heavy metal threaded cord fell in a snake-like heap.

36

———————

Reign | Mytholm

"You're running away," Reign told herself, staring ahead in a daze.

Running away from the murder she had just committed.

There was no guilt, only relief.

Reign didn't expect to take on her new role as a monster—one born of nightmares, the kind that haunted dark hallways and half-open closet doors. She was stronger now, more certain of what she had become since her body regenerated on Sheng's bloodstained patio.

Those gulps of blood that graced her throat had given her peace. It had been a long time since she could say that she felt that way, felt powerful enough to be terrifying.

Reign's muscles spasmed, her wings twitching from the constant speed she had to maintain, jumping through time in search of the place that could hold the weight of all her memories. She was growing tired; her view changed from day to night, from sea to skyscrapers.

"Finally, I've gotten it right," she whispered, elation flickering through her anxiety as she looked down at the clock tower. She was back in Mytholm. Dirt roads were now paved with stone. Buildings were sturdier, modern, and less flammable.

How many times had her jumps led her to these children? She might've rolled her eyes—but this was a chance to fix things.

This time, she wouldn't just leave them, especially as she took in the scene below where death loomed for any Kinnari blood spilled.

Sable, the one she'd turned in a frenzy, hovered above Amis. The look in her features, the rigid way she held her body, told Reign all that she needed to know: Amis was about to lose his head.

Maybe I should let him.

Sable would try to kill them, too: The kids.

Look at the monster I've created. The one that I've become.

Reign lunged forward, faster than she ever had, praying.

She had seconds to decide, and she did. Her fate would not dictate who she was—not now, not ever. If there could be such a thing as an ethical murderer, she'd be the first.

Her body collided with Sable's in a brutal tangle of limbs. The scent of Kinnari blue blood filled her nose. Sable's teeth grazed Amis's head as Reign knocked her off course.

The two tumbled to the ground, every bone snapping in Reign's arms. She screamed, landing on top of Sable, face shredded raw, nose likely broken.

Reign stood up without using her arms. They were already healing, but it wasn't fast enough. She had transformed into a Vrae without noticing, her skin the texture of rubber.

I'm never going to get used to this.

She could use more time to heal, but she didn't have that luxury. Reign forced herself to act like the lethal creature that she was, motivated by the horde of childlike Vrae that marched on Amis and the last kids of Waihema.

Useless. Amis is actually pretty useless.

If she didn't get a chance to protect her goddaughter—now a grown woman—Reign would defend them instead. Using her wings to propel herself forward, Reign landed between Amis and the horde of sharp teeth, red eyes, and adorable dimples.

Reign turned over her shoulder and smiled, hoping to reassure the kids, whose gray face paint was cracking and flaking on their skin.

Salome, Luca, and Ahora didn't smile back.

"You don't look like you," Reign reminded herself.

There was, however, a flicker of recognition in Amis's eyes.

Amis knew who she was, despite the changes to her body, the bloodlust, the malice simmering under her skin.

He did hear you speak.

That had to be why it took Reign so long to understand how her body had changed after her own slaughter. She avoided people. The Amises of the world with their petty, persistent needs—needs that always made her see red.

So instead, Reign focused her life on control. She controlled her magic with such finesse that it had become an art form, slip-ups only existing when there was a physiological need for it, something pulling her in a certain direction.

Like this. Like telling Hadley to be mad.

Reign wanted to be mad *for* Hadley: her poor goddaughter, her poor best friend.

"You will all go back to what you were doing before the fog cleared." She cleared her throat, looking directly into the eyes of all the Vrae before her. The group, once primed for attack, relaxed. All of them turned, walking away while conversing with one another.

"We always have a pink sunset after the fog clears."

"I wonder if anyone's awake in the feeding room for a bite."

Weather and food: didn't matter the species, the small talk was always the same.

Amis stood there, staring at her, mumbling to the kids.

"Are you going to get up, or are you pretty comfortable? You have no idea how relieved I am to be back in the right timeline," Reign said.

Salome gripped Amis's legs tightly. He carried Ahora in his arms.

Amis opened his mouth to speak, but then shut it upon hearing footsteps echoing with a rhythm that reminded her of the old clock tower behind them.

"Your venom runs through them," Tristan's voice echoed down the street. Reign watched as a boy, Luca, lay on the ground, now exposed. The Vrae that had surrounded him had now returned to their homes.

"They wouldn't have attacked you even if you hadn't given the command, Regin."

Reign watched Amis set Ahora down. He removed his jacket, revealing an injured Noah.

"Is he okay?" she whispered, the rest of the world falling away as her stomach dropped. She rushed forward, unfastening Noah from Amis's back and cradling him tightly against her chest.

"Monster," she heard him whimper.

Reign smiled, a combination of relief and nerves softening her giggle.

"I don't know why I'm so tied to you, to Waihema," she whispered to the child in her own dainty arms, "but maybe I am finally ready to stop running away from it."

She had failed Allienna.

Deep down, she knew that her best friend had cut ties because of Arryn. She'd known how her friend was treated. They all knew.

And yet they did nothing. Even worse, they left her alone with him.

When Allienna visited, she'd asked if Reign had ever wanted Arryn—romantically, sexually. But that had never been the real question. What she truly wanted to know was where Reign's loyalty lay.

If Allienna left him ... if she had his child ... would Reign have kept her secret?

If she had answered differently, if she had given the unconditional friendship that her only real friend was begging for, how different would Hadley's upbringing have been? Reign wouldn't have failed as a godparent.

Maybe, though, she could make up for it here.

Maybe she didn't hate Amis.

No, no, that was silly. Of course she hated Amis. He was still the worst.

Reign felt the shift begin—her skin tingling with that static prickle, like fear brushing down her spine. The cave-black hue of emptiness and lost time receded, peeled away, and the warm tones of her Kinnari skin returned.

Human again. Kinnari again.

"I'm not a monster now, see?" She cooed to Noah.

"Wheyn!" Noah whimpered against her. "Dank you."

"He's getting so big, so heavy," she said, smiling over to Amis, who kept turning his head between her and Tristan.

"Am I turning into a Vrae, too? Or can someone explain this all to me?" he asked, his face twisted into a smile. The tug in his voice told Reign he was still scared behind the mask. He did drop his protectiveness, but it was obvious he hated seeing Noah in Reign's arms.

Salome tugged on Amis's wing. He grimaced.

"Luca."

Reign watched Amis's face darken and, without hesitation, marched across the nearly empty street to where a boy lay on the ground, his hand still in the air as if he didn't have the strength to bring it down.

His blood was blue, fresh, and still flowing. And Reign suddenly was drowning in the scent, in the sight.

"Get her out of here. She's too fresh. She'll have little self-control," she heard Tristan say as her teeth lengthened, her body trembling and prickling toward Kinnari blood.

Hands grabbed her shoulders, pushing violently past her wings, the pinch bringing her back to her senses as she was yanked toward the nearest building. A heavy, round wooden door shut behind them, the heavy breaths of whoever had pushed her in huffing in the dark beside her.

Reign was still on edge, the distance possibly not far enough away.

She had forgotten—forgotten what it meant to be from Waihema. She had forgotten what that meant for her, now, in this body.

"I won't be able to help those kids," she whispered to herself.

"Well, it certainly doesn't get easier." Sable laughed.

Reign snapped her head up. Sable's face wasn't healed—red blood and pus oozed, her nose crooked, both eyes blackened.

"So, Vrae venom in a dead Kinnari creates . . . us." Reign said.

"Not necessarily," Sable replied. "I don't think the venom has anything to do with the transformation; it's the Kinnari death. Kinnari deaths are just so rare that it would be a good educated guess, though."

"How do you know then that it's any Kinnari death that triggers the transformation?"

"Oh, this is a juicy story." Sable's eyes lit up. "A few years after I was made, there were still some Kinnari in town. Most turned at once, but not all. One of the remaining Kinnari women was in love— but it was unrequited. She threatened to burn alive in a flaming barn unless the male came to save her. He didn't. A day later, she emerged with eyes like ours."

"She burned alive that long ... over a stupid male?" Reign blinked.

"I know, they're never worth it." Sable giggled.

"Why are you helping me? I murdered you," Reign blurted out.

Smooth.

"Honestly? Tristan is terrifying."

"Is he? Why?"

Sable ignored the question, walking up behind Reign and combing her fingers through Reign's hair like two girls at a sleepover. The tenderness was foreign—Reign jumped away, but Sable just kept going as if she hadn't noticed.

"I used to braid the hair of the children in our town," Sable said as she began to weave Reign's mess.

"Who were those children?" Reign dared to ask. "Were you able to have children?"

"Oh goodness, no. We are a barren species, Kinnari. Those children were mostly human. They begged on the streets, hoping somehow they could be made into Kinnari. I'm a little unsure how they got there, to be honest. So much was lost in all the years that passed. They're certainly not around anymore. Not since the great massacre and all."

"I'm guessing I was the great massacre," Reign said, frowning. The conversation helped. It was a distraction, at least.

"Not exactly. That was mostly me," Sable confessed. "I had no control after I first turned. Several Kinnari died by my hands, all transforming, all having the same reaction. I remember that bloodlust. I still have it, truth be told."

"But you can control it. How?"

"It's not that it's controlled. It's that we're so starved, there's almost a hesitancy. A worry to waste any drop."

"That must have been hard," Reign offered.

"It was," Sable agreed. "There, all done."

"Do you have magic?" Reign turned to ask. Sable shook her head.

"None of us here ever had magic beyond wings and an endless life. Fast healing, yes. But magic? No. We were told stories of you—of the original seven—like folklore. That a creator in another realm had left us here, forgotten. Tristan showed up eventually and played into that quite well. We hung on his every word."

Reign could easily imagine that. He had an ancientness about him, one that she didn't possess.

"You said he was terrifying."

Sable shrugged.

"He was magic. He'd enter our dreams and cause nightmares if we misbehaved. Some couldn't sleep for days. They'd go mad, finally complying with his orders. I have to admit, if he hadn't been here when everyone turned, I doubt Myrilosis would've survived. We stay here—contained. Hungry, but sustained. Just enough to live."

"To live," Reign repeated. "I'm worried that I won't ever live again. Not a life that I once loved."

"It's unbecoming, do you disagree?"

Reign blinked. "What is?"

"Missing what was."

"I'd like to head back outside," Reign said, moving towards the door.

"So you disagree, then. Pity for you."

Reign snapped around so fast, her irritation high.

"Oh, those pretty red eyes of yours—they spring on so fast now." Sable smiled. "I just mean ... keeping your soul, your heart, trapped in a life you've already left will stop you from growing into what could someday be really, really great."

"And what is great about this life?" Reign asked.

"Well, everything."

"You want for blood you can rarely have." Reign laughed.

Sable's eyes brightened. "It's worth the hope—the excitement—to pine after a delicacy. It makes the moment that blood touches my tongue pure ecstasy. Pure joy. The longing is half the pleasure, is it not?"

"The pleasure is all of the pleasure, I would counter." Reign said, hand on the door. "But I'm glad to know it's not that terrible here."

"No. Not terrible at all," Sable said through a smile. "We're a family here. We protect each other. We lean into being children. We daydream, watch clouds, and play silly games. Sometimes we hunt."

Reign paused.

The idea of being so carefree, after chasing autonomy for so long ... it might be good. Or it might just be a new box, something to define her in a way she didn't understand.

"It sounds like it could be beautiful." She opened the door.

"But it's not for you," Sable confirmed, walking up behind her.

Reign stepped out quickly.

"I'm not going to stop you. You're much older than me."

Reign shrugged her shoulders. "I guess it's cute that you think anyone could stop me."

"That's the Kinnari I know from the stories," Sable said. "I love to hear it."

Reign was taken aback. Sable was offering kinship, friendship.

"I don't know how to act around you," Reign confessed.

"That maybe makes two of us."

They walked back out onto the street. Sable grinned wide, practically glowing. Reign mostly stared at her feet, smiling—though she wasn't sure why.

"So, what are these stories about us?" Reign asked.

"There will be time for stories later," Tristan butted in, his voice pitched higher, edged with panic. "Reign, I need you to leave. Take Sable with you."

37

———————

Reifoel | Serelune

"What happened to my father?"

Gasher nervously grabbed the ends of her silver and blonde hair and twirled it, her jaw clenched.

"I don't know," she answered. "We should go into the royal dome and speak in private." Gasher turned away and swam along the pebbled path, not looking back.

This can't be good.

All the nerves in his stomach churned with a surge of guilt for Isadore's death. Breaking down was not something a royal son had the luxury of, especially when there was no king to rule their people.

"Is my mother there?" Reifoel raised his voice.

Gasher froze, her jawline parallel with the curl of her thick tail. "Just come with me. Please."

He didn't want to go. He didn't want to hear what she had to say because once he heard it, he knew he would never be able to unhear it.

Move, Reifoel. What other choice is there?

Reifoel's heart felt like it could shoot out of his chest. He began to worry he'd sprout legs this far beneath the sea.

He propelled himself forward, following Gasher toward the royal dome as the villagers warily returned to their routines.

Moments later, he passed through the familiar door made of bone and moss. Just as he had known it, it was still mostly empty except for the slimy wooden table in the center of the room and a sparse kitchen across from it.

This was home.

A home he hadn't seen in so long; too long.

Gasher floated opposite the council table, looking down and chipping at the sunken wood. Reifoel let her have her moment of silence. That's what his mother would have done: shown compassion, let others gather their words and courage.

His mother wasn't out there to greet him. She also wasn't inside. There was no smell of food being prepared. No mess of papers cluttered the table. Everything was clean.

Bare, like it had been abandoned.

Reifoel knew deep down what courage Gasher was gathering— what news she had to tell him.

Silence was no longer acceptable.

"What happened, Gasher?"

She looked up at him, removing all emotion from her face, as if it were armor.

"The moon exploded."

Reifoel's shoulders relaxed, just a centimeter or two. "I know. I was there."

"Were you really? I suppose you'll have several great adventures to share."

Reifoel smiled. He did. And Isadore would be highlighted in them all, made out to be a great hero in his people's stories. He would make sure of it.

"At first, the council stayed with your parents, checking on the village, doing perimeter swims, seeing what changes the explosion had on the water. All seemed calm, though everything was curiously a little darker."

Gasher kept her back to him as much as she could.

"And then what?" he whispered.

"Your mother was worried sick about you. She was convinced that even if we didn't see immediate effects, you would be in peril on the surface. Your father volunteered to go find you. We haven't seen him since. I had hoped that you were together. You haven't seen him, then?"

Reifoel shook his head.

"Do you know which direction he headed?"

Gasher chose to ignore the question. "There's more, Reifoel." She looked directly at him now, her lips tight, thumbs rubbing together for comfort.

"Not long after King Pires left, we started to feel the effects in the water. At first, the temperature crept up a couple of degrees. It was peculiar, but no action was taken. The queen and council didn't know the cause—or what it meant."

Reifoel's eyes widened.

"How was your first reaction not to scout the perimeter of the deep?"

Gasher smiled, but it did not reach her eyes. "You will be a good king, Reifoel. You believe in your mother's stories when most do not. Even the queen doubts them herself sometimes."

The deep was another world, another part of the ocean left unexplored. Anyone who went into those crevices beyond the seafloor did not return.

"The stories of the deep are of volcanic activity and beings meant to be left sleeping."

"I know the stories," Gasher replied with a sigh. "We all know the stories. But that's all they were. The queen hadn't even mentioned it."

Reifoel rubbed the spot between his eyes, his fingers pinching the bridge of his nose.

"Is that where she is? Did my mother go into the deep?"

"No, no," Gasher said. "The water temperature kept rising. It became so hot that the elders began to die, and the fish started floating to the surface. Other things began to float too. We were so close to the deep that we could see it—lava turning black as it rose higher from the floor."

"We are miles away from the deep. You could see lava floating above Serelune?" Reifoel clarified.

"Yes. Queen Pires decided that the town needed to evacuate. The water had to be cooler—bodies were piling up, young and old. She seemed to hold on only for you, for your father, for Serelune."

"But you're still here. And she isn't," Reifoel said.

"I'm just going to say it, because I don't know how to be gentle with this." Gasher looked up at the ceiling, a Serelune's way of crying. "Something came out of the deep during the evacuation—something big.

It was a monster, Reifoel.

A super-sized whale, an underwater dragon, lava coming out of its ears when it snorted. It opened its mouth as it moved quickly. Half of Serelune got swept up, swallowed.

Our queen was one of them.

I was in shock, frozen. We didn't know what to do. I'm the last of the council now. I led the survivors back to our home. We didn't get far."

Reifoel compartmentalized, breaking this story down like a pebble pointed list.

"What happened to the heat?"

"The monster disappeared into the crevice, and the heat subsided. We assume that it fell back into slumber."

Reifoel's chest rose and fell rapidly.

What do I do now?

"We were lucky, Reifoel," Gasher said. "I think that is the best way to look at it."

He nodded, the shock too fresh to let sadness in.

Moments ago, he'd been grieving Isadore in the street. He had been so nervous to look his mother in the eyes and tell her that he had been unable to protect Isadore. Now, he never would be able to.

Her arms, her protection, her love: all gone.

And his father was somewhere in a world falling apart—another name among the lost.

"Reifoel, it is your turn."

He didn't understand.

"My turn?"

"Your people need you. You're the last of your line."

"That's here," Reifoel corrected.

Gasher's face dropped; her empathy was too much.

He hated it.

"My father is just simply not here," he repeated.

"Reifoel," she continued, swimming up to him and bowing her head. "It's time. It's time to lead your people."

A chill passed through him, draining every bit of strength. He closed his eyes, letting the feeling pass.

He had gotten them all into this mess. That cursed ship had been his idea. He'd been a selfish child.

Reifoel cleared all thoughts of Hadley. Every desire, every door was suddenly shut. His heart couldn't be broken, not when there was real suffering right here.

They were hurting—his *subjects*.

Reifoel said the only thing he could think of to say.

"I accept."

Gasher raised her head and smiled. "They would be so utterly proud of you. Would you like a hug?"

"No."

The motherly instinct within Gasher was obvious, but he didn't want it.

He could handle this burden alone.

"Right." Gasher shrugged, "Well, as council advisor, I recommend that the first thing that we do is elect a new council—"

"The first thing," Reifoel cut her off, a new strength in his voice as he did his best to embody a king. "The first thing that we do is honor our lost."

Gasher's eyebrows shot up in surprise.

"While I appreciate the sentiment, the Serelune will feel more secure knowing that they have leadership. We should formally crown you."

"I am more interested in healing their souls. If our community is to regain its strength, then this is the path we will take. We will not ever be taking what we have for granted again."

Gasher let the silence build between them. She was no fool. There was no point in arguing with her leader, even if she was there to help him.

"I can get behind it. We can crown you at the end. Let's give Serelune its pride back," Gasher said. "I'll start the preparations."

"Do you mind... if I wait here for a moment? I need to—"

"King Pires," Gasher addressed him softly.

He wasn't ready for that. That was his father's title.

"Of course," Gasher said, redirecting after seeing his face. "Take all the time that you need." She put her hand on Reifoel's arm. "I'm so sorry for your losses."

He looked at the floor as Gasher swam away, through the moss-covered door, leaving him alone. This was his moment to finish breaking down, to purge the grief he'd started to unleash in front of the entire town.

Of what's left of the town.

Reifoel swallowed down the gulp, the cry that tried to sneak up his throat, and took his time trying to breathe.

Inhale.

Exhale.

Good job, Reifoel. Let's go get this job done.

Hours later, Reifoel drifted through the village, useless as a fish on land, floundering while others prepared the ceremony he'd ordered.

Reifoel didn't know how to decorate. He didn't know how to build a statue or something to remember them all by. He didn't even know how to cook. There was nothing he could do to help here.

You're a useless ruler, one that can only order but not act.

Gasher had dozens of Serelune adults in action, setting up the memorial for all of their fallen.

Children played around the pebbled streets. They giggled and chased one another. Serelune felt alive again.

"I was skeptical at first. But you certainly did give them a purpose, Your Highness." Gasher popped up out of nowhere.

"Not sure if I'm a fan of that."

"Giving them a purpose?"

"That title, *Your Highness.*"

Gasher grinned.

It was the first real smile he'd seen from her.

"You will make a speech, I presume?" she asked.

"This is for them. They should share their own stories and happy memories. A speech from royalty is just that: a speech, a lecture."

Gasher blew out, air bubbles streaming out from the corner of her lips. "Oh, sorry, I thought I was talking to one of my children. They like it when I do that."

"That felt oddly insulting."

"And do you find insults motivating? I saw the way you reacted when Isadore challenged you," Gasher said. "Forgive me if I am out of turn."

She was. But he didn't mind.

"King Pires, sharing your memories will help the Serelune connect to you."

"Were you trying to be like Isadore just then?"

Gasher smiled wryly and shrugged her left shoulder forward.

Reifoel didn't know if that made him sad or appreciative. Either way, it had worked. He felt a little more motivated. And though he'd gone to school with many of the remaining survivors, Gasher wasn't wrong—he didn't feel connected to the people, not in a way that mattered. He was the careless prince, the royal son who dreamed more than he participated.

"I think they might be ready," she said.

Reifoel looked at the center path, where all the pebbled roads intersected. Public ceremonies were not something their culture fostered. This all had to be made up, inspired by the hearts of the community.

Maybe that made it better.

On the far side of the cross was a pile of moss—soft, the green only visible in the dark when a Serelune swam past. On top of the moss were items that shimmered in the light of their bodies, like diamonds sparkling in the sun. Reifoel swam over to the memorial, his heart heavy as he studied what his village had done.

There was a collection of small items: shells that displayed layers of color and the history of love and relationships. Giving a shell to a Serelune, especially one so small and delicate, was a gift of love and intimacy.

These were love offerings—hearts letting go, but not forgetting.

Among the shells were other personal items.

Small tools made of carved whale and shark teeth. Rocks with remarkable etchings, marks that depicted a written language, ancient and secret.

Pearls of pink, gray, and white shimmered among bits of plant debris from the surface, dropped from birds above.

The effort put in here—the love—made Reifoel ashamed.

He didn't know how to show love like this. He was half the Serelune that his own people were.

A few began to gather, staring down at the memories that these objects represented.

Reifoel jolted away, gazes following him until he disappeared into the royal hut.

He hadn't had much from his parents. Both his mother and father believed in having little to no possessions. Trinkets were in short supply in their home.

The sparse kitchen had a small handful of items lined up where the wall and the surface space connected.

Reifioel studied them. He observed a gap in the otherwise precise line of items, spaced perfectly apart.

That was where the moonstone had sat.

His mother had tenderly gifted the item to him, placing it around his neck.

The other items were dull. They did not feel special.

He felt no life, no connection to his mother through them—but this was all that there was. A broken sea glass, thin and short, no bigger than his thumb. A plastic toy, shaped like a flower, the red paint dimmed as sand and time had settled onto the object.

A piece of hair was stuck within the teeth, black like his. It could be his mother's. It could be his father's. He had watched the queen comb the king's hair, and every time she was too tough with a tangle, he would playfully slap her on the back of her tail.

He smiled at the sweetness, their flirting, their love.

The comb would have to do.

Reifoel held the comb to his chest as he swam back out into the pebbled paths. With a few powerful flips of his tail, he rounded a turn and ducked into a different dome.

Isadore's dome.

Reifoel hadn't realized what his cousin was going through—not entirely—until now. That realization deepened his shame. His cousin had lost both his parents and lived in the same dome, alone.

Isadore did have more possessions than he did. Maybe collecting things had been his way of hiding the emptiness in his home.

Reifoel looked around at his cousin's collection of items. Unlike his own, Isadore's dome had a counter the entire way around. There wasn't a true kitchen, but bowls and utensils were lined up untouched, which would have made sense considering Reifoel's mother made most of Isadore's meals.

Dissolved papers sat in his line of sight, a book that had fallen under the surface and somehow managed to stay somewhat intact. Reifoel was scared to touch it, afraid it would fall apart with any movement.

There was a remote control for a television, gray and battered.

Gold, brass, and silver sat, begging to be dusted off and shown off to the world.

Treasure.

Had Isadore scavenged these from wrecks? Or were these a left-behind inheritance?

It pained him how little he knew about his cousin.

Reifoel picked up a coin from the pile and rubbed the grime off it. It was a circle, two inches in diameter, outlined in silver with a gold circle in the middle.

This will have to do.

Wasting no more time, Reifoel swam back out and over to the memorial where the rest of the citizens had gathered. Everyone's faces were solemn, filled with apprehension as an older couple spoke, saying goodbye to their adult child.

Reifoel had known their daughter. A loud, boisterous girl who went to his school, the one everyone had had a crush on. She never gave anyone a chance.

It was probably for the best.

"King Pires." Gasher moved beside him. "It's your turn to speak. Your community is waiting."

Reifoel felt like a fraud.

"Are you nervous?" Gasher asked.

He couldn't answer. His mouth hung open.

"Okay," Gasher rationalized, "what is your favorite thing about the surface? What makes you so happy that you always want to go back?"

Reifoel blinked at her question, not understanding the relevance. But her answering seemed easier than stepping up, than taking that couple's place as the memorial speaker.

"Had—" he started, but then stopped—the word, the name, feeling false in his mouth. Hadley didn't make him happy. Hadley made him terrified. Terrified of winning her heart—because she might change her mind. Terrified of losing her—because it would confirm he was always just a placeholder.

How could he see himself as a King if she couldn't?

"Burritos," he changed his answer.

"What in the world is that?" Gasher shook her head.

"It's my favorite thing to eat when I'm in the mortal realm, on land, of course. I didn't get one this last time around. I regret that."

"Burritos make you happy?"

"Yes."

"Okay, then. How about you pretend that at the end of this speech, there is the greatest, slimiest, most perfectly fishy burrito waiting for you on the other side of this."

"It's clear that you don't know what a burrito is, but I can play along," he said.

It did work.

He was grinning.

Reifoel let some nervous air flutter out of his lips and moved up to the couple, ready to take their place as they hovered there nervously, waiting for him.

"That was beautiful, thank you," he said to them as they offered their arms out, not giving him a real choice before the group hug commenced—before he could feel the sadness, the sobs that tried to escape from the mother's body.

They eventually let go and moved toward the audience. Reifoel turned to the memorial, laying down his mother's brush and Isadore's coin.

This is where his mother would have wanted to be—among her people. And if Isadore had truly hoped to lead, he belonged here too.

"This is something that I might get better at in time," he began. "At least, I hope I will. Speeches seem like the work of experienced leaders. Unfortunately, you have only me."

Reifoel looked at the faces watching him and saw the doubt settle across them.

Just say anything.

"We are here, all together, honoring those we lost. We carry them in our memories and in our souls—our lives and personalities are better, stronger because of them."

Not the worst ... Not the best.

"I want to speak about a few souls that I alone can likely speak about. My mother, Queen Pires, who died in front of all of you. And Isadore, my cousin, who died in front of me."

A few whispers came from the crowd.

"I watched Isadore die a hero—sent on a journey to save the world alongside myself, sent by my mother. He was blasted by fire from his bed when we were settling in for the night. It was unexpected. It was fast. But without my cousin, I would have never found Kinnari. I would have never had the courage. He gave me courage.

The last thing my mother gave me was a moonstone, for our protection. If she had not done this, I wouldn't have flown on dragons. I wouldn't have survived attacks from an ancient Goddess. I wouldn't have met a Vrae."

The last line broke out into full voices as the whispers gave way to disbelief, filling the crowd.

"Most importantly," he said, his voice raspy.

This is your mother's eulogy. This is her legacy.

"Most importantly, the moonstone my mother had given me is now in the Earth's atmosphere—serving as our new moon. Without the actions of my mother and my cousin, I fear we would have had to face a much harsher reality. I believe they helped save the world. I love them both. I love all of our lost. Each Serelune is a member of our family."

Reifoel didn't know how to add more without having another meltdown in front of the crowd. He was their king now. He couldn't show that kind of pain when he was there to harbor it for them—to protect them from the constant threats that surrounded them.

"He saved us," a voice said from the crowd.

"King Pires, Reifoel, saved us all," another voice echoed.

Murmurs of agreement spread as heads bobbed in unison, excitement reflected in the loudest voices.

"Hail King Pires," Reifoel heard.

"Hail King Pires," voices echoed again, and again, as his name—his father's name—was chanted through the crowd.

Gasher swam up to him, a crown of silver and white pearls, heavy in her hands.

"It's your turn, Reifoel," she said as she raised the crown and put it on his head, the weight bearing down on him.

But he felt no burden.

He felt only the need to not let Serelune down.

I will keep this place safe until you return, Father.

38

Djoser | Outer Space

The moon swelled before him, beautiful and unreal—like a pumpkin turning into a carriage in a fairytale. The light that poured from the sun was mesmerizing. Djoser thought of human tales of heaven and the afterlife.

They were all just atoms, recycled, repurposed—but being so close to this made him wish some of those stories were true. The beautiful ones. The ones that moved you. He always gave the people what they wanted, especially in his kingdoms. If he were a god to them, he would allow them to worship as their souls needed.

Trouble only brewed for the leaders who took advantage of that.

After tugging on the cord that connected them, Arryn and Djoser flew up from the ground. Djoser made a mental note to allow more slack next time—though he hoped there wouldn't be a next time.

Arryn worked, and Djoser floated there beside him, watching, waiting for the sign that he had grown too tired—that there would be no recovery without rest. If that moment came, Djoser would grab the cord and pull them both down until gravity did the rest.

He's so lucky to have me.

The moon grew larger.

Up close, it was hard to gauge scale—but it looked big enough to house cities.

Arryn's head started bobbing. Djoser took that as his sign to be ready for the collapse. Arryn might be intolerable, but he was causing himself a lot of harm to help fix this all. Djoser wouldn't forget that. He'd make sure the rest of the Kinnari didn't forget either.

Djoser looked at the Earth, glowing beneath them. It made him want to go home.

They had to be almost done. It looked finished.

A flash of white and red skittered across the edge of Djoser's vision. He turned and saw a glint—something reflecting off his helmet.

What … fucking … now.

Another flash went by. This time, he saw it: fire, rock—hurtling toward the moon. It missed by a hair.

Djoser rolled his eyes and crossed his arms.

"Arryn, I think someone is trying to destroy the moon again."

The cord on the back of his suit pulled tight. He looked over and saw Arryn floating aimlessly, upside down, doing micro-somersaults.

Oh great. Time to pass out. Perfect timing.

This time, a fiery red comet passed dangerously close. Djoser felt the heat warming his suit. Arryn's flipping worsened—and that's when Djoser saw it. The cord that made a T-shape in their tether had been cut.

Djoser watched the severed cord spiral away into space, drifting closer to the Earth below. One sudden move and they were dead. Arryn couldn't re-tether them, and who knew how long it would take him to wake without Celestine's tears.

We are fucked.

He went motionless, hoping Arryn would stop rotating like a floppy soccer ball. But it only got worse.

Another blast of fire blazed through—this one hit the moon. A silent explosion. A parade of heat, flame, and rock shot out violently.

A shard struck his knee.

Djoser cried out but shut his mouth immediately—his throat suddenly cold. There was a hole. A rip in his suit.

His skin slowly iced over. Oxygen hissed out. His breaths became ragged—like an untrained climber on Mount Everest.

"Arryn, wake up," he wheezed.

Arryn didn't wake. He just kept spinning, his cord dragging Djoser farther from both the moon and Earth.

This is how it ends. Immortality—but stuck in space, unable to breathe, tethered to someone I can only stand half the time.

He sighed, hoping Precession and Roksana would rebuild somewhere, and that Hadley would choose Reifoel. That Sheng would escape the Atheri. Sure, he didn't like the bloodsucking demon, but he didn't hate him enough to be blasted to death with light.

Multiple solar flares came at him—came at the moon—again.

He should have known it wouldn't be so easy.

Djoser watched as he got pulled further away, helpless, as more flares hit the moon, as more debris entered the area, as little by little everything they'd just rebuilt began to unravel.

A yellow light intensified behind him. Djoser resisted looking, resisted moving. Arryn's spinning was enough of a threat. Curiosity could kill them both.

The light was warm, and Djoser reveled in it as it drew closer. It was only when it passed him—when it was now in front of him—that he regretted not trying to figure out how to do this without going into space.

A figure—a woman, translucent and made of fire, of ember— glowed and hovered. She moved her arms, solar flares following her gestures. They slammed into the new moon.

Ayurveda was here. That meant they were close—so close—to finishing the impossible.

If there was one thing he wished he could fix in space, it was the silence. Djoser was too focused on staying still, on studying what the

Goddess was doing, on watching her mouth not move, her face blank —to notice the new body that hovered beside him.

Djoser would have yelled out in surprise if he'd had the air to spare, but he didn't. He simply accepted that Precession had flown up, the cord wrapped around her waist, the end of it clutched in her right hand.

Thank Gods.

His eyes flickered to Ayurveda.

Well, not you.

Precession smiled at the Goddess. Ayurveda had lowered her hands, but her stillness broke.

Nothing seemed to happen, but Djoser saw it—confidence blooming in Precession's posture, that subtle *fuck you* written in her body language. She was going to let go of the tether. She was going to fight.

Djoser couldn't imagine anyone equal to the Goddess in front of them. They had lost before—*together*—and still, Precession challenged her now.

Ayurveda began to grow, her body expanding, shimmering larger.

Precession didn't back down. Instead, she pulled her wings free and let her head fall back. Her red hair bloomed around her like petals.

So frail, like a rose. But with thorns sharp enough to make a Goddess reconsider.

A solar flare appeared, swirling through space silently, circling Ayurveda before redirecting—straight toward Djoser and Arryn.

Fuck.

This was going to hurt. This would shred his body, scatter pieces too far to regenerate. If Arryn didn't survive, the world wouldn't either.

Djoser reached for the atoms—for that magic, the destruction that lived in his core—and let it spread. The flare didn't slow.

There was too much at stake.

His mind flickered to a face he hadn't seen in days. A face he worried for.

Hadley didn't want to exist anymore.

She never had.

If he died again, if he didn't recover, Hadley would find her way into a darkness she could never return from.

This time, he had to live for her.

He wouldn't accept what was coming. He would deny the inevitable. This time, everything would work for him.

The air around him sparked—quiet but alive, alive with energy beyond comprehension—as he summoned his magic, an unseen force bending the world to his will. To the promise of death and decay. He floated in space, Precession to his left, Arryn still spinning, vomit fogging his helmet. Djoser reached toward the heat and fire plummeting toward them.

Precession lunged. Her eyes were clear. The haze she normally carried was gone.

She was a real ally now. A real partner. Someone he could trust in the moment.

She wrapped her body around his, anchoring them both—anchoring *all three* of them. Her movement pushed them further into space, but the cord wrapped around her waist held fast. It groaned, slicing into her—but she didn't let go.

Her skin began to turn blue—from the cold, from oxygen loss. Djoser would help later, once the blaze threatening to destroy every-thing was gone. Then they could worry about breath, Goddesses, and moons.

His hands trembled with the weight of his magic. It was barely containable. He gathered it all, ready to unravel what lay ahead.

A low hum resonated in his mind, vibrations through his body so deep they seemed to come from the marrow of the Earth below.

Precession's fingers curled into fists.

The atoms in the air shuddered. They met the flare mid-flight—already searing her skin, her clothes, his suit.

Oxygen, nitrogen, carbon dioxide—molecules unraveled, their bonds breaking apart in high-pitched fractures only the soul could hear. It was glass-shattering in slow motion.

His dark magic stripped them down to a vacuum—an ache of absence.

With the flare destroyed, with Precession trembling against him —her body screaming in silence but refusing to let go—Djoser dug deeper. Her will bolstered his own.

The strength he pulled from her caused his magic to surge, starving. He reached into the heart of matter. Protons and neutrons shattered beneath his intent. Flashes of light burst like dying stars. Quarks and gluons—foundations of the universe—tore free. A void followed in his wake, a hollow silence; the essence of creation had been undone.

Space. He was destroying space.

The air grew colder, the absence of matter stealing the sensation of life itself. Light twisted around him, bending and refracting. The laws of the universe could not bear to remain whole in his presence.

Shadows stretched into jagged, monstrous shapes cast by nothing and everything all at once. Particles caught radiation like dry grass caught fire.

Djoser's breath heaved, shallow gasps searching for the comfort of oxygen.

Ayurveda stilled, a glorious picture of power.

Her flames trailed behind in the darkness—a seductive promise of annihilation. Her eyes burned—not with rage, but with cold precision. She knew the cost, and she welcomed it.

When everything stopped, it stopped completely—a stillness that roared louder than any blast.

Precession's arms around his waist tightened. Her body cracked. A sheen of frost covered her face, her cheeks. Despite the fire he'd unleashed, she was freezing.

Djoser opened his hands, his fingers uncurled as if releasing the threads of the universe.

Around him was nothingness. Only a pure, unbroken void. And in it he floated, still forged in destruction and bound to its endless pull.

The moon was still there, though they had drifted far. New craters had appeared, but it was far from gone.

Their work hadn't been for nothing. At least, not yet.

Djoser knew he would never have returned to Earth if it hadn't been for the Kinnari curled around him, protecting both his and Arryn's lives.

Is that fool still spinning?

One.

Two.

Three.

Four.

Five.

Six.

He counted six solar flares heading straight for them.

Djoser reached out into the nothingness, searching for the first hints of radiation and particles approaching doom.

You can do this. Get pissed off.

He couldn't. He held more than anger—he held fear.

Death was scared.

Everyone he knew was heading towards an oblivion that could never be repaired. He would be lost in space with Arryn and Precession spinning into oblivion.

Could Precession even hold the tether if she ended up in a black hole, galaxies away?

The Goddess's laugh echoed across the void, sharp and cruel. The sound vibrated through him. The cold felt much colder. Motivation leaked out of his suit like the last of the oxygen.

This is her domain.

They couldn't win—Djoser could barely destroy a single solar flare.

Now six were coming.

Time slowed. Djoser looked down at Precession, her eyes frozen shut. She would cling to him until her body literally cracked apart.

The solar flares had burst forward—eruptions of plasma and magnetic energy spiraling toward them.

Djoser reached out, searching for the atoms, the matter he could unravel. If this was the end, at least he would go down trying.

Charged particles streaked across the void like dying stars, lighting space with unbearable brilliance.

Precession's heartbeat was suddenly vibrating through him. He didn't have time to look down, to check on her. The radiation from the nearest flare reached him. His skin seared, hissed, burned like acid. He began to deconstruct it.

And then, something broke his focus.

Precession let go of him.

She gently pushed him away. And in space, a gentle push was enough. He and Arryn drifted, the moon and Precession shrinking behind them.

The bright red light of the flares painted over her as they came nearer. Precession moved so slowly, a focus with unreal precision, arms rising, calm amid chaos.

Djoser watched her head tilt, as if listening to a song no one else could hear.

The solar flares slowed. He was sure of it. But he kept drifting, Arryn still attached, with no way to stop it.

She is pulling, he realized.

The Earth below spun on its axis, oblivious to the battle raging above. But Precession reached into that ancient, relentless motion, grasping it like thread between her fingers. Her body shuddered, her form vibrating with power.

The first solar flare tore across the void, a spear of blinding plasma and searing magnetism. The heat was suffocating; the brilliance consuming.

Precession didn't flinch.

The air around her shifted—not air, Djoser reminded himself, but the fabric of space, bending, rippling like water.

Precession's power thrummed through the stillness, and for a single heartbeat, everything froze.

Djoser had officially run out of air.

Then the flare hit.

But it hadn't struck her.

The space around her warped, folding into spirals so sharp and intricate they defied reason.

The flare screamed as it twisted, its power unraveling thread by fiery thread.

She watched it, her breath steady, her body taut with focus.

And as the last fragments of plasma scattered into harmless streams, streaking away into the endless void, she lifted her chin.

The silence that followed was deafening, heavy with the weight of what had just transpired. But Precession didn't allow herself a moment of relief as the other solar flares came for her.

Again, they didn't hit her.

Ayurveda's sneer cut through the silence. "You think the spin of a dying world will protect you?"

Precession's lips moved, though Djoser was too far away to hear.

It didn't matter; her body said enough.

Precession raised her arms again.

The next flare tore across space, larger, more erratic, its magnetic field crackling like lightning in a bottle.

She moved with elegant certainty, like a dancer mid-spin. Her hands guided the warped space to meet it.

The collision was unlike anything Djoser had ever seen.

The plasma buckled and tore. Its energy spiraled into the vortex as if devoured by a ravenous storm. Precession floated at its center, a singular, unyielding force. Each sweep of her arm fed off the Earth's rotation.

More flares erupted, Ayurveda unleashing her fury in wave after wave. The void burned, yet she held.

Precession's form flickered at the edges. The vortex around her spun—the pressure of velocity, gravity, time, all converging.

And then, it was calm.

The final flare dissolved—scattering like stardust in the dark.

The vortex slowed. Precession remained standing, her unwavering gaze fixed on the Goddess.

Djoser had seen that drive in her once before, when she'd let go of the tether and hurled herself into a fight.

But this—this wasn't the same.

She wasn't letting go.

She was holding on with everything she had, even as it broke her open. And still, she didn't flinch.

Precession had done it.

She had saved the moon, held the planet steady beneath her.

As Djoser drifted farther into the dark, the cold biting into his suit, gratitude surged through him like a second heartbeat. He was thankful, thankful someone still believed they could win.

39

———————

Allienna | Sacramento, Ca | 2006

The light was soft that afternoon, pooling across the blanket like it had been honey poured from a jar. Threads of Allienna's light brown hair clumped, tangled over her collarbone. Her eyes fluttered open and then closed again, too heavy to keep up with her thoughts. Everything felt far away—like she was underwater, or maybe dreaming.

Someone was holding her hand.

Warm. Familiar. Gentle.

"Where am I?" she asked, her voice barely a whisper. Her words, lisped through her missing teeth, tumbled from her lips.

A mortal death, just like I was promised.

Allienna turned her head slowly. There was a woman beside her —no, a girl. Blonde, beautiful, with a hard face, one that hid emotion like a stone.

"You're at home, Mom. In the hospice bed," the girl said. Allienna couldn't place the girl's name. But she liked her.

"Mom," Allienna's head was heavy. "I am a mom. I have a daughter named Hadley. She might be around your age, dear."

The girl squeezed Allienna's hand, and she could feel the deep bruising already starting.

You're so frail. When did that happen?

"It's me, Mom. It's me, Hadley," the girl said.

The words went over Allienna's head. It was so hard to focus, her thoughts slipping like water through her fingers.

Home.

That word she seemed to hear. It was filled with comfort.

"Good," was all Allienna could manage to say, her vision flickering in and out.

Behind them, two nurses stood near the machines, their voices hushed but not nearly enough.

"Liver's shutting down, now. Kidneys too. It's all so fast, just a matter of days, maybe less," one said.

"We'll manage the pain. She's not really here anymore," said the other.

Allienna heard the words but didn't process them. They passed over her like wind through lace curtains.

She was too busy trying to remember.

"My daughter," Allienna murmured, lips barely moving. "She writes stories. She will hold the world in her hands one day."

The girl made a small, broken sound—one that, just a year ago, would have crushed Allienna's heart.

"That's me, Mom," the girl whispered, tears sliding down her face. "It's me."

Allienna smiled faintly, though she didn't quite understand why. Her mind was softening around the edges now, memories melting into each other like snow in a spring rain.

"My magic, she's taking my magic," she said, almost to herself.

"How could you say that?" The girl's grip on Allienna's hand loosened. She pulled away.

"I want her to have it." Black spots painted Allienna's vision. "Because even when I am dead, I have to know that she's strong

—that she will be okay. I want her to fly faster than I ever had.”

"I will," the girl said. "I'll find a way."

Allienna let out a long breath. It felt like exhaling the weight of centuries.

Because it was.

She didn't speak again.

The light moved slowly across her blanket, and in her final quiet, Allienna dreamed of her daughter's laugh echoing through moonlit fields.

40

Hadley | Sacramento, Ca

A shriek, a roar—one that would send chills and nausea through anyone's body—rang out in the kitchen as the bullet buried itself into Sheng.

His eyes were closed, but when they opened, they found her.

"What the fuck," the shooter said, looking down the barrel of his gun. "Are these rubber bullets or something? Frank, did you fucking give me rubber bullets?"

Sheng opened his mouth, morphing to accommodate the transformation of his teeth—long, thick daggers sharp enough to dislodge heads from necks like tearing paper.

His skin rippled as he became something darker than vengeance—an abyss made flesh.

Hadley only nodded at him.

That seemed to be enough.

He sprang backwards, light on his feet. The shooter, who paid Sheng no attention, missed the threat as he walked away.

"Frank, where the fuck you at? There's a woman here, just like we wanted," he shouted, still peering down the barrel. "What games are you playing? Where you at?"

Sheng burst through the double French doors, wounds bleeding, a trail of crimson behind him as glass and wood splintered from their hinges.

"What the fu—" the shooter swore, but didn't finish. Sheng's mouth expanded, and his teeth clamped down on the man's neck. Skin, tissue, bone—gone. An entire head in Sheng's mouth.

He spat it out. Horror twisted his face as the body remained upright, spraying blood like an Italian fountain. Thick, copper-scented red soaked into the clay patio, bubbling and pooling.

Sheng showed no interest in feasting. But his terrifying Vrae form, blood dripping from his chin—a mix of his and the man's—smiled with all his weaponized teeth on display.

"What the fuck is that?"

A man yelled. A gunshot followed.

"Seth is missing his head! What the fuck! Everyone, get out here now!"

This must be Frank.

Large gardening pots—expensive ones that could fit several bodies—were overturned, chipped, creating obstacles for the group now running toward Sheng. One with torn shorts barely clinging to his waist came from the garden path. Another, wearing a long mullet and sunglasses and gripping a large shotgun, emerged from the patio's side.

Hadley counted six of them in total, all of them thin, frail, running slowly, but with attitudes the size of California—and mustaches to match.

"What is that?" Frank said, eyeing Sheng. His run slowed, nearly reversed.

"Shoot it!" another man yelled.

No one hesitated. Four guns pointed at Sheng, who stood beaming like a child seeing snow for the first time.

Hadley had never seen Sheng so alive, so sharp—as if protecting her made him whole.

It almost made her feel something.

Almost.

Instead, she watched, empty, unreactive, still in the kitchen, surrounded by her own bloody footprints. Her skin chilled—she knew only by the goosebumps on her arms and the stiffening of her nipples.

She stood unbothered, taking in Sheng in his element—a creature worse than the devil, her own personal nightmare, once irresistible.

Sheng leaped, grabbing the nearest man mid-air, his feet never touching the ground. Three bullets struck him—leg, arm, chin—but he didn't slow.

The screams from the man in the oversized shorts filled the space. Sheng curled his body around him like a shell.

The screaming stopped. Then came the sound of bones snapping, a gush of blood bursting like a shattered cranberry juice bottle.

One man dropped his pistol and ran, cursing.

Sheng looked Hadley in the eye and smiled, releasing the limp body in his hands. It dropped like a rubber toy. He opened his mouth and bit down, leaving a full bite mark in the man's arm. A chunk of flesh disappeared down his throat.

As he chewed, his human skin tone returned. His jaw shortened. Still seated over a mangled body, he swallowed, eyes going black.

"Now you're naked, too." Hadley, tilting her head, was reminded of the last time she was able to feel again.

"Should we do something about it?" He smirked.

The two locked eyes, ignoring the chaos. More men arrived, weapons drawn—some guns, some golf clubs, some chains.

"Get the girl," Hadley heard them shout.

"You're a bit messy." She blinked at him.

"I just needed a snack," Sheng winked.

Hadley watched twenty more men run up to Sheng. She was also very aware of the others who crept behind her.

There was no fear. No thrill. Only that black-eyed stare that consumed her.

That stare was worship.

It reminded her of the music festival—how followers used to look at her, filled with envy and loyalty she didn't deserve.

"It's not like you made less of a mess," Sheng said, standing. The rubbery body slid off him. He glanced toward the charging men. "This is my house," he said. Then to her, with another wink, "Let me revise: our house."

"Stop," Hadley said.

Sheng heard her. She hadn't shouted. Her tone wasn't urgent. But he stopped anyway.

Hadley scanned for the shimmer, the shadow.

There—her manic counterpart, spinning behind the counter.

Her shadow self turned translucent, awaiting permission.

Hadley didn't give it. Not yet.

The shadow tried again, returning to the form Hadley trusted. She gave the nod.

Internally, she felt the squeal of glee—though there was no sound—as her shadow self launched through the wall, through bodies about to strike Sheng, through hearts with fingers on triggers.

All motion stopped.

"What's happening?" Sheng asked.

Hadley said nothing.

Once again, the crowd was hers.

They belonged to her.

"You wanted less mess," she offered.

"How exactly?" he asked, thrilled. He wanted all of her—without restraint.

"No more breathing," she whispered.

Sheng's eyes widened. He stepped forward—then realized she wasn't speaking to him.

He looked around. Looters, thieves, and murderers surrounded them, men who overtook this neighborhood during the end of the world, men who took advantage. These men stood motionless.

Sheng watched their skin begin to change.

At first, it was subtle. Skin blistered red, then blue. The men fell, hitting the ground, not fighting. One by one, suffocation took their lives. The patio and grass became a graveyard.

Hadley walked forward, exiting the kitchen.

"What else can you do?" Sheng asked as more shouts, more yells rose.

"They're all dead!" someone shouted—her first time hearing a woman's voice.

"Kill that bitch!" her partner yelled.

The shimmer of her shadow self wrapped around Hadley, purring, aching to be used. Hadley closed her eyes, decision-making floating away like a balloon on a string.

"Go," she breathed—the word barely formed.

"Get off of our turf," said a man at the edge of the patio.

He wore a vest with no shirt, a full face mask covered his face. He held a baseball bat in his left hand. A trembling woman, purple underneath her eyes, clung to his shoulders.

Three other goons stood around them, massive heavy black guns pressing in.

"You must be the man of the house," Sheng offered.

"You can call me Rex," the man said. "We took over this neighborhood when the moon blew. You're trespassing."

"Sorry to hear that, Rex," Sheng said. "We're just here for one of my cars."

Rex's eyes bounced between them.

"Now, see, here's the problem," he said, pacing back and forth. "You killed most of my men. Food's scarce, so maybe you did me a favor. But I don't take favors from strangers. Leave the woman. Walk away. We'll call it even."

Rex licked his lips, unabashed and possessive.

"I am death," Hadley said.

Sheng turned to look at her, stunned.

Her shadow self plunged into Rex, translucent.

Rex hit the ground, and the shaking woman screamed.

Hadley moved forward, avoiding Sheng's touch. He watched her—hurt flashing in his eyes.

All she saw was the task in front of her.

She was empty, just like she had once wanted.

Her shadow self jumped right back into the body as Hadley approached. The group of humans was covered in dirt and oil. They had scavenged their survival.

The woman sobbed louder now, as Rex sat up—his eyes blank, his body now Hadley's.

"Holy shit," Sheng laughed. "This is incredible. My wife is the scariest, most amazing woman." He slapped his thighs and muttered, "Absolutely fucking ridiculously hot."

The undead rose. The others followed suit, forming a half-circle, linking hands.

Hadley lifted hers and placed a finger on her warrior's forehead.

A sound—glass clinking, ice in a shaker.

His body crystallized. Glass replaced skin. Sunlight refracted across the lawn.

The woman tried to pull away, but it was too late. The transformation spread—wrist, arm, shoulders.

Colors reflected on the grass all around her as the sun shone through the bodies, now heavy statues, relics, trophies to be kept—a stained-glass graveyard.

"I'd love to kiss you," Sheng said, "but who am I to assume I won't turn to glass?" He bounced beside her, loyal as a rottweiler. "Let's go. The garage is this way."

They moved, though Hadley was having a hard time recognizing her steps. She suddenly felt like she was not really there at all. The pulse of life was leaving her, a ghost trapped, cursed to haunt forever.

It was just as well; she had plenty of people to haunt.

Don't I?

She couldn't remember. She knew she had been someone once. She had a name. She needed to hear it again—or she might lose it forever.

"Hadley," Sheng said, "just through here."

That was it: Hadley.

They reached the other side of the garden and entered a large garage, painted white with sliding amber barn doors on black metal tracks. Rustic, camouflaged by the garden—Hadley had never even noticed it, though she once had been here for months.

Sheng moved to a small window and pressed a hidden latch.

Click.

A panel opened. He typed in a code. Seven soft beeps echoed in the silence.

"I don't see evidence of earthquakes, snowstorms, or anything catastrophic," Hadley said. "So why did they act that way?"

A heavy thud answered her. The scent of iron filled the air as the door groaned open, like a tomb being unsealed.

"Humans are hard, Hadley. Their reasons are not too different from your reasons. Why did you take the job? Why did you come here that first time?"

Hadley clung to the memory like a note in her hand being taken by the wind. "Because I needed to survive."

"Exactly."

They stepped inside. Sunlight filtered in through high glass panels. Dust floated in golden streaks. Vehicles lined one wall, motorcycles on the other.

Sheng looked at her and shrugged with a smile. "Just playing the part of a rich human. I had to get them."

He opened the passenger side door of the nearest car.

"Get in," he offered.

"What are we doing?" she asked. She genuinely couldn't remember.

"I promised I'd help you," he said, confused. "I choose you, Hadley. Especially now that you chose me. Let's go."

Hadley looked inside herself and found no reason to move. If she'd ever wanted anything, she'd forgotten it.

She got in anyway, folding into the red leather seat. Sheng shut the door and circled to the driver's side.

The engine purred to life.

"I'm not choosing you," she said. "You should know that."

His face didn't change, but his jaw tightened as he shifted into gear.

"Then what was that in the grass?" he asked as they pulled onto the driveway. "Doesn't matter. I said I'd take you home."

"Sex is what brought me into this, Sheng." She stared at his hand. Should she take it? Should she comfort him?

It didn't feel right. Nothing felt right. Even speaking required effort. Her vision blurred. Colors bled together into something new.

"It was a goodbye, then," he said, making a turn.

"It was," she agreed. "You're going to hit that man."

Sheng turned the wheel hard and slammed on the brakes. A wiry man appeared, slamming his palms on the hood.

"Wooohoo! Look at this beauty. If I'd known where it was kept, I would've stolen it first."

The man pulled a silver ninja star from the back pocket of his jeans.

"How about you two hop out and let me take over? I've gotten pretty good at throwing this thing."

Hadley didn't think—she obeyed, not from fear, but from detachment. She opened her door and stepped out.

"What are you doing? Stop!" Sheng shouted.

Her blonde hair caught in the wind.

"I like a woman who listens. I like any woman, to be fair," the man laughed. "And you're naked. This day couldn't get any better—"

The man froze.

He looked at Hadley like he had seen a ghost.

His free hand grabbed the cowboy hat on his head, bringing it to his heart.

"Darlin'?"

41

Arryn | Outer Space

The first thing he noticed was the smell—putrid, like vomit. Arryn opened his mouth; cold, dry film clung to his face. That's when the acidic burn rose in his throat. He realized he smelled bile.

His bile.

Arryn did the only reasonable thing he could think of—he brought his hands up to his helmet, vision blocked by the filth coating the visor, unclamping it with frantic fingers. His bones were sore, aching from the cold despite the burning that crept beneath his skin.

How long have I been out?

Truthfully, he was a little pissed that the group left him soaking in puke. The second the airtight seal loosened on his helmet, he choked as the air escaped his suit.

He was still in space. And he was spinning.

He couldn't stop.

Arryn let the helmet fly from his head, vanishing into the star-stained dark.

A new wave of dizziness crashed through him—this wasn't a magic hangover. He had been flipped like a pancake for Gods knew how long.

He needed to stop spinning. He needed the vomit off his face, out of his nostrils. He needed to breathe.

Arryn reached with his magic, finding what he needed—just enough to mold a reaction control thruster. He spun with it clutched in one hand for too long, nauseous, depleted.

The suffocation didn't help.

He counted rotations and found the rhythm. Then he waited for the precise moment to swing the pack over his shoulder and clip it across his hips.

It was large, and Arryn knew that if he were on Earth, it would be obscenely heavy. It wasn't a perfect fit; his oxygen tank got in the way. But after feeling confident in the timing, he slung the rectangular shape into place and grabbed the handle.

Arryn pressed down with his thumb. The thruster activated with a gentle but firm push. A controlled jet of gas burst from the nozzle. He aimed it carefully, firing bursts in the direction opposite his spin until the spinning began to slow and the stars settled, still, a tableau.

He looked ahead, Earth a far-off beacon of light.

How did we get so far away?

Another tug at the back of his suit reminded him he wasn't as alone as he had thought. Arryn turned to look, creating a towel and wiping his face.

Djoser was still attached to him, hovering at his back, his head tilted upside down. He didn't move.

Arryn rolled his eyes.

So dramatic. This isn't that bad.

He'd take this over the gladiator training center any day. Those showers were humiliating.

The human fascination with the abyss—the lifelessness where celestials mocked their creations—made no sense to him.

He would never be like that. When he created, he let things be. He didn't meddle.

Once this was over, he hoped the Kinnari would be back in the temple. They would see how they were stronger together than apart. It could feel like family again.

A new, airtight helmet appeared around his head, and oxygen flowed again. Arryn took a breath. The effect was soothing, healing. His lungs cooperated. The tightness in his chest eased.

"Are you out of oxygen or just wallowing in despair?" Arryn asked Djoser through the mic in his helmet.

There was no answer.

"Man, can you stop being so dramatic?" Arryn sighed and pressed the button on the thruster to drift toward Djoser.

Arryn reached out and grabbed Djoser's shoulder, pulling him closer. The Kinnari's eyes were closed. He wasn't breathing.

"I knew it," Arryn sighed, summoning oxygen with his magic and forcing it into Djoser's suit. He took his fist and punched Djoser's chest hard. The motion was dulled by zero gravity, but it was enough to get a reaction.

Djoser's eyes fluttered open, and Arryn heard the deep breath he took through the mic, the moan of relief, the pain that accompanied that first breath.

"There you are," Arryn said. "How in the hell did you run out of oxygen so fast?" Then again, Arryn had no clue how long he'd been unconscious.

Djoser's throat was raw, his words dry. "There's a puncture."

"Say no more," Arryn said. He sent magic sliding over the fabric until it found the breach. He found it in the left leg and filled it in, listening to Djoser's breath steady.

"Thanks," he said.

"Finally, a thank you from someone." Arryn chuckled, leaning back to float again. "So." He clicked his tongue. "We're floating in the middle of space."

"It seems so," Djoser groaned.

"How long was I out?" Arryn asked. "How long was I spinning?"

"I don't exactly have a stopwatch on me," Djoser said.

"What happened to our tether?"

"Ayurveda."

"Hm." Arryn hummed, his eyes drifting toward something large and dark. Earth glowed fiercely—uncomfortably small. He was just realizing how close they'd come to a terrible situation.

"Well, I think that's our moon over there. It still looks intact. Should we head back to Earth?"

"I never want to go to space again," Djoser said, grumpier than usual.

"Let's go home and get you a stiff drink," Arryn said. "Hang on."

They were going back to the temple. Arryn was done.

He could've woken up in an entirely different galaxy—lost forever.

He had done enough.

Using the jets on his thruster, Arryn directed his trajectory toward the glowing planet miles away. Djoser floated behind him, spinning in slow somersaults.

"Don't throw up," Arryn chuckled.

"I'm not spinning nearly as fast as you were."

Arryn hoped Djoser could hear his eye roll.

The stars and somewhere, Ayurveda—became smaller, distant, burning.

As they approached the dark side of the moon, a warmer light glowed from the opposite side. Arryn knew what it was without a doubt: Ayurveda, still hammering away at the moon. —something he had never realized how much he hated until now.

It was too much work, maybe, for any of this. The moon was too much to manage. Arryn needed to take some things off his plate, that was for sure.

Trying to decide if he should pivot or hide, Arryn slowed down. Djoser drifted ahead, tugged by the cord that connected them.

"Let's go," Djoser panted.

"Ayurveda is still there. I don't have a fight in me," Arryn said.

"Precession, she came to help us. She was there," Djoser said, his voice stuttering with each flip.

"We are not going to get the hang of moving around up here, are we?" Arryn grinned despite himself. "It doesn't seem like she saved us, though. Probably best to leave it."

"She held onto me after the tether was incinerated. She pushed me away only after multiple solar flares came straight at us."

"She pushed us out into space?"

"I'm sure she had a good reason. Let's go ask her," Djoser said.

"Why does everyone assume I'm so stupid?" Arryn scoffed.

"Because you are a beautiful blonde giant with blue eyes. Stereotypes, you know?"

Arryn let the silence pass between them as he contemplated.

"She would go back," Djoser said.

"Precession? I can't believe she can even stand up, let alone fly into space." Arryn shook his head.

"No, Hadley. Hadley would go back."

"And why for the Gods' sake do you think that would matter to me?" Arryn asked.

"Because Allienna would want it to. She would want Hadley to matter."

Arryn forgot to breathe, hearing that name on someone else's lips. He thought he was the only one who thought about her, the only one who bothered to remember what she liked, what mattered to her, who she was.

"She was too good for this world," Arryn said.

"Honor her, Arryn," Djoser said, his voice soft. "Honor her by making what mattered to her matter to you."

Gods damn it.

Would every Kinnari now try to get what they wanted by throwing Allienna in his face?

He had to admit—it worked.

Arryn looked at the moon, the glow, the hazing fire that carried out over the top of his view so vibrant against the blacks, against the darkness.

"Fine. But it's not for Hadley." He sneered.

"Of course not, why would it be?" Djoser said, not sounding as happy as he should be for getting what he wanted.

If there was ever a chance of getting Allienna back—like Djoser had come back—Arryn knew it would be through Hadley's death. It had to be. It was the only thing that made sense with Amis and his uncontrolled, unhinged magic.

Balance of the planet, my ass. Get real magic. Murder less kids.

Not that Arryn had anything against murdering kids. That would make him a hypocrite. And that, he would never allow himself to be.

True. I am true.

True to himself, maybe?

Yes.

He fell somewhere in there. That was good enough for him.

Time to be a hero. Again.

Djoser twirled behind him once he pressed the thruster again, arcing in a half circle to get a better look at what he knew was coming.

Precession would be tied up. Or passed out. Ayurveda would still be working to destroy everything they had tried to rebuild.

It was hard being the strongest one sometimes.

He would never say it out loud, but it felt great having Death somersaulting behind him, Djoser's fate tethered to his own.

So this is why people like pets.

He got it now. It made him feel powerful—not alone.

Ayurveda's head snapped toward him the moment he entered her view. And it took him a second to understand what he was seeing.

"Wow," Djoser gasped.

Precession hovered in front of the moon. Ayurveda was opposite her.

They weren't fighting.

They were watching.

Above them was a rip in space, a blur of motion and stars, a cloud of fear, unforgiveness, and judgment.

"The Life Gifter," Djoser said. "It came to take me again."

"No," Arryn breathed. "That's not—I don't think ..."

Ayurveda turned away from him, back toward the rip.

Precession was an ethereal beauty—blue like ice from cold and lack of air. A cord was wrapped and knotted around her waist. She looked like she could float away at any second.

Arryn had no desire to chase her like a balloon into deep space.

He moved toward her. Ayurveda and the Life Gifter loomed over them both.

"What the fuck are you doing?" Djoser asked.

"You wanted me to help," Arryn grumbled. "You might be scared of the Life Gifter, but he's basically my dad. And I'm one grumpy teenager."

"That might take the cake for the most ridiculous thing I've heard you say," Djoser choked with a laugh.

"I'm in hero mode here," Arryn said, closing the distance. The strangest face-off of his life now loomed before him.

Djoser somersaulted behind him.

Arryn grinned.

My own little animal sidekick. He's cute.

Arryn extended his hand, feeling the swirl of atoms around him. He reached for them, gathered them, then pushed them towards Precession.

She transformed like something out of a fairytale—white space-suit enveloping her, thermal, airtight.

Arryn heard her gasp through the comms.

"Thank you," her voice crackled.

"What did we miss?" he asked her.

"How in the world did you stop those solar flares?" Djoser cut in.

"Simple." Precession sounded tired.

She was once again the weak little girl he knew, not the warrior who stopped a Goddess from annihilating the Earth's moon. "Angular momentum."

The swirling black-and-purple cloud above them began to descend. Arryn's vision disappeared in wisps of energy. The magic under his skin burned, wanting to harness that creation.

It was a level of his power that he would never have.

But Gods, he wanted it.

He wanted it like an addict.

And then, like steam through a vent, the Life Gifter left—wrapped around Ayurveda, who boiled away like water.

42

———————

Precession | Outer Space

"Finish it," Precession gasped, watching the one who ruled over them with terror swept away.

That air felt like a luxury, a basic need that she would never feel again. Her body hurt less when moving, cracked less severely, and warmth was slowly returning to her limbs.

"What?" Arryn asked, still looking at the spot where Ayurveda had hovered. Moments before he showed back up, still attached to Djoser, she had been there—still throwing solar flares at the moon. But she had turned her attention toward Earth.

Precession wished she could have asked the Goddess, but she didn't have a voice in space.

You failed to capture Hadley, so you decided to destroy her world?

"Finish the moon. It's so close to being done. You can finish it now," she said through her mic.

"I think we could all use a little break, don't you?" Arryn laughed.

"Arryn," Djoser's voice came through his speaker. "As much as I would love to have control over my movements again, she's fucking right."

"Yes, I am fucking right," Precession sang.

"Thatta girl," Djoser said.

Arryn blew out a long breath. "I don't want to do this."

"Are you afraid you'll get lost in your magic, and never come back out?" Precession asked.

"Why would you think that?" Arryn scoffed.

"Because I'm afraid of that, too. I'm afraid of it so much that I've accepted it. That I am no longer a person, a living being. I am just a tether."

A long stretch of silence followed.

"Precession," Djoser's voice broke the silence. "I'm happy you're here with us."

"Me too," she said, wishing he could see the slight smile on her face through her helmet. To matter to anyone was all she could dream of. She had lived all her years supported only by her sister, ignored by everyone else. And she didn't blame them.

She knew how she came off in the world, in a conversation.

Others saw her as a lunatic.

But it was only because she was so tired. The weight of the moon and the Earth lived in her consciousness.

"Do you know why the Life Gifter pulled Ayurveda away?" Arryn asked, moving a bit closer to the moon's surface with his thruster.

"You can stop pulling me behind you. Connect me to Precession," Djoser hissed.

"Sorry, Djoser, your mic is cutting out," Arryn said.

Precession was sure it wasn't, and she laughed while Djoser cursed Arryn to high heaven.

"You seem better up here," she said to Arryn, "more at ease."

"Maybe I'm not," Arryn said over Djoser's continued protests. "Maybe I'm just trying to survive like everyone else. Maybe I don't get the luxury of anyone understanding my pain."

"Ayurveda kept changing Karmakara's time webs. I think she got tattled on."

"That is one Goddess I'm glad is not coming for us. She must have the most creative, scary mind if she created you and Roksana."

"I'm not sure that they think like we do. It seems more like animal instinct," Precession said, wondering how her mind might differ from her creator's. "I believe we have much more consciousness than they do, more feeling."

Arryn grunted in response and began what she had demanded of him.

He reached out, his magic collecting atoms and pushing them together as more mass was added.

Precession felt heavier and heavier. She could have been sinking in space—it was hard to tell. There was a stream of water above her head and something pulling her foot down as she got further and further from the Earth's surface.

Until she hit the bottom and couldn't take it anymore. Any more would mean she wouldn't be able to speak or function, which would mean she would turn into the very thing she feared. The very thing Arryn feared, too.

It was a wonder how alike they had been all this time.

"That's it," she shouted. It was the only way she could get the words above the water, heard from the surface.

Arryn listened.

"Precession," Djoser's voice came in through her mic, but it was wavy, or maybe that was just her head. "Are you alright?"

She was.

Because they had done it.

They had done something together more impossible than battling the Gods. She remembered that day they'd sat around the temple communal table, when Reign dropped the news, and none of it had surprised her.

She was so rarely surprised.

"It's the right size," she said the words with great effort. She was so heavy that she needed to close her eyes. "You saved them all—everyone on the planet."

Her head lolled, hitting the side of her helmet. She could leave it there. Rest by holding onto that heaviness, letting herself exist under that water.

That was who she was. That was why she was here.

"Let's bring her back down," Djoser said.

"No," Arryn replied. "Let's bring her home. Let's all go home."

Precession let her body go limp, focusing only on her magic—on being the perfect tool. She was aware of the cord connected to her suit being tugged on, of a sudden change in speed and direction. One with purpose. Her body followed without choice.

"You couldn't have made me one of these before you passed out the first few times?" Djoser asked. "I want space jets, too."

"You can't handle space jets," Arryn said.

"You just like watching others struggle. Admit it," Djoser shot back.

"I've never denied it. The thruster is about to be useless; we're about to break the atmosphere."

Precession opened one eye just enough to see the bright colors of Earth engulf her view. It was so beautiful—more vibrant and glowing than any magic she could encounter within it.

"Home," she mused.

Home would be lovely.

Feeding her chicken would be nice.

Walking around the estate with her sister on her arm would be a dream.

She knew this wasn't the version of home Arryn meant. And the poor soul would never understand anything else. He would never understand the joy of building your own life—when all he did was build lives.

It was something he'd always take for granted. Precession understood that. She pitied that. He would only appreciate what was, what he couldn't make.

He couldn't remake them.

That's why he refused to let go.

Precession suddenly felt like a doll tossed across a room, dropping down with no control.

They had hit gravity.

Her heart, her stomach, and her lungs felt liquefied and concentrated into her shoulder blades. They tensed, the tear of her skin stinging—a painful freedom that felt so natural, the closest she would ever come to giving life.

Her wings wanted to come out to support her. The spacesuit was too thick to rip, and the oxygen tank on her back was heavy. She was falling—still falling—gazing upon oceans and land masses, wondering which realm they might land in.

"Djoser," Arryn's voice sounded strained in her mic. Precession glanced left, then right, seeing the two males falling near her, their connection intact. The air brutally hit their suits. Precession smiled, thinking it looked like tiny invisible gnomes slapping them with wide but light hammers.

"Djoser," Arryn repeated, more urgently.

It was so loud—the sound of the freefall like static, like electricity. A switch flipped—like she had fallen into an electric fireplace, and flames engulfed her.

Fire.

She was literally on fire.

"Djoser!" Arryn yelled.

"I'm a little busy fucking surviving!" Djoser screeched.

He wasn't wrong. The suit didn't protect against the flames. It began to burn off completely. Her skin was already so unbearably hot that she screamed as fire licked it.

"I've got it!" Arryn yelled. The helmet and its microphone were the last things holding them together in free fall. She watched the Earth come closer, and now, with the freedom of her suit burned away, she worried if her wings came out, they'd catch fire too.

That fear eased. The heat began to fade, like turning a shower dial to the right, until there was no fire at all.

"Wings out," Arryn instructed.

She didn't hesitate.

Like hitting a brick wall, Precession's body violently jerked back. Her head spun. She couldn't let go of the tether—not again. But she could feel it slipping. She fought to smooth her glide, to lower her heart rate.

She got there.

She calmed.

The air supported her wings.

And like a skater across ice, she found her grace. They all did—recovering, reviving, their bodies healing while still in the sky.

"Why didn't we catch on fire the last few times?" Djoser asked.

Precession giggled.

Everyone was naked except for their helmets.

Arryn should probably fix that.

"A special kind of compression suit," Arryn said. "I forgot to give us one this time."

Djoser grunted.

"What?" Arryn sounded offended. "Like you could've done better?"

"Let's move this way," Djoser said, cutting to the right. At least someone was thinking about navigating.

"Where did the fire go?" Precession asked.

"Heat and cold are just atoms moving at different speeds," Arryn said. "I'm not great at fire manipulation—but I'm not worthless either."

Precession kept flying, wings pumping, holding the tether tighter than ever before. She pulled it close—maybe too close.

She wasn't that strong. She knew that could never happen. She was an anchor, and that was all.

Her dizziness worsened. Motion blurred in her peripheral vision —two or three versions of Arryn and Djoser guided her while her mind struggled to keep them singular.

It was so heavy, the moon.

So, so, heavy.

This had always been her role—holding it, feeling it, living with it. She'd carried it for so long she'd forgotten how much it hurt.

It wasn't tolerable. It was destroying her. She was strapped to a board, screaming for more bindings—so she wouldn't have to choose anything ever again.

This world would live on. This world would heal.

We could heal.

That was why Celestine stayed. Why Precession still mourned Percy—her chicken, her companion—burned to ash before her eyes. There was beauty down below—life that didn't even know they existed, didn't know about Gods or tethers or wars in the sky.

"What do you think, Precession?" Djoser's voice interrupted her train of thought. "Will you be a part of every action-packed venture from here on out?"

"Count me out," she said, a smile hidden underneath her helmet. "I will support you in my own ways."

She always had.

"I think you do surprisingly well in a battle. I never understood where it suddenly comes from."

"Phoenix tears," she replied. "But they wear off. I need to lie down. Are we even going in the right direction?"

"Shit," Djoser laughed. "She's right."

His laugh made her feel safe, like it was really over. Like she could finally rest—at least until the next god lost their mind. She hoped the Life Gifter would keep Ayurveda contained.

Hadley could stop running.

She and Roksana could start over—rebuild what they'd lost.

The property was still there, in Chartres, just waiting for them.

She could hatch a chick and deem it Percy the Second. after the previous esteemed Percy the Great.

And then there was the situation where her sister was in love.

Well—"love" might be generous. Either way, they'd need a better strategy to keep Precession from falling into another hormonal fugue.

They flew together, drifting on recovery. Everything except the weight—the exhaustion, the dizziness—was healing. Her burned skin, scorched by fire and frozen by space, mended as they moved.

"Thank you," she said to Arryn as new clothes formed and clung to her—loose, waterproof cargo pants layered over thermals, new boots, and a windbreaker that wrapped neatly around her wings. It was all black and gray, and she felt like a stuntwoman, parachuting through the sky.

Arryn and Djoser flew ahead, guiding her like brothers protecting a limping lamb. It wasn't like Roksana's fierce protection, all bite and threat. This was gentler. They let her try. Let her fail. And she cherished it—this rare taste of freedom, however fleeting.

Before long, they passed wetlands cloaked in fog. Precession nearly gasped—she knew this land. She didn't know how, but it pulled at her. A white brick clock tower appeared in the distance.

A city slept beneath it.

"We have to stop here," she said.

"We can't. We've left two behind," Djoser said.

"We have to stop," she whispered.

She turned to Djoser, then Arryn. The twist sent pain down her neck. Her muscles weren't made for this angle, not after flying for so long. Her vision tunneled. Her edges were a blur of pinks, blues, golds, and violets.

The colors overwhelmed her, flooded her senses. Her grip on the tether slipped—just for a second—before she gasped and yanked it close again.

"We can come back here, I promise. It's not too far," Djoser tried to convince her.

"But we have to stop."

They didn't.

43

Arryn | Outside of Ebonspire

rryn's feet touched the ground, his boots sloshing. The snow around the twisted trees outside the invisible dome was melting. The sun was shining, as if it could still represent the Goddess—restrained, angry, vengeful.

"Fucking land!" Djoser whooped, throwing off his helmet as he touched down. "I could kiss it. Roksana, I could kiss you."

"Don't you dare," Roksana hissed.

Arryn instantly felt the celebration turn vile, filled with malice.

Roksana was sitting against the twisted trees, tied up. The cord that had originally been severed was wrapped around her. Her arms were pinned, and her legs flopped out in front of her.

"Hello, welcome back!" Celestine jumped into Arryn's arms. Her happiness, her smile, and her breasts all gave her a much warmer welcome than the other female just gave them.

"What has happened here?" Precession asked, her voice a muted bell as she walked through the melted snow. Her steps were as graceful as Djoser's when he'd had a few bottles of liquor.

She was holding onto the moon again—that was the difference.

Arryn would miss that strong, strange creature. It was slightly disappointing that she was forced back into this box.

But she chose it.

Like he chose not to use his magic before.

He needed to choose that again.

The power, the manic surges that filled him when creating, turned him into someone he didn't like. Someone his lost love would never tolerate. He couldn't give that energy, that care, to everything he made.

He wasn't nurturing. Not everyone needed to be.

"Isn't anyone going to restrain her? She's clearly a lunatic," Roksana yelled. Precession jumped like a cat hearing a loud boom.

"Oh, we have to be so careful with that word, sister," Precession said, her hand to her heart.

"Why does she want you tied up?" Arryn asked Celestine, who swooned in his arms like a true damsel.

"Oh, don't mind her," Celestine said, smiling. "She wanted to go after her sister, so I wiped a few tears on her to make her sleep and then dragged her to the tree."

"And tied me up," Roksana added—her words long, bored, but with just a hint of poison.

"I did," Celestine said proudly, bouncing up and down.

"I didn't need protection. You needed protection," Roksana said as Precession looked back at her.

The twin moved up and began to untie the cord, and as soon as it slackened, Roksana jolted upright and pushed the rest of it off, letting it fall to her feet as she stepped out.

"If you ever put one of those tears on me again, I will rip your feathers off —"

"She means thank you," Precession interjected. "Well, I mean, thank you. Roksana, there would have been nothing you could have done."

"You were gone. You were gone for such a long time. More than a day had passed." Roksana threw her arms over Precession, who immediately fell under the weight.

"You did it." Celestine's lips pressed against Arryn's. Pleasure flooded him, and his stress lifted. "The moon is restored thanks to you all." She turned to Djoser. "You helped, too?"

Djoser nodded, and Celestine bounced to him and planted a kiss on his lips, too.

Arryn cleared his throat, unexpected jealousy pulsing through his veins.

"I don't share," he grumbled, though no one heard him—or at least they pretended not to.

"The sky is so clear." Celestine beamed. "I'm so proud of you all."

"Will you be returning to Phoenix Nest, or whatever it's called?" Roksana asked, her words drawn out.

"Phoenix Rest," Celestine corrected, jumping up and down. "There's no time for home. There is still so much healing to do."

"I won't be joining you for that," Arryn said. Celestine looked up at him, a spark of disappointment in her eyes. She thought so much of him, and he didn't know why.

He didn't want it. He didn't want to be loved in such an obsessive way.

"I'm going home. We left others behind," Arryn said, stomping his foot. "I don't plan on leaving. Maybe not ever again."

Heads snapped to him, expressions on faces that he couldn't quite make out.

How could he be a disappointment when he'd already saved so many?

"But you promised," Precession's meek voice rang out—a siren song that tugged at his heart.

"I promised nothing."

"Yes, you promised. You said that you would go back. We just needed to come here first."

"Djoser said that," Arryn shot back quickly. "I need to get everyone out of my temple. I'll have to go back to Glaciel and make it habitable again so everyone sleeping on cots has somewhere to stay."

Precession looked heartbroken. Roksana clutched her arm, steadying her. Arryn did his best not to roll his eyes. It had to be an act at this point. She was strong—he had just seen it. The tears were real, yes, but how much could they have done?

"Precession," Djoser said, "I know we promised, but I need to find Reign."

"Why?" Roksana scoffed. "Is that more important than this? When my sister asks for something, there is always merit behind it, even if she doesn't know what that is."

That was usually true. Arryn had to admit it.

Still—it was just too inconvenient.

"I think the Atheri are after Sheng. Reign went to find Hadley, and I'd bet Sheng did too. I don't like the idea of something like that coming so close to either woman."

"The Atheri only kill Vrae. You can relax."

Djoser didn't look like he was going to relax. Instead, his jaw tightened.

"You can all enjoy your small field trip, find the immortal powerful beings later, and everyone wins," Arryn said, flexing out his wings.

"You're not coming?" Djoser shook his head at Arryn.

"No. I'm going home."

"I'm coming." Celestine beamed. "I can help with those in the temple."

"I can't carry you," Arryn lied. "I'm too tired. I'm still recovering from my blackout."

"Oh, it's no worry at all," she smiled before spinning into a flame of gold and red smoke, a fire that wasn't hot, that didn't burn, leaving the phoenix, the bird that she had claimed this entire time to be.

Arryn forgot to breathe. Forgot he was supposed to be annoyed with this pet who wouldn't stop following him. When Celestine turned into that bird, he couldn't remember any of it. All he could do was stare.

A light shone brightly—but one that wasn't there at all. A hue, a glow, wrapped around Celestine's phoenix form and poured into his soul. Sadness, happiness, curiosity, loss, and relief all gathered in his heart at once.

She was impressively large, at least five feet from head to outstretched talons. Wings of gold and painted crimson feathers looked more like fine china—porcelain. A sheen gave the impression it would be impossible for her to fly.

"Sometimes, the beauty you create," Precession said to him, "is overshadowed by all of your faults, Arryn. She is truly magical."

"She's not creepy like those Atheri," Djoser huffed.

"I like the Atheri," Arryn grumbled.

His moment of appreciation—of basking in that ambiance—drifted away. He was back on land, back to his senses, back to his annoyances.

"You certainly always seem to have a solution," Arryn said, more irate than he intended.

"Hear, hear, to your grumpy old man era," Djoser raised a hand. "Although we probably entered that closer to your eleventh year."

"You'll take me." Precession turned to Djoser. "You promised. I don't know the way. You promised."

Roksana stood by her sister, a vicious dog ready to protect. "A promise is a promise."

"A promise is a promise," Djoser sighed. "Fine. I'll take you back to that swamping, foggy place. But then we must find everyone else."

"I don't think we will need to," Precession giggled.

Djoser rolled his eyes. Everyone knew that they wouldn't get any more explanation than that.

"Fucking great, then," Djoser said, slapping his hands on his knees. "Let's go."

"You mean *let's fucking go*," Roksana challenged.

"Let's fucking go," Djoser agreed, wings spread wide as he grabbed Roksana and Precession by opposite arms.

"I don't need your help." Roksana sneered. Precession stood there with her eyes to the sky, moving her head like it was barely attached.

Light and color and gold swirled around them, Celestine circling the group, waiting for Arryn to ascend.

"Meet me back at the temple when you're done." Arryn looked at Djoser.

"We won't."

"Then I'll see you in Egypt one day," he said, nodding.

"We'll see, old friend," Djoser said.

Five pairs of wings supported bodies in the sky, in two groups: one heading north, the other east.

44

Reifoel | Serelune

The water was progressively dropping in temperature. It was exactly what Reifoel had hoped to see. He assumed Arryn was making progress on the moon—that it was growing—and that the tides would return to normal.

He would pace back and forth inside the royal dome for most of the day, pretending to be stoic and serious whenever Gasher or a scout entered with updates.

Most of the time, the news was unimportant.

There is no way that this is all my parents did.

After a few more weeks, Reifoel began swimming around the perimeter of Serelune with the scouts, confirming no more beasts were emerging from the mysterious crevices that had once brought dangerous heat.

At least this felt like something—more than kissing babies, more than smiling and parading with a crown. His people were healing—

so was he—but he hadn't realized how painfully dull a process that could be.

"It's a good thing," Gasher said. "We should be focusing on the less exciting tasks, ones that take the skills of a diplomat. Why don't we worry about electing a full council instead? I cannot be your only advisor."

"Why not? You're doing just fine."

"If I told you we must go to war, then there is no one to dispute me."

"I would dispute you. That sounds incredibly ridiculous."

"Hmph," she said. "We could find you a queen. I might propose my daughter. She is of age and completely likely to be uninterested."

"That sounds like the proposition of a lifetime," Reifoel said, rubbing his eyes and forehead. "I think what I need to do is go to the surface."

"No."

"Hear me out, Gasher."

"No."

"I need to find my father."

Gasher huffed and put her hands down on the circular table.

"Listen, King Pires. I know that you love your father, but you cannot leave your people here alone, not for that."

"I remember you saying that before." Reifoel nodded. "But that wouldn't be the only reason."

"I don't believe you."

"Would that not be treason?" Reifoel smirked.

Gasher opened her mouth, then closed it. She sighed and said, "Go on, Your Royal Highness. What is this brilliant plan, oh kingly one?"

Reifoel laughed. Gasher pretended not to smile back.

"I want to go to land—to the nearest town in Myrilosis—and secure an alliance."

Gasher's eyebrows raised. She looked impressed. "Go on."

"When our evacuation occurred, no one knew where they were

going. There was no plan other than to flee. I want to find a place for us to go. Somewhere, we are promised safety if the waters prove dangerous."

Gasher floated out from behind the table. "That is a surprisingly good idea."

"I didn't mean to catch you off guard. I'll try not to be offended."

"Are you sure you wouldn't rather have a line of tail parading for your hand?" she finally asked. "I think we need to stick together. We need to keep morale steady, and we need to move on."

Move on.

How could he ever move on? That was not something he ever expected to happen in his lifetime. Reifoel was staring at a possibility he wasn't sure he wanted—to be stuck in this life, forced to be who he was deemed at birth.

"Are you sure this isn't about burritos?" Gasher asked.

Reifoel tried to choke down his hysterical laughter.

Gasher's face was dead serious.

"This is about keeping our kind safe and prepared. We need an emergency plan. It's been a miracle that nothing has ever happened before, especially since we are so close to the deep."

Gasher thought quietly for a moment.

"We can send scouts with a written message from you."

"It won't work."

"And why not?" Gasher was getting impatient. Reifoel imagined that if she had a foot, it would be tapping.

"Our paper doesn't transport into the air. It will be soggy, illegible."

"You're being difficult, Reifoel."

"Isn't that part of this whole king act? To be a little difficult?"

"Your father listened to his counsel." She took a deep breath. "Look—leaving no one in charge is a bad look."

"That's not what's happening. You'll be in charge. And while I'm gone, I expect you to assemble a new council."

Gasher narrowed her eyes at him.

"Fine," she said.

"Fine," he replied.

"Is there a ceremony or something we must do before I go?" Reifoel asked.

"Oh, would you just leave already? I have so much to do."

Reifoel chuckled and swam out of the dome.

45

Reign | Mytholm

"What is it doing here?" Sable said, her breath hitching. Reign looked over at her strange new friend, one who held no hard feelings over cold-blooded murder. She was staring ahead at the spot where Luca had been lying, his blood still fresh.

His body had moved. That was a relief.

Reign still clutched her jaw, her stomach gnawing at her over the scent of what she craved—what she suddenly needed too much of.

Her eyes flickered over to Amis, who sat on the ground not far away. Reign cocked her head. The idea of biting into him was entirely too appealing. She flashed her teeth as he looked up at her, his face betraying unease as he rose to his feet.

"You see it, right?" Sable's voice drew Reign's attention again. "Why are you not addressing it?"

"I just told her to run. How else am I supposed to address it?" Tristan asked.

"What is happening—" Reign followed Sable's gaze. The streets were long and clear except for a figure a few hundred yards away. It appeared alone at first, inching forward in shadow. No, not shadow—fog.

The air seemed to wrap around it. A ghost, perhaps? She was no fool. Ghosts were children's stories. Whatever this was, Tristan worried.

Demons—these Vrae—were scared silly of Tristan. Reign gulped, prepared for the worst.

Why is there something worse?

Amis walked over quickly. "The children are inside. Luca is being cared for. He heals slowly. The mortal blood inhibits—"

"Waihema children are not the ones to be worried about right now, Amis. Kinnari are not the ones to be worried about."

"Only us. It only comes here for us," Sable burst out, practically sobbing.

"This is your last chance, Reign. Run."

"What about you?" Sable interrupted. "What about us?"

Reign didn't run. She didn't know what to do. Her curiosity held her rooted. Her feet were entirely planted, her wings too heavy, useless. She stared at the figure in the fog, squinting.

"The fog is back. We can take cover." Sable's words were shaky. There wasn't a hint of confidence.

"They don't need to see," Tristan said.

They?

Reign could now see long torsos and tall legs moving within that blanket of fog.

Arryn was right. He should stop creating.

Reign blew her lips out, trying to regulate her nerves.

What could be so terrifying that even Vrae fled?

Reign had to know, despite Sable pulling and tugging on her arm.

"Stop," she said.

Sable's grip on her went limp.

"Reign, you don't understand," Tristan pushed her. "You will all die. We will all die."

Reign ignored him, watching the figures come closer. The fog that cloaked them gradually disappeared. There was a minute where she almost laughed.

What a hilarious joke.

"Is this a prank?" she asked, but as she got the words out, Tristan grabbed her and put his hand over her mouth.

A fog did not wrap the bodies that walked closer to them. It was light. Light so bright it nearly erased the bodies it emulated, even in the daytime. A beauty radiated from that light—not from any specific features, nothing biologically attractive—but the beauty of life, roses, stars, something ethereal and uncontainable.

The large eyes were windows to a heaven; their bodies were keepers of it. She wanted to reach out to them. She tried to flip her hand around in that light.

But why was Tristan afraid of something so beautiful?

"Atheri," she said, her voice muffled under Tristan's hand.

He let go of her then. His brown hair and youthful eyes seemed innocent, but his lips were a straight line. The slowness of his breath reminded her of his age, his stillness.

She still didn't understand. She still didn't know. But there was not one indication from the boy beside her that this wasn't serious.

"I found you," Meenio's words echoed across the distance between them. The voice—perfectly lovely, sweet, cheerful.

Tristan stepped forward, his arms slightly elongated at his sides as if preparing for a herd of Vrae to charge. As if he planned to stop them all.

Reign had never thought of Tristan as gallant before. She hadn't thought much of him at all. The poor boy was murdered in front of them.

He was the lost Kinnari.

All this time, he'd been here, protecting this place, protecting all of them.

"Tell them to leave." Tristan looked at her, his eyes pleading like a lost puppy.

He is terrified.

Reign didn't hesitate; she looked over to Meenio and said her command.

"You will turn around. You will take the Atheri you traveled here with, and you will all leave Mytholm."

Meenio smiled. The bright glow cast light ten feet around it. Tristan ducked, hands over his head. Reign raised an eyebrow—first at him, then at Meenio—as she realized the Atheri were not, in fact, leaving.

"We are not affected by Kinnari magic. Our creator—he seemed to know better when designing us."

Gods.

"Sable, grab every Vrae in the city and slam them inside. They are not to be touched by their light."

Their light?

Sable didn't ask questions. She nodded and turned, following directions perfectly.

Tristan was muttering to himself, his eyes closed, chin raised.

"Witchcraft?" Reign scoffed.

She didn't know what she should be doing. She didn't understand why she should be scared. But it had something to do with their light. That much was obvious.

"I'm praying. The Life Gifter sometimes listens to me."

That was the most surprising thing she'd heard all week. Her mouth popped open as she shook her head.

"The thing? The formation of power that completely ignores us?"

"It's the only God that doesn't. The Life Gifter has no agenda. No power needs."

This is probably the wrong time to talk about this.

Tristan opened his eyes, ignoring Reign's expression of disbelief. Instead, he looked toward the Atheri—toward Meenio—with a new determination painted across his puffed chest. A peacock, ready for the fight.

"You have no business here. We had an agreement. It has not been broken," he shouted.

Meenio drew closer still. The light grew brighter, highlighting more of the street with every step. Tristan stepped back. Reign followed, not willing to risk what she didn't understand.

"That's where you're wrong. This one here beside you came into our home—our hidden city—and wouldn't you know it, when she left, we followed her back. It was hard to track her. She kept disappearing. Don't let all our efforts go to waste."

"She's new. She didn't know the rules. She didn't even know what she was."

Meenio's extra-long fingers drew together in glee. That light reached for them, blinding.

It looked back to the other Atheri and nodded.

"I think it's time. We make no exceptions," Meenio said.

"Shit," Tristan said, then violently grabbed Reign's wings and threw her to the ground, jumping on top of her.

"What the fu—" Reign started to say as her head slammed into the pavement. But she stopped as screams and shrieks erupted from farther away. She heard the sound of flesh decaying, sizzling, as if hit with a laser gun.

An Atheri near the back of the group exploded. The heavenly light poured out, erasing everything from Reign's vision like a shield of invisibility. It was quickly approaching—about to reach Tristan's foot, the one not tucked into her.

"Their light kills Vrae. That is their only purpose," Tristan began.

"This is a crappy goodbye," Reign choked out. But as the light neared, as the screams grew louder, as she listened to Vrae still trapped in alleys, it pulled back.

It all happened impossibly fast. Her brain could barely register it. Her eyes could barely see.

Tristan must've seen it too. She could tell by the subtle shift in his body—the tension in his arms loosened. The light continued to recede. The shrieks of dying Vrae quieted.

Tristan pushed himself off of her, his knee pressing into her kidney.

Guess I don't need that.

She winced but said nothing, scrambling to her feet. Tristan had tried to save her—even when she was stubborn. Even when curiosity came to kill the cat, he still blocked the light.

"You would have died," she said to him, her words solemn, disbelief sitting there, a distrust in the gesture.

"I'm just not important enough anymore, Reign." His shoulders stiffened as they watched the light return to the Atheri who cast it. "With the secrets out, someone else can easily step into my place."

"Why did they stop?" She ignored that last part. Tristan seemed pretty damn irreplaceable to her—but they could argue later.

She was met with silence as she turned her head to see Tristan pointing and counting with his finger.

"One is missing," he said.

A chill ran through her. "Is it on the hunt?"

"What else can it be?"

The other Atheri were not staring at Reign victoriously as they had been before they cast their light. Instead, they were staring at an empty spot, a spot that the missing Atheri once stood.

"They are confused," Reign huffed. "They don't know."

"Try a command again," Tristan said.

Reign nodded and stepped forward, Meenio immediately turning its head to look at her. That bright-lighted smile, that cock of the head, told Reign that she had seconds before it was about to strike again. She would beat it to it.

But it choked. Meenio's light glowed brighter, reaching around it. Reign furrowed her brow, watching the smallest pieces of its body disappear. It began slowly—then, like a bubble popping, Meenio was gone.

The remaining Atheri stared at the spot, confused again.

Reign knew that magic. However, she didn't understand what it was doing here.

Tristan's lips twitched up too. They were likely thinking the same thing.

Another Atheri disappeared before their eyes, and then another, and another. With each one, Reign's confidence shone. They would be alright.

And despite the Vrae that likely died minutes ago, the ones that were not warned and didn't exactly know what they were up against, just like her, this city would be okay.

"You can come out now," Tristan said, smirking.

Without hesitation, the doors were thrown open, and children streamed out into the streets, smiling and celebrating.

"Tristan, you saved us," Reign heard among them.

Tristan looked at her and shrugged, a giant grin on his face.

You didn't do shit, and you know it.

Reign laughed and looked around, seeing Amis emerge holding a bright-eyed Noah in his arms. Salome and Ahora were skipping to keep up with him, his eyes finding hers before he rolled them.

"Luca will be okay," Amis told her once they reached them. "He's sleeping now. He's strong. He will survive."

"It looks like we all will," she said, smiling back at Salome, who grabbed her hand and jumped up and down. "What happened just now? Does anyone know?"

"Isn't it obvious?" Amis asked.

It was obvious, but Reign didn't see him. She looked around and saw no indication that he was there other than just having seen his distinct magic.

"Are you looking for me?" a gruff voice approached behind them.

Reign turned her head. The voice matched the magic.

"I can't believe we are all here, standing together, in my city," Tristan said, smiling as Djoser closed the distance. "Where did you come from, old friend?"

"We've all been here for the last half an hour or so," Djoser said. "It took us some time to decide to leave, but something about the Atheri made me suspicious. It wasn't hard to convince them to come with me."

"We?" Reign asked.

"Yes, we perched on the clock tower," Precession's beautiful voice wrapped around Reign like a warm hug.

"There was a lot of drama down here; it was like watching a soap opera," Roksana said, arm in arm with her sister, her nose held slightly higher in the air than was necessary.

"It is so, so good to see you all," Amis said, but his gaze was on Roksana.

The energy around them all, suddenly so heavy, filled with lust and pride.

"I was hoping I wouldn't see any of you again," Roskana smirked, pulling her shoulders back, still gazing at Amis.

Reign ignored them and turned to Tristan. "Thank you."

He only nodded and then excused himself. "I have to go find Sable. I don't see her here."

Reign watched Tristan slip away, as she was left with what she would consider the most combustible individuals of their Kinnari clan.

Djoser put his hand on Reign's shoulders, and she looked up at him. "Is Hadley with you?"

"No. I didn't find her."

46

———————

Arryn | Kinnari Temple

A touch so smooth, porcelain wrapped in silk, trailed along his neck. Celestine, in her phoenix form, sat atop his shoulder. Her tears rolled down his collarbone, and his skin drank them up like he was Reifoel in a desert.

Arryn had let her overtake him.

The fabric that clung to him was now soaked.

It was the first time Celestine's tears had made him feel like Allienna's touch.

His burning was gone—his anxiety, his despair, too.

He was a shell. He liked being a shell. They were strong.

The phoenix turned over, belly to the sky.

A storm was brewing in the distance; thunder crashed, and clouds illuminated. It was healing, resetting.

Amis was out there, unknowingly helping the Earth find balance again.

Arryn's biceps ached as the phoenix suddenly turned herself back into a grown woman. Celestine's face broke out in a smile, dimples etched into her soft cheeks. Her brown eyes were too easy to get lost in.

And yet, he still didn't want it. He didn't want her.

It wasn't like his relationship with Allienna—this wasn't true love. If he let her stay, it would only be to use her for those tears. No one deserved to live as a tool.

"Celestine," Arryn said, "It wouldn't be fair for me to keep you. You belong to the world."

Celetine's eyes widened. She always had the sweetest crease at the cross of her eyebrow and nose whenever she was surprised, but then, she smiled again, and he was grateful he couldn't feel anything, that the effect of her own tears stopped him from telling her that he was joking.

She could be mine. All mine. And she would choose to stay.

She would choose him.

She would choose him one hundred times; he did not doubt it.

"I will go." Celestine's voice didn't hint at sadness or insecurity. "I will go after we heal what's in front of us. After you feel settled, after we get you put away."

"You make me sound like a cat." He laughed, making sure that tall snow boots appeared, wrapped around her feet, ankles, and calves before setting her down in the powder-soft snow that danced in flakes around them while wind whipped it back up from the ground.

Arryn felt like he was in a snow globe, like the entire world could see the two of them, although they were isolated at the temple's exterior. A mountain hidden from the world, a mountain that couldn't be seen by technology, a mountain that contained one of the few portals that connected to two realms. It was home, this mountain, and he would hold on to that forever, even when the worlds were gone, leaving only him. He was confident there would be a future that looked like that. This one almost had.

"Your words would make me fear what's in that temple," he said.

"There is sadness in there." She looked at Arryn, her face gentle, composed, but the twitch of her fingers betraying her. "Bodies crushed, preserved by cold. We will bury them together. Please let me help you."

Arryn nodded to her, staring ahead at only an enormous mountain of snow before them. There was no reason to delay it, no point in procrastinating. His heart did not tug; the tears kept him held to logic, only.

He knew he would be grateful for that.

He knew that if he could hope, it would be that Amis, those kids, and more had gotten out before whatever destruction happened.

Arryn marched up to the pile of snow and stuck his hand through it until he hit something solid, only to shake the snow away from the temple wall, now a tiny part of it visible. His stomach lurched when he saw the etching on the stone, the brick part of the story of Reign, of her buying his freedom in ancient Rome. When he'd reconstructed it, he'd placed this brick near the top.

Arryn pulled his arm out of the snow, gathering the atoms in the air until he had enough to create a large barrel gun, connected to propane.

"This will make it faster," he said, primarily to himself, but he knew Celestine was behind him, watching, waiting while Arryn dug into the snow, hitting bricks, scraping and revealing more and more pieces of his fallen home.

This one wasn't on him; he hadn't abandoned a monster chained inside.

Not this time.

This time, picking up the pieces felt heavier, like he would never build his family's home again. It would be reconstructed, put back together, which wasn't much of a problem, but no one else would come back. At least, not anyone he wanted to come back.

Arryn knew that he was choosing solitude again. This time, there was intention behind it, no matter how much he might have wanted it to be different. This time, his form of self-punishment, his repentance, was taking a deeper turn. He would do what he had never done before, and really understand, really reflect on his part in all of this.

Allienna had chosen to leave, even though he loved her.

He wouldn't make the same mistake again, driving someone away without knowing why. He wouldn't fall in love. He would protect his heart and not let the burning control him, not let himself be a slave to his magic. He could be better. He could be different.

But he didn't know how to do that without throwing everything he knew away.

Out there, he would have a family. Out there was a daughter, his blood, and beings he'd shared so many years with, beings he loved even if they were infuriating, insubordinate, and mostly stupid. He wouldn't bother them; he wouldn't get attached. They would live. He would make sure by not being around, by not getting involved.

It felt good. He was being good. This is how he could love, from a cage of his own making.

More bricks with more fallen stories were uncovered until he got past the outward layer of debris.

You don't need permission to use your magic. You've been managing it. You can use it sometimes.

Arryn sighed, looking over his shoulder at a smiling Celestine, a literal ray of sunshine in an otherwise gray and cloudy storm. She was so patient, not making a noise, not asking questions. It was hard to let that go: a statue of a woman who could make him feel so good.

You don't want to fill that void, he reminded himself.

That void was for his one love, his remarkable counterpart, his Allienna. He would always keep it there, a reminder of her, her memory with him for eternity. The aches in his heart proved that it existed at all.

Arryn dropped the shovel, the clang of metal ringing out as it struck the surrounding bricks. He lifted his hands, calling on his magic.

Atoms stirred to life around his fingers, whirling like sugar in a cotton candy machine. Thin strands formed, weightless and pliable, dancing between his palms before being spun into something finer, stronger: silk.

He manipulated the speed of their movement, warming the snow at his feet. Slowly, the mountaintop began to melt. Steam rose even as the sky continued to snow, flurries drifting down in a spiral, brushing against him like the gentle arms of a twin waterfall—one hot, one cold—colliding midair.

The Kinnari temple was fully revealed when the powder around him melted into slush, a jungle of wet and crunch that attacked every fiber of clothing he wore, trying to find a weak seam to erupt through.

Arryn stared, listening to Celestine's footsteps as she walked up behind him, putting her hand on his left shoulder, followed by her head.

"More?" she asked.

"No more tears," Arryn said, though turning them down was almost an impossible feat with the ruins that lay in front of them both. Celestine slid her gloved hand into Arryn's, and he accepted that comfort. It might be the last he would ever receive.

"Djoser was right. Roksana was right. We should have come back," Arryn said. Before him, were bricks toppled and piled as if each one had been lifted into the air and violently thrown back down, its weight so crushing that the earth underneath, the hardened snow and rock, were indented and molded together, creating a bond that seemed impossibly close to cement.

"There was sacrifice here, yes," Celetine said, "but never forget how many more there could have been, should you not have found a safe place to create. You went to Ebonspire to see the damage, to heal. That's why I went with you. But instead, you mended so much more."

"Ebonspire didn't need healing. The Atheri were healthy; they could wipe out Vrae. That was all that mattered."

"I don't think it did," she mused, her accent changing the *O* to a *U*. What he'd once found so charming was now something that made the muscles in his stomach tighten, a punch to his gut.

"Come again?"

"Wiping out the Vrae—it was never vital."

Arryn furrowed his brow, recognizing a real need to be alone, where there was no one to disagree with him.

"That's where we find ourselves at an impasse." He shook his head, clearly appreciative of his choice to be alone. He didn't have to deal with the craziness of others.

Arryn recognized pieces of cots, benches, and the beautiful communal table that had lasted a millennium, maybe even longer.

Hours passed as he lifted bricks, some by hand and some by constructing, by shaping with his magic. There were bodies, yes, and he and Celestine used the shovel he'd thrown to the side to dig a grave for each one only a hundred yards away, a final resting place there among the Kinnari, the shapers of their world.

I'll make something beautiful, he promised each one while snow was neatly packed on top of each of them.

Arryn went to lift one more stone, wedged on top of what he assumed was a cot.

"Finally," a voice said as he carried most of its weight, lifting it only a few inches. The voice sounded on the edge of death, a love note serenaded while floating on the river to hell. Arryn nearly dropped the stone from surprise.

Someone lived.

Arryn quickly tossed the brick aside. A grumpy puffball with blue matted and frozen fur stared at him. Broken glasses were still pushed to his face.

"Balizar," Arryn yelped, kneeling to scoop him up. It was more of a job than he expected; the creature was surprisingly heavy. "What happened here? How are you alive?"

Celestine was immediately behind him, wiping her tears on Balizar where she could reach him.

"Your fur won't absorb it well." She frowned.

"I'm all fur," Balizar groaned. "It's like I was made on top of a mountain."

Balizar still managed to give Arryn his most disapproving look. Arryn only smiled.

"Are there others?" Celestine asked.

"Set me down," Balizar barked at Arryn. "If you're back, does it mean that it's safe? Can I go back to Glaciel?"

"There's so much to rebuild," Celestine said while Arryn propped Balizar on his feet. "No one has been back yet."

"But you did it? The moon is healed, the Goddess subdued, at least for now? I'm surprised she let you live," Balizar said, looking at Arryn.

"It's all done, at least for now," he agreed. "Did you see anyone else?"

Balizar considered, taking off his glasses and cleaning the cracked glass with his defrosted fur.

"I saw a few people, those kids with the long-haired Kinnari, go into the portal, to Myrilosis, I assume."

Arryn closed his eyes, processing that someone got out.

"I thought at first it was a massive earthquake, the way that the temple shook," Balizar said, "but then the roof overhead was gone, and I saw the tornadoes only when they hit. They were big, and there was more than one. It felt like they took up the entire sky. We couldn't hear each other scream, only the sound of the wind. Even the sounds of items crashing and flying were muted. It was as horrible as the attack from the Goddess, possibly even more so because there was no target. It was just weather."

Arryn handed Balizar a plate of food, hot steaming potatoes with a white drizzled sauce, and a hot cup of coffee.

"You might be scoring more points with me for that," he said, not looking Aryyn in the eye, but accepting the food. "Let me know when I can go through the portal. I'll be over here recovering."

Balizar walked away, flopping ten yards away in the snow and moaning much too loudly over his first sip of coffee.

"I don't think I've ever seen him so happy." Celestine laughed. "Brick by brick?"

"Brick by brick." Arryn nodded back at her, turning his attention back on the slabs of stone, as he polished and refined the stories and stacked the temple back up high.

When he was at the last stone, he stopped, staring at the story about how the Vrae had created a truce, about how a vengeful sun was their real enemy. Arryn amended it, with new carvings showing

Precession and Djoser alongside him, to heal a moon, depicting a team that saved this world with no obligation to do so.

Death and gravity are the real heroes.

The thought made him smile.

"Balizar," Arryn yelled out. "You can go through the temple now, through the portal. Take Celestine with you."

Celestine's face was in his instantly, her lips pressing on his, her arms wrapped around his head.

"Promise me you'll heal," she asked of him, a whisper in his ear, a secret just for them.

"I promise."

Balizar sulked as he stomped by, sloshed snow spraying at every step. "Get a room, you two."

Arryn watched Balizar and Celestine march through the temple door, fresh snow accumulating on the handle. Celestine turned around, one last look and one last goodbye, before they both disappeared into the dark, long hallway.

"Celestine, wait," Arryn yelled, running after them. He caught them right before they all reached the great room. Celestine raised her eyebrows, a hint of a smile, of some hope on her face.

"You called for me?"

"Here," he said, holding out his hand as a sleek metal and glass brick appeared in colors that matched the stormy sky outside.

"What's this?" She asked.

"If you see Reign, just in case, can you give her this? It's called a cell phone. I have a number programmed to this one." He showed her its direct counterpart in his other hand. "She will know how to use it."

"I will never lose it until it's delivered," she promised. Then, she turned and walked off, Balizar by her side, complaining about something under his breath.

47

Chapter Forty-Seven

He couldn't decide if he was suffocating, forced to be crowned a pompous king. That should have been Isadore's title.

Reiofel laughed. He once worked hard to contain his rage, not to erupt at the threat of his cousin's desire for the throne. Now, he wished for that reality.

Isadore deserved this role as much as I deserved my ship.

Back then, his cousin acted so entitled. Now, Reifoel knew that it was a cover to hide his loneliness. No one spoke to Isadore then, just as no one spoke to Reifoel now.

Here he was, King of Serelune, without a single being that he felt close to.

I might even miss Kismet at this point.

Reifoel was never the kind of Serleune to have casual friends he'd keep in touch with outside of school or sports. His brief stint in seaball was proof enough: celebrated, lifted high on shoulders after scoring the winning tail flip—and then forgotten.

His life was now performing, being Gasher's puppet, a doll paraded around. It was important work, sending a message, creating an image of strength and unity.

That light—how could he resist it?

Reifoel closed his eyes and his mother's face appeared. Her understanding smile turned into a disappointed frown.

That's how.

He could never dishonor her.

What she would want, what would make her proud, was to see him step into his role. Let Gasher parade eligible future queens around him, settle down and live out this life just like she had.

Reifoel's head broke the surface, the sun blaring down on him, and a huge grin spread across his face. He breathed in, smelling salt, smelling sky. The water around him wasn't angry. It felt normal, how it used to.

He could have been on his ship, about to pass through the portal over him. All it would take was a leap. He would move through Myrilosis to the mortal realm.

"Alright, Father," he said out loud, "which realm are you searching for me in?"

He supposed it made the most sense to go to the mortal realm since that was where his mother had sent him and Isadore to search for the one called Kinnari.

"There was a whole group of them, Mom," Reifoel said. "There wasn't just one; there were many Kinnari. The one you sent us to find was kind of an asshole. You might not understand what that means, but just assume it's an insult."

Reifoel wiggled his tail, prepping to make the jump. He needed to get high enough to hit the horizontal portal, one invisible to the eye.

A wall of fire flashed before his eyes—the memory of how everything had started, how his ship had been destroyed.

"I'm coming for you, Father," he said as he threw himself up into the air.

Instead of splashing into the ocean like nothing had happened, he slammed into something.

Reifoel wasn't even sure if he had reached the portal or where he was. What he was sure of was the weight of a heavy body forcing the air out of his lungs, his gills working harder as he hit the water.

His head throbbed, but his neck took most of the impact.

Reifoel floated there with his eyes closed, feeling slightly nauseated, wondering how badly his brain had hit the sides of his skull.

"Are you okay?" A voice echoed in the distance despite being underwater.

That can't be a good sign.

Reifoel held his head, his neck, trying to shed the pain so he could look up, see what had hit him, see who was talking to him.

Gods, he hoped someone was actually there talking to him.

"Can you hear me? Are you okay?"

There was definitely someone there.

"Reifoel, I found you. Oh, Gods, I found you."

He heard sobs, gasps of air, and felt himself pulled into an embrace.

Head on a shoulder, he focused—he knew that voice. It became clear as the throbbing in his head calmed.

Then he put it together and forced himself to open his eyes.

Reifoel ignored the black and gold spots on the edges of his vision. The only thing that mattered now was who had slammed into him. He looked into eyes mirroring his own. A chin that was strong. Nearly black hair sat atop his head. He looked like Reifoel—if Reifoel were twice as big.

"Father," Reifoel said in disbelief. "I was coming to find you, to bring you home."

If his father heard his words, he didn't show it. All he did was hug Reifoel and squeeze so tightly that if not for his gills, he would have suffocated.

"We were so scared, Reifoel," he kept murmuring. "You're alive."

There, in his father's arms, Reifoel cried.

"We are the only ones left," Reifoel said through gasping breaths. "Mother, Isadore, our family is gone."

He could feel his father's hug loosen at his words, and then his arms eased them apart. He didn't let go of Reifoel's shoulders, his face solemn.

"But you came back, son. You came back and took care of everyone. I am so proud of you."

The two of them swam back to Serelune together, while Reifoel told the story of what had happened — his mother, their home, and Isadore.

"Are you okay?" Reiofel asked.

"Of course not. But when the moon crumbled, when the tides changed, we were so scared, so worried about you. I've been searching for weeks, coming across too many dead ocean animals to count. There was so little life left in the mortal realm waters. I came back defeated. I came back telling myself that not knowing if you were alive was better than knowing that you were dead."

Reifoel had never heard so many words spoken by his father before. He was sharing so freely, like his mother used to—while his father had stood behind her like a silent statue, firm and expressionless, always listening.

"I hope one day I can be as great as you," Reifoel said.

His father stopped and turned Reiofel to face him. "My son, you already are greater."

The horizon of Serelune was before them now, and both males moved with hesitation as they swam nearer.

"I need to say goodbye to her, in my own way," his father said as they reached the pebbled path. "I need time alone in the dome. I can't answer questions from the council."

Reifoel nodded. "I'll make sure you're not disturbed."

"Good."

"It's King Pires! He's back!" the voices murmured.

"We have a newly crowned king." Gasher swam over to them, her eyes gentle. "Welcome back, Sebastian. I'm so happy to see you."

His father took her hand and bowed to it.

"And I, you. I heard the unfortunate details."

"Yes, and your son now sits on the throne."

"We don't really have a throne," Reifoel muttered.

"Anyway, I think it would confuse..." Gasher trailed off.

"Gasher, I am an old man these days. I'm nearing four hundred. I am ready for retirement and to grow my family."

"I agree. I have already had the wife conversation with your son."

Reifoel wanted to die.

"Gasher, my father will sit on the council with you."

"But I already formed a council." She blinked.

"Gasher..." Reifoel raised his eyebrows at her.

"Fine," she said.

"Fine," he said.

"Fine," Reifoel's father said. "Now, if you will excuse me, no one is to disturb me in my dome."

Reifoel swam his father to his dome and then guarded the door.

He stayed there for hours, swimming back and forth, thinking about his mother, listening to the occasional gasp escaping from the walls of the dome: his father's grieving.

He waved to various citizens who swam by, carrying baskets, children, or pets in their arms. Most looked away quickly, leaving only a strange loneliness.

"What are you doing?" a sweet, gentle voice asked. Reifoel looked behind him as a Serelune woman swam up. He recognized her—someone from a class below him. Her black hair made the darkness swim around her, a star in the atmosphere.

"I am giving my father space to be alone," he said.

She said nothing but did bite her lip, her eyes a deep blue, just like someone else he knew.

"Honestly, I don't know what I'm doing," he added.

She smiled at him, and there was no sadness, no empathy, just a sparkle and a dimple in her cheeks.

"I believe, My King, that you are supposed to be planning out your legacy. At least, that is what is expected of kings, is it not?"

"Legacy?" he questioned.

"Of course. What plans do you have for us? What will you build our community into?"

Reifoel hadn't considered that before. He cocked his head at the challenge she presented.

"I don't have a lot of experience being king just yet," he admitted.

"No." She shook her head, her dimples creasing. "But you have something that no other king here has had."

"And that is?" he pressed.

"Isn't it obvious? You've traveled the realms. You have seen so much. You know so much. How can you make it better here, now that you've seen all the possibilities?"

It *was* obvious. Reifoel couldn't believe he'd never seen that before.

"What's your name?" he asked.

"Sima."

"Thank you, Sima," he said.

"For what?"

"For inspiring me."

She smiled at him. He smiled at her.

"I was looking for my mother. Is she here?" Her eyes hit the floor.

"Oh, sorry. Who's your mother?"

"Gasher." She laughed in disbelief.

Now it was Reifoel's turn to laugh.

Of course.

"She's not here."

Sima let out a sigh. "She hasn't been home much, and I made a large meal tonight. Can you send her home when she's done with work?"

Reifoel instantly felt guilty. That was likely his fault.

"I will make sure she has the evening off."

Sima nodded and left with a soft smile on her face. Reifoel did everything in his power not to stare at the back of her tail.

You now have work to do.

Reifoel turned towards the royal dome's door and shrugged his shoulders.

"He'll be fine."

Without wasting another moment, he rushed a few pebbled paths over to Isadore's empty dome. He wouldn't let it sit empty. If Isadore had wanted to be king, this could be Reifoel's way of including him, of making sure that he was always part of his choices, that he would always be remembered.

Reifoel grabbed a few blank pieces of parchment made of bioluminescent jellyfilm and an ink pad from the counter.

"I'm going to make you proud, Mom," he said out loud, hoping his words could reach her, hoping her spirit remained there with him, with his father, with Serelune.

He put the thin piece of bone in his hand, dipped it into the ink, and made a line on the parchment that glowed like a jellyfish lighting the empty sea. He started by drawing out the paths. They were a testament to time—to the generations that built them, maintained them, connecting separate families into one strong and loving community.

He would see it become something more, though. A town that could survive an apocalypse with plenty of survivors, without structural damage, and with a royal lineage that rivaled the age of most creatures in Myrilosis.

Starting with where the royal dome stood, Reifoel began to draw, and then he pulled out a separate piece of parchment to sketch the interior of his vision.

After some time, he pushed himself back, hovering a few feet above his work.

He smiled, a spark igniting in his eye.

48

Hadley | Sacramento, Ca

"Darlin'." Grant sighed, the biggest grin plastered on his face. "You still slumming it up with this here dirtbag?"

Sheng pulled his chin back with utter disgust.

"Do you know this... thing?" Sheng asked.

"You don't remember me?" Grant laughed. "I remember you. You stole my girl right out of my roster."

"Ah, the elusive pimp." Sheng suddenly sounded bored. "Can you move out of the way? We have somewhere to be."

"Two things there, cowboy," Grant said, his brown leather boot now on the hood of the car, scratching the paint with the heel. "One, I prefer manager, and two, why is my girl's shoulder see-through?"

"What?" Sheng said, looking over to Hadley.

Hadley looked down, realizing how right Grant was. The skin around the curve of her shoulder, down to her navel on the right side, was there, but it reflected the light around her, existing like her wings, like Ayurveda when she was in her human-celestial form.

"I should tell you," Hadley said, looking over at Sheng, who was now getting out of the car, his movements frantic, his face disheveled as he nearly threw Grant to the ground to get out of his way as he ran to her, his hand hovering over her shoulder.

"What did you do?" His eyes flashed to hers in pain, in shock, as if he knew exactly what this meant.

"I'm still here," Grant said, waving after regaining his balance.

They didn't hear him, though. Instead, both Sheng and Hadley's eyes turned white, their pupils completely gone, their bodies shaking before they both fell onto the asphalt road on top of one another, their limbs tangled, their breaths in sync.

They didn't go anywhere, not really.

Hadley and Sheng stepped out of their bodies, staring back at themselves—Hadley's stare was blank, empty. Sheng, on the other hand, looked ill, his attention immediately returning to Hadley.

"What did you do?" he repeated.

She didn't answer.

A boy stepped out from behind the car, his curly brown hair the epitome of innocence, of youth, with his full, plump cheeks and care-free grin.

"Long time no see," Sheng said to Tristan.

"You killed me and then left me to watch over Myrilosis. I've been a little busy."

"It doesn't sound like you've done a great job," Sheng said. "Do you happen to know what Hadley isn't telling me? I feel like you know."

"I do," Tristan said. "But that's not why I'm here."

"I'd like to be a little more efficient here, little man," Sheng said, snapping his fingers.

Tristan rolled his eyes.

"They are all there."

"Where?"

"Mytholm. They all know, too, what I am. What Reign is."

"Great, we might as well all be cousins now," Sheng said, rubbing the smooth skin on his face.

"I don't think I've ever seen you unattractive before," Tristan offered. "You look like you might actually be a demon under that skin. Those circles under your eyes might indicate that you need to let go of some stress. Can I recommend a fidget spinner?"

"What's going on with Hadley?" Sheng looked back at her. Another centimeter higher on her neck was translucent. "She's changing. She's empty, she's barely responsive."

"She can't feel," Tristan said. "She's stepped into the fire."

"The fire?"

"Ayurveda's fire. Her transformation to celestial is nearly complete. She will have unrivaled power, rule over us all, forget us all."

"No," Sheng said, sadness and shock evident on his face. "I can let her go, but I can't lose her in that way. We have to do something."

"I can't help," Tristan said. "I have to go back. I have murders to prevent."

"Take us with you," Sheng said. "Maybe one of them can help her."

"You can't travel through dreams, Sheng. You have little time to get to the other side of the world."

Sheng looked at Hadley, the translucence another centimeter high on her neck. She stared back at both of them, but might as well have been watching a movie happen before her. She wasn't a part of it anymore. She had taken her seat.

"I don't know what else to do," Sheng said.

"Just go," Tristan said, turning around and walking away as Grant came back into view, shaking Hadley, running over and kicking Sheng.

"Prick," he said, over Sheng's body.

"I heard that," Sheng groaned, eyes opening. Hadley looked at him, seeing him tired, seeing him frazzled.

"We need to get back to the house," he said, blinking and jumping up like he remembered he was on fire. "We need to get you to Myrilosis."

"What can I do?" Grant asked.

"Keep those assholes out of my house," Sheng said, gently picking Hadley off the ground and setting her into the passenger seat. The seatbelt went around her, Sheng's gentle hands buckling her in before closing the door and jumping over the car's hood to get in the driver's seat as fast as he could.

Everything from that point was a montage of images. Hadley had a hard time deciphering whether they were memories or happening in real-time—maybe both.

She was carried up the pathway toward Sheng's East Sacramento mansion. She saw the fountain. The massive doors—splintered, as if someone had taken a hatchet to them. She saw Sheng's legs stride through the wreckage. Saw her own body in his arms, ascending the stairs.

Then the edge. The top floor.

Wind in her hair. And then—she was flying.

Thrown.

Her shoulder clipped the chandelier, sending out a chorus of chimes that followed her as she fell, as her body sliced through the glowing pentagram, through the portal. Until she landed—again—in the grass, gasping. Sheng had thrown her, and somehow, without meaning to, he had reminded her how to feel.

She saw Kismet, who swooped down on her immediately, taking her in her mouth and placing her as gently as a beast could on her back, in between her scales. Sheng was already there, his arms wrapped around her as they flew.

Hadley looked down, seeing her translucent hip against the burgundy wyvern scales. Soon, she would be no more; Hadley would no longer exist. It already felt like that, a walking ghost of a mind, of a heart.

Whatever her body did after without her, would never affect her in the way that everyone in her life had, constantly failing her, continually hurting her, pretending to care. She'd been an orphan that no one bothered to check on.

That couldn't be a world she lived in; if she had any need left, it would be to change that world. She suspected that she'd forget, that every face would be a haunting reminder of something that once was, that she would never know again.

It was still better.

It was worth the absence of pain. It was worth the disappointment and anguish that had surrounded her since her mom had told her she was sick.

Hadley looked down below her, at untouched scenery with hidden huts peppered in crevices. A city must be nearby.

She closed her eyes, expecting to float off Kismet, to float and never come back down. Then Ayurveda would welcome her with eyes wide open.

"Hadley," Sheng said against her ear. "Hadley, are you in there? Please still be in there." The raw pleading made her open her eyes again.

She could see her shin—half translucent—still on the warm hide of Kismet.

Hadley raised her chin to look at her wyvern, the animal she was so completely wrapped around. Kismet was her true soulmate, and even as a Goddess, she would find room to remember her.

Wouldn't I?

Kismet was sleeping.

They had landed.

Hadley looked around her, Sheng's hands wrapped around her waist, as if he had vowed never to let her go.

He will have to. I told him.

She didn't want it. She didn't want him forever. She could never trust, she could never forgive, no matter how much he proved they belonged together, no matter how much he worked to wedge his way into her heart.

She would have no heart now.

It was perfectly convenient.

"No touching," she said, and began to pull herself up, spreading out her glass-like wings, letting them soak in the light and gleam around her. She looked down at Sheng, who stared at her in awe, his hands on his shoulders, showing that he would follow her rules.

"Hadley," he said. "We are here."

She took in the scene—white brick clock tower rising through the mist, narrow streets curled between storybook cottages, the kind of town that felt borrowed from a Scottish romance. It was quiet.

Unassuming. Beautiful.

A veil of fog licked around Kismet's legs, and waiting just beyond was her shadow self—dark, still, hand outstretched like she was reaching to say goodbye. Then the figure shifted, shimmering into glass. It was the version of herself that had carried her this far—the one who taught her how to survive.

Would you not come with me?

"Hadley, I told them, they can help."

"Told who?" were the first words she uttered, though it no longer sounded like herself, her voice nearly echoing through the land for miles, a gasp from the trees and vegetation whispered back in worship to a power that was ancient, primordial, coming from that voice.

"The phoenix is here. She came," Sheng said.

Hadley looked down, seeing faces so familiar. Her eyes lingered on the dark brown eyes with green specks of a Kinnari with a broad chest, shaved head, and wings that matched his gaze. He stared at her back, his expression hard, the line in his forehead hinting at concern.

Djoser stood with Precession, Roksana, and Celestine. On the other side of the road, she saw Reign with that boy, the one with the curly hair. They were holding onto those children whom she had met in the temple.

Salome ...

"I can't help," Celestine said, her smile sweet yet sad. "There is nothing to heal. The universe will fully engulf her. She will be perfect, divine."

"There has to be something we can do," Sheng said desperately, sliding down off of Kismet, his hand outstretched to her.

She ignored it.

"We came here so you could stop it."

"What if she doesn't want to stop it? Djoser asked. "What if she wants to be nothing. What if stopping it is taking away her control?"

"I can't let her go, not like that," Sheng responded, his shoulders stiff, his stress turning into anger, his teeth bared at Djoser for the curious challenge.

"That's why you can't love her."

Sheng took a step back at that, and a stunned silence fell over them all. Precession put her hand on Djoser's shoulder for comfort, and walked toward Kismet, then toward Hadley.

"Hadley, my beautiful friend," she sang. "Are you in pain?"

"No," Hadley's voice exploded.

"Can you feel anything at all?"

"No."

"Then how do you know that this is what you want?" Precession turned back, Roksana welcoming her with open arms. The two whispered among themselves.

Djoser hadn't looked away from her, and she moved her attention back to him. He began to walk toward her.

"What are you going to do?" Sheng growled.

But at that moment, Roksana bounced up—well, bounced for her —as her bored and annoyed facial expression hinted at something more.

She put her arm in Djoser's and they moved together, stopping at the wyvern's tucked-in legs.

"Hadley, can I touch your hand?" Roksana asked.

"She doesn't like to be touched," Sheng barked.

"Down dog," Roksana said, stretching out her arm.

Djoser kept his eyes locked on Hadley, and he nodded to her, asking her to trust Roksana.

"I don't need to touch her if she's going to be difficult," Roksana scoffed under her breath.

"Would you take my hand?" Djoser asked.

Hadley wasn't sure.

She just stared at them, blinking, changing, becoming less and less, only to become so much more than anything could ever be.

"Oh, fuck it," Roksana said, clapping her hands above her head. "I can't remember the last time I got to do this."

The redheaded beauty closed her eyes and parted her lips, sucking in air, and blowing out. It couldn't be seen; there was nothing physical about it. It wasn't like when Hadley's shadow jumped into people, an apparent, sudden change. This was different, slow, a leak in a cracked vessel. The molten gold of Roksana's soul, of her power, was now a slow flow, reaching out to whoever it could burn.

It hit Djoser first, who stood with his hand extended to Hadley. Anger curled in his eyes, Roksana's default emotion. Hadley could nearly see the smoke. Sorrow swelled like an undertow.

"It's not enough," Djoser's husky voice struggled to make itself heard.

Sheng hit the ground, cradling his head in his hands, his chest heaving.

Roksana looked back, her gaze moving from her sister to Amis. She turned back to Hadley and let out a roar, an explosion of something inside her.

Djoser screamed too, hit with whatever she'd unleashed. He didn't move, though; he didn't break eye contact, his attention glued to Hadley's face. His face showed anguish, the pain of the worst heartbreak as he licked the tears from his lips.

There was something.

Hadley now felt something.

It was faint, but longing coiled inside her stomach, and she let it grow, waiting to see what would happen and how it would feel again. It felt like an experiment as she stared right back at Djoser. She could tell that she was breathing again, and that she had a heartbeat. She could feel that it was pulsing so rapidly that it might come up out of her throat and hand into the outstretched hand he offered.

"Death is enamored of you, Hadley," Djoser yelled out.

She wanted to reach out. She wanted to touch what was left of her hand, the fingertips that were not translucent, to see if she could feel his skin.

But she couldn't, because she would just disappear in a different way. Their touches erased one another, and they didn't know what that would do; she didn't know what that would mean.

Roksana moved closer, her steps tentative but heavy with meaning, as if every inch she closed between them carried the weight of her entire existence. Her voice wavered, fragile as glass, yet unrelenting. "Do you hear me?" she implored, her tone cracked and brimming with anguish. "Do you even feel it? This—all of this—is for you."

Hadley stood motionless, a monolith carved from shadow and silence. Her presence was an ache, a void that pulled at her insides with quiet, unyielding gravity. She wasn't cold, nor cruel—those were human things, and she was far from human. No, she was absence incarnate, a chasm so deep it devoured her light without reflection or trace. Her eyes were fathomless and unyielding.

Roksana's fury struck Hadley like waves against a cliff, each surge breaking apart into helpless spray before falling back into the abyss. Hadley's fists clenched, nails biting into her palms as she tried to hold herself together.

"You're a void," Roskana hissed, her voice trembling with the strain of suppressed screams. Her chest heaved as her breath turned ragged, each exhale heavy with the weight of despair. "I'm giving you everything, and you just ..." Her voice faltered, choking on the lump in her throat. "You just take it. Like it's nothing."

Hadley tilted her head with unnerving slowness, her expression as blank as a moonless sky.

But she did feel. She wasn't showing it.

Hadley stepped over Sheng, still distraught, unable to move, her hand outstretched but filled with trepidation, the blood under her skin boiling with Roksana's power pulsing through her, made her consider punching someone instead.

"Because I am nothing," Hadley replied.

The anger stopped.

Roksana was momentarily stunned, and then the sadness leaked through.

It was something Hadley had known too well in her human life. A blanket of cold, the world's hardness, fixated on her. All of the memories, those human emotions, flooded back into her, punishing her for trying to forget them in the first place.

That laugh of her mother, the last time she had held her freezing hand, the shame of sleeping on couches, of having nowhere to go, of having no one who wanted her. And then everyone wanted her, everyone who was wrong for her, who used her, who tossed her aside after and laid a few dollars down to end the transaction.

What was she worth, if not a few dollars?

I am nothing.

She cried. Tears of pure longing, longing for a world that was fair, one that accepted her as a teenage girl filled with hope, that supported her and guided her into anyone she wanted to be, into someone she could have been, someone that her mom would be proud of, so her sacrifice hadn't been in vain.

Hadley reached her hand out fully towards Djoser, who jumped forward to meet her, both of their faces sitting in pain that couldn't be measured, her looking for an escape, him looking for her.

49

Hadley | Mytholm, Myrilosis

Everyone who was there seemed to disappear around her, as she was caught in a cocoon of emotions, of experience, of life. Her memories came flooding back, everyone she was, everything she was, hitting her over and over again like she was the loser in a championship boxing match.

I'm Hadley, she reminded herself.

She was a person with light in her heart, willing to sacrifice to take care of people around her. She was a writer.

A writer. A daughter. A friend.

She created stories. She got joy from writing terrible jokes, from kissing scenes that were far too sweet.

She had forgotten that about herself.

She had forgotten it all.

And now, she didn't want to. She wanted to hold it all in, she wanted others to remember her that way. She couldn't be a shell of power hovering around this planet, nor anywhere else that could take her.

It would be better, maybe, to take his hand, to let him fulfill the promise he made to her on that rooftop. They could disappear together.

"Trust me," Djoser said, his hand outstretched to her.

She would be leaving Kismet behind, though. Kismet needed her.

But you also need Kismet.

Hadley's transformation was nearly complete, and the last few inches of her body still showed proof that she was once human, that she was once real, tangible, and something that could be touched.

No touching.

Hadley pulled her hand back, a reminder of what having that skin meant. That pain, embarrassment, and shame that came with it.

"Hadley, trust me," Djoser asked again. "Please. It could stop the transformation."

"You'll disappear," she choked out. "We erase each other."

"If you're gone, I'll disappear anyway."

Hadley bit her lip, staring into those eyes.

"I am death, Hadley. I am not afraid. I once made you a promise. Let me fulfill it."

Her stomach was tight, her heart was heavy, so heavy that she was reminded of why she had wanted this, why she had stepped into that fire, why she encountered physical pain that could not be survivable for anyone else, so she could get away from it all.

With her hand open, she reached back toward Djoser until he held her hand in his.

She watched him smile and got lost in the cadence of his breath. But then, just as it had been before, her skin began to disappear completely.

It started at her hands before moving down to her wrists.

This was no translucence; this was the promise he had made once upon a time.

And as she felt.

She felt so hard that she thought she might explode before she vanished,

Djoser turned into dragon glass, crystallized, reflecting light, the shadow of death, shadowed in glass, one millimeter at a time, faint cracking and popping as her magic crept through him as his did her.

Djoser grabbed Hadley's waist with his opposite hand and pulled her body in, his lips searching for her, for a goodbye kiss. It did not land on her mouth, instead, on her forehead—a gesture of innocence, of understanding, of compassion.

A gesture of love.

It was quiet.

There was little drama about it as they held each other, their bodies balancing the necrosis between them. Too much of the same energy, of the same magic, fighting each other as they both fought for her. Hadley and Djoser both fought so hard. Her shadow self's confidence was somehow embedded within her, promising Hadley that she could, that she should, fight for herself.

There are worse things than death.

"Of course," Amis yelled in the background, laughing like a lunatic.

Hadley kept waiting for a jolt of pain or a black tunnel that her soul would be shoved into for eternity, but it never came. Instead, there was stillness, the crystallization of Djoser's chest against her, his arms statuesque around her neck, shoulder, and head. Still, she thought she could feel the warmth of Djoser's chest, the slight puff out when he breathed in and out.

She could hear it—the popping, the breaking of glass that bounced off of her body, falling onto her feet.

Her body. There was a body there.

"Open your eyes," Djoser said.

She did.

Light blinded her momentarily until she could focus. A sleeping Kismet took up most of her view in the distance, and Djoser's upper body still hugged around her. The wyvern only snored soundly, unbothered.

"I'm still here," Hadley said, surprised by the disbelief in her voice, her monotone gone, a faucet that was simply turned off. "What happened?"

"We both died."

Hadley looked up at him and frowned, seeing a face that could be Djoser as they pulled away from one another. He was still taller than her, his shoulders still hunched over her, but he looked like he was barely a teenager.

"I was tall for my age," he chuckled.

She looked at her hand and arm, so little, her skin so soft and silky smooth, nearly hairless.

"We are children?" Hadley asked.

"We are Vrae," Djoser answered.

And then, like a blinding hot poker was shoved down her throat, Hadley was overcome with a thirst, with a craving.

"Woah. Whoah, slow down." Sheng walked up to them. "I'll have Sable show you the blood donation room."

Sheng bowed, bringing his eyes to her level, "I'm going to miss you, little wife."

"I'm still here," she said in disbelief. "I'm ravenous, but I'm here, and I'm . . . I'm good."

Sheng put his hand on her head. "But you're not mine anymore. Maybe you never were."

"I told you that. I told you so many times," she whispered, a part of her heart soaring from the strings being cut, the journey she had taken with him not something that she would write off, cast aside in the back of her memories.

Sheng held so much sadness in his eyes, like there was something he knew that he held back.

Sheng walked away, hands in his pockets, moving down the road as Precession beamed. Roksana scowled, and Amis stood beside her, bouncing up and down in excitement.

"Death wasn't chasing us," he yelled to the kids who clung to Reign and Tristan near one of the houses forty-five feet away. "Death was out of balance. There was too much of it."

Hadley noticed the micro-aggressive look Amis's eyes shot towards her and Djoser, a blame that was sifted between them.

That will be a conversation for another day.

"What does that mean?" Reign yelled at him.

"That means we are safe. Kids, you are safe." Amis's smile was infectious, his tone celebratory. He paused, though, as his gaze met Sheng's.

The two males walked up to each other, and Hadley listened.

"Do you think she would approve?" Sheng asked Amis, pushing his hair out of his face.

"I think Emere would have been very proud of you," Amis said, reaching out his arms and hugging the demon who would make the devil shake and cower in fear. Sheng hugged Amis right back.

"Thank you, brother," Sheng said. "Really, thank you."

Though everyone was smiling, hugging, and reuniting in triumph, chaos hadn't truly left the air. It only took a moment for the happiness to leave, for the breath that Hadley took to feel less like fresh air and more like embers sliding down her throat.

Hadley's heart beat rose as she heard Roksana's sultry voice grumble, "Can she not leave us alone?"

Roksana threw her arms around Precession, and Djoser adjusted to hold her in the same manner. It was a selfless love, the willingness to be sacrificial as the sun can blaze down from the sky.

The Goddess touched down thirty feet in front of Hadley, her expressionless face focused on her, taking in her new Vrae form.

Ayurveda, her translucent form surrounded by fires, blue and golds and molten reds, brought heat down.

"Don't touch her," Sheng said, running up from behind, the skin on his face disintegrating from the heat, his teeth gnashed together from pain. Djoser's protective stance around Hadley also became too aggressive.

She didn't mind.

"You've failed me," the sun's voice echoed through the city streets. Each footstep that she took scarred the bricks they stood on with blackened ash.

Hadley trembled.

She moved to step out from behind Djoser, his eyes filled with terror, and his hands not wanting to let go of her.

"Trust me," Hadley said.

Djoser nodded. He let her move forward.

"I created you to do my bidding. The king of my chessboard. Pawns defeated you, and then you changed colors completely."

I didn't realize you were such a fan of chess.

Hadley just smiled, walking toward the intense heat slowly, like a cat, with Sheng on her opposite side. The rest of the Kinnari and Vrae seemed to fall back. They were not there for another war with a Goddess.

But this was unresolved, and today, that would change. Today, Hadley's life would be free.

"I'm sorry that you didn't get what you wanted," Hadley said, her voice so quiet in comparison to the echoes of Ayurveda.

The sun cocked her head, like she'd just realized that Hadley was there all this time. Then, a smile. That terrifying smile.

"Oh, my daughter of choice, I might still have plans for you later."

Sheng's eyes locked on Hadley.

His arms spread wide. He mouthed something to her.

Was it goodbye?

And then, there were flames. No roar. No warning. Just fire, pure and silent.

It swallowed Sheng whole in a single, greedy breath.

The scream was soundless, but Hadley could still hear it.

That scream exploded inside her head, echoed in her ribs, tore through the marrow of her bones. Her knees buckled as the heat cracked the air, blistered it, turned it to glass. Her lungs refused to work—every breath scraped like shattered obsidian down her throat.

"No—NO!" she shrieked, surging forward, but Djoser's arms were already around her, iron and mercy, holding her back as she fought like an animal.

She clawed at him. Bit. Screamed again.

Sheng was burning. Not dying, burning.

The flames were unnatural. They didn't flicker. They consumed.

There was no smoke, no ash rising, just skin melting, teeth curling, bones glowing orange as if lit from within. A marionette of agony, writhing in flame.

Sheng's body convulsed until it didn't.

And still the fire raged.

"LET ME GO!" Hadley wailed, her voice splintering, her throat raw. Her fingers bled against Djoser's grip.

"He's already gone," he whispered, barely audible.

She collapsed in his arms, trembling, moaning, sobbing in pulses she couldn't control. The ash fell softly around her, finer than sand, lighter than snow.

It was him. It was Sheng.

His ashes clung to her skin, her lips, her hair.

Somewhere in her grief, Hadley *heard* him. A whisper between the flames:

You're free now.

She screamed again, not in rage. Not even in sorrow. Just the sound of something *breaking.*

And then the fire vanished.

I'm so tired of breaking.

Ayurveda rose, golden and burning, her work complete. "That's all," she said, indifferent as gods always were.

And with that, the sun was back in the sky. Ayurveda left silence, scorched stone, and Hadley on her knees in the wreckage of a relationship she hadn't wanted but that she didn't underestimate, either. And now that was gone.

Hadley's body curled in on itself. She bent over, hands on the blackened earth, forehead pressed to the cooling stone. The grief was too big for words. It bloated in her throat. Swelled in her chest. She couldn't hold it.

"He knew," she whispered, her voice gone hoarse. "He knew she was coming."

"He loved you," Djoser said. "He needed to make amends."

"I know." Hadley wiped her cheeks dry.

She sat back slowly, her hands now gray with soot. Sheng's soot.

The tears slowed.

Something inside her stilled.

There was no peace in it. Just a hollow silence. A space where pain had burned so hot it had nothing left to devour.

She wiped her face with shaking hands, smearing grief across her skin like war paint.

Hadley looked up. The sky above was blue again. Unforgivably blue.

"I won't forget," she whispered. "Not who he was. Not what he gave."

And somewhere deep inside her, a place darker than she'd ever touched before, something shifted.

She wasn't just mourning him.

She was becoming what he had died to protect.

A daughter of death with ash in her veins and a soul made of second chances.

Djoser hugged Hadley again, and she let her body be heavy in his arms. She was exhausted, but it was over now. It had to be.

"Are we supposed to be upset that he's dead?" Precession's dry voice asked, and a few chuckles rose from that.

Hadley was sad. She would be whenever she thought of her past. The journey had started and ended with Sheng.

But now was not the time to dwell on it. Now was the time to heal.

When she looked in the mirror, she saw a little girl who had been given a second chance.

A new life.

Thank you. She looked up to the sky, letting the universe fill with her goodbyes to Sheng, her heart pouring out in grief and gratitude.

"We had a complicated relationship," Hadley said out loud. Djoser nodded.

A looming feeling of bitter victory, in glory, swirled in the air.

Relieved faces on Kinnari and Vrae began to surround her as the town came alive, with anyone hiding in their homes creeping out as the heaviness of danger left the air.

Tristan looked at the Waihema children and mumbled, "It's not safe here for them."

"I will leave you all now. There are a few Articiren that need healing; their species is nearly extinct after the Glaciels' attack," Celestine said.

"I'll miss you. I refuse to think of this as goodbye, more like our penultimate," Precession said, embracing the barmaid-phoenix.

"Don't be jealous," Amis said to Roksana, who scowled at the two of them. "I won't let you be left out."

Amis pulled Roksana in and bent her backwards, moving with her into a swift, passionate kiss.

"Oh, Reign!" Celestine shouted, "I have this for you."

Hadley watched Celestine run over to Reign, handing her something sleek and metal.

"Is this a cell phone?" Reign screamed.

"It's from Arryn," Celestine said, jumping up and down until she was no longer in her human form, but flying in the air with colorful red and gold wings, a shimmer of magic behind her as she raised herself high.

The fog cleared, and the blue sky was painted with pink and gold streaks as Celestine flew across it.

"Look, you can see the wetlands, the bogs, there's so much water," Roksana pointed out to Precession.

"A sky, pink and blue, with a golden light shining down on a body of water that is so clear it reflects the sky."

"It's not an ocean, exactly, but a world without horizon." Her twin smiled and held her hand, repeating her vision, another instance of where her prolific sister knew it all. "Let's go home. It's time to rebuild, and get you a chicken, of course."

"Is he coming with us?" Precession asked, looking at Amis.

"Like you could stop me from following this little bit of chaos around the world," Amis laughed, his arms now over both girls.

"So, now what?" Djoser asked Tristan.

"We'll have to work on making Myrilosis a paradise, like it's always deserved," Tristan said. "It's all I have ever tried to do since . . ."

Djoser slapped Tristan on the shoulders. "I am quite relieved, brother."

Tristan laughed. "That your death was not as bloody as mine?"

"The title of most traumatized will forever be yours," Djoser smiled at him.

Hadley finally had the nerve to move out of Djoser's arms. He let go willingly, though his posture remained protective.

"Reign," Hadley said, not recognizing her voice, the youth it held. "Grant's alive. I saw him."

Reign shook her head in disbelief. "If there's one thing that survives an apocalypse, it's the cockroaches."

"What do we do now?" Hadley asked, surprised when a hit on her shoulder brought her answer back.

"I get to keep you," Djoser whispered, taking her hand in his. It was innocent, a protectiveness, a friendliness, no heat in their touch. And it set her free. No expectations were placed, and nothing was wanted of her.

Precession moved over to her. "See Hadley? I told you, you're soulkin. Even with a new taste for blood. Now that my sister's lips will be heavily occupied, you and I can enjoy some time together."

Hadley shook her head as she eyed Roksana and Amis, their noises uncomfortably close to progressing from panting to moaning.

"I would love that," she said, smiling up at her redheaded sister.

"Tag, you're it," Djoser said, gently slapping Hadley's shoulder, pulling her attention away from her redheaded friend.

"What?" Hadley blinked.

"If I get to be a child again, Hadley, I will take advantage of it."

Hadley smiled with all her teeth, her stress and uncertainty melting away while her eyes danced in pure delight. "You better run fast."

And as she chased him, bumping into childlike Vrae citizens walking through the streets, wind in her hair and hope in her chest.

Hadley could catch her shadow running beside her. Its smile was different, less lethal, and for the first time, Hadley understood that her shadow wasn't an exact replica of her. A vision of light brown hair, a smile wide as the sky filled her thoughts. She realized who she had been staring at all this time.

Who else had been there to protect her?

I'm strong, Mom, she thought. *And I will be okay.*

50

All his teeth sparkled, his smile so large that even his glowing skin seemed dull. Reiofel couldn't believe it, but he'd figured out how to be happy.

They hovered there together, his loneliness depleted. If anything, he had too many in his life, too many to love. Nearly a year had passed since he'd returned home to find out most of what had been left behind was gone forever. He'd been crowned, they'd chanted his name at the memorial, and he'd felt pride even though he had done nothing to deserve it.

Now, he felt pride because he had done everything. This time, the pride was his to claim.

"Are you ready?" Gasher asked him, her face betraying some hope, some excitement.

It was time for another speech, and he felt less nervous this time.

"When will I see grandbabes from the two of you?" his father asked with a bellowing laugh.

Gasher's daughter, Sima, wrapped her arm around Reiofel's and giggled.

"I think the marriage part is supposed to come first." Gasher eyed them both while crossing their arms.

"You two are the least professional council members we have, truly." Reifoel shook his head.

A past version of himself would be thoroughly embarrassed by all of this show, this parade, but he was no longer bothered by it. He had a secret, a surprise, that he would conduct after all of this. One that he would have never guessed that he would be doing when he'd decided to come back home, heartbroken, lovestruck, and filled with grief.

"Luckily, you have the rest of them you can rely on." His father pointed to the group of stone-faced council members that stood slightly off to the side, talking out of the corners of their mouths and taking their jobs phenomenally too seriously.

Reifoel looked ahead, at the faces of the community that had gathered in front of them, excited, clamoring to look past one another at what Reifoel currently hovered before.

"It's too bad our new allies couldn't join us. It is a bad look, really," Gasher uttered.

"The last time I checked, the residents of Mystmere couldn't survive this deep underwater without being squished to death."

"Well." Gasher still seemed ruffled. "They could have sent a gift at least."

"Don't ruin the moment." Sima tapped her mother's shoulder and gave her a wink.

Reifoel looked into Sima's eyes. They twinkled and reminded him of home, just like someone else's had, once upon a time. The difference, however, was that she *was* home. He was home and would be content never to leave, especially now that he had all of this.

"If I can have your attention," his voice echoed toward the crowd, "I wanted to thank you all for coming here today. More importantly, I want to thank everyone who participated and helped build it. I would like to thank the partners who supported their households while we worked tirelessly on this vision over the past ten months. This is the first, but not the last, representation we will complete that demonstrates to the world that Serelune is keeping pace with the times. We are not a small, humble town but a city that thrives, trusts one another, lives near the deep without fear, accepting that it is a part of our histories."

Reifoel turned to the stretched seaweed that symbolized a ribbon in front of a dazzling castle.

"I present to you the Serelune Citadel."

With hands wrapped around the slimy texture, Reifoel ripped the seaweed, letting its ends float behind them as the audience clapped and hollered.

"They're particularly peppy," Gasher said.

"They get it from you, Mom," Sima said under her breath.

Reifoel did everything in his power not to choke on his laughter as the group turned around to look at the first piece of the new Serelune.

"Do we think it's too much, perhaps?" Reifoel asked, staring at the structure that towered over the domes.

"I think it's perfect," Sima said, taking Reifoel's face in her hands and planting her lips on his.

Reifoel's father cleared his throat.

"That's not how you make babies," he grumbled. "Did we never have that talk with you?"

Reifoel rolled his eyes and craned his neck to look upon the real-life version of what he'd drawn in Isadore's dome.

Volcanic glass made up the vast majority of the exterior, hard and strong enough to not get crushed down too much over time. In the dark, it still gleamed, a black sort of glimmer in the distance. But when their bodies approached, it burst into shades of dark purple, blue hues, and blacks that rivaled the beauty of obsidian.

It was ethereal.

It was also haunting – an invitation as well as a warning.

A community, a city, survived and thrived here in the depths, coexisting with monsters that would terrify any faction of Myrilosis.

They were survivors, which he wanted this castle to convey, coming out stronger after any incident.

Spires sprouted around the outside of the structure, protecting an entirely too-large glass dome, adorned with shells to divert any sea animals that might accidentally ram into it. Thermal vents were built throughout the structure, not to provide heat, but to allow free-floating minerals to be cast around the interior, creating a sparkling illumination in the large central hall and common areas.

Reifoel planned for this to be a space for all, where any Serelune could freely come, contribute to the library, learn to cook in the absurdly large kitchen, support dreams, and find ways for the ambitious to grow, thrive, and be happy.

And of course, a set of private royal chambers were tucked away in one of the spires. A room for each council member below him. And one that he intended to share.

"It is phenomenal. For the first time, I see real potential for a different type of future for Serelune," Gasher said.

"Don't try to butter me up," Reifoel said while giving Gasher an appreciative look.

"Hail King Pires," a voice from the crowd started to chant.

"Hail King Pires," more voices echoed and joined in.

"I'll never get used to that," Reifoel chuckled, feeling too awkward.

"What's next?" Gasher asked. "I expect it will be something extravagant."

Reifoel imagined that the people could use some rest, time for a celebration, time to reflect with family, possibly attend a great party, the first to be held inside.

"Father," Reifoel held his hand out and nodded to him.

Sebastian Pires' eyes gleamed, and a smile that was more significant than his broke out. "I thought you'd never ask." He rummaged through his beard, toying with something small, untangling the hair that held it in place, had kept it hidden. Keeping the mystery by transferring it with a closed fist, Reifoel took the item in his hand, a gleam accidentally sparkling as it went into his palm with fingers clamping down on it.

Sima's smile dropped; her mouth opened.

She noticed.

Reifoel looked down, gathering his courage, knowing the surprise had been ruined. She knew, he knew that she did.

"Sima," he said, looking up into her eyes, those eyes that would forever be his home, if she said yes.

"Reifoel," she said, dimples appearing.

"Sima, I didn't think that I could ever be here. I didn't think that I would be able to live fully again. But then I met you, and you taught me within minutes the kind of leader, the type of Serelune, I needed to be. You don't scare me, but what does scare me is not having you by my side. I love you, Sima. I love your mind, I love your fire, I love that I could live the rest of my life trying to prove that I am good enough for Serelune, but also for you."

The crowd had quieted, his voice so soft, but he knew they could hear every word. He froze for a moment, the words getting stuck in his throat, his nerves getting the better of him.

"Are you going to ask?" Sima let out a laugh that was also a sob after he had paused for entirely too long. "Because I'm ready to answer."

"Sima," he said, blocking out everyone around them, pressing his forehead to hers, his voice barely above a whisper, their breaths tangling together. "Will you . . . come to the surface with me?"

Reifoel nearly flinched as the words left his lips. *Why is that how you would ask?*

"Is this?"—Sima cocked her head and laughed—"Is this about burritos?"

Reifoel wanted to die right there—he couldn't believe he'd messed up the proposal so badly.

"No," he tried to laugh it off. "I was more thinking of a honeymoon."

"Oh really? Are you asking me to marry you, Reifoel?"

He nodded his head fervently.

Sima answered by closing the already barely existing gap between them, her lips pressing against his. They pulled apart, her eyes still closed from the kiss, her dimples out in full force from her grin. She bit her lip before answering.

"Yes. I will marry you, and I promise that when we honeymoon, we will get you a burrito."

Those were the most romantic words that Reifoel could have ever hoped to hear, as he touched his forehead to hers and the crowd around them burst into cheers.

EPILOGUE

Reign | Sacramento, Ca

"Who's there?" Grant asked, his cowboy boots and jean shorts caked in dust and filth as he answered the side door in his Citrus Heights garage.

The screen creaked, announcing its resistance to the situation.

"Still haven't upgraded to living inside the house?" Reign asked.

"No, my friend just won't die—hey, aren't you that little shit? Reign's stepdaughter?" Grant squinted at the girl with jet-black hair who barely reached the doorknob.

Behind her stood a teenage boy who towered over her, carrying a toddler. A: a girl of similar size, with darker skin and the expression of someone who'd seen too much before breakfast.

"I am," she said. "Reign sent me here."

"For what? Did your house get looted? Is Reign okay?"

"They're all dead," Reign sniffed dramatically, eyes as dry as the Coachella Valley. "But her dying words were that Grant *will take care of all of you*. So here we are, in this hellhole."

The silence that followed was thick.

Grant blinked slowly. "God dammit, Reign. Why would she do this to me?"

"Been a while since you've had a conversation, I see." Reign raised an eyebrow.

"No, no, no," Grant said, nudging the door closed. "I can't be taking care of kids. I've got a business to run."

"You're going to make me do this the hard way, then?" Reign sighed, arms folding like a judge passing sentence. She stepped forward, the winter boots she still wore catching on the concrete lip of the garage.

"You will take care of Luca, Noah, and Salome like they are your children, like no one in the world matters more than them. You and I together will get you into a proper house. Reign's house might still be standing. I haven't checked."

It wasn't a request. It was a command.

"You haven't checked?" Grant questioned.

"Never mind that. Did you hear me? We are all now your children. Congratulations."

Grant stared, a man genuinely reconsidering his life choices.

A little late for that.

Her voice was calm, but something sharp glinted beneath it. They were here for a reason, and despite who he once was to her, to Hadley, Reign trusted him completely.

"You guys better come in; there are some dangerous people around here." Grant opened the door fully, ushering their group inside.

Noah ran to the massive couch Reign used to lounge on wearing her thigh-high leather boots.

He threw himself across it like a prince reclaiming his throne.

"Don't jump on that couch—it's older than you," Grant's parent voice wasted no time laying down rules.

"What else is he supposed to do in this dump?" Luca sneered, crossing his arms like a teen mafia don.

Reign shot him a look.

The rebellion has a spokesperson.

The boy always had a fire in him, but today, Reign was his warning flare.

"Shit, I gotta get a real safe or something for all those weapons on my desk." Grant looked over his shoulder, actually concerned.

Reign's eyes flicked toward the desk. Guns, blades, bits of scavenged tech. Nothing that surprised her.

He will do just fine, she thought.

Reign was the last to step inside, and she looked up at Grant. "Has the internet been restored? I'm going to start a damn website."

The phone in her pocket rang. She pulled it out to answer.

"Hello, Arryn. Lonely already?"

ALSO BY ELLE KAELEE

Glass Wings Series

1. Glass Wings

2. Burning Glass

3. Glass Shadow

Sweet Silver Bells

a gothic holiday romance

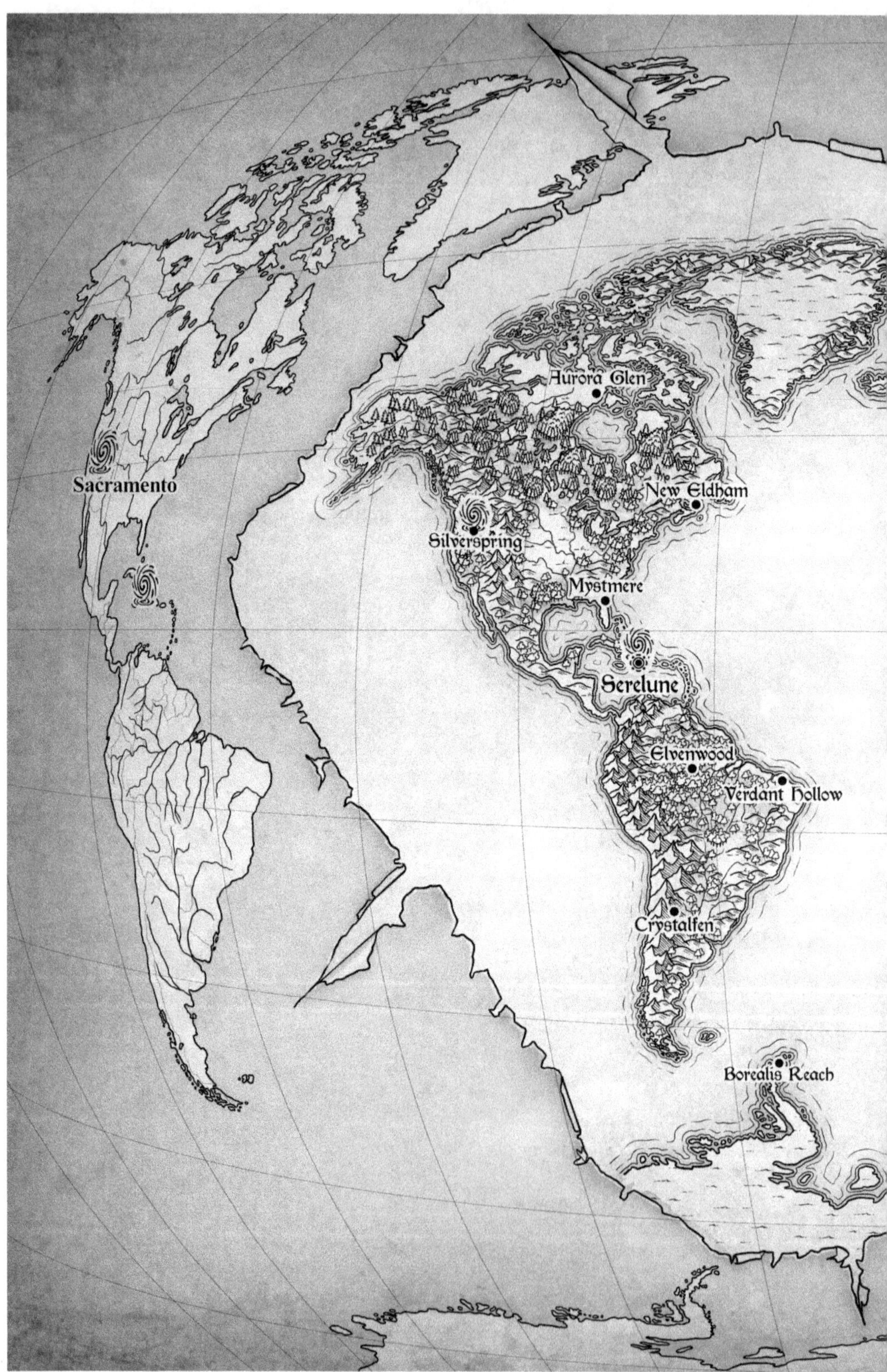

Sacramento
Aurora Glen
New Eldham
Silverspring
Mystmere
Serelune
Elvenwood
Verdant Hollow
Crystalfen
Borealis Reach

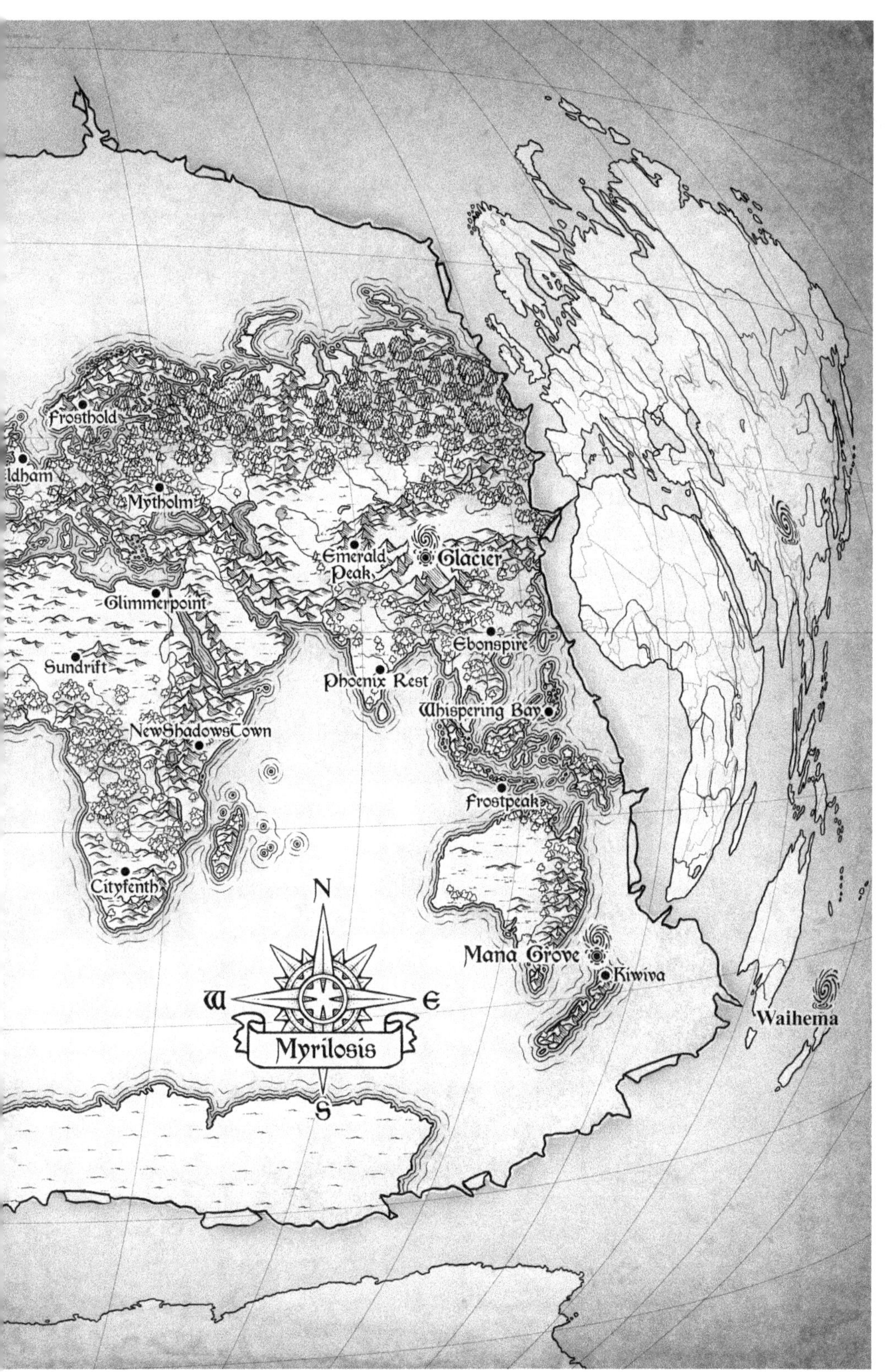

Frosthold
ldham
Mytholm
Emerald Peak
Glacier
Glimmerpoint
Ebonspire
Sundrift
Phoenix Rest
Whispering Bay
NewShadowsTown
Frostpeak
Cityfenth
N
W
E
S
Myrilosis
Mana Grove
Kiwiva
Waihema

GLOSSARY

Ahora

One of the last five Waihema children.

Allienna

Hadley's mother, a full Kinnari, is the one who dies, catalyzing the story. Ethereal and regal.

Amis

A complex Kinnari and caretaker of the Waihema children. Known for internal conflict, magical balance, and reluctant protection. Helps resurrect Djoser.

Aqurya

Hadley's original name for Kismet, a wyvern created by Arryn from sorrow and snow. Breathes fire and shares a deep, magical bond with Hadley. Kismet and Aquarya are the same creature.

Arryn

Hadley's father is a powerful, emotionally volatile Kinnari and the creator of Kismet. Capable of atomic-level creation magic. Grieves Allienna.

Articiren

Towering, dainty giantesses standing fifteen feet tall, with an otherworldly elegance. They resemble women with Victorian-style hair piled high, wearing wide floral skirts that make them appear to glide across snow. Their skin tones vary like the Kinnari, but are marked with imperfect rectangular patterns—similar to a giraffe's coloring—across their faces and limbs.

Atheri

Angelic beings in Ebonspire with radiant, genderless forms and ambiguous motives. Made by Arryn to destroy Vrae with their heaven-esque light.

Balizar

Cynical innkeeper in Myrilosis. Provides commentary on the Kinnari legacy and magical restoration.

Celestine

A kind, awkward barmaid in Myrilosis. Helps Arryn and Reign and shows affection for Arryn.

Djoser

A destructive but loyal Kinnari. Represents death and resurrection.

Glaciels

Species adapted to life in the town, Glaciel, is often emotionally reserved. Physically resistant to cold and attuned to Myrilosis's mountain realm.

Glaciel

A temple town in Myrilosis, carved into a mountainside. Closest in proximity to the Kinnari Temple.

Glass Wings

Translucent, painful wings, Hadley grows as a Kinnari. Beautiful but burdensome.

Hadley

The protagonist, a powerful Kinnari with a hidden past and evolving magic. Endures captivity, betrayal, and transformation. Also known as Hailey in her sex work scenes.

Hector

Hadley's close friend from her mortal life. His memory haunts her decisions.

Isadore

Aquatic noble from Serelune, cousin to Reifoel. Cynical, protective, and a skilled fighter. Distrusts Hadley and her magic.

Jenny

A cloaked follower of Sheng. A Vrae who serves him loyally.

Karmakara

Cosmic balancing force. One of the gods. Appears to Luca and offers glimpses of future paths.

Kinnari

Winged magical beings created to protect life and Earth. Their glass-like wings and powerful blood make them targets of the Vrae.

Kismet

Hadley's bonded wyvern, created by Arryn. Formerly known as Aqurya. Formed from snow and sorrow.

Kiwiva

The Northern New Zealand area of Myrilosis, destroyed by fire.

Life Gifter

The supreme creator god who governs cosmic laws, immortality, and the ability to create life.

Luca

A Waihema child marked by the Kinnari.

Lumes

Light-based ethereal bugs.

Marthrend

Crustacean-like beings who offer shelter in Emerald's Peak. Live in an icy region near Myrilosis.

Myrilosis

A mirrored magical realm of Earth. Connected by portals. Houses temples, sacred sites, and magical storms.

Noah

One of the five Waihema children. Survives storms and temple collapse.

Precession

Frail, prophetic twin sister to Roksana. Dreams of future events, receives visions.

Rangi

One of the Waihema children. Present during the exodus to Myrilosis.

Reifoel

An aquatic prince from Serelune. Has a growing romantic bond with Hadley. Calms the wyvern, possesses water healing.

Reign

Hadley's fierce, sarcastic godmother. A Kinnari who can regenerate into a child. Protective of the children.

Roksana

Blunt and protective twin to Precession. Amplifies emotions around her.

Salome

A Waihema child marked by the Kinnari. Protected by Amis. Loyal to Reign.

Saul

A Vrae cultist under Sheng.

Serelune

An underwater kingdom ruled by Reifoel's family. Suffers partial destruction, later begins reconstruction.

Shadow Self

Autonomous magical reflection of Hadley. Capable of moving independently, resurrecting, and manipulating life or death.

Sheng

The first Vrae, created by Ayurveda. Hadley's former captor and complex romantic antagonist.

Soulkin

A term Kinnari uses for non-blood-related family.

Temple

Original Kinnari temple located in the Himalayas. Contains ancient magic and serves as both a battleground and a sanctuary.

Tristan

A Kinnari boy, presumed dead, returned via prophetic dreams. Informs and guides others like Amis.

Vrae

Demonic beings created by Ayurveda to consume Kinnari. Can walk as humans or transform into monstrous forms with gaping jaws and red eyes.

Waihema

A remote village was created by the Amis to protect half-Kinnari children. Initially a breeding ground, later a sanctuary.

ACKNOWLEDGMENTS

Editor: Taylor Robinson

Cover Artist: Gretchen Cobaugh

Map Artist: @veronikawunder

List of commissioned artists for the series art so far:
    @foxlore_art
    @hexbayne
    @eburnsillustrations

TRIGGER WARNINGS

Glass Wings is a dark fantasy trilogy intended for **mature audiences** (18+) and readers who enjoy morally complex characters, intense emotional arcs, and dark fantasy themes. Please review the following content warnings before reading. These are a continuation from the first book of the series, and these themes continue for Burning Glass and Glass Shadow:

Major Themes:

• Emotional abuse — *on-page*, throughout multiple chapters

• Power imbalance / toxic relationships — *on-page*, significant throughout

• Trauma and recovery — *on-page*, central theme, appears in most chapters

• Identity, transformation, and loss of self — *on-page*, recurring motif

Explicit Content Warnings:

• Sexual content, including consensual and dubiously consensual scenes — *on-page*

• Graphic violence — *on-page*, including deaths and battles

• Blood and gore — *on-page*, throughout

• Kidnapping and captivity — *on-page*

• Drugging (coerced bite-induced intoxication) — *on-page*

• Physical abuse — *on-page*,

• Emotional manipulation / gaslighting — *on-page*, central to antagonist dynamic

• Death of a loved one / grief — *on-page*

• Cult behavior and forced rituals — *on-page*

• Self-harm imagery (symbolic/magical) — *on-page*

• Body horror (wing growth, transformations) — *on-page*

Psychological Themes:

• PTSD and dissociation — *on-page*

• Suicidal ideation (non-graphic) — *on-page*

• Panic attacks and anxiety — *on-page*

• Shadow self / fragmented identity — *on-page*

Fantasy-Specific Elements:

- Possession by magical entities — *on-page*

- Demonic beings / monstrous transformations — *on-page*

- Forced marriage / mystical bonding — *on-page*

- Betrayal by loved ones — *on-page*

www.ingramcontent.com/pod-product-compliance
Lightning Source LLC
Chambersburg PA
CBHW070306310726
48976CB00005B/1590